NO MAN SAVE ~~ONE~~ COULD TAME HER!

. . . the lovely Rosanna followed her desires wherever they led. And here are the men who lusted for her—and the woman who hated her—as she struggled for her dream. . . .

BERTO—the young shepherd who passionately desired both her body and her soul—and almost won them both. . . .

MARCO SORDELLO—Rosanna's dashing kinsman, who came nowhere to bring her a vision of a glittering future among the nobility . . . and whose interest in her was more reckless than was proper in a blood relative. . . .

UGO SORDELLO—the first to taste of her body —and the first to learn that Rosanna could be as demanding of her men as they were of her. . . .

BIANCA SORDELLO—to her, the beautiful Rosanna was a threat—and the cunning, seductive Bianca knew the best way to deal with such a threat. . . .

DUKE PAOLO—the proud, gentle nobleman who transformed Rosanna's life from bleak servitude to rapturous desire; the one love for the rest of Rosanna's life—*if* Bianca didn't steal him too soon. . . .

Seething with the human heat of explosive desires and diabolical intrigue, ROYAL CAPTIVE spans centuries of history to present a love story as vital and real as today—yet as eternal as the blazing sun!

ROYAL CAPTIVE

Patricia Phillips

PYRAMID BOOKS NEW YORK

ROYAL CAPTIVE

A PYRAMID BOOK

Copyright © 1977 by Patricia Phillips

Pyramid edition published February 1977

Library of Congress Catalog Card Number: 76-52567

Printed in the United States of America

Pyramid Books are published by Pyramid Publications (Harcourt Brace Jovanovich, Inc.). Its trademarks, consisting of the
word "Pyramid" and the portrayal of a pyramid, are registered
in the United States Patent Office.

PYRAMID PUBLICATIONS
(Harcourt Brace Jovanovich, Inc.)
757 Third Avenue, New York, N.Y. 10017

Chapter One

The sun was high and Rosanna brushed straggling hair from her damp brow as she called to her pet kid.

Pepe followed her voice, rounding a curve in the rocks and she fondled his silky head, smiling at the animal's soft, bulging eyes. "Soon we'll find water, then you won't be thirsty," she assured, hitching up her ragged skirts as she climbed higher on the rough, winding mountain pass, a wicker basket of herbs on her hip.

Below, the countryside spread far to the sea. On clear days she could see the masts of ships on the horizon in the harbors of cities many miles away, while stone towers of churches and castles jostled each other in the valleys. Today there was a mist and she could see no further than the first large city to the south—Lorenzo, its walls gleaming pink in the sunlight. Jumbled within the tall battlements were many buildings, their marble walls reflected in the silver ribbons of canals sparkling in the sun.

When she was nine, Rosanna had gone to Lorenzo with her mother, but they had been driven out by the crowd when her mother prophesied death for many inhabitants of the city. With a shudder, she recalled the terrifying day when they had fled through the gates, followed by clods of filth and sharp rocks. But her mother had been right. Within months the great plague of 1449 ravaged the city, soon to be followed by a bloody civil war which claimed many lives.

People called her mother a witch, and though she was feared, many came from the mountain villages seeking cures for their ailments, or for magic potions to work their secret desires. Tonight was to be a full moon: the only time when many spells could be used and her mother had sent her to gather wild plants from the high ground.

Rosanna began to walk, dragging her feet as she remembered her mission. Once Mother had allowed her to help with the magic brews, but since Pia came to live with them, they always sent her to gather the ingredients instead. She wished Pia would go away. Everything was much nicer before she came. When they found her, Pia was lying near death in childbirth agony, fallen from her donkey on the mountain trail. Rosanna's mother had nursed her back to health and Pia had never left. She was an ugly, dull-witted girl with a large, unsteady head and slobbering mouth. Pia's daughter was just like her. She had no name, just Girl. Pia's horribly deformed infant died a few days after birth. Rosanna had stared at its hideous face and wished it dead, willing the squalling, misshapen thing to die, fixing it with her large black eyes, until suddenly it was still. Slightly in awe of her powers at first, she later realized the potential they might have. Though she tried the same thing with Girl, however hard she concentrated, nothing happened. Girl tagged after her on her short bowlegs, whining to the women when Rosanna hid from her. Always she must look after Girl, until the long walks she previously enjoyed became hateful with the imbecile's presence. Several times she attempted to lose Girl on the rugged mountain tracks, but she always came back. In desperation Rosanna took Girl deeper into the hills, to a place she had never been before. Her mother had always warned her not to go beyond the foothills for brigands lived in the mountain caves, riding out from their strongholds to pillage villages, killing the men and raping the women. But Rosanna was not afraid of brigands, so she did not heed the warnings.

A gray mist rose from the tops of the hills, spiraling

6

into the air like smoke. She found a cave with a pool and when she dropped a rock into the black, silent water, there was no sound after the splash. She called Girl into the cave, showing her the bottomless pool and giving her rocks to throw in the water. Girl leant farther over the pool trying to hear the rocks hit the bottom, until suddenly she lost her balance and the ghastly creature splashed into the bottomless grave.

When Rosanna returned Pia did not ask about her daughter and she proffered no information. When Girl failed to appear the women assumed she was lost on the misty track.

For these past two months Rosanna was alone with only Pepe, the mountain goat, for companionship. And except for Pia, things were nice again. She had concentrated very hard on Pia's departure, but so far the half-wit stayed, never venturing from the tiny stone hovel where they lived.

With a cry of delight Rosanna spied the plant she sought growing on the grassy sod above her head. She scrambled up the crag, running over the flinty ground and knelt to pluck sprigs of flowers for her basket. Pepe found a clear stream sprouting through a crevice in the dark rock, and Rosanna splashed her face, wiping it dry with the skirt of her dress. Now they could go back, for she had everything her mother needed. They were high in the foothills of the mountains and she had not realized she had traveled so far.

Rosanna turned to pick up her basket and the long dark shadow of a horse and rider fell across her, blocking the light of the sun.

"Two little mountain goats," a man said.

She backed away, finding herself surrounded by a group of mounted men; the brigands about which her mother had warned her. Darting from side to side she sought escape, but one of them swung from the saddle and in a moment had imprisoned her in his enormous hands.

She squirmed and fought, while he clutched her shoulders in a viselike grip, his head thrown back with a bellow of laughter at her futile efforts.

"A goat, Tommaso, she is more like a wild cat," another called, as Rosanna hissed and spat at her captor. The speaker rode forward and dismounted, coming towards them. Tommaso released her, stepping back respectfully before his leader.

Rosanna glared at him. "Let me go," she demanded.

The brigand leader was a huge man, with dark hairy arms, his hands dangling loosely at his sides. A scar ran the length of his face, disappearing in the bush of coarse black hair on his chin. With a grin he opened his hands, flinging his arms wide. "I do not touch you. Go, little wild cat."

Taking a step forward, Rosanna glanced hesitantly at them, for they did not move, the horses forming a circle around her. Behind lay the steep crags of rock dotted with gorse and scrub. And she leant against a boulder, wondering how she could escape. The rock surface was rough, perhaps she could find a foothold and scramble to safety; yet she doubted if the men would let her get far before a dagger came whistling between the boulders.

"Aren't you going? I thought you wanted to leave," the leader mocked, and the others laughed at her.

Rosanna glared back, making her eyes as piercing as she could, willing a calamity to befall them. Perhaps a boulder rolling from above, or an earthquake to open the ground before them swallowing horses and riders without a trace. But they remained there, leaning on their saddles and grinning at her predicament. They knew she was cornered, and they tormented her like an animal with its prey.

The leader pulled her to him and Rosanna twisted in the crushing strength of his arms. He bent his face to hers, his mouth wet and reeking of stale wine and garlic, then he kissed her while the others hooted and clapped.

"She's only a girl child, *padrone*," Tommaso remarked sourly, "too small."

"Perhaps she has sisters," another suggested hopefully. "Where do you live, girl?"

"Down there." Rosanna pointed down the track to the valley where a thin curl of gray smoke was visible from the chimney of her home. If they took her to the valley, maybe she could hide from them, for it was familiar ter-

8

rain. Every boulder and cave she knew like the back of her hand. "There are others," she ventured hopefully.

"Older?"

She nodded enthusiastically. "Big, like this." With exaggerated gestures she described a voluptuous body with her hands, and they laughed in amusement.

"I'll take this one," the leader, said, stroking his bushy beard in contemplation. "I'll wager no other has had the measure of her. Have you food? Wine?"

"A cellar full," she lied.

"In that case, we'll pay your family a visit. It's a nice day for visits."

They shouted their agreement, moving back so the leader could ride at the front of the column. He dragged Rosanna to his horse and leaping astride, he pulled her after him, roughly dumping her across the front of his saddle like a sack of flour.

Down the trail they went, the animals slowly picking their way over the rough ground. Her heart thudded faster as they made the descent, while she wondered what she could do to save herself. Her head was swimming with the jogging movement and her hanging position. Blood seemed to flood her brain, making it difficult to concentrate. Eventually the man pulled her upright, sitting her before him, holding her close against his body. The mingled smell of him nauseated her; a mixture of garlic-tainted sweat and stale urine, wafting hot and acrid with each movement. His clothing of coarse homespun was stiffened with grime and dried sweat, and it chafed her skin as the scrawny animal stumbled on the unfamiliar track.

The passing landmarks were recognizable now, and Rosanna realized they were nearing home. While they rode, the brigand leader explored her body, his huge callused hands rough and clumsy on her flesh. And with inward panic Rosanna knew what he intended to do to her when they reached the dwelling. If only there were men at home who could fight the brigands and drive them away, but there was only Pia and her mother. Perhaps a couple of years ago she could have escaped unharmed, but she was no longer a child, a fact men noticed with appreciation.

Several months ago, when Girl was newly gone, she had been walking on the grassy lowlands in search of herbs. Berto, the young shepherd whose flocks grazed near her home, had stopped her on the road, drawing her into conversation. He wanted her to slip out to meet him later while he tended his flock, but she would not. When he tried to kiss her she was not afraid, only curious. But the kiss was disappointing. Rough and unpolished as Berto was, she had found some response to his maleness, attracted by his tanned physique, and the pleasure of his arms around her shoulders. When Berto wanted her to say she would be his sweetheart, she laughed at him, making him angry, so that he would have struck her if she had not darted amongst the rocks.

Berto still pursued her, becoming more persistent until she squirmed from him, wary of the possession in his eyes. Last week he cornered her against the boulders, determined to claim her. Rosanna's curiosity was almost her undoing, for she lingered too long, only managing to escape in time before he forced her to submit to his will. It was only when Berto tripped in his blind passion that she slipped away, scrambling over the boulders, fleet as a deer through the spring grass as she ran toward the safety of home.

Perhaps Berto would be on the track today. She would be pleased to see him and forgive him for his fierce embraces if he would save her from the brigands. She would call to him and Berto would rescue her. But though she searched for the shepherd, she saw only his sheep, bleating and staring foolishly at them as they rode past.

"Is that it?" the brigand leader asked, as a stone hut became visible at the end of the track.

Rosanna nodded, finding his arm tighten about her waist.

"Soon I shall have the measure of you, little wild cat," he promised with a leer, showing the blackened stubs of decayed teeth in his slack mouth.

Somehow Rosanna could not think what he threatened would come to pass, yet she knew of no escape. Sickness gnawed in her stomach as the only salvation she could foresee was how she might kill him.

In a moment they reached the hut. At the clattering

hooves Pia ran to the door, her gaping jaw hanging even lower as she beheld the fierce armed men. Rosanna screamed a warning for her mother, but it was already too late. A man leaped from the saddle and in a moment he had blocked the back entrance to the hovel. The women were trapped.

Her mother was dragged outside and the other men dismounted, thundering through the house, and Rosanna could hear them turning over furniture, smashing bowls and dishes in their search for food. The bounty was a wheel of goat cheese and two bottles of homemade wine, brought yesterday by villagers in payment for the full moon sorcery. Sullenly the brigand leader looked about at the miserable pieces of furniture which had been flung outside in the dust.

"You lied, wildcat bitch, you lied," he accused, until Rosanna cowered from the fury in his eyes.

"We won't waste our time after all," Tommaso shouted triumphantly. There was the sound of ripping cloth as he tore Pia's gray gown, the rags parting neatly in an opening from neck to hem. They all stared at her. It was a profanity to see the ugly, lolling head on her milk white body, for her form was as perfect as a sculptured goddess. "Maggot-head will warm us all."

The men's approval was a growing murmur and they stepped towards Pia, who whimpered and moaned in terror at the prospect of the attack. In an instant her head was wrapped up, her simpleton's face hidden in the folds of her torn dress. Tommaso fell upon her greedily, shouting like a madman, while the others waited their turn, grouping about to watch the spectacle.

Two men grabbed Rosanna's mother and she closed her eyes, unable to watch her mother's violation, desperately trying to think of a charm to save herself from the same fate.

The brigand leader ate some of the cheese, rinsing it down with wine, but his hand was still firm on her arm. At last he dragged up a broken chair and leant against the back of it, swilling wine and pulling her against him with his free arm. Then he stiffened, as above the cries and fury of the men's attack, her mother began to chant a spell.

11

With a curse, Tommaso threw his dagger and the blade sped true to its course, the metal hilt quivering, winking bright in the sun. Her mother was dead. But Rosanna felt no emotion, too stunned by the violent events to know sorrow.

Suddenly the air was filled with thundering hooves as a party of horsemen swooped down upon the hovel. The brigand leader released her with an oath of surprise, reaching for a weapon to defend his life. The horsemen threshed through the herb garden and the vegetable patch, the sound of steel upon steel shattering the sultry noon heat. There were men's cries and curses, the air thick with the sounds of dying. And just as suddenly, it was quiet again. The retribution had been swift as a whirlwind, so that at first Rosanna could not grasp what had happened. Strong arms lifted her from the ground where she had fallen with the force of the blow delivered to the brigand leader. Her rescuer was a young man in a green doublet and fine leather boots.

Rosanna stared up at him in awe, thinking he must be at least a duke by the grandeur of his clothes and the trappings of his horse. The others were in livery and she knew they were his servants. The party were strangers and it was as if they had swooped from the mists of the mountain top, so unheralded had been their coming, so mysterious, that at first she wondered if they were real men or whether they were an apparition created by her mother's incantations.

"Are you Rosanna?" the young man asked.

She nodded, her tears flowing, making rivers of white on her dirty face.

He carried her inside and laid her on the bed where she cried herself to sleep. When she woke he brought her a bowl of food. It was chicken broth; her mother's flock had found their way into the stranger's stewpot.

"Are you rested enough to ride now?" he asked, sitting on the edge of the straw pallet.

"Ride where?"

"To my home, Lorenzo."

"I can't go with you. I don't know you."

"But I know you, so that's different." He walked to the door and told his servants to saddle the horses. "You can't stay here. Your mother and her servant are dead. My men buried them behind the house. The brigands will be buzzard feast before tomorrow."

"Who are you that you know my name?" she asked in curiosity, placing the empty bowl on the floor.

"I'm your kinsman, Marco Sordello. Your mother was sister to my father, though for many years he did not know where she lived. I discovered it yesterday in the village. The journey was out of my way, but a force seemed to drive me here, beyond comprehension though it may seem. However, it proved to be a timeley intervention for you."

He glanced about at the broken vessels on the floor, the mounds of spilled herbs and puddles of colored liquid.

"My mother healed people," Rosanna explained.

A flicker of humor crossed his face, but he said nothing as she stood, pushing her straggling hair from her eyes, feeling weak and very tired.

"We must ride soon if we're to be inside the city before nightfall. Come, get whatever you want to take and I'll wait." He went out into the afternoon sun, ducking as he walked through the low doorway.

Rosanna washed her face and brushed her hair, changing the soiled dress for her clean one which hung on a nail by her bed. The only thing she took was an amulet her mother had given her to bring her luck.

Flies buzzed over the bandits' bodies which were sprawled in the dust. The riders were already mounted and the nobleman lifted her to his horse. She realized it was a hunting party, for one of the servants carried a large cage of falcons, squawking and thundering their wings against the wicker sides of their prison in an effort to escape. The birds of prey had been captured in the mountains to be trained for hawking.

Riding in the center of his entourage, the nobleman held her before him in the saddle. As they passed through the broken gates of the yard beneath a bush she saw the body: Pepe, the mountain goat, with his throat slit, his lovely soft eyes, bulbous and staring.

Though she tried to keep herself stiffly away from the man's body, Rosanna suddenly turned her face to his green doublet and wept, sinking against the comforting strength of him. For Pepe she felt more loss than for the death of her own mother. He had been the only friend she ever had, the only giver of unselfish love she had ever known.

"It was quick. He did not suffer," the man soothed, surprised by her reaction at the sight of the dead animal.

Leaving the stone hovel behind, they ascended the mountain path. Rosanna did not look back, there was nothing left for her there, everything was before her. The sun hung lower in the sky and the mountain air was sharp. A chill breeze cut through her dress until she shivered with cold. Far below, the valley was small, the dwellings of the villagers mere specks in the green sward.

The nobleman took a dark green, fur-lined cloak from his baggage and he pulled it around him, indicating she was to share the garment.

Rosanna nestled inside the soft fur, finding welcome warmth from the combination of his body heat and the cloak. She rested her head against his shoulder, closing her eyes, and as they jogged to the crest of the peak, she dozed. When she wakened the horses had already begun the descent. They had crossed the low mountain, dropping down to a valley where in the distance, shimmering on a plain, she saw the city of Lorenzo. The fading sun lit and burnished hundreds of windows, dazzling her eyes, even the rose pink city walls seemed to cast sparkles of light as if particles of diamonds were embedded in the masonry.

The party picked up speed, pressing the horses to reach the safety of the walled city before nightfall. Excitement gripped Rosanna as she wondered what lay ahead and where this man would take her. What would be her reception when he arrived home with so strange a burden? She moved in the saddle trying to find a comfortable spot, and smiling at her, he said:

"It won't be long now, you can already see the city."

Rosanna nodded, looking up at his firm jawline, at the tanned flesh of his throat disappearing into the folds of his green cloak. He was more handsome than Berto. Perhaps he was a duke, or even a prince. He said he was a kinsman of hers, yet her mother had said her family were dead. It was a surprise to find she was related to nobility,

14

and with a pang of unrest she hoped he had not mistaken her for another. The warmth of his body had a strange smell. A heavy perfume like flowers, and she sniffed the fragrance finding it unusually pleasant. Even the fur cloak was perfumed, almost as if she lay warm and content in a bower of summer flowers. With a sigh, Rosanna nestled against his chest, slipping lower in the saddle till her head rested against the steady thunder of his heartbeat, the sound a stirring rhythm in her blood. And she slept.

The cessation of movement wakened her and Rosanna discovered they were already outside the huge gates of the city. The hunting party filed inside, heading to the right, and she looked about with interest. Wide-eyed, Rosanna stared at the tall, magnificent buildings of marble, their many colors heightened by the rose wash of sunset. Between dwellings she glimpsed a wide canal, the water dark in the shadows. However, the city had an odor she did not find pleasant, the refuse in the gutters a startling contrast to the grandeur of the marble palazzos. Fascinated by the paving, she listened to the clatter of the horses hooves ringing over the street. There was no vegetation to be seen and she wondered if there was one growing thing in the entire city of Lorenzo.

Presently they rounded a corner and rode inside a walled courtyard with the strong odor of stables rising hotly in the heavy evening air. The fur-lined cloak had become oppressive and she cast it off, glad of the breeze on her arms. Grooms came out to take the horses and helped her dismount, staring at her with surprise. The nobleman swung from the saddle, directing his men, then inspecting the wicker cage of birds before turning back to Rosanna.

"Here we are, little orphan. Come, let me see about food for you and some water to wash."

Obediently she followed him through a tall archway and found herself in another courtyard, though it had blue mosaic tile flooring, it seemed to be a garden as well. Flowers bloomed profusely, spilling radiant color to the ground, and pink flowering vines climbed the walls, jostling espaliered shrubs and roses on the smooth buff surface. Trees threw patches of cool shade, their spreading branches weeping purple and yellow flowers. A fountain

15

in the form of a painted galleon spewed water into a mammoth bowl. The crystal jets were caught in the mouths of mermaids, strange creatures with scaly fishtails, yet they had beautiful faces and breasts like women. Rosanna stared in fascination at the exotic perfumed surroundings, surprised by the lush courtyard vegetation.

"You like it. I would not have thought you would." The man laughed, his hand on her shoulder. "The fountain is my father's toy. The jets can be regulated to spew high in the air. It's very ingenious, but come, there will be time later to admire my home. It is one of the finest in Lorenzo and Father thinks even his Grace, the Duke, is jealous of its richness."

Rosanna followed his swinging cloak, hardly able to comprehend the magnificence of the archways and pillars of blue and white striped marble. Twisting, turning through passageways, up flights of stairs, it seemed an endless journey until at last they entered a room with a huge, gold damask hung bed.

Two women cried out in alarm, startled by their intrusion. There was a girl and an older woman, who was dressed like a servant in homespun gown and white coif. The young one was a vision of gold, from her hair which was fine spun, to the gold slippers on her feet.

"See, Bianca, I've brought you a new toy. I found it on my travels."

The girl stared and backed away as Rosanna was gently thrust forward. "What is it, such a black, dirty creature?"

The man laughed. "She is your cousin, a Sordello like you, Sister."

"You lie. She's a beggar maid. What would Mother say if she knew you were bringing ragged creatures off the streets to my chambers?" Bianca cried scandalized, clutching a pomander to her nose. "She probably has the plague."

"Christ's blood, I hope not," he cried in alarm, stepping back. "I've ridden with her in my lap these past hours."

"I thought you were trapping falcons, not gypsy wenches," Bianca reproved, sniffing her pomander like a drowning soul.

16

"Don't be an idiot, Bianca, put that thing down. She doesn't smell that bad."

Bianca swung the pomander from its golden ribbon, studying the strange girl and passing judgement. "Are you sure she's related? You men are always so easily fooled. Oh, I wish Mother was here, or even our father."

"She's not going to attack you. I'll warrant when she's bathed and dressed more becomingly she'll be a beauty."

"Is she mute, doesn't she speak?"

"Yes, in a hill dialect, but she speaks. Cia, fetch nurse and prepare some water to bathe the child."

"Marco, are my servants to wait on a beggar wench? And bathe her. You must be mad," Bianca gasped, her blue eyes round.

"They're *our* servants, and yes, would you have her sleep in here in that condition?"

"She's not sleeping in here. I won't have such an ugly black creature in my room. I'd be afraid to go to sleep. How dare you suggest such a thing. Mother would never hear of it."

"Do you suppose she would like it better if I took the wench to sleep in my room?" Marco asked with a grin. "It might be more pleasant for all concerned."

"Marco, you shock me with your boldness."

He turned impatiently to the servant. "Go, do as you are bid."

With a hasty bob, the woman hurried from the room, her feet echoing down the hallway. The three young people stared at each other taking stock of Rosanna's appearance, and she of them. Now she found she did not like the man as much as she thought she would, for his attitude was unkind. She would not be treated like some curiosity he had found wandering in the streets. And the girl she did not like at all.

"How old is she?"

Marco turned to Rosanna studying her body critically, his lip curled in a smile. "Twelve, perhaps."

"What is your age, wench?" Bianca demanded haughtily.

"I don't know," Rosanna said.

"What does she say? How am I supposed to understand that hill mumbling?"

17

"She doesn't know how old she is. In the villages they don't always reckon time. She's probably your age. That's why I thought you'd like to have her, Sister. She can wait on you, if our father approves."

"I don't approve and neither will he."

"She is the daughter of his sister."

"What?" Bianca gasped, her pale face horror stricken. "She can't be, even though I've heard the servants say Aunt Lucia was . . . deranged, she was still a lady. This is a gypsy brat. Why, look at her black hair and how dark her skin is. Her eyes are like coals."

"She is burnt by the sun. Her skin could be as fair as yours in time," Marco dismissed, turning to the door. "Anyway, believe it or not, sweet Bianca, it is so. I have it from the priest in the village. Father Domenico says poor Aunt Lucia was possessed of the devil and would not enter the church to have her soul cleansed. She lived in a mountain hovel with her daughter and a half-witted servant girl. When I arrived they were being violated by a band of thieves. I was in time to save this child from being raped." Bianca gasped in dismay at his strong language, and the young man was pleased to shock her, though it had been unintentional. Daily she sounded more like his father's wife, Magdela, who was a seething mass of shocked femininity, falsely modest and just as falsely pious.

"I couldn't leave her with the carcasses in that barren place, what else could I do but bring her here? When Father returns tomorrow from Venice, he'll be pleased to have the child in Lorenzo. He always seemed to have great affection for his sister," Marco ended, his thin lips curled in a sneer.

The servant girl, Cia, reappeared with a stout, elderly woman, and behind them came two girls carrying jugs of steaming water. With a curt nod of farewell, Marco strode from the room, leaving Rosanna alone with the hostile women. She cast an imploring glance in his direction, but Marco did not turn around and the door was closed.

The servants pulled out a tub from behind a damask screen, dragging it to the center of the room where they poured in the hot water, followed by cooler water until the bath was the right temperature. Cia would have

18

sprinkled drops of colored liquid in the water, but Bianca stopped her with a shrill cry.

"Not my perfume for that creature, she needs a blend to kill lice, I'll be bound. I won't stay and watch, though it might be entertaining. It's the hour for my dancing lesson."

With a haughty swish of her golden embroidered skirts, Bianca swept regally from the room, slamming the door closed.

The servant girls left also, until Rosanna was alone with Cia and the nurse. They swore at her and roughly pulled her dress over her head, scratching her carelessly with their nails, tugging her hair as it caught in the folds of cloth. Humiliated, she stepped into the water, finding their curious eyes on her body, for she made a strange picture. Her legs were sun bronzed almost to the knee, her face, arms and shoulders the same shade, but the patch from chest to thigh was white. The fairness of her skin was begrimed, but flawless, and the servants remarked on the quality of her body for one of so lowly a station. Rosanna listened to their words without speaking, knowing they thought she could not understand them. The language was difficult to follow at first, being of a purer type than she was used to hearing, but not unlike her mother's dialect. The women scrubbed her flesh until tears of pain filled her eyes, then the nurse slapped her buttocks and they guffawed as she jumped: it was time to get out of the bath. With head down, not meeting their eyes, Rosanna took the towel to dry herself, but they snatched it away, rubbing until her skin was reddened. Several times she was pinched beneath the fabric and though it was meant to be an accident, Rosanna knew it was not.

Her black hair hung soggily wet down her back, dripping in a puddle on the floor. Roughly Cia seized the towel and wrung out her hair, tugging and scrubbing until the moisture was gone.

At last the ordeal was over and she was given a gown. It was one of Cia's and begrudgingly loaned. The bodice was too loose and the waist too big, but it was finer than any she had ever owned. They dragged her into the hallway and down passages and stairs, until they reached the dining hall. From somewhere in the house Rosanna could hear music and she assumed it was coming from Bianca's dancing lesson.

Marco was seated at a long polished table eating roast venison. Rosanna identified the meat from its aroma and her nose twitched, her stomach growling with emptiness at the sight of food. He motioned the young woman, Cia, to his side. Their exchange was in an undertone and Rosanna could not hear the words. Cia nodded, but with a scowl, and Marco grinned, reaching up to tweak her cheek until she smiled back, then with an impatient gesture, he dismissed her, returning to his supper.

Cia came to the nurse and told her to go, that she was in charge of the wench. Rosanna resented being called that.

"I am Rosanna," she said.

Cia stared at her, surprised by her words, realizing now that she understood their language. "Rosanna," she repeated slowly, taking the girl's shoulder. "Come to my room for tonight till our master and mistress return. They'll know what to do with you. Maybe send you to a convent to let the good sisters raise you like you ought to be raised," Cia suggested, leading her along the cool marble-tiled hallways.

At that idea Rosanna paled. It would be terrible to be shut inside a convent for the rest of her life. Never to be able to walk in the country, or laugh and sing, but to embroider all day, the monotony broken only by prayers.

They stopped before a wooden door in a part of the house that was less fine and much darker than the rest. The smell of cooking lingered in the hot atmosphere and Rosanna knew it was the servants' quarters. Cia's room was bare in contrast to the grand bedchamber they had just left. There was a low wooden bed and a trundle had been pulled from beneath it for Rosanna's use. Cia pushed the bed as far in the corner as possible, indicating it was for her, and Rosanna stretched out thankfully as Cia threw her a quilt.

"Now, Rosanna, you've come at a bad time for me. My Matteo has just returned after being at sea for many months. He's coming to me tonight. You will not say anything to the *padrone* about it; if you do, I'll cut your

20

black little throat," Cia threatened, a grin on her face, but her eyes were hard. "Agreed."

"Yes," Rosanna said, wondering what choice she had.

"You will sleep through it all?"

"Yes."

"Good ... and don't get too interested in Matteo, he has a big appetite after he's been at sea ... and I'd have to kill you for that, too."

In alarm Rosanna blinked up at Cia's pretty face, twisted in a scowl. What if Matteo would not be content to let her sleep through "it all"? This was almost as bad as the brigands.

"You're a good girl, aren't you?"

"Yes."

"With Matteo you stay that way," Cia pronounced vehemently. With a dawning smile she turned to the door. "If you're hungry I'll find you some food."

Rosanna said she was and Cia disappeared. She was gone a long time, returning at last with some bread and a bowl of soup, bringing her own meal with her. On her plate there was meat and saffron-colored pastry which she did not share.

It grew dark outside and Cia lit tapers. As the hour of the meeting with her lover approached, she sang gaily and smiled as she brushed her dark hair. In a moment of generosity, seeing Rosanna watching her, Cia offered her the brush for her own hair.

"Don't tell Signor Marco, either, he wouldn't like it. He acts as if he owns me," the servant girl complained.

The significance of the episode in the dining room became apparent to Rosanna; Marco was also Cia's lover. "I won't tell."

"When are you going to sleep?" Cia demanded, growing impatient as Rosanna tossed on the narrow bed. "He'll be here soon."

"I can't go to sleep."

"We'll see to that." With determination Cia marched from the room, to return a moment later with a cup of brown liquid. "Here, drink this," she said.

Rosanna hesitated, finding an unpleasant aroma wafting from the brew. But, as Cia impatiently thrust the cup to her mouth, she drained it and the girl nodded with approval. Within a few minutes the lumpy bed seemed bliss-fully comfortable, and soon the soft, even sounds of sleep made Cia smile with relief.

"Come in," she called softly, as the signal came at the window. And in a moment the swarthy Matteo was clasped in her arms.

Chapter Two

In the morning Rosanna was led to her uncle's study. Upon his arrival Marco had told him of the incident in the mountains, and Ugo Sordello demanded she be brought to him at once. Now he waited, pacing the room, smacking his gauntlets against the palm of his large-boned hand in agitation.

"This is the wench, *padrone*," Cia curtsied and withdrew, her cheeks flushing prettily with color at Marco's appraising glance.

"Come here."

Rosanna stared at the big man before her, slightly in awe of his rich clothing, but not afraid of him. She moved hesitantly across the room, twisting her hands together on the rough front of her dress. Catching her shoulder, Ugo Sordello drew her to the light which flooded clear and bright through the long windows. He stared intently at her face, turning her cheek, holding her dèfiant chin firmly in his hand. He was not as old as she had expected, but he did not look like her mother. Only in the dark eyes was there any resemblance. Long brown hair reached to his shoulders, soft and curled like a woman's, while on his hands he wore glittering rings. Her uncle's face was florid, the flesh of his cheeks sagging in folds, lax from dissipation and middle age.

"Mother of God, I think you're right. She is Lucia's daughter. There's an air about her I can't place, but she looks like her mother. You can be flattered, wench, my sister was a beauty in her youth. It's a pity such misfortune overtook you, but timely that my son happened on the scene. It must have been Providence's guiding hand, thanks be to God," he muttered, glancing piously toward heaven.

"Are we to keep her, Father?" Marco inquired, swinging from the corner of the table where he was perched. "Will she be of use?"

His father shot a warning frown as Marco reached towards Rosanna, and the boy dropped his hands. "We will place the poor orphan in our household. My lady wife will teach her the refinements as befits a lady's maid. Perhaps she will be company for little Bianca; they seem to be of a like age."

"She has no clothing but a ragged sack, and that thing is little better," Marco remarked, twitching the loose shoulder of her borrowed gown. "The child is swamped by it."

"I will ask Magdela to arrange some more suitable garment when she returns this afternoon. What a surprise it will be for her to find another daughter already full-grown."

Magdela's surprise was not of pleasure. "What do you mean, another daughter?" she cried with flashing eyes, as she flounced angrily about the room. "What if I don't want another daughter? What am I to do with two growing wenches to clothe and educate with only the paltry housekeeping sum you give me?"

"You shall have more, if it's necessary. The wench is orphaned, dear heart. She never knew her father."

"What care I for some baggage begotten in a ditch, and don't, 'dear heart' me. I'm not totally ignorant of the gossip about you and that sister of yours, Husband. Why, if the truth were known, she's probably closer related than I think."

Ugo raised his fist, thundering the dishes on the table.

"We will have no more of it. You clothe the girl, see to her education and keep your mouth shut. Those are my wishes, Madam, and this is my house. Perchance she will make a fitting maid for Bianca, and if not, we can always use an extra hand in the kitchens. Now get you gone."

Dropping a swift curtsy, Magdela departed in stony silence, inwardly seething at the imposition. Educate and clothe the wench, why Bianca said she was like a gypsy maid. It was unforgivable of Ugo to place such burdens on her good will. His latest appointment to the Duke's Privy Council had made him completely unmanageable, still, perhaps it was a small price to pay for the privilege of serving at court. Now her daughter would be able to make a far more profitable marriage than hoped, perhaps even to a man of royal blood. Just think, she might have grandchildren related to the house of Lorenzo. Then Ugo would not be forever comparing the blood line of his first wife, the saintly Lotta, when all she had produced was a wench-hungry idler. Why, there were times when she even feared for her darling Bianca, the way Marco entered the girl's bedchamber at all hours, and completely unannounced. More than likely taking after his father in that respect.

With an aggravated thump, Magdela knocked on Bianca's bedroom door and her daughter's sweet voice bade her enter. When Magdela looked about the room she beheld the strange wench standing by the window, the golden sun of early evening burnishing her dark face with a copper glow.

"Holy Mother, she is a gypsy brat," she gasped in dismay.

"This is Rosanna. Marco says she's going to be my friend," Bianca cried, running lightly over the tiled floor in her velvet slippers. "Isn't she ugly?"

"Yes." Magdela gathered her daughter in her arms for a swift embrace, then put her aside. "Does she speak in an outlandish tongue as well?"

"I don't know. She doesn't say anything. But Marco says she talks hill dialect," Bianca supplied helpfully, leading her mother to the strange new curiosity.

"I hope she's been bathed, she looks very dirty."

25

"Marco says she's sunburned and that her skin is probably fair like mine."

Marco seemed to know all there was to know about the brat, Magdela thought in annoyance. In truth, there were probably things he knew which Bianca would never dream. The black-haired thing looked as if she was already used to pleasing men. Magdela spun the girl around to study her face. Away from the yellow light, her skin was not as bronze as she had thought, but her eyes were black as coals and seemed to smoke with the same heat.

"I'm your Aunt Magdela. Have you no manners, wretch?" she demanded haughtily as the girl stared at her. "Don't you know how to curtsy?"

Lightly Bianca dropped to the floor. "Like that, silly."

With a shove from her aunt, Rosanna attempted the same thing, but she lost her balance and sprawled on the floor. Bianca's laughter pealed in the room and her mother joined in the humor. With a scowl, Rosanna picked herself up, refusing to meet their scornful faces.

"What a clumsy brat. It will be more than I can do to teach such an oaf grace and manners, I'll be bound," Magdela complained, turning up her nose. "Why is she in your room, Daughter?"

"Father said I could play with her, but she isn't any fun. She just stands there and glares at me."

Her mother patted her sulky face, agreeing with the complaint. She was a hostile creature and no mistake. It would not be safe to leave Bianca alone with her again. She would have the girl sent to the servant's quarters. "Don't worry, I'll have her sent to the kitchens. We can't keep such an uncivilized creature in our rooms."

"No. Marco said she could be my maid. I want a maid, I don't want an old nurse like a baby, I'm almost grownup. I want my own maid. Father said so too," Bianca wailed in anger, rubbing her eyes where tears were already forming.

"But, my dear, she's so wild. I'd be afraid for your safety," her mother pleaded in alarm, seeking to comfort Bianca, who wrenched away.

"If you don't let me keep her I'll scream. She's going to be my maid. I want her to wear a blue dress and have a cap, just like Cia. I want her. I want her. I want her."

Furiously Bianca drummed her heels on the floor, ripping out the elaborate hairdressing that her nurse had spent an hour arranging.

"Please, don't cry, Bianca. Your eyes will be all red and ugly, and you'll get wrinkles," her mother shrieked in distress. "Don't cry, darling, of course you can have the gypsy thing to play with if you want."

The favor won, Bianca's tears dissolved as if by magic, and a smile came to her tear-streaked face. "Do you mean that, really? Can I have her in here instead of nurse? Every day, to look after my clothes?"

"Yes, but she probably doesn't know how to look after anything. To please you, Bianca, darling, we'll let her try," Magdela appeased with a sigh of relief. In two weeks they would be leaving for their villa in the country; it would be easy to find an excuse to leave the wench behind. Probably by then Bianca would have lost interest in having a maid. After the summer was over, perhaps they could hire a suitable wench, for Bianca would be thirteen next month; it was time to dispense with nurse. "Are you happy now, darling?"

Bianca nodded. "Make her speak to me, Mother. She won't say anything."

Magdela viewed her daughter with dismay, such a favor was beyond her control, so to distract the child, she said: "I have a length of lovely blue velvet for you. We brought it with us all the way from Venice. And I have some silver slippers, and all kinds of ribbons for your hair."

"Make her talk," Bianca demanded defiantly, glaring at Rosanna.

"But, how can I?"

"Make her talk."

In desperation Magdela stepped up to the girl and slapped her hard across the cheek. "Say something, you wretch. Speak!"

Tears spilled from Rosanna's eyes and she gasped in pain as Aunt Magdela repeated the action. Then her own anger boiling, she wrenched away, slapping her aunt's hand from her face and she screamed all the curses she knew. Aunt Magdela reeled back, her face white with shock, but Bianca laughed and clapped.

27

"You made her talk. She did talk."

"It would be better for her to be mute than utter such filth. She shall be whipped. I will inform your father that she must go. We can do nothing with her."

After her whipping, Rosanna went back to Bianca's bedchamber. Although she ached from the blows of the switch, she experienced a certain triumph that Aunt Magdela had been overruled. Her uncle had laughed when her words were repeated, until Aunt Magdela was gray with anger. But Rosanna was to stay. Secretly she wondered if Uncle Ugo would have liked to call Aunt Magdela those things himself, for he seemed to be highly amused by the profane recital.

A dress had been found, blue, as Bianca requested. It was too tight in the bodice and the skirt too short, but her aunt said it would suffice until a new one could be made. There was to be a bed for her in Bianca's room, begrudgingly vacated by the rheumatic nurse, who had given her a sharp pinch as a parting gesture. And now Rosanna waited for further instructions from Bianca, nervously standing by the great bed in the center of the room. Bianca was a spoilt little baby and Rosanna would have dearly loved to slap her during her temper tantrum. Bianca watched her, a triumphant smile on her pretty face. She always got her way eventually after going through a few hysterics.

She skipped to the window, and opened it, leaning far out and she waved to someone below. Then she turned around and said: "Why don't you do something? Don't just stand there."

Rosanna thought she would go to sleep, perhaps tomorrow her situation would appear better.

"You sleep over there; I sleep in the big bed," Bianca informed her as Rosanna approached the carved fourposter in the center of the room. In a lordly manner she waved her hand towards the small wooden bed pushed close against the wall, far from the breeze blowing through the high arched windows. It was not as bad as she thought having the wench in here, at least she was rid of her old nurse. Now she was a grown-up lady with her own serving wench instead of a child with a nursemaid in attendance.

Rosanna stood silently in the shadows, far from the pool of light, watching Bianca flounce around the room importantly arranging her belongings and smoothing imaginary wrinkles from the rich brocaded bed cover.

"You're really very lucky to be able to live with us," Bianca continued. "My father's one of the richest merchants in Lorenzo. We're received at the palace, you know. Marco's mother was the Duke's cousin, so we're actually related to the royal house."

"I want to go home."

"Home! Don't be silly, you haven't got a home," Bianca reproved. "Mother's right, you are ungrateful. She said you were a blackhearted, ungrateful baggage." The insult was repeated with pleasure, rolling easily from Bianca's rosebud mouth. Then, with a sigh, she was a little girl again. "Rosanna, don't you want to be friends with me? I've never had a friend before. If you say you'll be my friend I'll let you play with my dolls."

Unmoved by the pleading tone, Rosanna however was not impervious to the bribe. "What are dolls?" she asked, coming into the light.

"You don't know? Haven't you ever had one?" Bianca gasped in amazement, slithering from her perch on the big bed.

"No."

Crossing to the chest in the corner, Bianca opened it and chose two dolls. "I'm going to let you have Teresa—she has one arm missing, but I still like her because she came all the way from Rome," Bianca informed, studying the effect of her words, but she was disappointed by Rosanna's reaction.

"Where's that?"

"Don't you know anything? It's hundreds of miles away to the south. Father brought her for my ninth birthday, so you see I've had her a long time. You must promise to be careful with her, for if you're unkind, I'll take her from you."

Rosanna held out her arms and the doll was laid reverently against her bosom.

"Isn't she pretty? Her dress has gold embroidery."

The girls bent over the little figure in a pink velvet dress embroidered with gold lilies. Pearl earrings swung from the doll's ears, and a miniature necklace hung around her neck. Rosanna stared at the beautiful dress, more taken by it than the doll itself, for the painted wooden face was unlifelike with its fixed simper and staring eyes.

"Her dress is lovely. I'm going to have a dress like that someday," Rosanna vowed, stroking the velvet skirt, feeling the softness of the fabric like flower petals under her fingers.

"You'll never have a dress like this," Bianca laughed scornfully, snatching her doll. She put Teresa on the chest and held up another doll. This one was larger and had real hair looped in circles over her ears. She was dressed in red silk with silver undersleeves, and Rosanna gasped at the lovely dress.

"This is Bella, but you can't play with her. I've got another doll I'll show you, but you mustn't ever touch her, your dirty fingers will soil her gown."

Humming a gay tune, Bianca danced to the cupboard and opened the door, returning a moment later with a third doll. "This is Gilda. She's the prettiest doll I have. We don't play with her, she's just to look at."

Rosanna gasped again at the doll's beautiful gown of white embroidered with pearls and sparkling jewels that winked fire in the candlelight.

Bianca was pleased by her reaction and she smiled smugly with pride, holding the doll nearer to the light. "Do you know who she is?"

Rosanna shook her head, longing to handle the lovely doll, but knowing she could not.

"She's Duke Paolo's wife in her wedding gown . . . at least she was, she's dead now," Bianca dismissed, stroking the doll's golden hair.

"Why did she die?"

"Having a baby," Bianca said, taking the treasure back to the cupboard. "It must be terrible."

"Dying?"

"No, having a baby. When I'm grown-up, I'll never have one," Bianca vowed, shutting the cupboard door. "I don't want to die when I'm still young and pretty like she was."

"You don't just die from having babies," Rosanna reflected, sitting on the carved chest where she examined Teresa more closely. "You can die from being stabbed and your blood comes gurgling out of your mouth, all dark and frothy . . ."

"Stop it, this instant, you terrible girl. Give my doll back," Bianca screamed, repossessing her poor Teresa. Crooning softly she soothingly patted the bright-painted face. "You'll frighten my poor little girl."

Sullen, Rosanna stared at the floor without speaking. She had not intended to upset Bianca, but everything she did seemed to meet with her disapproval. "Did the baby die too?" she asked at last, morbidly possessed by the memory of death on the windswept mountains of her home.

"Yes. It was while Duke Paolo was away at the war with Milan. My brother fought with him and he was very brave too," Bianca said, smiling again. "Marco's the Duke's friend and sometimes he goes to balls at the palace. And he even goes to Castel Isola and hunts with the royal family," she boasted, patting her long golden hair. "I look like them, everyone says so. You might see the Duke someday at our house. He comes here, you know. We even entertained King Alfonso of Naples once."

Rosanna was not interested in the Duke, or King Alfonso, she only wanted to look at the doll's clothes. And while Bianca's back was turned, she fingered Bella's sumptuous skirts. Touching the stiff, plaited hair, she shuddered, wondering suddenly if it came from a dead woman.

"If you're really lucky and you behave, we'll let you watch the procession next week. The royal family will be riding in it."

"What's a procession?"

"You don't know about anything, do you? Everyone dresses in their best and rides through the streets, and there are floats with flowers all over them, and pretty girls dressed up as goddesses and things. Afterwards there's a ball at the palace, but we can't go to that yet. The Duke is the handsomest man in Lorenzo, even more handsome than my brother."

31

With a groan and a stretch, Rosanna got up. "Can I go to sleep now?"

"No, not until I'm ready for bed. You have to help me."

Bianca haughtily instructed her, but the fastenings of her dress were difficult to manage. After much struggling between them they managed to take off the red silk dress. At Bianca's bidding, Rosanna hung the dress in the deep cupboard, searching quickly for the bride doll, Gilda. It was on the third shelf, the shimmering white skirts spread around the doll's stiff little figure like a bell. Someday, when Bianca was gone, she would take out the doll and look at her; she would comb the beautiful golden hair and pretend Gilda was her own.

"You're going to have to learn a lot if you're to be a lady's maid."

I don't want to be a lady's maid, Rosanna wanted to shout, but she only nodded in agreement, waiting to be dismissed to her own bed.

"When we go to our villa next month, Mother is going to have you sent to the nuns for the summer. She hopes they will make a lady out of you. It's terrible not being able to embroider or play a musical instrument, it's positively barbaric, she says. Father doesn't like the expense of it, but she says he'll do it anyway."

Rosanna was alarmed by this information, for she had no desire to learn to sew or play an instrument and the awful thought of a convent made her stomach pitch with dread.

Finally Bianca was ready for bed. She brushed her long golden hair, not trusting Rosanna's clumsy hands with so delicate a task. As she knelt on a crimson silk cushion before the huge crucifix, Rosanna thought she looked like an angel with her flowing tresses and white shift—like the holy paintings on the walls inside the church in the mountains, at which she had stared with awe, until pious villagers drove her from the hallowed sanctuary.

The prayers Bianca repeated were strange to her, and she hurried through them so mechanically, Rosanna could not catch the words. In a few moments her cousin was scrambling into bed, settling herself regally in a mountain of white covers.

32

"You may kiss me on the cheek if you wish," she announced languidly, as if she were doing a great favor.

"I don't want to," Rosanna said, turning away, ignoring Bianca's outraged snort of annoyance at her words. At last she could retire and thankfully she lay on her own lumpy straw pallet, the wooden bed creaking in distress as she wriggled about until she was comfortable.

During the following week, Rosanna learned many things; though she spent part of each day with Bianca, she did not immediately assume her role as lady's maid. Cia explained the intricacies of a lady's rich garments to her, how they fastened and what was put on first, also how to brush and braid her mistress' hair, and how to arrange an elaborate coiffure with false hair pieces for special occasions.

Uncle Ugo rode to the mountain village north of Bergamo in the Venetian Republic to talk with the priest who had directed Marco to her home, and from records kept at the church, he learned she was born in the summer of 1440. Rosanna found she was one month younger than Bianca; a fact which greatly pleased the other girl, who was always anxious to lord it over her, though Uncle Ugo demanded she be treated more like a relative than a servant. On Bianca's saint's day there was usually a ball at their villa to mark the beginning of the summer season. But Rosanna would spend her saint's day in the convent of Our Lady where she was to learn some refinements and become a Christian.

"She's positively heathen," Aunt Magdela cried, when Ugo suggested she might travel to Villa Sordello with the family. "I wouldn't want it on my conscience to take in such a godless brat. No, she'll go to the sisters who I hope can teach her a little piety and a great deal of manners."

There was one week left before the family departure and the highlight of that time was to be the festival. Bianca prattled about the glorious parade and was in such a good mood, she even allowed Rosanna to hold her precious doll. Sometimes when Bianca was at her music lesson, Rosanna took down the bride doll to examine her gown, careful to place her back on the shelf before Bianca returned. Rosanna dreamed about the dead Duchess,

33

wondering what she was like, and she imagined herself inside the palace dressed in gorgeous jeweled gowns. She would be named Gilda too, and instead of her own black hair, she would have golden tresses as fine spun as the doll's hair. It would sparkle brightly in the sun until people remarked on her beauty instead of thinking her black and ugly.

On the day of the festival Rosanna was given a new gown. Aunt Magdela presented the gift grudgingly, reminding her of the immense sacrifice she had endured to allow the seamstress to make a dress for an orphan child, instead of working on her own important summer wardrobe.

Rosanna slipped the gown over her head; it was too big, but her aunt said that was to allow for growth. The smooth, closely woven material was a rich beechnut brown, while beneath there was a white gathered shift.

"Mother of God, she looks even more like a gypsy in that," Aunt Magdela gasped, her hands to her pudgy face. "Perchance the weeks in cloisters can bleach her face. I shall see to it that she be kept out of the sun."

When her aunt had gone, Rosanna admired her appearance in Bianca's mirror. She looked very strange, for she had never seen her reflection before, except in the mountain streams. Her face was dark with high, well-defined cheekbones and her black eyes seemed to slant upwards at the corners beneath dark brows. Her hair was long and so ugly, it was easy to see why they thought her unbeautiful. She wasn't even dainty like Bianca, but wide-shouldered and full-breasted, even at twelve. Bianca was right; she was born to be a peasant, even though she didn't feel like one inside.

"If you're very nice, I'll let you have a ribbon for your hair," Bianca offered generously. "What color would you like? Red?"

"No, I like green, the color of the grass."

"All right, I've got a green one."

With a gasp of pleasure, Rosanna accepted the ribbon, and she braided it in her heavy hair, finishing the end off with a small bow.

Bianca applauded, pleased by her cousin's appearance. "You're not pretty like me, but you look much better in that dress," she allowed generously. "Would you like a flower for your hair? I have a basketful to throw to the riders."

Rosanna took a bunch of violets from the ribbon-decked wicker basket, for they were the only flowers she recognized. Their perfume was delicately sweet, filling the room with a lingering fragrance. Dividing the blossoms she hooked some in the lacing in the front of her dress, the rest in the braid of her hair. Now she looked almost attractive, Rosanna thought, looking back at her reflection.

"If you weren't so tall and big, and if your hair was another color, you might be pretty."

Bianca's words dashed her self-confidence and sadly Rosanna slunk to the corner to await the festivities. In a few minutes Uncle Ugo came to wish them good-by, for he was to ride in the parade. His expression was one of surprise when he saw her, and with buoying spirits, Rosanna read admiration in his dark eyes. Bianca was wrong, she thought with pleasure—men found her attractive. It was strange that women did not.

"Good-bye, sweetings. Don't forget to throw a big flower to me, Bianca. I'll wear it in my hat for you," he promised, kissing his daughter's cheek.

"I'll wait till you're under the balcony, Father. Oh, isn't it exciting?" Bianca squealed, clapping her hands.

"You too, Rosanna. Will you watch for me?" he asked, his hand lingering on her shoulder as he studied her face.

"Yes, Uncle."

With a wave of his jeweled hand, he was gone, the metallic thread in his magnificent robes glittering in the sunlight as he walked past the window. Rosanna watched him go down the steps from the balcony, his plumed bonnet bobbing above the wall as he walked.

"Come on, let's go to the balcony," Bianca urged, catching at her arm. "You can carry my basket."

The girls hurried through the house which was unusually quiet, for the servants seemed to be either in the kitchens, or watching the parade. The family was gathered on a large balcony overhanging the street. Chairs were grouped about and the stone wall was hung with colored bunting and streamers. Aunt Magdela indicated Rosanna

35

was to stand by the wall, but Bianca began to pout, and fearing another outburst, her mother said if Rosanna was very quiet she could sit with the family.

Bianca grinned triumphantly as Rosanna came to sit beside her and she squeezed her cousin's arm, bubbling with excitement.

"We'll see the duke, won't that be exciting?"

"Will the duchess be with him?" Rosanna asked with interest, thinking about the magnificent doll on the cupboard shelf.

"No, silly, I told you she's dead," Bianca corrected scornfully. "Don't you remember?"

"Well, I thought maybe there was another duchess by now."

"No, Duke Paolo hasn't remarried, although many would like to be his duchess. All the girls in Lorenzo are in love with him."

Rosanna digested this information, and the other snippets of gossip which Bianca whispered while they waited for the parade to begin.

A shout went up in the street; the first banner was visible, bobbing down the middle of the road as a man on a white horse carried the standard of Lorenzo. For over an hour Rosanna stared and gasped at the magnificence of the spectacle. Dozens of floats with beautiful maidens went by, and the sumptuous display of color dazzled her eyes. The floats were decorated with hundreds of colored flowers, while more flowers were thrown to the riders from the balconies of houses along the street.

Bianca bubbled and laughed as she pointed out famous people to Rosanna, whose mind was a jumble of names and titles.

"Here, look at the woman sitting in the seashell," Bianca squealed, as a float depicting the king of the seas moved past. A buxom woman in a floating, sea green gown reclined on a pink plaster seashell, her long golden hair a silken cloak around her shoulders. "That's Flora Dati, the Duke's mistress."

"What's that?"

Bianca snorted at her cousin's ignorance. "Don't you know? She has his babies, but she isn't married to him," Bianca informed in a sophisticated drawl. "Really, you are ignorant. I don't think she's pretty and she's positively middle-aged. Do you know she's twenty," Bianca related in aggrieved tones. "They say he'll be tired of her soon and then he'll have someone else. See that girl there, the one with the wings, sitting on a cloud."

Rosanna nodded, admiring the pearl-encrusted gown the lady wore. It must be worth a fortune. "Yes, who's she?"

"She's Betta Peruzzi. Her father's the leader of the *condottieri*. Everyone says she'll be the next one, but the Dati woman won't let him go. Betta's pretty, isn't she?"

Rosanna agreed, admiring the girl's lovely auburn hair. She had not seen one lady with black hair in the entire procession. "Why doesn't anyone have hair my color?" she whispered to Bianca.

"Because it's not pretty. Everyone wants to have hair the same color as Duke Paolo and Flora Dati. All the women dye their hair if it isn't the right color. It's just not fashionable to be dark haired this year," Bianca declared with a conceited smile, patting her own fine golden locks. "Oh, there he is now. Isn't he handsome?" Bianca squeaked as the Duke's household came in view, with prancing steeds and fluttering pennants. A huge white satin banner flapped on a gilded pole, depicting a strange animal shimmering in gold embroidery. When Rosanna asked about it, Bianca said it was called a lion. She was so fascinated by the creature, Rosanna barely glanced at Duke Paolo, beyond noting his magnificent garments of cloth of gold.

"He often wears gold because he's a golden ruler from head to foot," Bianca supplied, craning over the balcony as the ducal party moved up the street, until she caught her mother's disapproving eye and drew back.

When the last float was out of view, the family party withdrew to the cool interior of the house to rest for the afternoon. There was to be a banquet and reception at the palace later in the evening which Aunt Magdela and Uncle Ugo were to attend.

All day Rosanna thought about the wonderful parade, wishing she could have been one of the lovely girls on a flower-decked float. Maybe when she was older she could dye her hair like they did to make herself more attractive, but at present she did not know how.

As a treat the girls ate their evening meal in their room, whispering and giggling about the parade and with surprise Rosanna found Bianca was not so bad if she was happy.

Chapter Three

The day was overcast and before breakfast a drizzling rain began to fall. Rosanna surveyed the gloomy morning with apprehension, for it seemed to duplicate her own dreariness. Soon the family would be on their way to Villa Sordello while she would be thankfully deposited within the forbidding, iron doors of the convent. In her wildest imagination she could not visualize the monotonous boredom of three months in religious seclusion. Last night, in a rare mood of kindness, Bianca had tried to comfort her by saying most girls of good family were boarded in a convent at some time in their lives. She had spent three years there herself and it was not so bad; you just had to behave and be attentive to your studies, and above all, pious. Rosanna had only the vaguest notion of religion and she was sure the sisters would be shocked to learn of her ignorance.

"What's wrong, Rosanna? You look as miserable as the weather," Marco greeted, as she trailed disconsolately inside the dining room.

"I don't want to go to the convent."

"Is that all. They won't bite you. The sisters are supposed to be wise and gentle ladies. Cheer up, I'm sure you'll be so ladylike when I return, I'll never recognize you."

"That's what I'm afraid of," she replied with a scowl, moving past him to her chair.

"What if I promise to visit you?" he suggested, slipping his arm about her waist. "Will that be something to look forward to? I tell you what, I'll get written permission to take you riding on your saint's day."

"Will you, really?"

"If you'd like," he agreed, drawing her against his shoulder. "Come now, give me a kiss, sweetheart, and smile."

Rosanna kissed him, surprised by the warmth of his mouth. For a moment she stared into his eyes, puzzled by the change she sensed within herself. Her heart thudded faster and she felt a burst of heat within her stomach, the way she had felt when Berto held her, or when she rode to Lorenzo clasped tight against Marco's body. She suspected Marco too noticed the difference, for he did not release her immediately, and his hand toyed with the fabric of her gown.

"Do you promise to come for me?"

"Yes, I promise."

The shrill tones of Aunt Magdela's voice could be heard beyond the door and Marco gave her a pat. "Back to your chair before Magdela suspects me of seducing you at the breakfast table," he joked, turning back to his plate as his stepmother came into the room.

"Well, up early for once, Marco. Or is it that you never went to bed?" Magdela asked with sarcasm, stooping to plant a reserved kiss on the boy's cheek.

"Good morning, Stepmother."

"Rosanna, did you pack your bag as I instructed?"

"Yes, Madam."

"I'll be glad to have you safely inside the convent. It will be such a relief to my conscience to know you are in God's hands," Aunt Magdela said with a smile, settling her dark traveling skirts demurely as she sat in her chair.

Rosanna stared at the food on her plate, her stomach revolting against the thought of eating, even though Cia had placed a choice portion of meat pasty and fresh, honeyed bread especially for her. Maybe at the convent they

40

would put her on a ration of bread and water to cleanse her soul of its wickedness. The thought spurred her laggard appetite. This might be the last decent meal she would have all summer.

With a hurried greeting Bianca and her father joined them at the table and Rosanna was ignored as the meal progressed. Outside the windows rain swished gently against the glass and with a thunderous glance towards the gray sky, Aunt Magdela complained, "One would think I had been lax with my devotions that the saints should send such inclement weather for our journey."

"The farmers' devotions must have been more sincere, sweeting," Ugo suggested, and Marco spluttered in his wine cup at the remark.

Magdela glared, ignoring her husband's humor. "It really is unfair, my new headdress will be ruined, and I shudder to think what will become of the baggage."

Rosanna listened to her aunt's multitude of complaints, her stomach churning nervously as the hour of departure approached. Finally it was time to leave. With dragging feet Rosanna went for her bag and cloak, feeling as if she were to be imprisoned. Perhaps they would forget about her and leave her in the convent for the rest of her life.

"Ready?" Marco asked behind her, taking the small trunk from her arms. He smiled reassuringly as she blanched, desperately glancing about for a means of escape. "I'll go with you, if you promise not to run away," he offered.

"All right," she agreed after a long silence.

"Good." Marco strode back to the dining room, his voice drifting to her ears as she stood trembling in the cold, damp passageway. "I'll take the child, if you wish, Father. It will save your new robes from the rain," he suggested.

"A good idea. What think you, Magdela?"

"I think it's a disgraceful idea to allow a young girl to ride abroad unchaperoned with your son."

"Cia will come, I cannot enter the sanctuary, and she can see that the child is safe before we leave the city."

"I don't like it. People will think the girl's a wanton riding abroad with a man."

"Enough," Ugo snapped with a sigh of exasperation.

41

"Take the wench for me, Marco, but be back promptly. We leave within the hour."

Whistling, Marco came out of the room, an expression of triumphant accomplishment on his face. "All ready, come on."

The streets were dreary in the chill rain and Rosanna huddled inside her borrowed cloak, trying to stay dry. Marco spoke to her and joked, making the time pass quickly, until it seemed only a few minutes before they stood outside the forbidding doors of the convent of San Lorenzo.

Marco boldly strode to the door pulling a dangling rope beside the entrance to announce their arrival. From inside the dim, stone interior the great bell clanged hollowly, and Rosanna shuddered at the sound; the place had all the warmth of a tomb. At last a small grill in the door was opened and a woman's old, wizened face peered through to see who stood outside.

"It is the girl from the Sordello household," Marco announced, striding up to the opening. "Hurry, you old crone, it's wet out here."

The door was unlocked, its hinges grating with an eerie, creaking sound. Rosanna passed through a small door cut within the larger one and she wondered if the main door to this prison was ever opened. The interior was gloomy and cold. A few austere stone benches were ranged along the walls of the long narrow room, and an illuminated picture of Our Lady was visible at the far end of the corridor. With a curt word the old woman shuffled away, disappearing around the corner, her footfalls echoing for a few minutes in the awesome silence. Marco placed his arm reassuringly around Rosanna's shoulders, winking at Cia over the girl's head.

Soon a nun came with outstretched hand to welcome them. "I'm Sister Veronica," she said with a soft smile, her small gray eyes surrounded by a criss-crossed sea of wrinkles.

Marco bowed, doffing his cap, then turning to Rosanna, he introduced her to the sister. "I believe my father has told you the sad details concerning the girl's arrival in Lorenzo, Sister."

Sister Veronica agreed, reaching for Rosanna's arm in

a gesture of comfort. "That he has, and we must thank our blessed creator for His intervention on the child's behalf."

"Amen," Marco agreed, glancing towards the ceiling.

"Now, come with me, child. I shall see that your stay with us in not unpleasant."

Rosanna hesitated, glancing towards the closed door and back to Marco. Cia had remained dutifully in the background while he spoke with the nun, and now she came forward, carrying Rosanna's bag.

"Bid your cousin good-day, child."

Marco held out his arms and in a moment Rosanna was clinging to him fiercely, whispering: "Don't go, please, dear Marco, don't go."

"You know I must. Come now, what did we decide this morning," he reprimanded, but there was a twinkle in his eyes. "We decided on smiles, didn't we . . . and a certain promise."

Tight-lipped, she nodded, fearful lest she should cry before the sister. The two women stared at her in surprise, and Sister Veronica impatiently cleared her throat.

"Good-by, little cousin." Marco kissed her, and reluctantly she released his arms, stepping back as he put on his cap.

All too soon he went outside and the door closed behind his familiar figure. At least Cia was still with her, and the servant girl gave Rosanna a reassuring smile. Sister Veronica led the way while they trudged through what seemed to be miles of endless stone corridors. From somewhere in the distance came the sound of organ music and the notes of a choir, but beyond that the convent was silent as a tomb.

Finally, after climbing a winding flight of stairs, they reached a dormitory where Sister Veronica instructed Cia to put the bag. It was a long narrow room with six beds, all neatly topped by serviceable gray covers. Rosanna's bed was near the window, and she was glad of her good fortune—at least she could look outside at the world of freedom. Brushes and combs were arranged on small bedside chests, with a crucifix and kneeling cushion beside each bed. The only other decoration on the austere stone walls were two portraits of Our Lady, and in the corner by the door was a statue in a niche, a bowl of white flowers and a flickering candle before it.

Cia stood by helplessly, until Sister Veronica assured her it would be safe for her to leave; the child would be taken good care of. Rosanna kissed the servant's rosy cheek, finding to her surprise large tears trickling from Cia's dark eyes.

"Good-by, little one. Be brave," Cia whispered as she departed, sniffling and dabbing her eyes.

Sister Veronica quietly closed the door, leaving Rosanna alone in the strange, cheerless dormitory. Outside, the steady drip of rain was loud in the silence and she went to the window, raising the black curtain to peer out. The view was disappointing. The window overlooked a low roof and the cloister opposite, yet if she stood at the very edge of the glass and craned her neck she could see the busy streets of the city. With surprise, Rosanna realized part of the convent overlooked the piazza before the ducal palace, for a liveried guard was visible on a flight of steps across the square. Perhaps she could find another window which gave a better vantage point, she might even be able to watch processions and the royal household leaving for mass. The choir and music she heard in the corridor must have drifted from the cathedral, which was probably adjoining the convent building. All would not be seclusion after all.

Feeling much better, she allowed the curtain to fall in place. Now she had to wait to see what her dormitory companions were like before she could be at ease. She hoped they were not highborn girls like Bianca, but orphans like herself who had been brought to the sisters for safekeeping.

It was cold in the room and Rosanna huddled in her damp cloak, perched on the edge of the bed. The mattress was hard and lumpy and the pillow smelled of mold, even the bedsheets were musty, as if fresh air had not entered the room in years. She shuddered to think what the convent of Lorenzo would be like in the cold of winter, it was miserable enough in summer.

By now Bianca and her family would be journeying to their villa, looking forward to a season of entertainment, while she was imprisoned in a tomb of correction. It wasn't fair. When she willingly left her home with Marco she had not bargained for such an unjust fate. She could have stayed by herself on the mountain, and maybe Berto would have come to look after her. She might even have married him if she had not come to Lorenzo. It would be nice to be married to someone, to belong and know you were loved, and he had said he loved her. Tears of self-pity gathered in her eyes, slipping down her brown cheeks, to plop coldly on her hand. No one in the Sordello household really wanted her for herself; Aunt Magdela whipped and scolded her; Bianca made fun of her, and Uncle Ugo yelled at her clumsiness when she displeased him. Of all the family, only Marco was kind, and even his motives were suspect. Still, he had promised to take her riding on her saint's day; she had almost six weeks to wait for the outing. That length of time would probably seem like six years in a convent.

Footsteps beyond the door jerked her back to the present, and alert, she straightened up, hastily dabbing her eyes with the edge of her cloak.

Five girls trooped obediently inside the room, followed by a young novice in a gray habit. The girls stared in surprise at Rosanna, and the nun smiled at her. "This is Rosanna Sordello," she announced to the others, who smiled politely and went about their own business. From their bedside chests the girls withdrew bundles of embroidery, replacing their prayer books in the drawers. They kneeled devoutly on the cushions beside their beds and repeated a small prayer for the safety of their day.

" 'Tis a pity you were too late for mass," the novice said, her mouth pursed in a disapproving circle as she eyed Rosanna's brown ankles, projecting immodestly beneath her dress. "You must be outfitted in a regulation gown. Come with me."

Rosanna trailed after her fleeting steps, and one of the smaller girls stuck out her tongue as she passed. As the door closed, she heard them break into giggles and she was sure they talked about her behind her back. It did not matter, she would keep to herself, she did not need their friendship at all.

When she returned, Rosanna was outfitted like the other students. She hated the scratchy material of her

45

dress, and when she moved, its roughness chafed her skin, even the waist was spiky, her shift too thin to protect her body from discomfort. They had bound her hair about her head and fastened it beneath a white head covering. Now she was unrecognizable from the others, except by the darkness of her skin—a situation, the sister assured her, which would soon be remedied inside the convent far from the damaging rays of the sun.

Facing her dormitory companions was an ordeal. She had been determined to ignore them, but somehow, now she was dressed in their same modest uniform she felt lonely and afraid, her bravado gone. The other five girls stared back at her as she stood hesitantly in the doorway, urged forward by an impatient novice, who had other more important tasks to complete before noon.

"Say hello to the other girls."

"H . . . hello."

"Good morning," they chorused loudly, bobbing curtsies, their impish grins betraying a secret.

With a nod of satisfaction, the novice left. In fright Rosanna stared at them, for they had collapsed in a giggling heap of gray dresses and white caps.

"What a terrible beast she is. Look at her skin," one of them said, walking up to Rosanna and staring impudently, inches from her face.

"Oh, Battista, maybe she'll bite you." It was the little one who had stuck out her tongue and she danced about, pulling faces and deliberately popping her round brown eyes, staring unblinkingly.

"I'll tell Mother Superior. How can you be so unkind to a new girl?"

"Oh, shut up, Esmerelda. She hasn't brought anything to eat," Battista dismissed, turning around to shove a fat, fair-haired girl to the closest bed. Esmerelda lost her balance, sprawling on the bedspread with a shriek of anger.

"Off my bed, you huge . . ."

"Don't you call me that again, or I promise, I'll send for Mother Superior this minute," Esmerelda threatened, looking very undignified with her fat legs thrust upward. Smoothing back her fair hair which had fallen from beneath her cap, with great effort, she rolled to a sitting position.

"Why don't you look at your bed?" another girl suggested to Rosanna, her voice deliberately sugary.

"Yes, do see what happened to it," the others chorused.

Rosanna walked to her bed in the corner, wondering what could possibly have happened, for when she left, there had been nothing amiss. A huge wet patch covered the middle of the gray covers, and even as she stood there, more rain blew in a drenching gust through the open window. Leaping to the casement, she slammed it closed, knowing they had deliberately opened the window to wet her bedding.

"You'd better not tell anyone," Battista said, with a smug smile. "Or we'd have to tell what you did to the vase of flowers by the votive candle—knocking it over and putting out the candle, really, that's quite sacrilegious. If you don't cause trouble we'll probably say the wind blew it out, but if you run crying like a baby, we'll have to tell the truth."

The others agreed, watching Rosanna's reaction. She wanted to hit them all, at least the action would relieve her anger, but she thought it better to ignore them instead.

After several similar incidents, the senior members of the dormitory decided to call a truce, much to Rosanna's relief. She found the rigid discipline of the convent difficult enough without having to endure constant friction with her peers. One evening, after lights out, they came to her bed and introduced themselves to her, offering their friendship. For the first time, Rosanna felt she belonged somewhere, and though she still wanted to be free, the companionship of the others softened her temporary imprisonment.

Leonora Miserotti, the one who had stuck out her tongue, became her closest friend. Rosanna discovered these girls belonged to Lorenzo's leading families; but Leonora soon dispelled any feeling of inferiority in their friendship, sometimes putting the others in their place if they became too snobbish towards her friend. From Leonora, Rosanna's education in the gossip of the city was completed. She knew which families were rivals, which were in favor, or out of it, and which women the Duke had been in love with. The city's commerce appeared to be controlled by her own uncle, while the banks were operated by Leonora's father, Guido Miserotti. The Dati's were the noblest family in Lorenzo, and looked down their well-bred noses at anyone from the merchant class, whom they regarded as upstarts.

At first Rosanna found the convent sewing lessons difficult, but once she mastered the art of making tiny stitches, instead of the gigantic ones she first produced, the sisters relaxed their vigil on her work. Reading was more difficult, and the others laughed in amusement at her first attempts at writing. With pleasure she discovered she could sing in a sweet, true voice, a talent the sisters exclaimed over in delight. They were not as pleased, however, about her total lack of religious instruction, clucking and gasping over her pagan bliss. A rigid catechism was set up for her, and when the other girls enjoyed the warm summer evenings in the sunny courtyard, Rosanna was brought before Mother Superior to recite the day's catechism.

Before the month was out Esmerelda had a miraculous vision. The other girls awakened by her cries and thinking she was ill, trooped to her bed. By the bright moonlight they could see Esmerelda threshing and twisting, the bed frame groaning beneath the punishment.

"I'm having a vision," she gasped in reply to their urgent questions. "The Holy Mother came and spoke to me."

The others scoffed at her story, but Battista went for Sister Veronica at Esmerelda's tearful insistence. Reverend Mother herself came to investigate, and Esmerelda was taken away to be questioned further about the miracle.

The next day the convent was buzzing with excitement over Esmerelda's holy vision. The Duke was to hold an audience with her in Mother Barbara's presence to hear for himself Esmerelda's account of her miraculous experience.

As Esmerelda's dormitory companions doubted she had been blessed with anything more than a dream, the prospect of the Duke's visit was far more exciting. And they waited expectantly to see him, hoping they would not be caught away from their needlework.

"Here, I've a sweetmeat to share," Leonora whispered.

With pleasure Rosanna ate the unexpected gift, enjoying the strawberry flavor of the sugar comfit.

"I think they're coming now," someone squealed.

With a rustle of skirts, the girls clustered round the window to see the royal party. First came Mother Superior leading Esmerelda by the hand; the plump, fair-haired girl was simpering, puffed up with her own importance as she minced along the flagged path, basking in her moment of glory.

"I don't think she has visions at all. I bet she makes it up," Leonora suggested scornfully.

"It's probably because she wants to meet the Duke," Battista added. "I wonder if I had a vision whether I could meet him as well."

"He wouldn't do what you want him to with Reverend Mother there."

The others giggled, pressing against the leaded glass.

"Oh, there he is now, isn't he lovely," Leonora sighed, clasping her hands against her plump bosom in ecstasy.

Duke Paolo passed beneath the windows, striding across the courtyard, his gold embroidered robes glittering in the sunlight. Rosanna gasped at his sumptuous garments of sapphire blue embroidered with gold. And when he turned, she saw his doublet was sapphire blue also, contrasting beautifully with his own coloring. To her surprise she realized the Duke was a young man, not middle-aged as she had expected. His hair was dark blond, wavy and thick, and he wore it cut short above his collar. Now he accepted the kisses of homage from Mother Superior and Esmerelda, raising them both from their knees where they knelt on the chill paving. His hands flashed with jewels in the sun, and when he smiled, Rosanna thought his smile matched the brilliance of the gems. She stared spellbound at the Duke, fascinated by his appearance for he was like no one she had ever seen before. Now she realized why the other gilrs were in love with him.

"Don't you wish you were Esmerelda?" Leonora asked, pressing against her for a better view as Duke Paolo led

Esmerelda to a bench beside the lily pond. Then he bent forward, head down in earnest conversation as Esmerelda revealed the nature of her latest vision.

The other girls chattered about the marvel of seeing the Duke at such close quarters; how fortunate Esmerelda was to have the honor of being presented to their royal master, and to enjoy his company, even if it were only for a brief time.

Rosanna watched his bent gold head, seeing the curve of his profile and the gestures of his ringed hands. She thought of kissing his sensual mouth and of being caressed by his slender hands. With quickened heartbeat, she substituted the Duke for Berto in the romantic fantasy she constructed. At last he stood, the interview at an end. Beneath his blue tights his legs were strong, and as his robe gaped open she noticed the muscles ripple beneath the material which fit tight as a glove, displaying the tautness of his body. Though the Duke was only of medium height, his straight-shouldered carriage made him appear taller.

"Now, are you in love with him too?" Leonora asked, digging her in the ribs. "You don't think we're all half-wits now, to adore him, do you?"

With a smile, Rosanna shook her head, watching the Duke as he bade his leave. When he was beneath the window he glanced upward and seeing the girls, he smiled at them. Everyone squealed, clutching each other in delight, so that he laughed in amusement at their reaction. All except Rosanna, who stared boldly back, fascinated by his appearance, her lips parted breathlessly, her pulses quickened to hold his gaze.

Duke Paolo winked at the saucy, black-haired wench who stared at him so impudently, and for a passing moment he wondered if her body matched the sensual promise of her face. Then Mother Barbara was at his side and the girl was thrust from his mind.

The girls raced up a flight of stairs, scurrying breathlessly to arrive at their vantage point before he departed.

"We're in time, he's still here," Battista gasped as she saw the ducal party below in the street. "His Grace is on the steps talking to Reverend Mother and that sickening Esmerelda is with them, staring at him like a loon."

"And what are we doing?" Rosanna challenged with a grin, making Battista glare at her in annoyance.

"Look, isn't that Flora Dati?"

A woman walked swiftly towards the building, arriving just as the Duke came down the steps to his waiting horse.

Rosanna felt a wave of nauseous emotion at the sight of the elegant figure below. In her newfound appreciation of the Duke she had forgotten his mistress, and the discovery made her seethe with jealousy. When she held his gaze there had been a communication between them, so wonderful and intense, Rosanna had fallen head over heels in love with her royal master. But now that lovely feeling was shattered, replaced by gnawing dislike of Flora Dati as she smiled at her lover. The Duke stroked her cheek, leaning down from his mount to speak to her, and as he straightened up there was a grin on his mouth. Flora Dati moved away, disappearing in a doorway across the piazza. The party of riders started towards the palace, the horses moving slowly, their hooves clopping over the cobblestones until they were lost from sight.

"I don't think she's that beautiful," Rosanna said with a scowl, turning her back to the window.

"No, and she's getting old too," Leonora added.

"She's given him two children."

"Both girls. My father says Paolo needs a son."

Battista curled her mouth in scorn. "He needs legitimate sons. What he really needs is a new duchess, but the Dati woman has him under her thumb. I'm to be presented at court next season, wouldn't all of you be jealous if he chose me to marry him?"

"You're too thin. He likes fatter girls than you."

"My brother says Flora Dati has great big . . ." Leonora stopped, glancing about to make sure they were not overheard before she spoke a forbidden word.

The others squealed in delicious shock at her language and Battista nodded, leaning forward conspiratorially to add her own revelation to Leonora's story.

"Hurry up, here comes Sister Annunziata," Leonora squealed, picking up her skirts and making a mad dash down the corridor to the empty classroom.

When Sister Annunziata walked through the door, five

51

heads were bent dutifully over their tapestry frames, only the flush on their cheeks betraying the excitement of the past hour. If Sister suspected anything to be amiss, she did not speak of it, and Rosanna breathed a sigh of relief, sinking joyfully into a dream about riding beside Duke Paolo on a lavishly caparisoned horse, her jeweled headdress gleaming in the sunlight. Esmerelda did not return to her classmates till afternoon, when she was besieged by their clamors of excitement.

"Tell us what he said?"

"Did he touch you? Oh, do tell, please."

Esmerelda sat upon her bed, arranging her skirts in leisurely fashion while the other girls pleaded for her to speak. At last, with a smug smile, Esmerelda cleared her throat.

"Actually he was impressed by my holy visions," she announced importantly. "He thinks perhaps a miracle could happen in Lorenzo, for such things are often presaged by visions. I'm to go to the palace the next time I have one to speak to Fra Domenico in an audience with the royal family."

The other girls gasped at her exalted status, gazing with envy at Esmerelda, who gloated at the impression she was making, patting her dress, her puffy cheeks almost hiding her small currant eyes in a smile of satisfaction.

"What happens when they find out you don't really have visions at all, that you're just cheating?" Battista asked with a spiteful scowl. "I think I'm going to tell Mother Superior you make everything up."

"I do not."

"Yes, you do. Remember after we read about the saints and you said how lovely it would be if you could have a vision too; then, right away that night you had one."

"I didn't make it up. Don't you dare say anything to Reverend Mother, don't you dare make up lies about me," Esmerelda cried, her face creased with dismay. She grasped Battista's long plaits pulling until the other girl screamed with pain. Esmerelda pushed Battista to the floor, where she sat upon her, grunting with the exertion.

"Get off, you fat monster, you're squashing me," Battista protested in anguish, attempting to push Esmerelda over.

"Say you won't tell Mother Superior when I had my first vision, promise, or I'll sit here all day."

"All right, I promise, you cheat. Just wait, you'll be found out."

"There's nothing to find out," Esmerelda said, getting up so that Battista could breathe again. "I'm telling the truth."

Angrily Battista brushed her gown, straightening her hair and she stuck out her tongue at Esmerelda, who was kneeling piously before the crucifix by her bed, murmuring a prayer.

"If it wasn't a sin to injure someone at their devotions, I'd hit her on the head with a chamber pot," Battista vowed in anger, glaring at Esmerelda's fat body. "You big liar," she hissed, going to her own bed, and Esmerelda stuck out her tongue in retaliation.

"Well, even if she does cheat, I'm glad she does, or we wouldn't have seen his Grace this morning," Leonora said with a grin. "Wasn't he beautiful?"

There was murmur of assent. Leonora danced between the beds, swishing her skirts and bowing with a smile, as she pretended to dance with a handsome gallant.

Rosanna sat upon her bed, though it was against the rules, and she clasped her hands around her knees, resting her head on the nobbly mound. She was transported to the sunny courtyard in the heart of the convent where she talked with Duke Paolo. If she were clever enough to produce imaginary visions perhaps he would come to visit her as well, though it would seem strange if the girls in this dormitory began to have divinely inspired visions. It was a pity Esmerelda had thought up the idea first, it really was a good one.

"When are you going out with that handsome cousin of yours?" Leonora asked, coming to her side. "Isn't it next week?"

"Yes, so it is."

Rosanna had not forgotten the promised birthday treat, but what if Marco had. What a fool she would appear after boasting to Leonora about the outing.

Her saint's day was a special day, and Sister Veronica presented her with a gilded marzipan replica of the

Duomo, which Rosanna kept in her drawer, thinking it too beautiful to eat. The morning lessons were handed out and she wondered if Marco had forgotten his promise. She had just sadly resigned herself to this fact, when Sister Veronica beckoned from the door of the classroom.

"You have a visitor, Rosanna."

With a smile of delight, Rosanna walked to the door, forcing herself to be sedate, though she wanted to run in her eagerness to be free. Before she reached the common room she could see Marco impatiently waiting at the door, looking tanned and handsome in a new blue doublet, his quartered hose embroidered with the arms of the house of Sordello.

It was a glittering morning. The warm sun spread golden fingers over the piazza, shining on a hundred windows winking like diamonds in the pink marble facade of the ducal palace.

"How lovely," Rosanna gasped, her face wreathed in smiles as she enjoyed the wonderful feeling of freedom. "Don't hurry, Marco, I want to smell the air, to feel the sunshine."

"You sound like a prisoner," he laughed.

"I am a prisoner. You don't know what it's like to be closed up in a convent night and day for six weeks."

"No, but I'd like to try it."

Rosanna grinned at him. "You'd be very popular."

"Thank you," he acknowledged with a grin. "We mustn't dally, your warder only gave you two hours."

"I know. I suppose it will be long enough to go outside the city walls, won't it?"

Marco nodded, his attention attracted by a commotion at the canal steps as a party of riders came from the entrance to the palace. "Would you like to see the Duke?"

"Yes, I've never seen him except from a window."

"Come on, we're just in time. He goes riding at this hour every morning."

They rode across the piazza into the shadows of the buildings by the palace steps, finding it uncomfortably cool in the dense blue darkness where the sun had not yet warmed the morning air. The ducal party rode in a small group, skirting the impressive flight of steps before the palace. As they passed before them, Duke Paolo saw Marco, and he reined in, raising his hand in greeting.

"Good morning, Sordello."

"Good morning, your Grace."

Rosanna stared in awe at the Duke, realizing she did not really know what he looked like, after all, finding him much different close up, not the way she had pictured him since his visit to the convent. His gold hair waved crisply beneath the edge of his crimson hat. His gray eyes were framed by lashes far darker than his hair and there were age lines running from his nose to his mouth. She was so close to him she could see a cut high on his cheek which must have happened while shaving, for blood settled sticky along the edge.

The Duke returned her searching gaze, his eyes smiling, his mouth lifted at the corners in a grin of appreciation at what he saw. Then, with a polite nod to her, he raised his hand in farewell to Marco, motioning to his gentlemen to continue their ride.

Rosanna stared after him watching his figure broad shouldered in the saddle, his red and white striped doublet bright in the morning sun. His horse's trappings were crimson velvet with tassels of gold, all hung with tiny gilt bells which jingled musically as the white stallion pranced haughtily over the broad piazza.

"Mother of God, don't tell me you're in love with him too?" Marco said with exasperation. "What in God's name Paolo has that fascinates women, I'll never know."

"He's very handsome, and he's a Duke," Rosanna pointed out with a grin. "Why shouldn't women be in love with him?"

Her cousin smiled, shaking his head at her reason, finding no worthy challenge. "Come, let's take that ride. How would you like to go by the warehouses and see them unload a barge?"

"Uncle Ugo's warehouses?"

"That's right, our warehouses."

She agreed in excitement, seeing the last of the royal party disappear through the alley from the square, and with a sigh, Rosanna followed Marco.

They spent so much time at the family warehouse admiring the cargoes of expensive damask and velvets, there was no time to ride beyond the city walls as Rosanna had intended. Marco gave her a length of ribbon for her hair. It was silver gilt and very grand. With a squeal of delight she tied her braids together, feeling splendid in her new hairdressing. It was with reluctance she began the journey back, not anxious to exchange the exciting sounds and smells of the city for the peace of a convent.

The weeks to follow seemed quieter than ever after her brief taste of freedom. Though the other girls went out quite frequently with their families, Rosanna knew she would have no other visitors till September.

One Saturday in early August she found herself completely alone. The Dati family had staged a tournament at the tilt field and all the others had been invited by their families to attend. Classes for the day had been suspended, but Rosanna still had her daily religious instruction. The material was brief and soon memorized, though not as readily understood, and now she sat disconsolately staring through the window wondering what to do.

A bee droned outside, breaking the silence in the common room. It was only early afternoon, but Rosanna felt as if she had been there for hours. The others would not return before supper. If only someone would come to take her out. Perhaps Aunt Magdela would relent and send a message, but she knew it was no use hoping, all the wishing in the world couldn't make a visitor materialize. Besides, the other girls wouldn't know, even if she did have one. They'd scoff at her story, telling her not to tell lies, because no one ever visited her.

Though she did not want to cry, Rosanna felt a hot tear of self-pity slide down her nose, then plop to the scarred wooden table before her. There was probably no other girl in Lorenzo who was as lonely as she. Wistfully she thought about Marco and how he had taken her riding. Was Marco perhaps a little in love with her, maybe not as much as Berto had been, but just a little? It would be wonderful to have someone rich and important in love with her. That would be a story to tell them. Oh yes, today I went riding with my betrothed, he's very important in court circles. That would be something to tell them. But it would be a lie.

"Rosanna, all alone?"

She glanced up to see Sister Veronica standing in the doorway, an armful of flowers colorful against her dark habit. With a wan smile, Rosanna greeted the sister, self-consciously brushing the trickle of tears from her cheeks.

"You mustn't stay here by yourself. I didn't realize you were the only girl left. Do come with me, we can talk to each other. Sometimes I'm lonely too."

Sister Veronica held out her hand and shyly Rosanna reached out. She was not usually shy, but the sister was so good and holy, she felt terribly sinful by contrast. The sister's fingers were dry and cool, but her handclasp was warm with friendship.

"I would have been all right," Rosanna mumbled.

"No, you wouldn't. About ten minutes ago you felt so lonely you began to cry. Am I right?" Sister Veronica asked, with a kind smile.

Wide-eyed Rosanna nodded, wondering how the sister knew.

"There you see, I was right." Sister filled a large urn with blossoms, handing Rosanna a spray of fragrant pink roses to hold. The blue figured bowl held a mixture of flowers: spicy carnations with frilly pink edges, pure white lilies and yellow roses. Trailing greenery spilled from the urn, the fine leaves fluffy like hair.

"That's fern," Sister Veronica told her, as Rosanna touched the plant, wondering what it felt like. "Do you like flowers?"

"Yes. And grass. And trees. I like the mountains. The way it feels when the wind blows my hair, and the rain on my face."

Sister Veronica smiled, watching the rapture which suddenly lit the dark little face. Poor girl, such a child of nature, primitive and unspoiled. It was a pity to cage her, to force her into the mold of a proper, high-born girl.

"Those are things your Aunt Magdela wants you to forget," she reminded quietly.

"I know," Rosanna sadly agreed, finding a note of sympathy in the sister's voice. It was almost as if she understood how she felt inside, but she couldn't, because Sister Veronica liked being in a convent. She must have been here for years. Rosanna watched as the sister arranged

57

the flowers, standing back to admire the lavish display. There was a smile of pleasure on her lined face as she sniffed the fresh scent of the blossoms.

"Such lovely things, aren't they, Rosanna? Sometimes I wonder if God really wants us to cage ourselves within cities, hemmed in by walls where flowers and trees have to be coaxed to grow. I think perhaps he really wants us to live in the woods, or on the mountain tops where the air is pure and the wind blows free. We're far closer to Him there than within the walls of a convent."

Some sprigs of flowers had dropped to the tiled floor and Rosanna stooped to retrieve them, surprised by the sister's words.

"Would you like a spray of roses for your dormitory?"

"Yes, thank you, Sister."

Rosanna admired the perfumed blossoms clustering along a reddish thorny stem. The roses were perfect, the loveliest flowers she had seen since she came to Lorenzo. They reminded her of summer when she gathered wild roses from the mountain tracks. Those were pink and very thorny, but the beauty of the blossoms was worth a dozen torn thumbs.

"Come, we'll put the rest of the flowers in the sisters' dining room."

Sister Veronica led the way, gliding down the long deserted corridor to the room where the sisters took their meals. Sunlight shone in wide, square-patterned banners, lighting a wooden crucifix on the wall, showing all the torment of Christ's agony on the cross. Rosanna stared in fascination as the sister found a vase for her flowers. It seemed very strange if Jesus was the Son of God that He should die in such pain. He could have stopped everything that happened to Him with His Divine power, yet He had not. Religion was certainly very baffling, not as simple as she had believed. When the sisters drummed new information into her, shocked by her pagan mind and anxious to save her soul, she usually had not even understood the previous lesson. Rosanna could not really believe as they did, she had too many questions left unanswered. But whenever she asked them, they scolded, and told her to believe as a child, not to doubt the teachings of the scriptures. She would probably go to hell.

With a sigh Rosanna turned around, finding Sister Veronica watching her.

"Such pain . . . and for us, Rosanna. Do you realize that? We are so unworthy."

"Yes, Sister," Rosanna agreed obediently, seeing the reverent expression which flooded the sister's lined face, brimming her nearsighted eyes with tears.

"Don't you find a love of God in nature? Isn't it wonderful how everything has a season to grow, each in its place?"

Rosanna nodded; she had never thought of it like that before. Perhaps God was around her in the flowers and trees instead of the agonized wooden carving on the wall of the sisters' dining room. That was much more holy a picture; His presence in beauty rather than pain.

"I have a garden behind the kitchen where we grow some of the vegetables for table. Would you like to see it?" Sister Veronica offered, drying her hands on a linen towel which was tucked in the tie about her waist. "Maybe it will remind you of home."

The kitchen garden was small, but Rosanna thought it lovely to see the neat rows of growing things. The sunshine felt pleasant on her face, and when Sister Veronica asked if she would like to help tend the plants, she eagerly accepted the offer.

Between them they hoed and weeded the vegetables and while they worked, Sister Veronica talked to her. Rosanna was surprised to learn the sister herself was a poor relation who had been placed in the convent because her relatives could not afford a dowry. Uncle Ugo had a lot of money, so Rosanna breathed a sigh of relief, glad that poverty would not thrust upon her a similar fate though the family's choice of husband might be as unpleasant.

Voices drifted from the building, and Rosanna found with surprise the other girls had returned. Her afternoon had passed quickly and Sister Veronica assured her she need never be lonely on visiting days, for there was always room for a willing pair of hands in her vegetable garden.

All week Rosanna looked forward to helping Sister Veronica, but on Saturday she found that only one girl was to visit with her family, so lessons continued as usual.

After noon various dormitory housekeeping chores were assigned to them, making Rosanna too busy to help in the garden. The task of changing bed linen was taken by Battista and Leonora, who asked if Rosanna could help them in place of Maria, who was in the common room awaiting her Saturday guests. Rosanna could not understand the other girls' eagerness to undertake that particular task, for changing beds was not to her liking.

"Don't be so cross, you'll see, it's fun," Leonora whispered, leading the way up a narrow staircase to the linen closet.

The other girls' movements were furtive as they glanced about on the landing. Finding everywhere deserted, they dived towards the double oak doors of the closet, dragging Rosanna with them.

"We thought a long time about letting you into our secret," Battista explained, opening the door.

The lingering fragrance of lavender met them in a wave, mingled with the smell of cedar and fresh-laundered clothes. The cupboard was large as a room, with shelves piled with neatly folded bedding.

"What's so secret about this?" Rosanna asked in disappointment.

"You just wait, you'll see."

The girls moved aside the bedding on the shelf at the end of the room to reveal a small door.

"Where does that go?" Rosanna asked in surprise.

"That's the secret. Come on."

They opened the door to a flight of cobwebby stairs and Battista led the way, groping along the wall to steady herself, for there was no handrail. A shaft of light shone down on them from somewhere above and Rosanna felt her heart quicken with excitement. The girls led her to a small cubbyhole of a room, high in the building, which was almost bare and heavy with dust.

"This is it. We're the only ones who know about it, except Maria. We took a board from the back of the cupboard. I bet they've forgotten all about this place."

"It was probably a prison for a princess," Leonora breathed romantically, imagining herself forlornly waving her hand to passers-by from the window.

"We have another secret too," Battista revealed, opening a wooden chest in the corner of the room. "We keep treats up here to eat." With an exclamation of annoyance, followed by an unladylike oath, she held up a bundle of tattered white fabric. "Mice! Everything's gone," she reported in disgust, slamming the lid closed.

"Ssh, someone will hear."

"I wonder how mice got in there?"

"I don't know. What shall we do now?"

"We could spy on the soldiers," Battista suggested with a wicked grin. "That's always fun."

"What soldiers?" Rosanna asked.

"Stop asking so many questions and help move the chest."

They pushed the wooden chest beneath the window, climbing on top to look outside. The view was disappointing.

"It's just an alley and an old stable," Rosanna voiced with disappointment. "What fun is that?"

The others giggled. "You'd be surprised what we've seen," Battista grinned. "It's the garrison stable."

"Are the soldiers *condottieri?*"

"No, silly, the garrison are royal troops."

Rosanna stared at the drab alleyway where nothing was visible beyond some broken wagon wheels and a pile of wood. A soldier appeared with a bowl of slops, which he hurled on the ground, the soapy liquid running down the narrow cobbled channel in the center of the alley.

"He's handsome, isn't he?" Leonora whispered, craning up to the window, her short frame at a disadvantage. "Sometimes you can see all kinds of things from up here," she whispered, nudging Rosanna as she winked with sly meaning.

They watched the soldier's movements, each totally absorbed in their occupation of spying.

"I wonder what he'd say if he knew we spied on him?"

"We're not spying, we're watching."

"I'm glad he doesn't know. He'd probably want to do something bad to us, soldiers are all alike." Leonora pulled a face and shifted her position. "I don't think I'll ever get married, it would be awful to have to put up with the tortures women have to endure. My mother says . . ."

"I might like it," Battista interrupted, "especially with a man like the Duke."

The other two snorted at her words, watching the soldier as he disappeared inside the barracks. Then they went downstairs. One by one they crawled over the shelf and pushed the blankets back in place on the cedar paneling.

"If we don't put the panel back before they take the winter blankets, someone will find out," Battista gasped as she rushed about the room counting sheets and pillowcases. And staggering under their burden the girls scurried back to the dormitory to finish their job before someone came to investigate the delay.

Their secret was discovered the next day, but no one admitted the crime. The board was put back in place, and just to make sure the guilty did not go unpunished, extra devotions were ordered for the entire dormitory. But Rosanna did not mind. In two weeks it would be September and then she would be free.

Chapter Four

Rosanna waited nervously in her new dress wondering what her reception would be. The September sunlight streamed warm and mellow through the long windows, slanting across a red-patterned rug from the Orient. She practised a curtsy in preparation for her aunt's arrival. It was a disappointment to learn it would be only Bianca and Aunt Magdela who were coming home, for she had wanted to see Marco and show him how finely she could curtsy. Cia had told her the men would stay in Venice till the new year.

"So they've civilized the little hoyden," Aunt Magdela sneered, coming into the room where she stalked around Rosanna with swishing skirts.

From the doorway Bianca laughed. "She's not quite as black now, is she?" she commented, joining her mother in the scrutiny and she made a face at Rosanna.

"Let's see you curtsy. Cia tells me you do it well. Go on, wench, curtsy."

Panic-stricken, it seemed her legs refused to move correctly so that Rosanna squatted in an ungainly fashion on the floor.

"Saints preserve us, what a clumsy performance," Aunt

Magdela screeched unkindly, shoving Rosanna until she sprawled on the tiles. "Come, Bianca, it's time to sup."

And Rosanna realized nothing had changed at all.

For the next week she was instructed in dressing and undressing a lady in preparation for her duties as lady's maid to Bianca. She was treated with haughty disdain by her cousin, much to Rosanna's disappointment, for she had hoped Bianca would be more willng to accept her after she tried so hard to improve at the convent. To cover her loneliness Rosanna lapsed into a world of daydreams, constructing wonderful romances about Duke Paolo, adding newer and more exciting scenes until her imagination was a colorful pageant. Sometimes at night she woke trembling, the memory of his body crushed against hers, the imagined taste of his mouth on her own. Then, remembering her surroundings, she was often moved to tears.

At last the great day came when she was to move permanently into Bianca's chamber. Her first ordeal was to be a bath, Bianca's first since her arrival in the city. The servants brought water to fill the metal bath, and Rosanna poured a bottle of scented oil in the water, sniffing the delightful fragrance that arose from the steam. The oil colored the water a pink-violet, and as she swished her hand through the warmth, she wished it was for her instead of Bianca.

"Don't put your hands in my bath," Bianca shrieked.

"I'm testing the water, so you won't be burned," Rosanna replied evenly, watching Bianca unwinding her elaborate headpiece. The time in the convent had given Rosanna a new outlook on her place in this household. She was not a stupid, clumsy peasant as Bianca imagined, for she was just as intelligent as the daughters of Lorenzo's prominent citizens. Inwardly she could think whatever she wished, while she maintained an impassive expression, infuriating both Bianca and her mother. They went into hysterics at the least provocation and Rosanna found it amusing to goad them to fits of tears. It was really very easy to manage, and they never guessed the difference between what happened by accident or by design.

"When I learn how gentle you are, I'll let you do this for me," Bianca announced as she rolled the false golden

64

braids and placed them in a painted box. "I don't want to be scalped by your rough hands."

Rosanna brought towels and laid them out without answering, while Bianca brushed her hair.

"I had a marvelous birthday ball."

"Did you?"

"Yes, everyone who was important was there."

"Was Duke Paolo there?"

"No, that terrible Dati woman kept him in the city an extra month because one of her brats had the sweating sickness. I could have killed her," Bianca complained, banging down her hairbrush with a vindictive thud. "Fancy, I'm thirteen, that's old enough for a suitor, you know."

"Do you have one?" Rosanna asked with interest.

"No," Bianca snapped, loath to admit the truth, "not yet. But I will soon. I'm too pretty not to have."

"Many of the girls at the convent were to be betrothed on their next saint's day," Rosanna said, with spite. "Leonora Miserotti was my best friend."

Bianca snorted in disgust, though inside she was envious. "I wouldn't be friends with a Miserotti. They're upstarts, 'tis only by their treachery they have such a large bank. Just common moneylenders, Father says."

"They have a lot of influence with the royal family."

"That doesn't matter. If Father expands his fleet like he wants to, we'll be richer than anyone in Lorenzo."

With a gloating smile Bianca stood up, shaking back her hair. "Then we'll see how many suitors ask for my hand."

Rosanna was silent, wondering if what Bianca said was true. She had been told by Leonora that Uncle Ugo was buying more ships, but she had not realized the purchase would bring such wealth. "Will I have a suitor as well?"

"You?" Bianca cackled in a most unladylike manner. "What a foolish idea. No one would have you, except perhaps some mercenary in Luca Peruzzi's band of ruffians. You don't need to start putting on airs because you were patronized by the Miserotti baggage. She probably just wanted to learn our secrets. Hurry up, you useless girl, help me with my gown," Bianca shrieked after a moment, as she struggled with the fastenings.

Rosanna came to her unhurried. It took so little to ruffle Bianca's composure, and Aunt Magdela's as well, that she took fiendish delight in the accomplishment. Marco and her uncle were different; men didn't dissolve into hysterics.

"Hurry," Bianca demanded, twisting to be free of her binding skirts. "My bath water will be cold and it'll be your fault."

Rosanna unhooked and unlaced, accidentally pinching her cousin till she shrieked in pain. "Did I catch your skin? I'm sorry."

Bianca wrenched away, taking off her own shift. Rosanna stared in curiosity at the other girl. Its the first time she had seen Bianca without her clothes and she discovered they were different.

"What are you staring at me for," Bianca cried, covering her nakedness. "Stop it, you're not to look at me." Picking up an empty water pitcher, she hurled it at Rosanna's head, but she ducked adeptly and the pitcher shattered against the wall. "You wait, I'll make your life miserable before you're through."

Rosanna was silent; her cousin was already most adept at causing her misery, surely things could not be any worse.

But she was wrong. During autumn and the winter that followed, both her aunt and Bianca increased their demands for perfection to such extremes, Rosanna stopped trying to please either of them. If she was going to be accused of being a clumsy, rebellious wretch, then she would be one to satisfy them.

It was late spring before Uncle Ugo returned. He appeared older and more haggard than she remembered and his manner was surlier to match. Only Marco was unchanged, always laughing and flirting with her, until Aunt Magdela accused her of doing many things she had not. The meetings with her cousin were quite harmless, though sometimes Rosanna wondered if he intended to keep them that way.

One sunny morning, Marco approached her in the orchard, bringing her a handful of sugared green walnuts. Bianca was perched on the orchard wall, screaming and wailing, almost obscured from view by the new leaves on the apple trees.

Marco laughed and helped Bianca from the wall. "Don't plague your cousin so, Rosanna."

"She could have jumped."

"You know I'm afraid of heights. I only went up the ladder because you dared me," Bianca shrilled, wiping her tears dry on the hanging sleeve of her gown. "You wait till I tell my mother."

"No, say nothing." Marco's tone was sharp and Bianca blinked in surprise. "You weren't hurt. She meant no harm."

Bianca glared at him and flounced away, still sniffling.

"She's silly," Rosanna said with a grin. "Put me on the wall."

He obliged, swinging her up. "*Donna* Magdela would not approve."

"She's with her confessor, telling such terrible sins like ... forgetting to say her rosary last Monday, and keeping too much back from the housekeeping money for the private purse in her room ... and not telling Uncle Ugo about the message a servant brought him."

Marco laughed. "How do you know that?"

"I saw the servant come and she said she'd give the message, but she didn't. When I reminded her, she told me to shut my mouth, so I did."

His brows drew together in a puzzled expression, then he laughed as an idea came to mind. "It was probably from a woman."

"Maybe," Rosanna agreed, looking over the walls into the garden of the neighboring palazzo, where at this hour a kitchen wench usually entertained a young solider from the garrison.

"Who are you spying on now?" he asked, following her gaze.

"Carmela has a sweetheart."

"Who's Carmela?"

"The pretty red-haired one, the one you look at when you think no one's watching."

"I know the one," he smiled, looking with renewed interest at the overhanging tree branches. In a moment their vigilance was rewarded as a young man in the Duke's livery swung over the high wall of the garden.

"I think he's handsome, don't you?"

Marco shrugged. "I like her better."

The couple clasped each other tight, kissing hungrily, until Marco turned Rosanna's face away. He would have liked to watch himself but thought he had better preserve some of his dignity and her innocence.

"Marco!" she shrieked, "I want to see what happens next."

"You don't need to know," he said sternly, holding her defiant little chin in a firm grasp so she could not turn back. "How old are you?"

"You know I'm thirteen. My saint's day's a month after Bianca's."

"You should be playing with dolls, not watching lovers."

"I don't like dolls; anyway, even Bianca is too old for dolls."

Marco had not realized the girls were beyond that stage. He studied Rosanna, finding she was indeed no longer a child. Her face had fine, high cheekbones and her neck was slender. Her bodice was generously filled, and with quickened pulse, he noticed the material of the gown stretched tight over her straining bosom. And now he recalled, when he had swung her to the wall, her waist had been well-defined beneath her gray dress.

"Forgive me, Rosanna, I hadn't realized how grown-up you were."

She smiled with pleasure, thrusting her shoulders back proudly. There was silence in the Corelli garden, but Marco glimpsed the flash of a bared leg and he knew what they did. The thought, and the sudden discovery of his cousin's maturity, brought a surge of painful heat stabbing through his loins.

"Now you're a lady you'll have to act like one."

"I'm not that old yet. I still like to climb walls," she pointed out scornfully.

"And men will like to watch you, so you must not."

Rosanna pulled a face, looking for Carmela and her lover but she could not see them. "Would you look at my legs, Marco?" she asked curiously.

68

Tempted to lie, he changed his mind. "Yes, but I'm your cousin and it doesn't matter," he explained, trying to convince himself. "Have you ever been kissed by a man?" he asked suddenly, his face close to hers as he leaned against the wall.

"Yes."

"When?" he questioned in disbelief.

"Before I came here. His name was Berto and he was a shepherd," Rosanna proclaimed in triumph.

"What else did he do to you?"

"Not that."

Marco grinned at her swift retort, and his hand stole to her waist, gripping the warm softness of her body. "Did he put his hand on you like this?"

"Yes."

"And like this?"

Now his hand rested below her breast and Rosanna smiled slightly. She was not as naive as Marco thought, but she would allow him to think he deluded her, though she was aware of his next move. It would have been simple just to take away his hand, but the novel excitement of the game lured her on.

"Yes," she said, finding the blood flooding hot through her stomach.

Suddenly he bent his head and kissed her mouth. Clinging to his shoulders, Rosanna kissed him back, excited by the intimacy of his hands and the smell of his body so close to hers. She could hear his breathing, quick and harsh against her ear, then came the echo of footsteps and Marco disentangled himself from her embrace, dropping his hands as if she was on fire.

They stared at each other and Rosanna wondered what he would say now, surely he would not still pretend this was just a game.

"There, you see what can happen," he reproved, straightening his doublet and running his fingers nervously around his sweat-soaked neck. "A man's not always in command of his feelings." Marco glanced about furtively, wondering if they had been observed. "So in future, Rosanna, you mustn't let a man kiss you," he ended, attempting to sound aloof and calmly adult.

"I won't," she replied meekly, trying not to smile. "I promise."

"All right, we'll say nothing of this, then?'"

"Of course not."

He smiled, believing himself undiscovered, protected by her girlish inexperience, and as his father approached he nervously patted her skirts in place about her slim ankles.

Ugo Sordello glanced at them suspiciously, knowing something to be amiss, but not sure what it was. The two figures had seemed to be close together when he first glanced up, yet his sight was not what it used to be, so he could not be certain. Marco looked pained and his face was darkly flushed and sweat beaded on his brow. *Madre di Dio*, had he interrupted a seduction? He glanced at the girl who sat perfectly composed on the wall, her skirts drawn modestly around her slippers. As usual her face was darkly impassive as she met his gaze, though he sensed a certain tension in the air.

"Did I interrupt something?"

"On the contrary, Father, I was leaving. I have an engagement," Marco excused, bowing politely, and he hurried away.

"Magdela will be abroad within the hour. It would be better if you went inside the house," Ugo suggested, extending his hand to the girl.

With a slow, easy movement she came off the wall. He did not know if she jumped or slithered, her descent was so sudden—like a huge cat, agile and haughty. He would have gripped her hand if he could, but with a disdainful sweep of her trailing skirts, Rosanna declined his assistance.

"I will go inside, if that is your wish, Uncle."

"Stay there. It is unseemly to be sitting atop a wall. We have benches if you're tired."

"I will remember," she answered unsmiling and she walked away, leaving him angrily disturbed.

The emotion stayed with him for the next few hours, and Ugo was unable to concentrate on his accounts for thoughts of the girl. Angrily he closed the ledger, placing it in the secret compartment of his desk, and withdrew another, slimmer volume. This one was his official ledger kept for tax purposes; the other was a secret, but far more accurate accounting of his wealth.

Magdela forever scolded him about his son's behavior, perhaps he should return Marco to their Venice branch, though the suggestion had always met with the boy's disapproval. Having Marco in the house complicated matters. The wench was a marriageable age, but he was reluctant to betroth her just yet, money aside. Her wildness promised hidden delights and he could not overlook such opportunities. A time would come soon when he need speculate on the delight no longer, for he would own it. And with a smile of pleasure, Ugo returned to his accounts.

Bianca's marriage chest bore a carved picture of two lovers reclining on flower-strewn grass, each sheltered by an apple tree, its branches loaded with gilded fruit. The heavily laden tree signified fertility, for the high twining branches met in an archway crowned by a lover's knot. Rosanna admired the two richly dressed figures, picturing the wooden images come to life and clad in sumptuous garments. The girl would wear a white, pearl embroidered gown like the bride doll Bianca had kept in her bedchamber when they were younger. And the man would wear sapphire blue velvet like Duke Paolo had worn when he visited the convent.

With a dreamy sigh, Rosanna fingered the polished wood chest imaginging it was her own. Wondering what Bianca kept in her dower chest, she lifted the heavy lid and peered inside. It was almost empty. Besides a length of white embroidered brocade and a bundle of crimson satin, there was only a small wooden box. The satin turned out to be two sleek pillowcases, and Rosanna gasped in admiration as she stroked the fabric, picturing them upon the pillows of her marriage bed. The box was carved with a crude interpretation of the Madonna, but the sides were inlaid with a pearly gem which showed all the colors of the rainbow when she turned it towards the light. The working of the design reminded her of Aunt Magdela's coveted blanket chest which had come from a mystical land far across the sea. Perhaps this little box came from there too. Bianca said things from that country

71

often possessed a magical power, so Rosanna carefully opened the gold-hinged lid, almost afraid to discover the contents. They proved to be disappointing, for there was only a ring with a square-cut emerald, and a crystal necklace, pretty, but no prettier than Bianca's other jewels.

"What are you doing, you thief?"

Rosanna whipped around with alarm, startled by the anguished shriek. Bianca descended on her like a fury, snatching her possessions away, slapping and pinching in anger.

"I was just looking at them. I didn't hurt anything," Rosanna protested, shielding her face from the onslaught, remembering only too well the length and sharpness of her cousin's fingernails.

"You thief . . . you thief," Bianca screamed, beside herself with rage. "Don't you know a person's dower chest is sacred? Those things aren't to be handled. You wait until I tell my mother. She'll whip you till you bleed."

With gold hair streaming down her back, Bianca battled her cousin, tears of righteous indignation on her cheeks. Rosanna ducked beneath her flailing arms, and picking up her skirts, she dashed for the door, escaping thankfully into the corridor.

It was silent in the passages. Fortunately Bianca's outburst had not summoned any assistance from the servants. Not knowing where she ran, Rosanna darted along a twisting passage and up a flight of stairs, glancing over her shoulder to see if she was being pursued. Bianca was nowhere in sight. She could not even hear her squeals of rage. Good. Maybe she had given her the slip after all.

"Christ, what ails you!"

With stunning impact she ran headlong into Marco's arms. Panting with her exertions, Rosanna stared up at him, her breath knocked sickeningly from her body by the unyielding hardness of bone and muscle.

"What happened?" he asked, holding her from him at arm's length, looking over her shoulder to see who pursued her.

"It's Bianca. She's after me," Rosanna panted, "she'll kill me if she catches me."

"What crime deserves such violent punishment?"

"You don't need to laugh, I mean it," she retorted in

indignation, seeing his amusement. "I looked in her old marriage chest, that's all."

Marco clicked his tongue in disapproval. "Now, that is a grave crime. I think I ought to turn you over to the proper authority."

"What!" she shrieked in dismay. "You wouldn't do that, would you? I expected you to be on my side."

"I said I ought to, but I didn't say I would." His grin was different now, and he drew her against the soft velvet of his doublet. "If you promise to be nice to me, I'll hide you where Bianca will never find you."

"Where's that?" She was at once suspicious of his offer, recalling clearly the incident on the balcony last Friday.

"In my bedchamber."

"No!"

"Don't hesitate much longer, here she comes, a veritable whirlwind of revenge."

In horror Rosanna listened to the shouting, sobbing advance of her cousin, who had to be almost at the foot of the stairs by the strident pitch of her voice.

"Yes, or no," he whispered, holding her tight.

"Yes."

A moment later Rosanna was bundled inside the room at the top of the stairs and Marco barred the door. It was not a minute too soon, for Bianca's voice came from the staircase.

"Are you up there?"

Rosanna listened, giggling as she pictured Bianca's flushed, tear-stained face, wearing that baby tantrum expression.

"Aren't you going to answer?" Marco asked.

"Of course not. How do you know she doesn't mean you?" Rosanna suggested, slipping out of his encircling arms.

Going to the door, he called: "Is that you, Bianca? What do you want?"

"Have you seen that terrible gypsy thing?"

Bianca's voice was right outside the closed door and Rosanna stuck out her tongue, finding a heightening sense of intrigue as Marco grinned, his finger to his lips.

"No. Why would she be up here?"

"She ran away from me. She came this way. Where do you suppose she's hiding?"

"I don't know. Maybe she turned into a cat and jumped from the window."

Rosanna giggled, hearing Bianca's loud gasp of dismay at his suggestion. In a moment Bianca recovered, for she had heard the giggle and was at once suspicious.

"Are you lying to me, is she in there? Come on, Marco, I heard her. Open this door at once," Bianca cried, pounding on the heavy door, gasping with pain as she bruised her hands.

"Go away, I'm busy, you are a nuisance . . . stop it . . . stop that, wench, or I'll . . ."

Marco acted his role very convincingly and Rosanna giggled at the appropriate moments. There was silence from the corridor.

"Have you got one of the servants in there?" Bianca whispered, her voice hushed with shock.

"I told you I was busy; there are certain things you shouldn't interrupt. Go away."

"You terrible thing! I'm going to tell my mother what you're doing up here, you just wait." The indignant threat was followed by a thudding sound as Bianca ran down the stairs. And then it was silent.

"Well, that got rid of her," Marco sighed in relief. "She's such a little prude, she'll raise the entire house if she gets the chance."

"What will I do?" Rosanna questioned in alarm, not realizing before the consequences of his joke.

"Magdela is visiting the poor; it's the morning for her gracious lady charity visit to St. Alo's. Father is at the warehouses. So you see, there isn't any danger."

"What about the servants?"

"They won't pay any attention to her. God, I'm a man, aren't I? Do I need a thirteen-year-old chaperone?"

His face had darkened with anger, and Rosanna realized Marco was just as swift-tempered as his father when crossed. "Don't be angry with me," she pleaded, assuming a tearful expression.

"I'm not," he assured, coming to her with a slow smile. "Sometimes Bianca makes me puke."

"Me too," Rosanna agreed, letting him draw her in his

arms. She had not intended to find herself locked inside Marco's bedchamber with no chance of rescue from outside. This was an unforseen problem to which she must work the solution. As his hand softly caressed her neck, she was suddenly alarmed. What if this was a problem she did not want to solve by guile, for he already had a perfect solution, a very appealing one ... "You'd better stop."

"Why?" he grinned, turning her face around to kiss her soft mouth. "Don't pretend you don't like it."

"I might tell someone."

"Don't forget, you came willingly. I gave you a choice," he reminded, searching for the fastening of her gown.

"I only said I'd come in your room, nothing else."

"It's what you implied, not what you said."

He caught at the bow which secured the lacing of her bodice, pulling it undone. "Come on, let me see what you kept hidden last week."

Clutching the edges of her brown bodice together, Rosanna backed away. "No. You shouldn't ask me to do such a thing."

"Why, you know you want to?" Marco argued, pursing her, but his movements were lazy. This was a very tantalizing game she played, highly arousing and most enjoyable. He was in no hurry.

Glancing behind her, Rosanna realized his windows opened on the balcony which circled the upper story. There was her means of escape.

"But it's wrong."

"Since when do you worry about things being wrong?" With an eager stride he reached her, taking her close against him thinking to claim her at last, subduing her complaints with a kiss.

The window catch was set low, and with effort she reached it, hoping it would open easily. It did. Marco did not seem to notice her action, assured now of his conquest as Rosanna drew a kerchief from her skirt.

"If you put this on, Marco, I'll take everything off," she promised with an inviting smile.

He paused, his breathing shallow, mentally reviewing her astounding statement. "Why should I hide my eyes," he whispered at last, "when I want to see you?"

75

With downcast lashes, Rosanna whispered: "Because I've never done this before. I'm very shy."

For a few moments he hesitated, his desire quickened by her unexpected offer. "All right," he decided at last, "but hurry. I'll turn my back," he vowed with a grin.

The knot tied, Rosanna kissed his cheek, turning him about to face the door. She could hear his laughter, and to make everything appear authentic, she rustled the fabric of her skirts. "Not yet," she cautioned, as he half turned at the sound. "Wait a minute."

She had the window open now and silently she slipped onto the balcony. "Not yet," she protested again, as he moved. "Wait."

"How long?" Marco demanded impatiently, tiring of her game.

"Not long," she assured from the window. Then hoisting her skirts so that she could run faster, Rosanna raced along the balcony. "Now, Marco," she shouted as she descended the first flight of stairs. He raced to the balcony tearing the blindfold from his eyes in rage, but she was already gone.

Marco remained angry with her for the next couple of weeks, but his goodwill returned as the time of the Duke's birthday tournament approached. Everyone in Lorenzo would be there to watch the mock battles and skilful displays of weaponry, for this would be the last public spectacle before the summer heat, and the constant threat of plague, emptied the city for the season.

Chapter Five

For days the household buzzed with excitement about the forthcoming tournament. Uncle Ugo generously allowed Rosanna to remake one of Bianca's festival gowns for herself after Aunt Magdela had insisted she could not afford new dresses for both girls. The dress was too small in the bodice and her uncle gave her a piece of yellow velvet to enlarge it, and a bunch of yellow ribbons to trim the sleeves. The velvet was too bright a color choice for the blue gown; nevertheless, Rosanna was thrilled by the gift. This gown would be even more attractive than the brown one Aunt Magdela gave her last year.

The day dawned misty, but soon cleared to reveal bright blue sky. Clattering feet and closing doors heralded the important morning, and with a squeak of excitement, Rosanna scrambled from her bed. The day smelled fresh, and the sun had not yet roused the flies from their hiding places, nor sent the hot, unpleasant odor of refuse from the gutters wafting through the large rooms of the palazzo. With eagerness Rosanna dressed, finding her excitement mounting as the horses were readied for their departure. Then her pleasure was shattered by the angry voice of her aunt echoing like an imperious bugle through the house.

"That creature shall not come with us, leaving my daughter's best shoes outside. Look at them, Husband, they're completely ruined."

In alarm Rosanna remembered she had been carrying Bianca's shoes last night when she went to the kitchen for milk. She must have left them in the courtyard.

Seeing her in the doorway, Aunt Magdela descended on her like a madwoman, wielding a switch. Rosanna tried to duck, but her aunt's fingers held her in a viselike grasp, biting into her flesh. Uncle Ugo came to the doorway where he watched the beating, wincing at her cries of pain.

"Magdela ..." he interjected as the blows became more violent, and stepping forward, he took his wife's arm. "Enough, come, we'll be late."

Snorting with anger, her puffy face flushed, Aunt Magdela turned to Rosanna. "You stay here by yourself. You've displeased me once too often, so I think to miss the tournament will be a fitting punishment."

Uncle Ugo cast a backward glance at her huddled, weeping figure, then clearing his throat in discomfort, he followed his wife down the staircase.

Hours later her tears were dry, her disappointment turned to cold hate for Aunt Magdela. Rosanna hunched her knees to her chin, staring over the rooftops, hearing an occasional roar from the crowds at the tilting field beyond the city walls. The streets were deserted. Everyone was at the festival, even the servants and the old women who usually nodded in the courtyards beneath hanging arbors.

Rosanna thumped her fist into the purple-tasseled cushion beside her, imagining the soft yielding substance to be her aunt's puddiny face. That blow and that for last week's beating, this for the punishment yesterday, and this for today's humiliating scene.

The velvet cushion plummeted down, a bright splotch of color on the floor. There was some satisfaction in beating the pillow, but not enough. Rosanna screamed, loud and piercing. No steps came running for the house was deserted, save for Antonio, who was deaf. She screamed again, her back and legs tensing with emotion. There, she felt a little better, but it was still not enough to release her tension.

With a sigh she swung her feet to the floor, kicking off her slippers and wriggling her toes on the cold marble. Her foot looked white and slender against the dark surface and she admired her ankle, turning it this way and that, twisting her foot and setting it down daintily. Soon she began a graceful dance, humming a tune. She would have her own festival by herself in spite of them. Her coif was hot and impatiently she pulled it off, shaking her black hair down about her shoulders. Smiling, she bowed to her imaginary partner, speaking in deep tones, the way Duke Paolo addressed the ladies at his court. Next she curtsied, perfectly today, for Aunt Magdela was not here to watch, and Rosanna grinned, almost wishing her aunt could see how graceful she could be if she wanted. She moved up and down the room in perfect rhythm, smiling graciously to courtiers who gaped at her beauty, now at her partner, the Duke. How handsome he was in cloth of gold with slashed sleeves embroidered with jewels; his hand strong in hers; his fingers straying to her wrist. . . .

"Are you mad?"

A voice broke into her make-believe and with a whirl of blue skirts, Rosanna spun to face the door. Her uncle stood watching her, a look of surprise on his face. Flustered, she dropped a curtsy low before him.

Ugo stared down at her, finding his pulse racing madly at the sight of the fair young body, her flesh gleaming above the bodice of her gown, her black hair billowing as she sank to the floor. He stepped forward and raised her face, his hand grasping her chin.

Rosanna stared up at him. His handsome, florid features were flushed with drink, and as he bent over her, she smelled the wine on his breath. His ribbon-looped bonnet was askew, and his brown hair, curled and scented this morning, straggled sweaty across his face.

"Get up, you don't have to bow to me. Not when we are alone."

Alone. The word had a ring of warning as she realized he spoke the truth; they were alone in the house, almost

79

alone in the city. And the knowledge brought a pang of unrest.

"Why came you back, Uncle?"

He hesitated, and turning away, made a lame excuse about his horse casting a shoe; yet he had ridden back to the city, and hard, by the dust on his fine satin doublet.

He caught her arm, the pressure of his fingers bruising her as he turned her to him studying her face. Ugo saw the dried tears and the redness of her eyes, not entirely faded. "My wife is a bitch. If I could have stopped the beating, I would." And at that moment, standing close against her, he believed it.

"It was not my fault," Rosanna said, making her defense.

But he was not listening. He smiled and glanced at the empty expanse of floor. "You dance well. 'Tis a pity to dance without an audience."

She flushed, casting her eyes down, wondering what he thought of her foolishness. His expression puzzled her, for Uncle Ugo never spoke softly to her, or looked at her that way. He was usually gruff and angry.

"Sometimes I hide and watch Bianca's dancing lessons," she admitted shamefaced. "When I lived with my mother the gypsies taught me to dance like they do. Their dances are fast and I like them best."

"I've never seen the gypsies dance. Will you dance like that for me?" When she hesitated, he chucked her beneath the chin. "Come, Rosanna, it's almost like being alone. I'm just your uncle. I wouldn't laugh at you."

Slowly she went to the center of the room and he sat on the padded bench under the window, casting aside his gauntlets and bonnet. Then he nodded for her to begin.

Rosanna closed her eyes, concentrating on the hillside where she had seen them dance, seeing the whirling skirts and flying hair of the gypsy girls, hearing the exciting rhythm of their music. Her movements were uncertain at first, but in a moment she had gained momentum, as more of the tune came singing through her brain. Clapping her hands, she stamped and twisted, moving swift as an animal; bending, writhing her supple body, snapping her fingers, effortless as a reed in the wind. Her skirts billowed higher until her legs were visible beneath the twirling blue. Her hair fell over her face and she tossed it back, coming closer to him as without realizing she began their high chant, the words coming from the past, though she had not known she remembered. Ugo was watching her, his breathing shallow, his face a mask. In an instant the knowledge of his need came to her. Instead of repelling her, it excited her, speeding the dance and she came closer, bending towards him, whipping back as his arm would have encircled her. She arched her body, the material straining to her breasts as she backed from him laughing. The dance was faster and faster until at last, with a final shout, she dropped to the floor, a tangle of hair and skirts.

With her breath regained she also won her sanity, knowing with a lurch of her stomach what she had done. Alone; he knew it and so did she. Fearfully Rosanna glanced towards the window, remembering his expression. Knowing, with sudden instinct, what it was he wanted. Scrambling from the floor she backed away as he rose from the window bench. She darted and bobbed as he pursued her, like an ancient dance. He grew clumsy in his haste and tripped, but still he was between her and the door. It was no use. She stood still and let him come to her.

"You witch, to dance so, to torment me and now to elude me. We will have none of it," he cried, but his tone was not of anger, rather of jesting laughter.

"No," she cried, as he caught her to him, but her voice was muffled by his lips, his beard alien to her face. And she squirmed to avoid it.

"It's no use struggling, you little wild thing, we are alone. I'm far stronger than you. You can fight and scratch, bite me, scream your head off, but when you are done I'll still be here and then I'll take you."

"I'll scream," she threatened, shaking with fear.

"No one will come. Antonio is deaf. Besides, if anyone should hear, this is festival time. They'll think it's some drunken soldier and his maid."

Rosanna stared sullenly back, seeing his brown eyes hard, yellow-tinged, secure in his mastery. And she knew he was right. When a woman struggled a man beat her, for she had watched it; the attack one of her clearest memories of home. When you fought they were more cruel, they forced and tore. . . .

"That's better, my dove, docile and obedient," he mocked, kissing her again, his mouth hard, her lips bruised by the pressure. She stared up at him, seeing the enlarged pores in his skin, his face pock marked down the left side. At last his eyes opened looking into her own. "You're a bold one." He laughed. "Aren't you afraid?"

"No," she lied, though it was not completely a lie, for with her anxiety was a mixture of curiosity. What would it be like?

"Come." He caught at her dress, pulling the shoulder.

"Don't tear my gown, Uncle, please. I have no other as fine. I'll take it off," she pleaded, as his large hand broke stitches in the yellow ribbon trimmings.

"Then do it," he demanded, his voice harsh as he led her to the padded bench against the wall.

"It's torn already."

"I'll get you another if you say nothing about this day. Would you like that?"

"Could I have a green silk one like Bianca's, with silver gauze and embroidery?" Rosanna asked in wonder.

"Yes, if you keep your mouth shut. You shall have it for your saint's day."

"I want a darker green than hers, the color of moss."

"*Madre di Dio,*" he cursed, "haven't I said you shall have it. Whatever shade of green you want." Panting, he reached for her and pushed her to the cushions.

Rosanna did not take off her gown, remembering how the brigands had stripped the women. Always it was naked women and clothed men; the woman's body turned to an instrument of pleasure, her dignity stripped away, until she was reduced to an animal to be used, while the man retained his place as master.

"You first," she said.

"What?" he echoed, stupefied.

"You undress first."

Ugo stared a moment, then threw back his head with a great peal of laughter. "You want to look at me?"

Laughing, he tore at the fastenings of his doublet, his ardor increased by her strange request, heaping coals upon the fire of his lust. She wanted to see his body, to touch and admire him, she had wanted him all this time and never spoken of her needs. . . .

Coolly Rosanna watched him, foolish in his tearing haste and she despised him. She reclined upon the cushions to see this new form of entertainment. He was a massive man, barrel chested and muscular, his body thickened with middle age, but he was not as ugly as she had expected. Dark hair matted thickly over his chest and stomach, curling and speckled with gray.

"Am I not a man to be proud of, little niece?" he breathed, watching her curious eyes travel downward and stop in unabashed scrutiny.

Rosanna carefully took off her dress, folding it neatly and placing it on the floor beside the couch. He did not wait for her to take off the shift, but impatiently dragged it from her, his mouth slack with desire. And in the generosity of his need, he whispered, "You shall have a cloak to go with your gown, a headdress too."

Then with a grunt he seized her, welding her to his body.

Rosanna bit her lips, but the pain was soon over and not as severe as she had expected. That was lovemaking; it was disappointing. And as he got up from her, she hated him.

Ugo glanced at her impassive face and seeds of worry filtered through his mind. What if he had impregnated her, what then? He would have to think of a story to protect her, for when Magdela knew, she would have her beaten. In her pain, the girl might reveal her violator. He would deny it of course, but Magdela would be swift to believe any story of his infidelity, even from Rosanna.

"Remember, keep your mouth shut," he growled, grasping his clothing, holding it before him as he realized his nakedness.

She laughed at him, stripped of his mastery. "Don't forget my dress, it's the price of silence," she reminded impudently.

Struggling into his doublet and hose he glared at her. "You're your mother's daughter, all right, bitch," he spat. But she only laughed.

Angrily he finished dressing, charging from the room with his doublet half fastened. Rosanna moved slowly, her bruised body aching from his hands. She dressed, carefully smoothing the wrinkles from her gown, and walking to the window, she retrieved her headdress. A sense of power over Ugo Sordello made her smile. She had discovered his weakness and she also knew he would pay the price of his deed.

Knowing what she must do before the servants arrived home, Rosanna moved from the window. Her uncle had noisily clattered from the stables, riding as if the devil were at his heels. She must go to the herb garden and pick what she needed. Long ago she had learned the secret of the herbs from her mother. There were potions to be taken to prevent conception; for the first time she would brew one. Her uncle would never know and that was another weapon she could use on him during the next few months. With a flash of hatred for him, Rosanna cursed beneath her breath: she would rather die than bear his brat.

The sun filtered in patches on the walls as she went through the silent palazzo, swiftly moving through the winding maze to the servants' quarters. She took a basket and some scissors from the kitchen, then walked to the herb garden, the sun caressing her face and distilling the mixed fragrance of the plants in the breeze. After a search she found the plants she sought and clipped a generous bunch, deciding to dry some as protection against possible future visits of her uncle.

Inside the kitchen she heated water to brew the herbs, and carrying the hot liquid in a cup, she went to her chamber. As she drained the cup, she saw a cloud of dust on the Via San Lorenzo; the revellers returning from the tournament.

For the next week, her uncle kept his distance, though Rosanna found him watching her, or attempting to catch her eye while they ate.

On Tuesday, true to his word, seamstresses came to measure her for her gown. Aunt Magdela was visiting the poorhouse that day and was unaware of the intended gift until Rosanna actually received her present.

The first day she wore her moss green, silk-embroidered gown, her fingers shook so much with excitement she could barely fasten it. Twisting and turning she

84

preened before Bianca's mirror admiring her reflection. Her headdress was green and silver and she gasped aloud in admiration when it was in place.

When her aunt saw the dress, her face turned a sickly hue. "It's becoming, and very expensive."

"The cost is from my purse, Magdela, not yours," Ugo added, as Rosanna turned around to show him her dress. "You are a beauty, niece, as fair as any in the duchy."

Magdela snorted with displeasure at his compliments dismissing Rosanna with a curt nod, waiting only until the girl was outside to unleash a torrent of wrath.

"How dare you dress that urchin in gowns as costly as your own daughter's?" she screeched.

"Peace, Magdela," he sighed wearily, "would you have the girl abroad attired like a kitchen wench?"

"You have an unseemly interest in her welfare of late."

"She is our own flesh and blood."

"Your flesh and blood, not mine. You also have a concern far exceeding that of an uncle. Was your part in her begetting unbrotherly also?" Magdela hissed, her eyes narrowed to slits in her puffy face. "They whisper she is your bastard on your half-wit sister."

His face paled, then flushed brick red with anger. "Will you repeat every piece of slattern's gossip? They also whispered her father was one of the Egyptians who roam the hills, or the devil himself. God knows, Lucia was senseless enough, it could have been any passing yokel. You will say no more."

"She's not the get of a yokel, though at times I swear she's clumsy enough. I think she does it just to plague me," Magdela complained, brooding, as she watched Rosanna run across the courtyard, her green dress billowing behind her. "Look at her, no modesty, and in here she creeps noiselessly like an animal, forever spying on me."

Magdela leaned out of the open window to see who it was the girl greeted, brimming with excitement over her new gown. Horses clattered into the yard, harnesses jingling, and a man's voice rang out in greeting; Marco had returned from the chase. With a scowl Magdela watched his admiring glance and smile of approval, the way he swept Rosanna about in a laughing dance as soon as he dismounted.

"Your son forgets himself," she snarled. "And her flirting with him like a kitchen drab. If she's not careful your lusty son will have her belly swelled, then you'll listen to me. You'll see what I've been telling you, Husband. She's a wanton just like her mother."

Ugo followed his wife's spiteful, disapproving gaze, to see Marco with his arm round the girl, laughing with her. The young couple disappeared beneath the arches of a doorway, and with anger he wondered if his son had bedded with her also.

"He's a Sordello and no mistake," Magdela flung, as the couple went inside the house. "And so is she."

"Do you accuse me of incest?" Ugo growled. "Do you think I would be guilty of so grave a sin?"

"There is no sin created that I would not suspect you of, my husband," Magdela purred, and with a swish of her skirts she was gone.

In anger he strode to the dining hall where the noon meal was laid. He picked absently at a plate of biscuits, pouring a full glass of choice muscatel wine. Marco did not join him for over thirty minutes and Ugo simmered with resentment as he pictured what was probably taking place. That was likely the reason the wench had not invited him to bed with her. Marco was far younger, and knowing his son, he probably made himself readily available. When they moved to the country it would be even more difficult to watch them. And suddenly he had an inspiration.

At last Marco came to the table, sunburned from the morning's chase. Cia brought a soup of peppers, followed by roast mutton and chicken pie. She served a generous portion to the men; then, with a curtsy, she retired.

"God, how glad I am that Lent is past," Marco remarked, heartily devouring his meal.

"Where were you? You're late!"

"Talking with Rosanna. What a difference the gown makes, she'll have a suitor yet."

"Perhaps 'twould be for the best. Magdela makes such a burden out of the girl's presence," Ugo muttered, staring at his wine glass, his florid face sunk in heavy folds which bulged above the snug collar of his black velvet robe. " 'Tis a pity she's not a boy, we might have placed her in Duke Paolo's household . . . or Bernardo's, he has an eye for pretty boys."

"Paolo has one for pretty girls," Marco added with a grin.

"But what use will that be. A couple of romps and he'd be tired of her. A page would be far more valuable. I always dreamed of having a son serve in the royal household."

"I served them on the battlefield."

"Aye, but a boy of sixteen's fighting is soon forgot."

"It's unfortunate I am too old for a page," Marco reminded, his face tight as he looked at his father.

"You must have some use beside wenching, though I'm damned if I know it." Ugo pushed away his plate reaching for more wine. "You ride, you hunt, you exchange silly talk at Paolo's gatherings. What have I got from that? If you were some use in the business, I wouldn't mind the frivolity and expense. If you would take that position I offered you in Venice. . . ."

"I don't like Venice, I like Lorenzo. Besides, Father, I've no head for figures. You know that."

"Perhaps not on paper," Ugo added sourly, "but in a skirt it seems you're an expert from what I hear. Even at the countinghouse. Have you forgotten you go there to work?"

"I do work. I'm sorry my efforts don't meet with your approval. I've no interest in sharks and moneylenders."

"No, your interest is in pimps and whores. How in God's name can you work with your hand in some wench's bodice."

Marco blanched at his father's thunderous voice, wondering if Magdela were in hearing. To battle with his father was bad enough, without accepting Magdela's shrewish gauntlet to boot. "Do you want me gone from your household?" he challenged, tight-lipped.

"Aye, but only to Venice," Ugo said in softer tones. "Will you not please me in this one thing? A man takes pride in his son's achievements. He likes to know there'll be one to follow in his footsteps when he's gone. I'm not a young man, Marco. I want you to carry on the business when I'm dead. You're my only male get, perhaps the only one I'll ever have."

Marco looked at the painted cherubs on the ceiling. God, how he hated it when his father waxed sentimental. He probably had another thirty years in him, and as many bastards. "Father," he began, but Ugo would not listen.

"Only yesterday I had one of my spells. Father Francisco was like to give me extreme unction before I recovered."

"You must have received the last rites more than any man in Lorenzo. You will be virtually sanctified when you finally go," Marco remarked sarcastically and his father rose from his seat in anger.

"Are you so godless you jest at the sacraments of the church?" he questioned in hypocritical piety. "If your lovely mother could hear you, she'd weep in her grave."

"Forgive me," Marco sighed, picking up his gauntlets from the table. "The hunt was tiring. I'll withdraw if you will permit, Father."

Seeing the signs of Marco's nervous strain, Ugo delivered his death lunge. With a smile he waved his son back to his seat. "Not yet, first there is something I must warn you about."

"Warn me?"

"Aye, perhaps warn is too mild a phrase, beg, plead, beseech. The house of Miserotti is a vengeful one. Rumors have come to my ears that you pay court to the lovely Ginevra."

"Who told you that?"

"I have my spies. When her father questioned me, of course, I denied the charge, for I have no wish to find my only son impaled on the end of a sword. But in the interests of my own salvation, I must make a true confession. If it were to prove I was in error, then I should have to admit my mistake."

"Come to the point," Marco snapped, leaning over the table, his eyes fixed on his father's stony, unmerciful face.

"The point being, my fine peacock, we have the same confessor who I'm sure can be made to chant every word to the Miserotti for a purse of gold."

"Are you blackmailing me?"

"Blackmail is a strong word. Persuasion is a far more appropriate choice. Ginevra Miserotti is betrothed to another who has a quick sword. If they even suspected the height of your involvement with the wench they'd set upon you this very night." He stood up, the interview at an end. With a sly smile, Ugo patted his son on the head, smoothing the fine hair which lay damply against his brow. "You are handsome, my son, very like the house of Lorenzo. I trust you will find many willing females in Venice. The climate is excellent this time of year." With a short bow, Ugo left the room.

Tense with anger, his fist clenched about the hilt of his dagger, Marco watched him stride through the door, hearing the heavy steps until they died away in the silence of the marble-tiled passage.

"Damn you for being such a treacherous dog," he spat, unleashing his emotion in a thunderous blow which sent the venetian glass ringing and splintering upon the floor.

Chapter Six

"Our villa is one of the most expensive in the duchy," Bianca boasted with a smug smile. "We have green lawns, and all kinds of flowers. There's a pond with lilies and a golden cupid. You're very lucky to be related to us."

Rosanna listened, glancing about the rolling countryside, wondering how much longer it would be before they reached Villa Sordello. Bianca was regaling her with a tireless description of her summer home, until Rosanna wished she would be quiet. If Bianca suggested she was fortunate to be related to her once more, she would push her from the saddle.

"Bianca, darling."

It was Aunt Magdela's voice drifting to them over the party of servants, the familiar weary note already present.

"I know what she wants. She doesn't like me to ride in front in case we're set upon by thieves," Bianca grumbled, urging her horse forward, increasing her pace.

"Bianca, come back."

Aunt Magdela was shrieking now, and she shouted to one of the manservants to go after her. Rosanna thought it was fun riding so fast, it was even fun to anger Aunt Magdela. She was surprised to find Bianca had the courage to race her horse, and with a gleam in her eye she challenged her cousin.

"I can beat you to the bend in the road."

"No, you can't. My horse is better than yours. She's one of Father's best horses. Yours is just an old nag."

"Prove it."

Rosanna pulled ahead, and with a squeal of rage, Bianca urged her mare forward. With flushed face she gained on Rosanna, pulling abreast. Bianca's headdress slipped from her head hanging down her back by a ribbon, while her elaborate gold plaits spilled loose around her face.

Strong hands grasped her shoulder as Taddeo raced ahead to stop the girls. "Sorry," he said with a grin, "I have my orders."

Angrily Bianca pulled her arm free, her chest heaving with the exertion. "Take your dirty hands off me, you stableboy."

He touched his forelock, obediently releasing her. And he winked at Rosanna. "You beat her," he whispered, as they rode back to the litter.

"I know."

After a tearful scolding from Aunt Magdela, Rosanna rode behind the litter, while Bianca was forced to dismount and ride inside. It was dusty behind the horses and soon her face was covered with grime, but it had been worth it to prove Bianca wrong.

In a few minutes the gates of the villa came in sight; she knew it was the right one by Bianca's excited squeal. Now she would see Villa Sordello for herself. The picture which greeted them as they rode through the wrought-iron gates, was one of the loveliest Rosanna had ever seen. The house gleamed pale against a dark background of trees and bushes. Gardens seemed to stretch in every direction, colorful with scented flowers nestling at the feet of giant horses and cockerels, elaborately fashioned from rows of clipped hedges.

The interior of the house was just as splendid, with Oriental carpets scattered about the intricate tile-patterned floors, and costly paintings on the walls. The furnishings of the rooms were lavish, far grander than the palazzo in Lorenzo. And Rosanna found herself looking forward to the summer months which lay ahead, for this was an adventure; a whole new world to explore.

"Which is your bedchamber?" Rosanna asked, glancing through the long windows to the lawn which rolled gently down a slope to a fringe of leafy trees.

"Any one I want. There are twenty bedchambers and I can choose the one I like best. They've all been redecorated, so I don't know which I'll like."

"Can I have a bedchamber too?"

"Of course not, you're not a member of the family."

"But if there are twenty, surely there's one to spare for me," Rosanna said in disappointment.

"You'll have to ask my mother, but I doubt if she'll think you deserve one after trying to make me hurt myself on the journey. Racing like that, you know it's really very dangerous."

"But it was your fault. You were the one who started it."

"Of course I wasn't. What lies you tell."

Bianca flounced from the room, and Rosanna trailed after her. Down the corridors they went, peering inside the empty rooms, exclaiming over colors and the luxury of the furnishings.

At the head of the stairs they met Uncle Ugo and Bianca skipped towards her father with an impish smile. "Good day, Father, darling," she bubbled. "I'm looking at the bedchambers, trying to decide which one to take."

"What's wrong with the one you used last year?" he asked with a smile, patting her golden head with his huge hand.

"It's decorated in purple, and I don't like purple."

"Can I have a bedchamber, Uncle?" Rosanna asked, coming to stand at his side where she stroked the softness of his velvet sleeve. Immediately his eyes were on hers, and his voice rasped as he spoke.

"I see no harm in it. Bianca?"

"No, she's my servant. She can't have a bedchamber."

"Come, sweeting, what harm can be done? It will be only a small one, not nearly as fine as yours."

Bianca pouted, pulling from his reach as he attempted to embrace her and she walked down the corridor. Rosanna watched her, wondering which room Bianca would choose as she stopped before an open door. If she chose that one, the room next door was small. And most important of all it had a bolt on the door.

"This one."

Rosanna's face broke into a smile, Bianca had chosen the right one after all.

"I can take the next room, Uncle," she said, patting his hand, eluding his touch as he tried to capture her fingers. "I'll be next door when Bianca wants me, and the room is small."

"If you wish," he mumbled, as he mentally placed the location of the room. It would be easy to find at night and it was a long way from Magdela's suite.

"Let me look at yours, just to see how small it is," Bianca snapped in annoyance, wrenching open the door.

The room, which overlooked the lawns, had a perfect view of the magnificent flower beds where brilliant scarlet flowers splotched the grass with color. The deep windows had intricate patterns of stained glass in the upper panes, tinting the rays of sunlight blue and crimson as they fell across the bedcovers. On the bed was a spread of moss green, trimmed with gold, the canopy and bed hangings of matching fabric. Beneath the windows was a bench padded in saffron velvet, and a carved oak chest stood at the foot of the bed.

"Is it small enough, Daughter?" Ugo asked with impatience, waiting for Bianca's approval.

"Oh, all right, but you'd better come every time I call you," Bianca grumbled, walking into the dressing room which joined the two rooms. "Mine's much prettier and grander."

Bianca's shrill voice drifted from the other room as she walked about, exclaiming over the richness of the bed hangings.

"Do you like this room?"

"Yes, Uncle, very much."

"Then you shall have it," he smiled at her, his glance searching and lecherous as it swept the bodice of her brown dress. "Do I not deserve some reward?"

"A reward?" Rosanna whispered in mock innocence, knowing full well what he meant. She moved towards the open door, hiding the bolt with her back, as she smiled at him, running the tip of her tongue over her red lips. "Why, Uncle, I don't understand."

Ugo took a step toward her, his mouth curved in a smile. His hand was hot on her neck, and he tucked a finger neatly in the warm hollow between her breasts, until Rosanna squirmed from his touch. But he held her firm with his other hand, bending over her, the sweet perfume from his clothing strong in her nostrils. And he kissed her mouth. "That is but a token payment."

In his voice was a promise, yet she smiled still, secure in her secret as she felt the hurting pressure of the metal bolt in her back. "Thank you for the room."

"Thank *you* for the room." With a meaningful laugh, he released her. Glancing about, he asked: "Is it the one you wanted?"

"Yes, the one I'd already chosen for myself."

"But ... Bianca only just made up her mind," he pointed out with a bewildered frown. "How could you know?"

Rosanna smiled at his words, brushing her hand slowly over her skirts, smoothing the crumpled fabric. Ugo stared at her: then, with an intake of breath, he noticed the color of the bed hangings.

"Green ... the bed is green."

"A restful color, Uncle."

Backing away a pace, Ugo regarded her with a mingling of emotion, fear seeping through his desire as she smiled in her strange, secret way.

"I will come ... later," he promised gruffly, turning on his heel, and he strode through the dressing room to his daughter's bedchamber.

A bird sang liltingly in the bushes beneath her window and Rosanna listened with delight to the magical song, her knees hunched beneath her chin as she stared at the moonlit night. Silver beams slanted over her bed, reflecting on the walls like arrow-straight flares. And she sighed with contentment, breathing the fragrance of the bedding, which was clean and smelled of summer flowers.

There was a sound outside in the corridor, followed by a discreet tap on the door.

"Rosanna, open the door."

She knew her uncle's voice, and she smiled as he hoarsely whispered her name. With another sigh she stretched luxuriously beneath the covers, ignoring him.

He called her name again, then the door handle turned, but the door held fast. He rattled the door as heavily as he dared, afraid someone would hear, but the bolt was snugly in place. After a few minutes his footsteps receded into the night.

Rosanna did not see him alone until noon the next day. While she tidied Bianca's gowns, laying out her riding habit for an afternoon ride, she heard his heavy tread in the corridor. Uncle Ugo appeared in the doorway, a scowl on his face, glad to find her alone at last.

"You little bitch, you deceived me," he growled.

With wide eyes, she stared at him in innocence. "Deceived?"

"Aye, you scheming baggage, you didn't tell me there was a bolt on that door."

"But you didn't ask me, Uncle."

Much to Bianca's rage, because of the increased threat of plague from the city, the annual birthday ball was not held. The only social highlight of the summer was a surprise visit from the Duke on the way to his hunting retreat. Rosanna was not allowed to be present with the family to greet him, not being considered worthy to be introduced to his Grace. It was a great disappointment to her, but she was determined not to display her feelings before her aunt, who had probably made the rule out of spite.

The royal visit was intended to be brief, but on the afternoon of the Duke's departure, Uncle Ugo persuaded him to stay and examine some fine German manuscripts he had recently acquired. The sky was dark, threatening rain, and the royal party delayed their departure because of the impending storm.

After supper, which she ate in her room, Rosanna was summoned by Bianca to stay with her. The other girl was terrified of storms and at each clap of thunder she burrowed beneath her bedcovers, screeching a fervent prayer for deliverance. Soon conversation with her became impossible as the storm moved closer. The wind rose, blowing cold through the open windows, sending Bianca permanently beneath the sheets to whisper a tearful paternoster for their safety, while Rosanna went to the window and watched the storm.

The sky flashed white and orange, the wind cutting tree branches and bowing them to the lawns. Thunder rolled nearer and the walls seemed to shake with the violence of its echo. Rosanna felt the whip of the wind, cold and damp upon her face. Storms exhilarated her, exciting her with a power that was beyond herself, the force outside seemed to draw with a strange magnetic pull. If she had been a child again, she would have walked in the gardens, feeling the drench of rain upon her hair when the torrents finally came. Perversely she would laugh at the might of the elements instead of cowering afraid like Bianca.

There was a knock on the door and Cia stood on the threshold. "Your uncle wishes to see you."

Rosanna sighed, wondering what it could be at this hour, unless . . . "I'll come." She glanced at her shift, light and transparent. She had no robe, but Bianca did. In her cowering foolishness she would never miss it.

Picking up the blue-furred garment Rosanna slipped it on and followed Cia into the darkened passage. Ugo waited beneath the sputtering sconce at the landing. Curtly dismissing the servant, he drew Rosanna into the alcove by the window.

"Duke Paolo has decided to stay the night," he confided in a harsh undertone, lest they be overheard.

Rosanna remained silent, watching the lightning flash behind her uncle's head, streaking a brilliant path through the midnight sky.

"Well, have you no tongue?" he growled, angered by her silence.

"Our house is honored."

"Sometimes I think you're as touched as your mother."

Faintly a smile glimmered and Ugo clenched his fist in rage at her secret expression. "I have many wants in this life, imbecile, many of which can be provided by our royal master. My hospitality will be remembered by him. The night is cold and wet . . ."

"It isn't raining yet," she interrupted.

Ugo glowered at her correction, his hand raised to strike and she drew away to avoid his blow. "It will, before long. As a host it's my duty to send a woman to lessen the chill of the night, understand?"

"Yes. Shall I fetch Cia?" Rosanna asked, rising, but he thrust her back to the stone seat.

"Not Cia."

"Who then? I thought she was the prettiest of the servants."

"There's one prettier and more fitting."

"Bian . . . Me?" Now the answer was clear. Not Bianca the sainted, but Rosanna the damned.

"Of course. Not my daughter. Bianca will make a fine marriage. She must stay virgin till her betrothal is arranged. Whereas you . . ."

"Are not virgin, as well you know, Uncle," Rosanna spat, her mouth twisting with the words. In anger he struck her, but it was only a glancing blow with the flat of his hand.

"Shut your mouth."

Subdued, she waited, eyes downcast, fighting the sting of tears.

"Go to him . . . and please him. If you don't, I'll have you flogged," Ugo promised, gripping her shoulder cruelly with his huge fist. "And remember, if he asks, you are virgin. He'll probably be heated and never notice, least of all remember in the morning."

"What will you give me for this? A green gown?" Rosanna taunted, raising her eyes to meet his.

Ugo stared at her, his brown eyes stony. "What do you want?"

"A furred bed robe like this."

"You shall have it, if you please him. Green, I suppose."

"How did you know?" Her smile was baffling, and seeing her face lit with the brilliance of the lightning, Ugo shuddered in a wave of fear.

"It is the witch's color," he said.

Rosanna waited outside the Duke's bedchamber, hesitating, the key to the door clutched in her chill fingers. Beyond the windows rain drenched the panes, violent and forceful. The sound gave her courage and she inserted the key.

To her surprise she found Duke Paolo awake, a candle burning beside the bed. He was propped against the pillows reading one of her Uncle's priceless volumes, the gold leaf glinting beneath the candlelight. A fire burned in the hearth and moisture fell to the logs, spitting and hissing on the coals. He wore a bed robe and a thick quilt was pulled high beneath his arms.

"My uncle hopes the accommodations are pleasing, your Grace," Rosanna said in a clear voice as she closed the door behind her.

The Duke glanced up at her entrance. "They are fair. The fire dispels some of the chill. You may convey my approval."

Rosanna stared at him sitting in lordly command in the bed, his burnished hair appearing dark in the weak light of the candle. His face was lit by a slanted reflection which wavered in the draft, the brightness shifting from his eyes to his mouth and back again. He was so handsome. How many times she had dreamed of being held in his arms, of pressing his lips with her own.

"Well, what are you waiting for?"

Rosanna blinked. His voice when it came was not soft, not tender; it was commanding, annoyed by the invasion of privacy.

"I . . . are the volumes pleasing also?"

The Duke smiled, glancing down to the heavy book against his knees. "Yes, they are indeed treasures. I'm jealous of your uncle. Such fine volumes should be in my possession, not his. What say you?"

"I think so too, your Grace," she agreed, moving towards the light. "May I see? I can read a little, but he won't let me handle the manuscripts."

She sensed his hesitation, then with a beckoning movement of his bejeweled hand, he nodded. "Come."

Moving to the bed, Rosanna found her heart thudding wildly. To stand so close to him in the intimacy of his bedchamber, to be alone in the night, while the storm raged outside, was the realization of her most fantastic dream.

She bent over the parchment, marveling at the brightly

colored drawings of flowers and birds, at the lifelike animals and gilded saints. Painfully she stumbled through the first passage, finding the embellished letters hard to decipher. At last she glanced up to find Duke Paolo's eyes on her face. She could read nothing in their pale brilliance as he regarded her a moment before looking away.

"They are truly wonderful, your Grace," she breathed with shining face. "So beautiful."

"There are many things in this house that are beautiful."

The meaning behind his words sent her heart racing until she was sure he would hear the sound. She stepped back a pace in a primitive, protective gesture, but he did not reach for her.

"Why did your uncle send you?"

"He . . . I . . . to warm your bed, your Grace."

"It is warm enough. Send him my thanks, but I've had a long and tiring journey," he dismissed, turning back to his book.

Catching her breath, Rosanna faltered, her heart continuing its deafening rhythm, but now in fear instead of excitement. She would be flogged if she went back now. Perhaps her uncle waited in the passage outside; he would know she had not pleased the Duke if she came from his room so soon. Loosening the bed robe she let it fall, until she stood in her thin shift.

He looked up at the sound of the falling garment. The storm had abated for the moment and it was quiet, so much so, Rosanna heard his intake of breath as he saw her body visible through the material, made almost transparent by the background of fireglow. He closed the book, deliberately placing it on the table beside the bed. With the movement his black and silver-furred bed robe opened until she could see the matting of brown-gold hair on his chest. And he smiled, but the expression was without humor.

"So you are the sacrificial virgin of Ugo Sordello's household. What is it he wants from me, wench? Do you know?"

"No, your Grace."

"Of course you do," he contradicted sharply. "What

99

does he discuss at table, or behind the doors of his chambers? Is it lands he speaks of, or . . . ?"

"Ships, your Grace."

"Ships," he echoed in surprise, then a smile of enlightenment dawned. "Have you heard him mention Algordo?"

"Gennaro Algordo? Yes."

"Then I have it. Algordo will soon be put to death and your uncle wants his fleet. He must think the wares are valuable indeed. Are you worth a fleet, wench?"

Rosanna dropped her eyes from his, hurt by the expression she saw. She stared at the floor, sweetened with herbs and crushed flower petals for the Duke's stay.

"What is it they call you? I like to know the names of my whores."

"Rosanna," she whispered in shame at the word he used.

"Are you virgin?" When she did not answer, he rephrased his question. "You have not known a man?"

"I understand, your Grace. My uncle told me to lie, but I cannot. I am no longer virgin."

Duke Paolo threw back his head with a peal of laughter. "So, Sordello bargains with soiled goods. Wait till the court hears that. How many other weary travellers' beds have you warmed?"

"None, your Grace. It was . . . my uncle."

He stared at her, sobered and she dropped her eyes. "If I send you from here?"

"He will flog me."

"What a sweet and gentle man is our noble Sordello." The Duke stirred in the bed reaching to her simple headdress and he took it off, dropping it on the floor. Her black hair fell in a shimmering cloud to her waist, falling over her brow and he lifted the glossy strands. "And what will he give you for this night?"

"A furred bed robe, your Grace."

His mouth twisted in a smile and pushing back the covers he got out of bed. Rosanna watched him cross to a trunk in the corner by the clothespress and he opened the clasp. He returned with a trailing organza scarf shot with silver, and a pair of embroidered gloves.

"They were for my lady mother, but she will not miss

them," he said, handing the articles to Rosanna, who stared in stupefied silence at the expensive gifts. Impatiently the Duke pulled the scarf from her grasp to drape it over her head, arranging the folds about her face and he stepped back to admire her appearance. "You are a vision," he complimented, his eyes traveling to her body beneath the shift. "Too lovely for a whore."

Again the word and Rosanna found tears of shame in her eyes. It was not what she wanted him to say. He had almost begun to be tender, but now his eyes were hard, empty and brittle, his smile of scorn.

"I shall save you from a beating, Rosanna Sordello. I am to be thanked for that, am I not?"

Before she could reply, his mouth was on hers, bruising and hot. His fingers sought her breasts beneath the shift which, a moment later, he impatiently pulled over her shoulders. She found her body throbbing, but with Duke Paolo she wanted love with the passion. She was not a whore, she wasn't.

He turned towards the table and leaned over the candle. Before he snuffed out the light she saw his eyes. They were dark with only one expression. And it was not love.

In the warm sea of bedcovers when she wanted him to hold her, when it should have been time for kisses and whispered words, he turned away, thrusting her aside. Rosanna trembled with silent sobs, her love a painful thing. When she thought he slept, she moved to the edge of the mattress but his hand came out detaining.

"Don't go yet, the chill of the night is still on us," he said, irony and scorn in the words. "Why do you weep? Did I hurt you?"

"No."

His hands caressed her arm and Rosanna found the pain of stifled sobs agonizing in her throat. For a time he was quiet, yet she knew he was awake by the movement of his hands. She moved on the pillows to see his face, but his head was turned towards the window where the storm raged with renewed fury. She wanted him to kiss her, to say he loved her as he did in dreams, but the night was not for that. To Duke Paolo she was nothing. Tears spilled in a silent river down her face, her grief betrayed by the slight shudders as she gasped for air through the choking blanket of tears. His hand moved to her face, touching the wetness of her cheeks.

"I am sorry, Rosanna."

His voice came through the thunder of her tears and she was surprised by its gentleness.

"I should not have used you cruelly, it is not my way," he said, his fingers gentle on her face. "Why do you cry?"

"I don't know, your Grace."

"Are you afraid? You said I did not hurt you."

"Not afraid," she murmured in reply, seized by an impossible idea. Tonight would be all she would have of would he do? Would he tell her uncle, or have her beaten? Rosanna thought it would be neither of these things.

"What then?"

She reached for his hand upon her cheek, trembling at the warmth as she pressed her mouth to his fingers. Her arms went about him and now the salt taste of her mouth was on his as she touched his hair and face as she often did in dreams.

"Mother of God," he whispered against her face, trembling at her touch. "I didn't know. What a fool, I didn't know."

"Paolo." There, she had said his name, without title, without deference to his nobility, just Paolo, her lover. "Please, again, slowly so I can remember it."

In the darkness she heard his soft laugh, but there was no scorn and her body sang with joy at his touch.

"It will be slow as I can manage," he promised with a grin, drawing her close. "This is not for Ugo Sordello. This time it's for Duke Paolo."

When Rosanna woke, it was with his golden head cradled against her face and she wanted to weep from the pain of her love for him. Tonight she had for herself after all.

Silently she slid from the bed, trying not to disturb him. When she took away her arm she expected him to wake, but his sleep was deep and satisfied. She stood beside the bed and watched him in the dying glow of the fire, then she picked up the discarded blue robe from the floor and slipped it on. It was quiet outside, the storm finished. From the corner of her eye she saw the scarf and gloves tumbled from the bed and she stooped to retrieve them as she tiptoed to the door.

The hinge creaked, but he did not wake, and she went into the cold passage. At the end of the hallway she saw a figure swathed in a fur robe. It was Ugo.

"In the name of God, how long does it take him," he muttered, shivering in the numbing, damp cold. "You've been hours."

"He's asleep now."

"And pleased?"

"Very pleased."

Ugo smiled and placed his arm around her shoulders. "You shall have your bed robe. Tomorrow I'll have them bring bolts of stuff to your apartments. Don't say anything to Bianca."

"I won't."

He left her and she wound through the twisting passages to her own room, her heart bursting and her body heavy with pleasure.

In the morning the royal party left, riding grandly down the wide, beech-lined driveway, sunlight glancing fire off the men's weapons and the metal pieces of the horses' trappings. The royal standard fluttered proudly at the head of the party, and behind the standard bearer rode the Duke.

With a sigh Rosanna watched him until the party of riders was a speck in the distance, wondering if she would ever see him again.

September came and they returned to the city. The ships of Gennaro Algordo became the ships of Ugo Sordello, and Rosanna was given a pearl cross on a chain as a belated birthday gift by her grateful uncle. Aunt Magdela suggested that betrothals for both girls be arranged as they were fourteen—the perfect age for marriage. Rosanna quaked at the thought of the husband her aunt would probably choose for her, but apart from this anxiety her life resumed its monotony. If she told Aunt Magdela of that night with the Duke she would not believe it; however, Rosanna was not tempted to reveal the secret, for she had already felt the strength of her uncle's wrath.

Every outing was a new opportunity to see his Grace, but though she watched for him, she did not see the royal party until the feast of St. Francis when she accompanied her aunt and cousin to the Duomo to hear the holy day mass.

The congregation was luxuriously dressed and Aunt Magdela clucked over the shameful presence of a number of ladies of the town, their heads covered by yellow silk scarves. Rosanna knelt in the incense-laden gloom with head bowed, her eyes tightly closed. The beautiful nave of the church was filled by singing voices, rising in a chorus as pure and heavenly as the song of angels. The chanting of the priest was loud as the chorus ceased and he raised the sacred chalice. When she looked up at the glittering gold to adore the host, Rosanna encountered a man's eyes fastened upon hers. Above the bowed heads in the rows of pews, Duke Paolo watched her as if they were entirely alone in the magnificent cathedral of San Lorenzo. He did not smile and his pale eyes were troubled, for what seemed an eternity their gaze was locked, broken at last by the shuffling passage of communicants to the high altar. The Duke was lost from sight, and when mass was over, Rosanna discovered he had already left. The discovery gave her a momentary feeling of frustration. Did he remember the night of the storm? Yet he had not returned to Villa Sordello, nor had he visited the palazzo since their return to the city. Could it be perhaps that Paolo was just a little in love with her? His eyes betrayed nothing, beyond their distress. Did his own lust cause him distress, or dare she hope he felt more than that in his heart?

Aunt Magdela jabbed her sharply in the ribs, glaring at her abstraction. With a swift bob, Rosanna genuflected towards the holy atlar, moving into the stream of people filing through the massive bronze doors of the cathedral.

Outside the sunlight was intense and Rosanna squinted her eyes against the glare. A flock of pigeons had fluttered from the cathedral steps as the doors were flung back, to perch on the nearby buildings; now they boldly returned, strutting importantly about the broad piazza before the cathedral.

The early morning air was fresh and Rosanna glanced towards the pink and white marble towers of Palazzo Lorenzo, shining across the square. If she could have willed herself to be invisible she would slip inside the grand archways, run through the winding, high-vaulted corridors and seek out his room. There, held safely against the thudding of his heart; the demanding strength of his arms locked around her . . .

"Daydreaming again, what a useless wench," Aunt Magdela hissed, turning an iron grip on her shoulder. Bianca smiled triumphantly, mincing along, basking in the warmth of her mother's approval. And behind her aunt's stiff, unyielding back, Rosanna stuck out her tongue at the other girl.

Chapter Seven

Spring sunshine patterned the courtyard with lace as it shone through the new green leaves, the pattern changed as a breeze stirred the branches. It was cool in the shade, so Rosanna sat beside the fountain where the sun slanted directly on her back. Everywhere was quiet. Too quiet. It was going to be another boring day. Bianca and Aunt Magdela had already departed for mass, refusing to take her with them because of her unladylike behavior yesterday. Well, at least that was one stroke of good fortune, she wouldn't have to sit through hours of prayer in that stuffy cathedral. What could she do? Cia had promised, with cook's permission, to show her how to make a cake, but her lover, Matteo, had unexpectedly arrived, so that was that for a few days. Not that she was really anxious to learn how to bake, for domesticity was not one of her virtues, but at least it would have been something interesting to do.

She plucked a pink flower from the border at the base of the fountain, absently plucking its petals. "He loves me, he loves me not, he loves me . . ." With a sigh of aggravation, she cast the mutilated blossom into the splashing fountain, where it floated a moment before becoming trapped against a mermaid's scaly marble tail. Now she was thinking of Paolo, which was much worse, remembering the way he had touched her, the feel of his kiss.

"No ... no," she muttered, jumping to her feet. Instead of mooning, she'd go to the stables and look at the horses. Since their journey to the villa last summer, she had made friends with Taddeo, the chief groom; he was rather dense but could be good company when she was desperate. He explained the care of the animals to her, sometimes allowing her to groom Bianca's horse, though Aunt Magdela would have been shocked to learn of her back door accomplishment. That in itself was a spur to continue the impromptu lessons.

Rosanna hurried over the deserted outer court, stopping to examine the ripening fruit in the orchard. She sampled an apple, pulling a face at the sourness of the fruit. This could be given to Tisa. The mare would appreciate the green apple far more than she.

"Does your aunt know you're here?"

Rosanna pulled a face at Mari, the stableboy, a very junior stableboy at that, but because he was her own age he thought he had the right to dictate what she should do.

"No, she doesn't, but that's no concern of yours," she answered scornfully, turning up her nose at his dirty clothing. "Where's Taddeo?"

Mari inclined his head toward the harness room. He wouldn't talk to the uppity baggage if she was going to be like that. She could get caught for all he cared.

Rosanna opened the door, finding the smell of saddle soap and leather pleasant in the fresh morning air. "Taddeo."

The groom's tousled head appeared over the shelves of saddles and bridles. He grinned as he saw her, coming into the middle of the room. "What do you want?"

"I came to talk to you, *outside*," she replied, determined to keep him in his place before he got other ideas. Taddeo was not on her list of possible admirers.

"Too bad. I hoped you came for some other lessons," he quipped with a suggestive grin, hoisting a saddle over his arm.

"I don't need any of those lessons."

"No, I bet you don't, at that."

Rosanna grinned at the appreciative tone which crept into his voice, following him outside to the stableyard.

"I want to give this apple to Tisa first. Where is she?"

"In her stall. Come on."

The bay mare whinnied with pleasure at their approach, thrusting her velvety nose over the side of her stall.

"Here, Tisa, see what Rosanna's brought you."

The mare gently accepted the tidbit from her hand, brushing her soft, wet muzzle against Rosanna's fingers. While Tisa ate, Rosanna stroked her black glossy mane, wishing she was her horse instead of Bianca's. If she had such a lovely horse she'd ride every day, cantering over the fields outside the city. How lovely it would be to feel the wind blowing through her hair and to smell the grass. Here in Lorenzo, though they did have a garden within the courtyard, everywhere was paved. There was no feeling of space or freedom, just miles of stone and marble.

"She needs exercise, poor girl," Taddeo joined, rubbing the mare's velvety muzzle with a whispered endearment in her ear, which Tisa enjoyed, pushing against him to show her appreciation.

"Don't you give her exercise?"

"Only round the stableyard; sometimes we go to the tilt field but there usually isn't time. When the master's away there's not much care taken of the animals. *Donna* Magdela doesn't trust horses, so she doesn't bother about them. We're lucky *Signor* Marco has the stallions with him, they're harder to manage than these old girls."

"When's he coming home?" Rosanna inquired, patting the mare's glossy red coat.

"It ought to be some time today."

Rosanna was silent, inwardly her mind raced with a marvelous plan. Why didn't she ride out to greet Marco. She could take Bianca's horse and give her a run at the same time.

"Can I ride out to meet him?"

"You? God, no, it would be more than my life's worth to let you go alone," Taddeo protested, picking up a bucket of water. Then he walked outside into the sunlight, collecting brushes and combs on his way.

"Come with me," Rosanna suggested helpfully.

"I couldn't."

"Why? You said the horses needed exercise. *Donna* Magdela is at mass. Today's a holy day so they'll be gone for hours. Oh, come on, no one will ever know."

The pleading note in her voice moved Taddeo, and he pursed his lips in concentration, trying to gather his wits to think over her suggestion. He could take her along, it would probably be all right, yet somehow he could not help thinking it very wrong. *Donna* Magdela had never actually told him not to let the girl ride, but on the other hand, she'd never said he could.

"What are you waiting for? Please, please, Taddeo, say we can. Just think how lovely it would be to ride out of the city. See, Tisa knows what I'm saying, listen to her."

The bay mare whinnied from her stall as if she knew the proposed plan, endorsing the suggestion with enthusiasm.

"All right, but you tell them it was your idea if anything's said. And no farther than the tilt field, then we come back," he decided, weakening before the brightness of her smile.

With a squeak of pleasure, Rosanna raced toward the stall, calling Tisa's name in excitement. Taddeo shook his head, smiling at the answering voice from the stall.

"Can I use Bianca's saddle? Can we put the trappings on, the ones she used to ride in the procession?"

"Not those, you'll have me skinned, and no mistake."

"Which ones then? How about the black velvet one with the red roses and gold fringe?"

He nodded, a worried frown creeping between his eyes, and he glanced into the stableyard to make sure they were still alone. "Come on, but I hope to God we don't get caught."

"First I have to change to my habit. I'll hurry. Don't go without me."

Taddeo leaned against the stable door, watching her streak across the courtyard in the sunlight, her dress bobbing like a brightly colored bird amongst the urns of greenery. Perhaps he might extract a small payment for his generosity; he knew the wench was lonely, and she'd been friendly enough towards him. To have her would be something to boast about in Romano's place. It would be almost as good as *la Bianca* herself, and probably far more satisfactory.

Sitting straight in the saddle, Rosanna felt like a queen with her grand trappings, proud of the spirited mare who moved so daintily over the ground. At her urging, Tisa increased her pace until they were cantering over the broad, grassy reach of the tilt field. Taddeo raced after her, cautioning her about her recklessness, reminding her it was time to return.

"Could we just go to the bend in the road to watch for Marco?" she pleaded, sensing his reluctance to take his charges home.

Taddeo knitted his brows, wondering if he could take the chance. It was still early, and no one was about. "All right," he agreed, riding close beside her, and he grinned impudently at her pretty face.

Giving him an answering smile, Rosanna pulled ahead, sending him thundering after her. The ribbon of the Via San Lorenzo stretched white and bare, winding over the plain, disappearing in the grassy foothills of the mountains. Marco's hunting party was nowhere in sight. Ignoring Taddeo's admonitions to return, Rosanna headed Tisa along the dusty road, flying to the next turn, and the next, with Taddeo racing after her in hot pursuit. Suddenly she saw the hunting party and her heart leaped, for at the head of the column the royal standard flapped in the spring breeze; Marco had joined the Duke for the morning hunt.

In excitement she hailed the riders and Marco waved back, surprised by her presence. With a triumphant glance towards Taddeo, who was slumped in the saddle with a scowl on his face, Rosanna rode forward to meet her cousin.

"You're just in time, we thought to stop at the inn for refreshment," Marco said, maneuvering his horse alongside hers. "Does Magdela know you're here?"

With a wicked grin, Rosanna shook her head, leaning forward to obtain a better view of the Duke, who turned to smile at her. Her heart thudding, she smiled in reply as he swept off his hat to greet her, before he turned back to

Marco. Pained disappointment flooded through Rosanna at his polite indifference.

"My cousin, your Grace," Marco said, as an afterthought, as she rode at his side. Again Duke Paolo smiled, his mind elsewhere, and Rosanna fell back a few paces allowing the men to ride together.

But later, when Marco was speaking to the falconer, the Duke waited at the crest of the road. When she drew alongside him, he fell into step beside her, his high-spirited white stallion prancing and sidestepping beside her bay mare.

"Are you Rosanna?" he asked, his voice soft, so that she barely heard him over the noise of the riders.

"Yes, your Grace."

His eyes were upon her, sweeping over her russet habit, coming to rest on her face. "I trust the storms have abated for the season, *madonna*," he said with a slow smile, then he spurred the stallion forward, drawing away, leaving her face a rose flushed warmth of pleasure.

Sometimes he watched her, for she could feel his eyes on her back, but he did not speak to her again. It did not matter. He had remembered, and the knowledge made her tingle.

The inn was shabby, the innyard almost too small to accommodate the large hunting party, but eventually everyone was served. The wine was bitter, and Rosanna gave hers to Taddeo, whom she felt deserved some slight reward for his pains.

In an hour the party was on the road, turning the horses towards Lorenzo. Marco did not speak to her, his attention on the Duke, but Rosanna did not mind, for riding with them was part of her adventure.

At the crossroads the hunting party separated, the Duke's party heading to the east, while they turned their horses back towards the west gate of Lorenzo. The sun was hot and the heat bore down from a cloudless sky, the dusty road brazen beneath the horses' hooves. Behind them the powdery ribbon stretched far to the horizon over sloping, gentle hillocks.

"Marco, could we rest? I'm so hot," Rosanna asked, reining in beside him.

Marco glanced towards the inviting cool shade of the

trees and nodded. "Of course, it was thoughtless of me. I thought only to reach home before dusk."

He wheeled his horse back to the dusty column of servants and by their eager exclamations and laughter, Rosanna knew she was not alone in her fatigue. The party dismounted and Marco brought a blue saddlecloth emblazoned with the Sordello arms for her to sit on.

"Let's go to that clearing through the trees," she suggested, anxious to retreat from the acrid smell of sweat and horseflesh which rose from the steaming company.

The clearing was gloomy, lit by flickering light from the sky, shining between the moving tree leaves. Apprehensively, Marco glanced about him at the deep forest, suspicious of the unknown reaches. He could see the servants from here. If anything befell they were within the sound of his voice; so he nodded agreement, picking up the saddlecloth and a flask of watered wine to quench his thirst.

"We must not stay long. I want to be inside the city before nightfall."

She nodded, dropping on the mossy ground with a sigh, stretching her limbs, slowly uncoiling from the long hours spent in the saddle, until Marco laughed at her.

"You look like a cat."

She accepted the flask of wine and drank from it, handing it back to him. "I wish I was going to the ball tonight."

"Bianca isn't even going."

"That's only because she has her woman's time, she's such a ninny, that one. I wouldn't miss a chance to go to the palace."

"Even if you dripped blood on Duke Paolo's marble floor, I know you." Marco laughed, but his words were not unkind.

"Will you take me?"

"Take you? Of course not."

"It's masked. No one would know me."

"I'd know you."

"Oh, Marco, I've never been there."

"There are hundreds of girls in Lorenzo who've never been inside the palace."

"Am I not beautiful enough?"

"It's not that. I just couldn't take you. What would Father say?"

"He doesn't have to know. I could borrow one of Bianca's gowns. She wouldn't miss it. Oh, please, Marco."

"Maybe a few years from now, when you're quite grown-up."

Rosanna scowled and sat up, hunching her knees to her chin. "Are you going with the Miserotti woman?"

Marco turned quickly, gripping her arm. "What do you know of her?"

"That you slip out at night to see her," she answered smugly, seeing his discomfiture, and knowing she had the advantage.

"How?"

"I've seen you when the others are sleeping, going the back way with your boots in your hand."

"You don't know where I was going." He sighed in relief, releasing her arm.

"I do now."

Angrily he glared at her, then his anger dissolved in a smile. "If you think to frighten me into taking you, you're wasting your time."

"I wasn't going to get you in trouble, Marco," she said with a sweet smile, watching him over her russet-covered knees. Slowly she swept her hand down the dusty material, her eyes slanted and secret, so that he turned away in sudden discomfort. He was a little like Duke Paolo to look at after all, she thought with renewed interest. Marco's hair was darker and his eyes were different, but the rest was very similar. He was even taller than the Duke, she had noticed that when they stopped at the inn. If she danced at the ball with Marco she could pretend he was the Duke, for he would be masked also. If only she could persuade him to take her with him.

"Do you want some more wine?" she asked sweetly, offering him the flask, but he shook his head.

"When I come back." Marco left her, disappearing between the trees, his feet crunching on the undergrowth.

The rustling sound stopped and Rosanna glanced in the direction he had gone, catching her breath. In that spot the screen of shrubs and trees were sparsely leaved and his brown doublet was visible through the branches. Her

113

face flushed hot with blood and she looked away, conscious of that feeling she knew so well thundering through her body. At that moment she desperately wanted him, but it was not Marco Sordello she wanted, it was his maleness to assuage the hunger within herself.

Lacing his hose, Marco reappeared through the trees, to find Rosanna demurely threading flowers to form a chain. She glanced up at his approach, her cheeks prettily rose-flushed, her black eyes luminous and smiling.

"Your wine," she said, giving him the flask.

He accepted the drink, stretching on the soft moss, his hat over his face.

Rosanna went on with her task until she had threaded a long chain, then she moved to him, snatching away his shield. He grinned good-naturedly as she draped the pink flowers around his head, threading them through his hair.

"You would make a prettier model," he said, sitting up and drawing the chain from his head. He trailed the garland over her hair, placing the flowers in a crown, allowing the ends to drape across the swelling of her bosom. And with triumph, Rosanna saw the changed expression on his face as he met her eyes, puzzled, yet at once eager.

"It's time to leave," he said gruffly, moving his hands.

"Already. It's such a short time."

Marco glanced towards the servants who were sprawled in various attitudes beneath the trees at the side of the road.

"So you promise to take me to the palace when I'm grown-up, then will I be pretty enough for you?" Rosanna laughed, completely aware of her unsettling effect on him.

"You are already pretty enough ... and I think grown-up enough."

"For the palace, Marco?"

"No, I did not mean for the palace."

"For what then?" she demanded innocently, marking his shallow breathing, the flush of his face.

His eyes held hers, and his expression she knew; it was a replica of his father's. She watched him and willed him to touch her, her eyes black and fathomless, until he moved forward, his hands eagerly demanding.

"For this," he whispered, bearing her back on the moss. "Say you will have me, now, before we return."

Rosanna forced her limbs to remain steady, though the weight of him and the pressure was almost unbearable. "You want to do *that* to me?"

"Yes, God, yes."

"Very badly?"

"It is agony."

"And if I say no?"

"I can take you by force, but I'd rather you say yes." He smiled, his face on her own, his mouth hot and soft against her cheek.

"Marco, if I let you do it, will you take me to the ball?"

He hesitated and her hand stole into his hair, brushing over the flesh of his neck, slowly, softly, tormentingly. . . .

"Will you? If you promise, I'll let you do it, Marco."

He hesitated, wondering if he could manage the idiocy of her scheme; its very insanity interested him. It would be novel and she was very lovely. "Yes, we will go together."

"And will you treat me like the Miserotti woman, instead of your cousin?" she asked, finally allowing the release of her control, so that her legs strained against his until he pressed her harder into the moss.

"Yes."

"Then you can do it. I won't tell anyone, if you don't hurt me."

Triumph flickered in his eyes. At first he was surprised by her eager movements beneath him, the knowing, intimate touch of her hand and the heat of her kiss. Then he smiled, looking down at her face beneath his on the ground, her eyelids tightly closed, her red mouth soft. He had stirred her with his virility. His prowess as a lover had wakened hidden passion in her virgin body. And he claimed her, feeling enormous pride in his masculinity.

Spent, he rolled from her, sprawling wearily in the grass. In a few minutes he had recovered and he sat up, finding her leaning against a tree trunk, a smile on her face.

"Don't tell my father," he cautioned, belatedly anxious.

"I won't, if you take me to the ball."

"I said I would," Marco paused, grinning at her. "I'm good, aren't I?"

115

But she only smiled, feeling nothing for him as a person. Inside, her body was quenched; let him enjoy his moment of triumph.

"Aren't you glad I took you?"

"I took you, Marco." She laughed, springing up to dart between the trees, her skirts bobbing over the ground until she reached the road.

On the return journey Marco was disconcerted by her aloofness. If he had not known otherwise he would have sworn he dreamt the heated interlude in the forest glade. His cousin was like another woman, remote and mysterious, not the panting, clinging creature he had pressed so willingly into the cushion of moss, scant distance from the snoring servants. When he attempted to make conversation she replied in monosyllables, or not at all, until he retired in moody silence.

Sunset was a glorious, crimson backdrop as they rode through the city, and down the winding streets Rosanna saw the gleaming towers of Palazzo Lorenzo. It was unbelievable to think in a few hours she would be inside those faceted marble walls, mingling with a glittering throng of nobles. She would see where the Duke lived, and if she was very fortunate perhaps he would dance with her, for her identity would be hidden beneath a mask. With a shiver of delight, she imagined his hand in hers, his eyes lit by a smile; he might even draw her to the shadowed arches by the canal and kiss her. Anything and everything was possible on this magical night.

She abruptly left Marco at the stables, eluding his arm, no further interest in him. All her senses were absorbed in the reconstruction of her daydream.

For a moment Marco had the inclination to deceive her. He was not bound to take Rosanna to the palace, and what could she do if he left without her? Yet the thought gave him a swift chill of foreboding. He was sure she would find a way for revenge; the form that revenge might take made him grow cold. He glanced up at the full circle of a pale golden moon as it struggled through the wispy clouds of night, and he wondered if the townspeople were right about Aunt Lucia. Was she a witch? Had she imparted her satanic influence in the heart of his lovely cousin? It was insane to even contemplate taking

Rosanna to the palace, yet as he stared at the tossing moon, he realized he was completely powerless to go against her desires. He would take her, but not from his own choice, from a force beyond his control. And with a shiver of apprehension, Marco strode into the courtyard, attempting a faltering whistle of confidence.

It seemed an eternity before Bianca was safely in bed. As Rosanna stared through the window, her thoughts on the ball, Aunt Magdela came storming through the door.

"What is this I hear, that you were abroad with his Grace, and your cousin?" she demanded, her face a mask of rage as she slammed the bedchamber door closed.

Rosanna said nothing, barely looking at her aunt, her eyes fixed on the moon. Her mother had told her the power to make people obey her will was strongest at the full moon.

"Answer me, you wretch."

"It is so. I rode into the countryside to meet Marco."

"You shameless hussy, wait till your uncle hears of this, the latest escapade in a list of things you do deliberately to plague me. As soon as he returns I'll tell him."

"No, for I too have things to tell. It should be interesting to see which he finds the gravest complaint, what I shall tell, or you."

Magdela's gasp was audible in the silent room, and her face set in a frown. Rosanna turned from the window, the moonlight shining full on her face, her eyes glittering as if they burned with fire. Falling back a couple of paces, Magdela dropped her hand. She had been ready to strike the insolence from her niece's face, but that expression prevented the action.

"We shall see," was all she said. Kissing her daughter good-night, Magdela swept from the room without a backward glance.

With a smile of triumph, Rosanna knew she had won.

"You should not speak that way to my mother," Bianca reprooved, scandalized.

"She should not speak that way to me."

"But she is mistress of this house."

"I've done nothing to cause her distress. I rode out to greet your brother. Is that a crime?"

"You were not given permission. Always you must have permission to go outside the house; it's unseemly to ride abroad like a man," Bianca reminded with a virtuous smirk.

"I will do what I want," Rosanna declared defiantly, throwing herself down on the bed in the corner. And she wondered how long she would have to wait for Bianca to fall asleep.

"Did you really see his Grace?" Bianca whispered.

"Yes."

"Was he very handsome?"

"Of course, the handsomest man in Lorenzo."

"I wish I could go to the ball tonight and see him," Bianca sighed. "It's terrible to be a woman and have to put up with these terrible pains each month."

"You could have gone if you wanted. I'm sure you won't be the only woman there in that condition."

"I can't dance when I'm like this," Bianca whined tearfully. "You know how I suffer. You act like a peasant woman, you have no shame. Ladies aren't like that, they suffer terribly. Mother says . . ."

"Don't treat me to one of your mother's lectures, I've had enough to last a lifetime," Rosanna interrupted. "You'd better go to sleep or I'll tell her you talked all night, then she'll scold you for ruining your complexion. You'll have big black circles under your eyes."

"Oh, you're awful. I'm sure no other girl suffers like I do. Nature is cruel enough, without having to endure you as well."

Sniffles and sobs erupted from the big bed. With a sigh of exasperation, Rosanna turned to the wall wondering what hour it was. Surely it must be close to the time of departure, yet she'd heard no sounds from the stable. At dinner she had whispered to Marco she would meet him in the outer courtyard and he had nodded his agreement.

Soon the sobs turned to snores; Bianca had cried herself to sleep. Good, now she could begin her adventure. Rosanna crept to Bianca's clothes chest, the moonlight making everywhere as bright as day. Apprehensive, she glanced towards the bed, but Bianca's snores were even and profound. The clothes chest creaked and it seemed hours before she finally had it open. The dress on top was a deep sapphire blue. The color would be attractive enough, Rosanna decided, pulling out the stiff brocade. This must have been what Bianca had intended to wear to the ball before Mother Nature dealt her such a cruel blow. With a grin, she let the lid down easily, carefully pulling the trailing skirts free.

It was difficult to fasten the dress by herself, for Bianca was more slender than she and the bodice was tight. With much panting and struggling, Rosanna managed the task, pulling the material as modestly high as she could. The undershift was stiff with silver embroidery and it scratched her flesh as she moved. With a sigh of delight at her magnificent appearance, glimpsed in the long mirror on the wall, Rosanna put on her best slippers. They were not as grand as Bianca's, but today she had tried her cousin's silver shoes and they were too tight. Better to be unfashionable and still able to dance. What agony it would be if the Duke asked her to dance and her feet were so painful she could not.

She plumped her pillow and shift into a mound beneath the bedcover, in case Bianca wakened in the night, she would not know the bed was empty. Then picking up her silver mask, Rosanna tiptoed to the door.

In the passage it was silent and her footsteps echoed though she tried to be stealthy. At last the winding journey was negotiated and she stood outside in the fresh coolness of night. Making sure she was unobserved she ran over the inner courtyard, through the connecting passage and into the garden. A dark shadow moved by the archway to the stableyard and she knew it was Marco.

In a moment she had run to his arms and he whispered urgently, "I thought you weren't coming. I almost left without you several times. What took so long?"

"Bianca wanted to talk, then she started crying. I thought she'd never go to sleep. I hurried as fast as I could. Will we be late?"

"A little, but it doesn't matter. We'll slip in and mingle with the guests," he assured, glancing at her appearance in the moonlight. "You look lovely," he breathed in admiration. With a swift tug of memory, his body responded, until he would have taken her in his arms, but she moved away.

"Come on, Marco," she urged impatiently, running towards the waiting horses.

"I'm almost sorry I wanted for you," he hissed, "if you're going to scorn me."

With a disarming smile, she stroked his face. "Don't be sorry you waited, Marco, dear. You would have been sorrier if you had not."

For a moment his brows knitted at her words, but she was laughing at him again and with a swift smile, Marco swung her to the saddle. Taddeo and a couple of boys came out of the shadows of the stables to join them, and the small procession passed through the archway into the dark street.

Palazzo Lorenzo was a blaze of lights, shining so brilliantly through the streets that the remainder of their journey to the palace was lighted. Liveried pages stood on the wide, shallow steps holding aloft huge, flickering, gilt candelabras to light the way of latecoming guests. Rosanna had never seen pages in such rich attire. Their tunics were of gold embroidered velvet with the arms of Lorenzo emblazoned on chest and back. Their hose was shot with gold, even their shoes were gold, with foolish, elaborately long toes with a lion's head at the curled point.

There was little time for gaping at the beautiful marble exterior of the palazzo, for Marco was urging her up the steps. A herald stepped forward to take his name and rank, but Marco waved the man away, his finger to his lips to disclose the secrecy of the occasion.

Young Sordello was known to the herald, so he did not question the move, only nodding with an approving grin at the mysterious lady who accompanied him.

"Rocco thinks you're a duchess at least," Marco whispered, leading Rosanna to the crowded ballroom. "I'm sure he thinks some leading citizen of Lorenzo will wear the cuckold's horns tonight."

She smiled, nervously clutching his arm, drawing strength from her cousin's assurance. Her mask was in place, and now, so was his, as they moved inconspicuously amongst the richly attired guests. The ladies' beautiful gowns glittered with jewels, sparkling in the light from hundreds of sconces flaring along the walls; while the men wore satins and velvets of such sumptious colors, her breath was taken away by their magnificence.

The ballroom was painted with murals depicting scenes of mythical gods and goddesses, beautiful and unclothed—the work of the Duke's protégé, Pandolfo Ricasoli. Once Marco had told her Ricasoli was the lover of Bernardo, the Duke's brother, but Rosanna puzzled over the relationship, for they said he was handsome and sought after by the ladies of the court. She glanced about, wondering who was the artist. The royal family had not yet arrived, and the expectant hush heightened to a murmur of anticipation as a loud fanfare of trumpeters announced their arrival.

Craning her neck to see, Rosanna gasped at the magnificent attire of the royal brothers. She knew at first glance which was Duke Paolo, even though he was masked; the assurance as he strode amongst the assembly, the way he inclined his head and his gestures were all firmly embedded in her memory.

His younger brother was shorter with a slender build, his fair hair already thinning at the temples. Bernardo wore purple velvet with heavy gold embroidery, his short cloak lined with gold damask, but it was at Duke Paolo Rosanna stared. His doublet was of rose-pink velvet lavishly trimmed with gold and jewels; a short cloak of the same color swung jauntily from his shoulders, lined with wine-colored satin in startling contrast to the velvet. His hose were gold, the metallic threads catching the light as he walked, his strong, muscular legs rippling beneath the tight fabric. She sighed at the sight of him, wishing he would come to speak to Marco, but already Marco's interest had shifted to the nearby women.

"Who's that?" she whispered, tugging his arm as a tall woman in black moved to a dais at the end of the room.

"The Dowager Duchess Maria; the Duke's mother."

"I don't like her," Rosanna said with a shiver, seeing the Duchess' narrow, cruel eyes flickering over the assembly, forever shifting.

"You have much company in that emotion. Duchess Maria is not the best-loved woman in Lorenzo. They say she poisoned her own husband to gain control of the

121

throne through Paolo," Marco confided in a whisper, not anxious to be overheard in such treachery.

Rosanna was jostled aside as people pressed forward to gain vantage points to watch the entertainment. For the first time she noticed a curtained dais at the opposite end of the room. Grasping her hand through the crush of spectators, Marco drew her before him, so that she might watch.

"What's going to happen?" she asked breathlessly, staring with awe at the velvet and gold curtains which remained closed.

"There'll probably be a masque."

"What's a masque."

"A play with musicians, you'll enjoy it," Marco answered, clasping his hands on her waist.

A herald mounted the steps to the stage where he trumpeted a fanfare. The royal family were seated on their thrones at the opposite end of the room; the guests and courtiers lining the walls on either side. Duke Paolo raised his hand for the spectacle to begin.

"The royal trio: a murderess, a whoremonger and a pederast. What a blessed trinity." A voice mocked from the shadow of a pillar beside them and Marco turned to find Sandro Miserotti leaning against the gilded molding.

"Your tongue will be your undoing," he warned urgently, glancing about, but only Rosanna was in hearing.

"What use is a tongue, my friend, if it cannot wag?" Sandro asked with a laugh. "Who is your lovely companion? Will she unmask so that I might see if her face matches her body?" he asked, boldly ogling Rosanna, for he had discarded his mask.

She shook her head, smiling at his disappointment.

"I've promised to guard her identity with my life," Marco revealed dramatically.

"My sister Ginevra will be sore affronted. She sits home this very hour sobbing into copious handkerchiefs."

"It wasn't possible to invite Ginevra, especially after the way your father feels about me; besides, she's betrothed."

"But that doesn't stop you rolling her when the opportunity arises, eh?" Sandro grinned, digging him in the ribs, while Marco glanced with aggravation towards Rosanna to see if she had caught the exchange. "The lovely lady will keep our secret, won't you, *donna?* Or we will not keep hers," Sandro suggested. "See, Marco, the beauteous Flora Dati. Won't Paolo be jealous of that costume's appearance. Now all the gentlemen are acquainted with the lady's charms, plentiful as they are."

All heads turned at the sight of Flora Dati as Venus, reclining on a gilded papier-mâché cloud borne by winged cherubs. Her flimsy white gown was almost transparent, revealing her long, full-fleshed legs and rounded hips. The bodice of the garment consisted of a narrow band of the same material, joined at the waist and rising to a gold circlet at the neck, completely baring her breasts. Her nipples had been gilded and rose erect, glittering like suncrested mountain peaks.

Rosanna could not see Marco's face, but she heard his intake of breath at the sight, and the quickened pace of his heart thudded against her back.

"It would take both hands to capture those," Sandro whispered against his ear.

Marco replied with a knowing grin, his eyes glued to the languid, reclining Venus borne down the center of the room to be placed, subservient, at Duke Paolo's feet.

The assembly applauded and Rosanna craned her neck to see as the Duke leaned down to speak to Flora Dati. After a moment he straightened up, a fixed smile on his face, motioning for the entertainment to continue. But as she watched him, Rosanna saw his smile fade, replaced by a flush of anger. Throughout the entertainment, she watched to see if he spoke with Flora Dati, but he did not even look at her. And his voluptuous mistress smarted with humiliation at his public indifference.

The curtains parted to reveal nymphs in diaphanous draperies who danced from the lighted stage, which was decorated with shrubs and a carpet of grasses. Flowers trailed from magnificent painted urns. In the background, water splashed over rocks in a moving stream which had been specially constructed for the entertainment. Two lambs with large satin bows round their necks wandered amongst the foliage, cropping greenery on the stage. A singing maiden in a filmy pink gown strewed the floor with flower petals from her basket, while concealed musicians played behind a painted canvas backdrop of pastoral tranquility.

The twelve nymphs moved through the center of the ballroom, their pale green and lilac gowns fluttering as they danced to a wild, abandoned rhythm. A youth playing a pipe followed the maidens, portraying the god Pan in flesh-colored tights with animal hair glued to his legs. As the girls danced to his haunting melody, their garments revealed enticing glimpses of shapely legs, much to the delight of the gentlemen present, who laughed and applauded the spectacle.

With a final burst of enthusiasm, during which one of the plumper maidens lost the top half of her gown, the dance ended. The dancers' departure was greeted by thunderous applause. As the masque continued wine was served to the guests by pages dressed in gold-striped hose and white satin paltocks. They carried engraved silver trays bearing fine venetian goblets filled to the brim with heady, sweet wine.

Rosanna was fascinated by the magnificent surroundings and the excitement of this unusual entertainment. She looked towards the Duke, pleased that he still did not acknowledge his mistress. And when the masque came to an end, he stood abruptly, walking down the red-carpeted steps from his throne without a second glance toward the sulking Venus at his feet. Couples formed in the center of the huge ballroom and the musicians struck up a chord for dancing as Duke Paolo selected a partner to lead the opening pavane.

The sweet wine made her giddy with excitement, and Rosanna found many laughing partners eager to dance with her. She accepted their lavish compliments, at the same time listening to the gossip buzzing around her. Flora Dati had left the palace, at Duke Paolo's request, for he was greatly angered by her unseemly dress. Other women flirted with him, anxious to be noticed, laughing gaily at his sallies and replying in kind.

Soon the heat and noise of the ballroom made Rosanna dizzy, and glimpsing a dark patch of sky beckoning invitingly through an archway, she escaped to the banks of the canal. Here it was cooler; though the odor of the tainted water somewhat marred her pleasure.

"I saw you come outside, *madonna,* are you bored with my reception?" A man's voice sounded at her elbow, and with a gasp of pleasant surprise, Rosanna realized it was Duke Paolo.

She backed further into the shadows as she answered, "No, your Grace, I find the entertainment stimulating."

"It was my intention to stimulate." He laughed. "To arouse the senses to fever pitch."

Suddenly his hand was in hers, his fingers caressing her wrist. "Will you not remove your mask? Come, let me see your face."

"I cannot, your Grace. My identity must be kept secret," she murmured, her heart thumping with excitement at the urgency in his voice.

They were in the shadows of the archways where the soft night was purple and still while beyond the steps the water of the canal lapped gently in the breeze, the creak and bang of gondolas coming from the moorings on the bank.

"If you remove your mask, perhaps I would steal a kiss."

"But my husband is very jealous," Rosanna lied, snatching at the first plausible excuse.

The Duke laughed softly, his arm stealing about her shoulders. "I am an expert with jealous husbands," he said. "It is very dark beneath the arches, come, I promise not to betray your identity. I will not even look into your face. My lips ache for yours, remove the mask so I may kiss you," he invited huskily, his hand already on her hair as he undid the fastening.

Hastily Rosanna stepped back in the deepest shadow as the silver mask fell away in his hand. He pursued her on the pretext of handing back her mask, but instead trapped her against the cold marble pillar.

"One kiss, you have no more excuse, *donna.*"

She waited for him to hold her, trembling at the heat of his arms, at the pressure of his hands on her face, then the scent of his body close against her own. Eagerly Rosanna slipped her arms about his neck, as he kissed her, his ardor increased by her mystery.

With a shocked exclamation he stepped back, his hand to his mouth, as if he had been scalded.

"You," he gasped, a smile breaking on his face, but she slipped from his grasp. "Rosanna," he called, darting after her, but he was too late. Already her mask was in place as she ran inside the ballroom, her blue brocaded skirts lost from view amongst the dancers.

Chapter Eight

The forced ban of sobriety during Lent was lifted for a
day and the excitement of the crowd was infectious, their
voices and laughter rising to a crescendo of noise. At last
the head of the procession rounded the corner of the
street; a gilded wagon bore beautiful maidens in floating
chiffon draperies, garlands of spring flowers wreathed
about their heads. Behind them came the billowing,
blood-red banners of the house of Peruzzi with its grisly
emblem, a human skull on crossed swords. Luca Peruzzi
was at the head of his fierce *condottieri,* their plumed helmets glistening in the bright sunlight, swords clanging
against their armor as they rode. He was stern and grim
as befitted his profession, but at a sally from one of the
girls in the wagon, he laughed, answering in like form
with an erotic wit which made Bianca gasp.

Behind the *condottieri* came a beautiful white and
purple float of massed lillies and violets. A lovely,
golden-haired girl who personified spring, reclined on a
green bank, throwing flowers to the crowd. She was followed by splendidly dressed gentlemen of the court who
jostled their horses alongside the float, ogling the buxom
maiden and whispering ardent praise to her beauty.

From the nearby balconies came showers of bright-colored confetti, dropping like brilliant snow upon the heads of the riders. In the balcony directly across the street the women of the Dati household threw scented flower petals. The courtiers noisily greeted Flora, who was seated in a gilded chair, her infant son held by a nurse in the curtained window.

Rosanna waited impatiently, craning over the balcony to see if the ducal riders approached. She caught Flora Dati's eye and the other woman glared hostilely at her, deliberately turning her back on their family.

"How dare she flaunt herself in public, and just brought to bed of a child," Magdela grumbled, with a spiteful scowl. "Tis a wonder she's not riding naked as Venus, but I suppose her belly is still too big."

Cia grinned at her mistress's remark and leaning out over the balcony, the servant squealed; "I see him, it's the Duke's banners. He's coming."

Her voice brought an expectant murmur from the crowd. Across the street, Rosanna watched Flora Dati grab a mirror from one of her women to study her face, pinching color to her already rouged cheeks. With a final pat to her golden hair, the Dati woman handed back the mirror with a serenely smug smile, and settled herself to wait for her lover.

With thudding heart Rosanna waited, clutching her bouquet of white Easter lilies tightly in her hand. She would throw the flowers to Marco when he passed. If only the Duke had been watching for her instead of Flora Dati. Perhaps she would wait and save the flowers for him, but she could already see the nosegay of blooms being handed to his mistress by her serving woman.

"Here they are." The shout rippled over the heads as maidens craned from balconies, laughing and waving at their handsome ruler. The Duke's banners floated, bouying in the wind like fluttering sails; the gold lion of Lorenzo on white satin banners, glittering in the sun. Trumpeters announced his passage. Through the rain of flowers from the houses the cantering horses slowed to a walk in the press of people and floats backed up the street, waiting their turn to cross the Ponte San Lorenzo.

"Marco," Bianca shouted excitedly, waving her blue

kerchief to her brother who glanced up, and seeing the girls, raised his hand in greeting.

With a gasp of surprise Rosanna saw her cousin rode beside the Duke. If Duke Paolo looked up, he could not fail to see her.

Leaning over the balcony, the draperies of her gown flapping in the breeze, Rosanna called to her cousin, her cheeks rosily flushed, eyes sparkling with excitement. The deep blue silk of her gown enhanced the blackness of her hair, which she had braided with red and white flowers, wearing a gold circlet upon her brow.

Marco turned at the sound of her voice, sharply catching his breath at her beauty. And he waved, standing in the stirrups as Rosanna threw a lily to him. Reaching far out, he caught it with a triumphant cry. Suddenly Duke Paolo looked up at the balcony, and by the slow smile on his face, Rosanna knew he recognized her. For a moment the procession stopped beneath the balcony, and taking careful aim, she threw the last two lilies to the Duke. Adeptly he caught the flowers, waving his hand to acknowledge her gift. He pushed the lilies into the band of his jeweled bonnet and as the horses moved forward, he kissed his hand to her in parting.

Almost swooning with delight, Rosanna leaned against the wall, watching the bobbing banners as they moved down the street. Duke Paolo darted his head from side to side as if looking for someone, and she realized he had missed the Dati woman. With triumph she looked across the heads of the riders and met Flora Dati's eyes, seeing the expression of hatred there. Rosanna had caught the Duke's attention and he had ridden past his mistress without acknowledgment. And she smiled proudly as Flora Dati withdrew from her balcony in angry humiliation.

"Oh, Rosanna, he saw you," Bianca squealed, clutching her arm, her nails biting into the flesh. "He's wearing your favor in his hat. Oh, you're so lucky. Why didn't I think of throwing a flower to him."

As she mentally recalled Duke Paolo's appearance, Rosanna smiled. He had worn scarlet velvet, his cloak trimmed in ermine, a gold breastplate winking in the sun. But most of all she remembered his scarlet jeweled bonnet

129

where he had fastened her flowers, and the swift recognition in his pale eyes as he saw her.

A week before they were due to leave for the summer villa, Bianca drew her excitedly to the courtyard, bursting with news.

"Rosanna, I must tell you, though it's supposed to be a secret, I can't keep it to myself any longer," Bianca cried, in excitement, her eyes bright as she drew her cousin to the marble bench beneath the cascading golden laburnum.

"What is it?"

"You'll never guess, so I'll tell you right away. I'm going to be betrothed."

"How wonderful for you!" Rosanna exclaimed with genuine pleasure, finding she almost liked Bianca tonight. The other girl was curiously transformed with her flushed face and shining eyes. "Who is he?"

"I don't know, but Father says he's very rich and important. He might even be a member of the royal house. Just think of it, he says I'll be the envy of every girl in the duchy. He won't announce it yet, but I'm to start my dower chest. Seamstresses will come tomorrow for fittings."

"Aren't we going to the villa?" Rosanna asked with surprise.

"Yes, that's the strange part of it. Everything's just as planned, except the Duke is coming to my fifteenth birthday ball," Bianca squeaked with delight, clutching her porcelain hands together in rapture.

As Rosanna viewed the possibility of seeing the Duke, her heart skipped a beat, but her joy was overshadowed by a terrible sense of foreboding. Surely Bianca's mysterious suitor could not be he. Cia and nurse had been whispering about Duke Paolo after he left last week, but they would not tell Rosanna anything. Bianca always had what Rosanna wanted, surely she would not get Duke Paolo too.

The garden seemed suddenly chill. The pleasant cool shade of evening had grown damp and forbidding, even the splashing fountain was jarring to her nerves, until Rosanna stood abruptly with a mumbled excuse. Bianca was too engrossed in her dream future to notice anything amiss as she gazed at the fountain, humming a song to herself.

Though long ago Bianca had drifted to sleep, Rosanna could not. She lay wide awake with her distressing thoughts for company. The more she reviewed the events of the past weeks, the more she was sure of the identity of Bianca's suitor. Was this the reason new livery for the servants had been ordered? And her own gowns? Even the grand draperies in the reception rooms must have been in preparation for this event. Still, she could be wrong; there were other unmarried men in the royal household—their relatives ruled the nearby cities. It might not be Duke Paolo at all. Surely he would marry a woman of royal blood, not the daughter of the city's richest merchant.

Rosanna heard Bianca's tinkling laughter peal out, followed by the sound of the Duke's voice. She stretched as high as she could to peer over the clipped hedge. Her cousin was sitting beside the Duke on the stone garden seat, while Cia stitched an apron near the lily pond, at a discreet distance from the pair. Though the two figures kept to their own ends of the bench, the scene held an aura of intimacy which stabbed Rosanna with a painful thrust of jealousy.

"Oh, your Grace, how witty," Bianca laughed again, with fluttering eyelashes, a perfect example of modest girlhood. And when the Duke would have taken her hand she drew away, flustered by his boldness, her pale cheeks flushing.

She isn't like that, Paolo, not really, Rosanna wanted to cry. She's only pretending so you'll fall in love with her. Really she's selfish and spoiled, she whines and tells lies . . . and she can ever love you like I can.

Climbing from the bench, Rosanna sank to the wooden seat in misery, holding her face in her hands. If she could only tell him what Bianca was usually like, but he probably would not thank her for it. Instead he would be angry because he would not want to destroy the image he cherished of a pretty, shy maid. To him Bianca was possessed of all the virtues befitting a well-born young girl—his perfect Duchess.

With a sniffle, Rosanna dried her eyes, for she found tears trickling beneath the fringe of her lashes. Tears, what use were they? With impatience she tossed her hair defiantly from her face and marched down the path. At least Bianca would not enjoy him any longer this afternoon, she would see to that.

The couple glanced up at her approach, and Bianca allowed a frown of aggravation to crease her brow. "Yes?" she inquired haughtily, as Rosanna curtsied.

"Your lady mother wishes to see you."

"What for ... ?" Bianca began, but remembered the Duke's presence just in time. "Of course. I must leave, your Grace, my mother must always be obeyed."

With a smile, he stood and kissed her hand. "Tonight then, at supper."

"I am always your servant, your Grace." Bianca dropped a perfect curtsy, but as she turned her back to the Duke, she scowled at Rosanna.

In triumph, Rosanna glared back, watching Bianca depart with great pleasure. "Your Grace."

He raised her from the gravel walk, his fingers warm in hers. And he smiled, watching Bianca's silver skirts disappear round the corner of the hedge.

"Did you really bring a message from *Donna* Magdela?"

"No."

"I thought as much ... you know, you're really a forward baggage. I should be angry."

"Are you?" she whispered in concern, which changed to a sigh of relief as she saw him smile, not only with his mouth, but with his eyes as well.

"No."

"I'm glad," Rosanna said, glancing towards Cia, who was bent dutifully over her sewing, paying no attention to them. "Have you seen the fountain in the rose garden?"

"No, should I?"

"Oh, yes, your Grace, Uncle Ugo is very proud of it. It's newly installed this year. It's supposed to be the three graces, but the women look just like the mermaids on the fountain at the palazzo, without their tails."

"Probably the same sculptor, don't you think?" he laughed, striding over the walkway beside her.

132

Rosanna nodded, hugging herself with pleasure. It was far pleasanter to be able to talk to him like this, instead of having to simper and feign a ladylike air, when she really didn't want to at all.

Before them the elaborate rose garden spread in perfect order, radiating from the fountain like a huge wheel with walkways of pink crushed rocks for the spokes. Banks of blue and yellow flowers swept gently from the surrounding hedges to the outer rim of the wheel, each spoke divided from the rest by low clipped hedges which formed wedge-shaped beds.

"It's very pretty, isn't it?"

"Very impressive," he agreed, taking her hand as they walked down the shallow flight of steps to the rose garden.

Butterflies lighted on the blossoms, their pale blue and white wings contrasting with the strong reds and pinks of the roses. In the distance could be heard the murmur of men's voices as the Duke's gentlemen continued their game of skill, but apart from that, the solitude was broken only by the steady running of the fountain.

"There, what do you think of it?"

"Magnificent, but I agree with you, they do look like mermaids minus their tails."

She grinned, leaning against the cold marble basin, watching him out of the corner of her eye as he studied the figures. The Duke's clothing outshone the flowers with its brilliance. He wore gold and crimson-striped velvet embroidered with jewels; his hose were crimson, his shoes gold, and a heavy ornate chain about his neck caught the rays of the sun, flashing with a blinding dazzle.

"Why are you staring at me?"

"I was thinking your clothes were even prettier than the flowers, and twice as bright."

The Duke threw back his head, laughing at her answer. "You always surprise me, Rosanna," he said affectionately. "It's a rare lady who will speak her thoughts honestly, whatever they are."

She looked away from his eyes, finding the light of memory kindled with his words, and her heart skipped a beat as the pressure of his fingers tightened. "I take pleasure in your approval," she murmured.

"Now, that's not Rosanna speaking, that is Bianca," he

chastised, leaning closer, the beading of splashes from the fountain dampening his embroidered sleeve. "Tell me, what does Rosanna think?"

She stared at his pale eyes, so close to her own, at the firmness of his lips, curved in a smile as he watched her. The fragrance of perfume from his clothing was in her nostrils, distinguishable above the rose scent, while the movement of his breath stirred her hair against her brow. It seemed as if they were drawn closer and closer, though neither of them moved.

"She thinks how much she'd like you to kiss her." The words seemed to escape unbidden from her mouth, but when she would have taken them back, with an exclamation of dismay, he only drew her closer.

"Now those are sentiments that meet with my approval," he jested, his hands moving on her back. Then he kissed her, his mouth like fire.

Somehow they had turned so that his body pressed her against the side of the basin. Rosanna stared into his eyes, her knees growing weak as he leaned against her. Her head went back, perilously close to the fountain, until suddenly she was caught in the deluge from the jets of water. With a shriek, Rosanna twisted away, her hair thoroughly doused, water streaming down her back.

The Duke laughed at her accident, pulling her against him, squeezing the weight of her sodden hair in his hands, trickling puddles on the path.

"I'm sorry, forgive me." He laughed, eyeing her dripping appearance. "You're still lovely, but now you're more like a mermaid than they."

Exploding in annoyance at his humor, she struck him hard against the chest, scratching her hand on the jeweled embroidery. The Duke grasped her wrists, laughing at her anger, and he kissed the blood tracery on her flesh.

"Now what does Rosanna think?" he inquired, releasing her hands as she struggled to free herself from his grasp.

"She thinks you're an oaf."

"Saints preserve us! You hussy, what are you thinking about . . . Oh, your Grace, forgive her."

In alarm, Rosanna looked up to find Aunt Magdela

running along the walk, with an angry Bianca waiting on the steps.

"She meant no harm. It was all in fun, even her drowning," the Duke replied, still laughing as Aunt Magdela sank to the ground before him. "Don't scold her, *Donna* Magdela."

By quivering, pointed finger, Rosanna was dismissed. Behind her she could hear her aunt's apologetic voice, catching the words, barbairc ... hoyden ... shameful. But the Duke seemed to take it in good humor. Anger blazed in her face as she mounted the final flight of steps to the lawn, knowing they watched her departure. She tried to appear dignified, but it was difficult to manage with sodden hair streaming over her back, soaking the thin fabric of her gown. At last she was out of their sight, and hoisting her skirts, she fled to safety.

Drying her hair in her room, Rosanna wondered what would happen now. She would probably be forbidden to dine with the family, perhaps even forbidden to attend Bianca's birthday ball. It was really her own fault everything happened. She should never have told the lie to Bianca in the first place, but she did want to see him again. And he had taken her side against Aunt Magdela over the incident. Maybe he loved her a little after all. Last summer seemed far away, so far in fact, she no longer thought of him as Paolo. It seemed as if the incident during the storm had never happened.

Before supper Aunt Magdela came to her room, her face dark with anger. "You may eat here, wench," she cried, slamming the door behind her. They faced each other, Rosanna staring back at her aunt in defiance. "I shall expect you to apologize to his Grace before you retire. Is that clear?"

"Yes, Madam," Rosanna meekly replied. A meeting with him would be quite in order, but it would not be solely to please her aunt.

"Very well, you will be sent for," Magdela said, with a sigh of relief, her face assuming a smile. When she first came in the room she had not expected this subdued manner from the wench, perhaps the immense disgrace of her conduct had finally sunk into that black little head of hers. And with a curt nod, she closed the door.

Rosanna dressed carefully for her meeting with the Duke, selecting her best gown of blue silk. It was the one she had worn for the parade at Holy week. With it she would wear the silk organza scarf he had given her.

When a servant brought her meal, she picked at the food, excitement robbing her of her appetite. Soon the girl returned to take her downstairs, and with pounding heart, Rosanna followed.

It was already twilight, the sky milky turquoise above the golden haze of the setting sun. Through the windows she could see shadows in the garden grown long and purple, while darting fireflies shone their twinkling lights against the black silhouette of the giant cedar walk. If only the Duke was seated on the balcony the enchantment of the summer evening would form a romantic setting for their meeting.

Unfortunately he was being entertained in the small reception room at the side of the house where the furnishings were gloomy. A young page sang a plaintive love song, accompanied by a minstrel on a lute. As the song ended, Rosanna was triumphantly led forth by her aunt, who had been waiting for her outside the door.

"Here is the repentant baggage, your Grace," Aunt Magdela announced, thrusting her forward with a vindictive push.

"Repentant? Rosanna?" the Duke repeated, waving the entertainers away. The twinkle in his eyes echoed the dawning grin on his mouth as she knelt before him, head dutifully bowed in penitence. "How strange. Tell me, girl, are you truly sorry for your unforgivable outburst this afternoon?"

"Yes, your Grace."

"And will you promise never to repeat the offense?"

"Yes, your Grace."

Aunt Magdela beamed in approval, hardly able to believe the sudden change in her young niece. The sisters had taught her much. Last summer had been spent profitably after all.

"She is truly repentant, your Grace," Magdela added, taking the girl's hand to draw her up, but the Duke stopped her.

"Let me speak to your niece about the behavior expected of a young lady, if I may, *Donna* Magdela. If it would not be unseemly of me?"

"Oh, no, of course not, your Grace. Cia will stay." With a flutter of her white hand, Aunt Magdela summoned the servant girl, directing her to a chair in the darkest corner of the room. Then, with a curtsy, she backed from the room leaving Rosanna kneeling dutifully on the cold tiles.

"You may rise, though it's pleasant to find you submissive at my feet," the Duke whispered, bending over her.

Rosanna scrambled up, seeing the smile on his face as he offered a cup of wine, which she accepted with whispered thanks.

"Now, I promised to lecture you about your unseemly behavior," he began, indicating a low, tapestry-covered stool at his feet. Obediently she was seated, finding she could not see Cia, and she was likewise hidden by the back of the Duke's massive gilt chair.

"It is unseemly, even treasonable to insult a member of the royal house," he continued, taking her hand while he spoke. "And to call me an oaf ... why, it's a grave insult."

"I'm sorry, your Grace. I spoke in anger," she whispered.

He drew her head against the embroidered material of his hose as he spread her hair in a black banner over his knees, admiring the texture of her hair. "Your hair did not suffer from its impromptu washing?"

"No, your Grace."

"In future, wench, I shall expect the strictest obedience."

"Yes, your Grace." She nodded, allowing him to take her face in his hands, and stooping, he kissed her.

"You may leave now. You can tell your aunt I'm not angered."

"Yes, your Grace," she replied, kissing him back, her mouth lingering on his an instant too long, until he quickly put her from him at a movement from the corner.

Cia was waiting in the shadows. Rosanna curtsied and departed without a backward glance. Cia assured her anxious mistress that no impropriety took place, for she was

137

present throughout the conversation, and his Grace told the girl only what she should have been told.

With a sigh of relief, Magdela rang for the minstrels, even mindful of her exalted role as hostess to the Duke.

Rosanna was left more to her own devices as time for the birthday ball drew near.

The Duke hunted with his gentlemen, spending much of his day in the surrounding countryside. It was only in the evenings when twilight made the garden magical with towering shapes, he returned, tired and dusty from the chase. Sometimes in the early morning Rosanna heard him leave, with much clattering of harness and men's laughter. The richly caparisoned horses streamed over the chalky path from the stable, clopping down the sweeping drive with its border of beeches, to disappear into the dense green forest. When the last rider was gone from view, she was left with a feeling of loneliness which brought tears to her eyes.

If only she could have gone with them. Twice Bianca had ridden to the hunt, but she always returned before noon, complaining about the heat of the sun, searching in the mirror for freckles. If the Duke had invited her she would have stayed till dusk, undergoing any hardship to be at his side. But he did not invite her.

Her own ball gown was fitted, and at each session the seamstress reminded her of Aunt Magdela's generosity in allowing her to have a new gown. It was maroon silk, a color which her aunt had thought would be unbecoming to her complexion. Instead, it flattered her, a fact which Magdela scowled over in annoyance when she discovered it, though it was too late to change her selection. So, vindictively, she ordered the gown to be made as plain as possible, while Bianca's was to be in figured, leaf-green silk with overskirt and sleeves of silver tissue, jeweled and embroidered, slashed and puffed, quite the grandest gown Rosanna had ever seen.

Not to be completely outdone, Rosanna persuaded her uncle to allow her to have a silver headdress. He was very generous lately, overcoming his annoyance at her refusal to allow him in her room. Perhaps he thought this new approach would soften her resistance to his advances, Ro-

138

sanna did not know, but whatever his reasons, she was determined to make use of the situation. Aunt Magdela had been furious when she learned of the gift, especially after Rosanna's shocking behavior towards the Duke in the rose garden, but her uncle dismissed his wife's protests with a scowl.

Even Uncle Ugo's sudden generosity gave Rosanna a strange feeling of unease. Throughout the household there was an air of great anticipation, more than was usual for the annual birthday ball. Marco was to return from Venice especially for the event. Rosanna could not help wondering if the Duke was to announce his betrothal to Bianca at the ball. The thought was agony to endure, and she fought against its acceptance. Cia reported Bianca's marriage chest was bursting with riches. Everything seemed to point to Rosanna's worst fears, but to refuse to accept it was her last protection.

The day before the ball Bianca was in her room complaining of a headache, a cold compress to her forehead. In anger she sent Rosanna away, leaving her free to wander in the garden. The Duke had not hunted today because of his concern over her cousin's health. If he had asked her she could have told him what was wrong with Bianca. The headaches were just a ruse for attention. Her ailment was always miraculously cured when she got her own way. Rosanna knew the Duke had intended to hunt today, for Cia whispered some of the gentlemen left without him. Maybe he walked in the gardens and she could pluck up enough courage to ask him if he was secretly betrothed to Bianca.

She walked over the springy turf, nervous with anticipation, scanning the lawns for a sign of his courtiers, but saw no one. Rosanna stopped at the lily pond. Leaning over the railing, she watched a large frog croaking as he floated in splendor on a gigantic lily pad, enthroned in the heart of a snow white blossom. Perhaps he was a prince who had been turned into a frog by a wicked witch.

Kicking the railing with her brown leather slipper, Rosanna turned away, trailing disconsolately up the shallow steps to the lawn. What a silly dreamer she was. She was long out of childhood so why did she cling to such foolishness? It was reassuring to daydream when things went wrong, to escape to her land of make-believe where everything could be the way she wanted. There she had a woman's dreams mixed strangely with those of a little girl; confusing and stirring, until sometimes she had to think very hard to distinguish reality from imagination when she woke in the night, her mind vividly alive with pictures from her sleep.

She heard the crunch of footsteps on the gravel walk, and two men walked round the corner of the hedge, greeting her with courteous smiles. It was the Duke, and his favorite, Rinaldo Viverini.

"Good morning, your Grace." She curtsied, suddenly conscious of her shabby gown and tousled hair. "Good morning, *Don* Rinaldo."

The men politely acknowledged her greeting, then resumed their conversation, unconcerned by her presence. In pained surprise she watched them sit on the bench beside the pool where Viverini cast a shiny pebble at the bullfrog, sending him leaping for shelter into the murky water. Rosanna felt suddenly alone and she turned away, stumbling on the hem of her gown, catching herself on the curving, wrought-iron balustrade.

The Duke glanced up at the sound, watching her depart. His face creased in a frown as he twisted the enormous signet ring on his right hand, brooding, staring at the royal seal without actually seeing the heraldic device; his mind straying back many months.

"Why is it, Viverini, there are women we marry, and women we hunger after?"

Don Rinaldo laughed. "I don't know, your Grace. How fortunate it would be if they were the same. Still, hunger can be readily appeased, whereas marriage is far more difficult to arrange."

"Can hunger be appeased that easily?" the Duke questioned with a sigh, and standing up, he joined his companion at the edge of the pond.

"Mine always is, your Grace."

"Ah, but you are not a duke, Viverini."

Chapter Nine

Bianca's fifteenth birthday ball began with a beautifully dressed masque depicting the story of Paris and the three goddesses. Bianca was Venus and she basked in the attention of the audience as the handsome actor portraying Paris presented her with a golden apple filled with rare perfume from the East. A young boy, dressed as an angel, was let down on a gilded rope as if flying from heaven to present Bianca with a circlet of pearls; thus she was crowned Queen of the Ball. The crowning was the signal for the musicians to begin the music. With much laughter and chatter, the house guests took their places for the opening dance, which was to be led by Duke Paolo and the queen of the evening.

Rosanna watched the proceedings, finding little pleasure in them. Her new gown was very flattering. A fact that was confirmed by the multitude of admiring glances she received from the male guests, but though she danced with them, smiling at their compliments, her heart was heavy. Not once had his Grace looked at her, except when she was presented with the other guests, and then his face had been a polite mask.

Before the first hour was over Rosanna had her worst

fears confirmed. From all sides she heard whispers about the actual purpose of this lavish ball; Ugo Sordello had sold his beautiful daughter as a bride to Duke Paolo. The public announcement relied only on the arrival of his latest cargoes, which bore all manner of priceless treasure, many of the riches for Bianca's dowry. The rumors made Rosanna faint with shock.

From the shadows Guido Miserotti watched her, and though Rosanna constantly moved away, he always followed, an evil smile on his face. It was as if he knew the secret of her heart and gloated over her misery. Though he was Leonora's father, there was little family resemblance between them. He showed none of Leonora's lively humor, giving the impression instead of someone already decayed; as if the burning intensity of his eyes shone from a living corpse. Sometimes the banker dined at Palazzo Sordello and the unwavering scrutiny of his eyes made Rosanna afraid. She did not fear his amorous advances, for the expression was not of lust, rather of satanic power. And when he fixed her with those flickering yellow-tinged eyes, it took her utmost will power to look away.

Although it was impossible for them to know her heart, others watched with the same curiosity—Leonora's brother Sandro, her sister Ginevra and many others. Surely her own emotions were not that apparent. When his tongue had been loosened by wine, had her uncle told Miserotti of the reason for his Grace's generosity in appointing him comptroller of the fleet? Miserotti even called her witch to her face. To be true, it was half in jest, yet there was a seriousness about it not entirely masked. The guests probably knew what a fool she had been, perhaps they had even discussed the subject in laughter with the Duke. Nausea gripped her at the thought.

Stumbling blindly from the ballroom Rosanna fled to the dark safety of the balcony, far from the beautiful dancing couple, in their rich, bright-colored clothing—and the painful surveillance of Guido Miserotti.

A perfumed breeze fanned Rosanna's brow as she wiped her hand over her moist skin. The sounds of the ballroom, pulsating with music and laughter, were faint in the background. Soon the guests would go home, their feet trampling the dew-fresh grass, drunken jests echoing

142

in the sweetness of the dawn. They would be gone and she would be left to remember how, with their bright, false smiles they had paid homage to her milk-white cousin.

She leaned on the balcony wall, the stone cold to her bare wrists. The fragrance of flowers wafted from huge urns which spilled their bounty generously on the stone balcony, while heads of hydrangea shone ghostly in the moonlight which flooded the lawns with silver. Moonlight shone for lovers, at once concealing and revealing. Even the beauty of the night was a mockery, and she turned from the sight of flitting shadows amongst the trees as lovers sought sanctuary from prying eyes.

Tonight had been a torment. She had waited for the ball, dressing with care to accentuate her beauty, dreaming of his compliments. But it was all for naught. When he smiled at her, his eyes were guarded. His lips alone curved in a polite gesture of welcome, while Bianca clung to him with a fixed simper on her face. He had danced only with Bianca, while she had been forced to partner lecherous old men and half-grown boys who panted and drooled at the beauty of her. While he, who it was all for, ignored her.

A movement and voices below the balcony attracted her attention and Rosanna craned over the wall to see who it was. In sickening dismay she beheld a couple weaving amongst the bushes, the girl's bright skirts like a brilliant plumaged bird. The man held her hand. His doublet was sky blue, shot with gold, a short cloak swinging from his shoulders, the girl's dress leaf green, with draperies of silver tissue . . . God, spare me this. Must you be so cruel?

She recoiled in horror: it was Paolo and her cousin. In numb misery she heard his voice, soft, husky, the way it had never been for her, whispering endearments. The bushes rustled and she was so close she could have leaned down and touched them. Bianca replied, her words betraying her fear. But he assured her of his love, his gentleness, until her apprehension melted beneath the warm passion of his kiss.

The figures moved, merging with the shadow of the trees, and she knew they lay on the soft turf directly below. Rosanna looked down, seeing the shadowed colors blended in the moonlight. She listened to Paolo's impassioned words with morbid fascination, each endearment a knife in her heart.

She did not watch, but she could hear, and the sounds were agony to endure. Weakly Rosanna leaned against the balcony, drawing into the shadow lest he should glance up and see her. The pain of her discovery was a physical blow, as wounding and cruel, making her breathing painful as she fought the agony of tears. Noiselessly her lips formed his name, wanting to scream aloud her presence to spoil the magic of their lovemaking. I hate her. I hate her, Rosanna breathed, teeth clenched against the force of her emotion. She wanted to kill Bianca, but even the pleasure of revenge could not stifle the pain of spurned love.

It was quiet now and their two shadows emerged from the bushes, the Duke's arm round Bianca's tiny waist. They stopped for a moment in a patch of moonlight and Rosanna thought she would die from the pain in her heart as she saw his face as he tenderly caught her golden hair in his fingers. Rosanna turned from the sight of his burnished head close against the other: the golden ones.

"Why were you watching them?"

She started in alarm as a figure emerged from the shadows beside the urn of flowers; a man swathed in a dark cloak. It was Miserotti.

"Why were *you?*" she countered, fighting to keep tears from her voice, though the effort was more than she could manage.

"I take pleasure in watching the saintly *La Bianca* fall from grace." He smiled, seeing her pain.

Rosanna hated him, hated his knowledge of her weakness.

"He will wed her soon," Miserotti said. "Sordello had everything planned, this too, 'tis in the form of insurance against a change of heart. With *La Bianca* deflowered, Paolo cannot back out. Sordello has already schooled the girl to request a vow of chastity until their public betrothal. Everything has been taken care of."

Rosanna did not speak, unable to stop the tremble of her mouth. His words were a shock.

144

"The bastard he gave her tonight should hasten the nuptials."

Mutely Rosanna watched him through a haze of tears, seeing the bony, sallow face, the cavernous eyes.

"It would be a calamity to join Duke Paolo with the house of Sordello. Ugo Sordello already has too much power. Your uncle does not always handle his affairs peaceably, with the armies of Lorenzo behind him, no noble in the land would sleep safe."

"What are you saying?" Rosanna questioned, his meaning drifting through a thousand painful miles of tears. "Would you kill my uncle?"

"Not your uncle, for without his white one, he has no bargaining power. I think you can suggest a more appropriate victim."

"Bianca?"

"Exactly, *La Bianca*." Miserotti smiled, his skin stretched taut like a skull and Rosanna shivered at his appearance. "Come now, the same thought was in your mind moments ago. How readily her name sprang to your lips. You want Paolo. Without her your way is clear."

"He would never marry me. We both know that."

Miserotti moved closer, his hand clawlike as he gripped her wrist. "I did not say marry. As many women know, the pleasure of a man's bed is not with his wife, but with his mistress. Would that position not suit you, or are you too ambitious for that, Rosanna *Bruna*?"

"Don't call me that," she snarled, pulling from him.

"It is your name."

"No, it's only the name you've given me. You let them think me a witch. I know it's you who spreads rumors."

Miserotti smiled and was silent.

"Leave me. Can I not at least be heartbroken alone? Must you gape and gloat?"

"Our bargain is not yet struck."

"And never will be."

"You lie, and prettily too. Paolo spurns you as the whore your uncle made you when he sent you to his bed; Bianca is like the Madonna to him. We must change that. Until he is not sure if the whelp she carries is his or no."

"Whether you blacken her virtue or not, it will not bring him to my bed."

145

"No, but we cannot have him grieve too strongly over a dead woman. If he doubts the parenthood of the child he will not suffer overmuch. Paolo is thirty. He must marry soon and beget an heir. I have a scheme . . ."

"If your plot harms him I'll have no part of it."

"I assure you, Paolo will be safe. There are certain factions who want an alliance with Savarese. Such a powerful spokesman in Rome could prove invaluable, don't you think?"

"The Savarese? Who have they to offer? Teresa Savarese is already betrothed to the Medici sprig."

"She has a sister Giulietta."

Rosanna threw back her head with a laugh. "She is ten years old, hardly bedable with Paolo."

"His own mother was thirteen when he was born. There is little difference."

"Will he accept such a marriage?"

"I think he will, if he has you to warm his nights. He will have no use for the child, except to beget an heir in a couple of years. I think he would be pleased with the arrangement once *La Bianca* is food for the worms. Your servant, Rosanna *Bruna*."

Almost as mysteriously as he came, he withdrew, leaving Rosanna puzzled and angered at once. Her hurt had become rage directed against Bianca and her father, whom she now knew was responsible for tonight's happening. Whatever scheme Miserotti planned, if he included her, Rosanna knew she would be forced to do her part. She could not help herself.

The former pleasure of her own bedchamber was lost, though she was thankful for the opportunity to be alone, safe from prying eyes, so that she might regain her self-control. She did not know how many hours she spent there, nor if the sun shone, or if it rained. If she could have succumbed to a noisy fit of weeping, her pain would have been lessened. Instead she sat in a state of exhaustion, her legs weak and aching, as if she had walked a thousand miles. Tears slid silently down her cheeks, stopping and beginning without her knowledge. If only she had realized the impossibility of her dreams, but she had not. And disillusion made her pain complete. To think she had imagined he loved her. What a fool! Why would he

146

care for her, so black and clumsy, while Bianca was dainty in all she did. Her hair was like spun gold, her complexion delicately pink, even her hands were tiny, with small pearly nails, not strong like her own. Bianca was the exact way the Duke wanted his duchess to be, while she was little more than a servant with her begrudged finery and cast-off gowns. Those things were the worst of all to endure because they were things she could not help.

At last her pain was eased, as if the tormenting hours finally burned out the core of her emotion, and Rosanna washed and dressed, deciding to join the family for the noon meal. No one had bothered to investigate her absence. It seemed as if they did not notice whether she ate, as if she did not really exist for them. There was no one in the world who cared.

When she reached the dining room, Rosanna discovered the meal was over, but the board had not yet been cleared. There was a dish of roast capon in white sauce, so she served herself a small portion, carefully picking off the gilded pomegranate seeds which garnished the fowl. The dish was highly spiced and after a few mouthfuls, she laid it aside. Slipping an orange in the pocket of her apron, she left the room.

As if by instinct she took the circuitous route to her bedchamber in order to pass the Duke's private suite. The door was open, and she saw him standing beside the empty hearth watching her, his hand toying with a jade figurine on the mantel. Without smiling he inclined his head, indicating she could enter.

Rosanna hesitated, finding her emotions not stifled as she had imagined, for the sight of him sent her heart racing desperately within her breast.

"Are you really going to marry her?" she blurted.

Paolo turned from the fireplace. "Yes, Bianca is to be my Duchess."

Rosanna heard her own gasp, loud in the silence.

"We are soon to be betrothed. Don't come to me again."

The summer wind racing through the trees and her own heartbeat were the only sounds, until she managed: "You love her?" Her voice sounding distant and alien.

147

"I worship her," he replied.

In numb misery Rosanna heard his words. Hadn't she seen them in the garden when Bianca was afraid. How sweet were the words he had used in comfort, how patient, until Bianca's will was his own.

"Will you lie and say you do not want me?" she groaned, her cheeks streaked with tears.

Paolo steeled himself not to look at the sweet curves of flesh displayed provocatively above her amber gown.

"Please . . . leave me."

"Say it. Tell me you don't want me."

His eyes regarded hers, the lines on his brow etched in a deep frown. "I told you to go," he said evenly, tremors of suppressed anger sounding through the words. "Am I to call the servants?"

"You can't say it, your Grace, can you? Because you do want me. If I lay on that couch and bade you come to me, you could not help . . ."

"All right, damn you, yes. Now get out," he spat. "Stop tormenting me, you black-hearted witch. Leave me alone."

An unexpected peal of laughter greeted his words and with a deep, billowing curtsy, Rosanna was gone.

Paolo leaned upon the mantel, his head in his hands, fury coursing through him. Forever she tempted. This morning in the chapel to please Bianca and her father. he had vowed celibacy until their marriage. It would not be as difficult to uphold if that wench would leave him alone.

Chapter Ten

The family returned to Lorenzo during the middle of August. Summer heat shimmered in waves over the dusty road and a cloudless sky stretched far to the horizon. Bianca rode in a gilded litter, stretched languidly upon silken pillows, but the swaying movement of the conveyance nauseated her. Twice they stopped at the roadside while she vomited. Assisting her unwillingly, Rosanna hated every twinge of sickness, for she alone suspected the cause of her cousin's indisposition. Bianca was pregnant.

"Be careful, don't move about, you're making me sick," Bianca shrilled, clutching her stomach, her face white and pinched beneath her elaborate headdress.

"You shouldn't eat so much," Rosanna snapped.

"Everything I eat makes me sick, It must be this terrible heat, I don't know why Mother insisted on coming back to the city so early. We always stay till September at least. His Grace will do anything I want him to. He would have been willing to wait a few months till it's cooler, until spring if I wanted him to."

Rosanna treated her cousin to a withering glance. Fool, she thought, stupid fool, she doesn't even know. What a

149

novel wedding it would be with the bride nine months gone with child. Turning towards the red hanging curtains of the litter, Rosanna allowed herself to think about the Duke. Usually she tried not to think about him, it was too agonizing. Maybe he was as ignorant as Bianca about the child, though surely he would suspect and hasten the date for their wedding. Perhaps Aunt Magdela already guessed at her daughter's condition and so curtailed the summer holiday, but it seemed to be more at her uncle's urging.

"Give me some water. Hurry," Bianca demanded, propping herself on her elbow against the mountain of pillows.

Taking the flask of chilled well water, Rosanna poured some in a cup to give to Bianca. Just then the litter lurched violently and the water spilled, soaking the front of her cousin's cherry red dress.

"You clumsy idiot, look at my gown."

Recoiling from a sharp smack, Rosanna nursed her reddened cheek, wanting to strike back, but knowing she must not.

"When I'm Duchess I'll have you punished for your clumsiness. I'll betroth you to the ugliest, cruelest soldier in the entire *condottieri*. And I certainly won't have you in my household. There'll be no place at the palace for such an ugly creature."

Rosanna attempted to mop up the water, but Bianca pushed her away, taking the flask herself and refilling her cup. How dare Bianca treat her so haughtily, as if she were already Duchess. For a moment Rosanna was tempted to reveal what took place on the night of the storm when she had owned, for a few hours at least, Bianca's betrothed. And how Duke Paolo had not found her ugly.

"I did not expect to serve you at the palace."

"Good, then you won't be disappointed, will you?"

"Do you think you'll be happy married to Duke Paolo?"

"Of course, any girl would be happy married to the Duke."

"But I mean Paolo, not just because he's the Duke."

"You must not speak so familiarly about his Grace. Besides, Paolo is the Duke. He's always Duke Paolo. He isn't an ordinary man. He's royalty every minute," Bianca declared importantly.

"But when you kiss him don't you think of him as a man?"

"Well, I suppose," Bianca admitted, "I hadn't really thought about it. We're only betrothed, you know."

"Yes, I know," Rosanna agreed as Bianca closed her eyes. Was it the wine that made Bianca submit, or just obedience to her father? Today she spoke about the Duke as if he was a great figure of state and not her lover at all. Perhaps Bianca was incapable of loving anyone besides herself. With a glow of satisfaction Rosanna knew Bianca did not dream of that night with pleasure.

Their destination reached, Bianca was carried up the steps of the palazzo, and Aunt Magdela accused Rosanna of making her poor suffering daughter's journey uncomfortable by her presence. She received a cuff on the ear when Bianca complained of the accident with the water, but she did not cry. Aunt Magdela should not have the pleasure of seeing her weep, even if she must bite her lip till it bled.

When Bianca was bathed and settled in bed, Rosanna brought her a meal which was refused with a petulant cry of, "Wretch, you're trying to make me ill again. Take it away."

Instead Rosanna took the tray to the balcony where she ate the food herself beneath the twinkling stars. The night air was warm and humid, damply fragrant against her face. From inside the room Bianca called to her, but she pretended not to hear. When the food was gone, she leaned against the stone wall and watched the stars, idly plucking a spray of flowering vine from the stonework. Alone with the vast night sky there seemed to be so much promise to life, so much yet to come, though in reality the future was dim. When Bianca was gone she would probably be sent to the kitchens. Or perhaps she would spend the remainder of her days trying to avoid the sexual advances of her uncle, or Marco. Though Marco's attentions were preferable, she was only a plaything to him, a black-haired servant to amuse him when he tired of the high-born women of the city.

Miserotti's words suddenly echoed in her brain, repeating his evil suggestion: if Bianca was gone, Paolo would be alone. Once she had pleased him, perhaps she could do so again.

When Miserotti contacted her the next day, Rosanna was prepared for his visit. When he beckoned to her in the deserted hallway, after a business conference with her uncle, she went obediently to his summons.

"You've blossomed in the summer sun," he complimented, drawing her inside the small antechamber beside the palazzo entrance. Quietly closing the door, Miserotti turned her around before him, allowing the yellow sunlight to stream full on her face while he assessed her beauty.

"Were you afraid I had the pox, or grown cross-eyed since our last meeting?" she snapped.

"I merely wish to acquaint myself with the merchandise with which we bargain. To see if it is worthy."

"It's worthy enough."

"Yes, I believe it is," he agreed, smiling so that his thin lips drew back to expose long, animal-sharp teeth, yellowed like fangs against his skin. "But then, a witch always has the power to make herself beautiful, doesn't she?"

"If you are so convinced I'm from the devil, aren't you afraid of me? I can just as easily cast a spell on you."

"Ah, there you are wrong. I have no fear of you, for you see, I'm your master. I am Lucifer himself."

Again that smile and Rosanna shivered before the evil expression, convinced the boast was not an idle one.

"I knew your mother well. Why, I might even be your father." And he laughed at her shudder of revulsion. "Enough, let us to business. Do you still want to take a step on the path of destiny?"

"I did not agree. Then, or now."

"I already have your consent. It is in your eyes and face. All that remains is the detail. How it shall be done, and where. I already know by whom."

"It . . . Bianca?" she whispered, suddenly afraid.

"Bianca." He pursed his lips, then a slow smile dawned and his tongue peeped out thin and pink, like that of a wolf. "I think you can serve as message bearer. A partner in romantic conspiracy. The type of intrigue that sets the girlish heart pounding with delight."

Not understanding, Rosanna questioned him, but he only shook his head, slipping into the passage. She would have detained him had not a manservant appeared from the staircase as Miserotti left through the side door.

For several days Rosanna waited apprehensively, wondering how she was to be contacted and what her duty as message bearer would entail. Bianca was feeling recovered now she was home; consequently, she was more congenial towards her. Sometimes when Bianca was exceptionally pleasant, Rosanna felt a smattering of guilt for her knowledge of the proposed crime.

On Saturday the house was thrown into turmoil by the message of an unexpected visit from the Duke who would dine with them at eight.

All afternoon Bianca primped before her mirror. She decided to wear her newest gown, soon changing it for another and another, until every dress she owned was spread in gaudy disarray on the bed. At last she decided on the cherry red figured satin, with a silver headdress with floating gauze veils. Her long blond hair was elaborately braided in square crossing patterns and coiled within silver net cauls. The tall cone glittered at every turn, defying gravity by the precarious pitch of its angle, making her face appear tiny and very white by contrast.

With lurching heart, Rosanna heard Duke Paolo's voice below and when Bianca went downstairs to the feast, she hung back lest she should see him. While she waited for her cousin's return, Rosanna tried on various headdresses, looping her own thick hair inside Bianca's jeweled cauls. After she had replaced the expensive gowns in the dressing room, she lay across the bed staring into the darkness.

Laughter drifted from the dining hall. She could picture them at the banqueting table with its huge salter shaped like a turreted castle, eating from the choice gold plate and sipping Uncle Ugo's best wine from engraved crystal goblets. Paolo would openly admire Bianca in her lovely gown and smile affectionately at her when he thought no one was looking. Perhaps later he would inquire in secret about the outcome of the interlude in the garden. Maybe then the empty-headed fool would realize what caused her recent ailment. There would be pleasure in her shock, but it was a doubtful benefit. To have Paolo ask such personal questions, to see his tender smile at Bianca's surprise, would not be worth enduring for a moment of triumph.

Rosanna slept, to be awakened by the clatter of servants and jingling harness from the courtyard as the guests departed. Link boys illuminated the stable yard and she perched in the high windowsill to watch him mount his white stallion with its elaborate gold trappings. Tonight Paolo wore a dark color, possibly brown, but in the light cast by torches it was hard to distinguish. The night sky was overcast and a gray mist clung in dense pockets between the dark shapes of bushes in the courtyard, hovering in halos of white around the yellow burning lights. The royal party turned from the stable into the dark street and Rosanna moved from the window.

Bianca came back voicing her usual whining complaints. The new headdress had given her a blinding headache, and she was sure the highly spiced dishes would make her vomit before morning. When Rosanna tried to help her take off the silver hennin, Bianca pinched her arm vindictively and flounced away, insisting she would do everything herself rather than suffer beneath her clumsy handling. With a shrug, Rosanna retired to a padded chair in the corner watching Bianca unbraid her long golden hair.

There was an unexpected knock on the door and Rosanna went to answer it, thinking perhaps Aunt Magdela was being unusually polite out of deference to her daughter's exalted station. A page in the royal livery stood outside, his finger raised in warning to his lips as he glanced furtively about the corridor, and he handed her a note addressed to Bianca. She thanked him and closed the door. Bianca hurried eagerly to her side, her unbraided hair fluttering about her shoulders.

"What is it? For me?"

Nodding, Rosanna gave her the note, watching her cousin read the paper by the light from a taper beside the bed.

"It's from his Grace," Bianca gasped in delight. "How

exciting. He wants me to meet him tonight, masked and cloaked."

Rosanna experienced nausea at the news. Paolo was so eager for her cousin, he was not content with the social visit of this evening; he must arrange a secret tryst.

"Will you go?" she asked heavily, moving from the light.

"I don't know. I'm afraid of the dark. Will you come with me, Rosanna, dear? Please, say you will. We are to follow the page. It's all so exciting, I don't know what to say."

Bianca danced about, her hands clasped on the note and she kissed the parchment in ecstasy.

To watch them meet, to see his eager smile, the way he would sweep Bianca close would be too painful. She would not go. Bianca could find another companion.

"Do come. If you do I'll give you my new headdress with the pearls, the one you admired so much," Bianca promised, catching her arm. "Say you will, you know you're my friend, Rosanna. I've always thought of you as my friend."

Her cousin's cajoling had little effect on her, but perhaps it would be exciting to go to a secret meeting. It would be mysterious to creep outdoors in masks and meet a man unchaperoned in the dead of night.

"Please. Here, take the headdress."

Bianca thrust the glittering cone in her hands and Rosanna gasped as she fitted the pearl-trimmed gold shape upon her dark hair, adjusting it before the mirror. Now she was grand.

"All right, I'll come."

With a squeak Bianca kissed her flushed cheek, urging her to hurry. They fitted their masks in place and Bianca thrust her hair haphazardly into a net before she pulled on a cloak. In the darkness no one would guess who they were except he who had sent the message.

"Ready? Come on, don't be slow. He might get tired of waiting."

They tiptoed into the passage, glancing about for the page who emerged from the shadows beside the window, and he beckoned for them to follow. He appeared to know the house well, and Rosanna was surprised by his fleetness in the dark, twisting corridors, though Bianca did not notice, too preoccupied by her exciting adventure.

The mist had thickened until it was difficult to distinguish shapes through the murky dampness. Clutching each other for courage, the girls followed the Duke's page who had also donned a cloak to hide his distinctive livery. He led them through the streets where fog swirled gray and wispy, moved by the breeze. Visibility was decreased as they approached the canal where the vapor seemed to rise in ghostly, shrouded figures, moving and swaying noiselessly. Rosanna grew afraid as the page moved ahead in the gloom, leading them down cobbled streets, twisting and turning until she was completely lost. They encountered no one on their journey and though she spoke to him, inquiring about their destination, he did not reply. Suddenly he disappeared inside an archway leading to a darkened palazzo, telling them to follow. They were close to the canal because Rosanna could smell the slimy wetness of the bank, foul with decaying refuse, and to her left came the loud creaking of moored boats.

Fog shrouded them, and with a forced air of bravado, she stepped through the dark portico drawing Bianca with her. No one was there. Realizing they had been tricked, Rosanna turned about with a cry of alarm, to find a masked face loom out of the darkness. A hand was capped tightly over her mouth and she was drawn into the deep shadow. Bianca looked around in terror, realizing she was alone and she cried feebly for help, wrapping her cloak about her in a childish attempt at protection. From the deep, fog-shrouded shadows came a swift movement, followed by the whistle of a knife through the air. Then the thud. A shrill cry of surprise as it found its mark. And Bianca slumped to the ground.

Figures emerged from the fog, lifting her body, wrapping the cloak about her face. Wide-eyed, Rosanna watched, knowing now the messenger had not come from the Duke, but from Miserotti instead. And foolishly she had not suspected treachery until it was too late.

The man who held her released his grasp, knowing she would not cry out. "Who are you?" she whispered. "Speak to me."

"Why such urgency, *donna*?" he said, his voice vaguely

156

familiar, though it was muffled beneath a mask and swathed in the concealing shroud of his cloak. "Must we always have the fate to meet when you are masked?"

Then she recognized the voice with its mocking, jesting words. It was Sandro Miserotti. She spoke his name and he laughed low, his voice sounding chillingly evil in the fog-wreathed archway, buried far into the black shadow.

"Partners in crime do well to conceal their identity. 'Tis a lesson well learned by those who would live. I'll see you at Palazzo Lorenzo. Remember me generously, won't you, *donna*?"

He was gone, disappeared suddenly in the night and she shivered in fear, wondering what she would do alone on the streets in this eerie fog.

"Follow me. Your part in the masque is over."

Rosanna shuddered at the voice, husky and close, turning to find a hunchback huddled against the marble archway, smothered in a dark cloak.

"Beggars know the streets by night as well as day."

Unprotesting she followed, knowing this was no ordinary beggar, and when he left her at the side entrance to Palazzo Sordello, Rosanna was sure the hunchback straightened and walked whole.

Sunday morning began with a symphony of church bells calling the faithful to mass. Every church within the city had its own distinctive chime, while each clock seemed to be set differently from another, so that the clanging voices began minutes apart. First was Santa Maria Novella at five to the hour, the chimes of its campanile sweet and pure. To be followed by the cracked voices of San Croce and Gran Madre di Dio, joining in unison three minutes later. Exactly on the hour, San Bernardo chimed in, followed a moment later by the deafening boom of the huge bell of the Duomo, set high in its campanile overlooking the city. For a full five minutes the deafening crescendo rang forth, rousing all laggards from their beds, noisily heralding the dawning of the holy day.

Rosanna stretched, yawning and rubbing her eyes. When the bass echo of the cathedral bell drowned out the voices of the others, she covered her ears, deafened by the clangor. She would have to get up. In a few moments Bianca would be shrieking and thumping her, accusing her of being a good-for-nothing laggard; then Aunt Magdela would be outside the door, reminding them the first mass was already begun. She would probably insist on traveling across the city to the cathedral because the royal family worshipped there, instead of going to San Bernardo at the corner of the street.

Still rubbing her eyes, Rosanna swung her feet from beneath the covers, shivering as she touched the coolness of the marble tiles with bare toes. Wondering why Bianca was still alseep, she glanced towards her cousin's bed to find it had not been slept in. Then she remembered. Bianca was dead.

Rosanna lay back on her pillow a moment to gather her wits. The shock of her discovery left her shaken, almost afraid of the hours to follow, when the deed would be learned. How long would it be before they found Bianca? Miserotti would probably handle everything, she need only feign ignorance, pretending she slept while Bianca stole away. No one knew the truth, for last night their departure had been stealthy. Perhaps it would be less likely to arouse suspicion if she rumpled the covers on her cousin's bed.

There, she stood back to view the bedding, thumping a larger hollow in the down pillows. A knock on the door sent Rosanna scurrying to open it, drowsily rubbing her eyes.

Cia was in the corridor, bearing a large bowl and jug of steaming water. "Come on, you'll be late. Where's *Donna* Bianca?" the servant girl asked, as she placed the washing utensils on a marble-topped table.

"I don't know. Maybe she's in her dressing room."

Cia bustled into the small adjoining room, finding it empty. With a puzzled frown she emerged, carrying a sable-trimmed gown which she laid carefully on the bed. "You'd better get out her jewels, Rosanna. You know what she'll be like when she finds you aren't dressed. Maybe she went to the privy, but I didn't hear anyone. I'll ask *Donna* Magdela."

Rosanna nodded in agreement, opening Bianca's jewel box. The gown on the bed was saffron brocade, her cousin usually wore her pearl necklace with that, and the heavy pearl rings. As if nothing was wrong, she laid out the jewelry, placing Bianca's gold-engraved hairbrushes beside it.

When Aunt Magdela arrived, Rosanna was already dressed, her own hair neatly braided. She waited dutifully beside the bed, eyes downcast, her hands folded demurely in her lap. Now she was more sure of herself, for the few minutes alone had given her time to formulate a story.

"Get out of that chair, you lazy wench," Magdela demanded in anger. "Where's my daughter?"

"I don't know, Aunt Magdela. When I woke she was gone. I thought perhaps you knew where she was," Rosanna answered quietly, coming to stand at the door.

"Go and find her. Have the servants search the house. Perhaps she's in the courtyard. What a selfish girl, she knows I don't want to be late for mass, going off like this without a word ... well, don't stand there. Go and find her."

Bobbing a curtsy, Cia and Rosanna scuttled from the room, heading in different directions. Each time Rosanna met a servant in the corridors she told them to leave what they were doing and join the search for Bianca. Soon the entire household was in turmoil, searching every nook and cranny for the missing girl.

Ugo joined the hunt, bleary-eyed and yawning, his head throbbing painfully; the unpleasant aftereffects of overeating mingled disasterously with vast quantities of choice wine. He belched several times, tasting the spiced roast eel he had relished at dinner, its flavor not as succulent after a night of rest.

"You ought to know where she is," he yelled in accusation as Rosanna entered the solarium.

She found the family seated in the sunny room, perched uncomfortably on the edge of their chairs. Cia and nurse were there, and even Father Filippo, Aunt Magdela's confessor.

"I told you, she was gone when I woke."

Father Filippo nodded, his face creased with fine lines, and with a smile he stretched out his hand. "Of course, child, no one accuses you. We are distraught. Forgive us."

A flush crept up Rosanna's neck traveling to her

159

cheeks at the priest's words of comfort, for he had made her experience the first pangs of guilt she had felt for last night.

"Shall I look again, Father?"

"No. Come, let us inquire further afield, *Donna* Magdela," Father Filippo suggested, taking a crucifix from the pocket of his gown. He handed the article to Aunt Magdela, who was openly weeping, while her husband made a clumsy attempt at consolation, patting her heaving shoulder with his huge paw.

Father Filippo passed close to Rosanna and gripped her hand with his parchment fingers, the flesh stretched translucent over the bones like a holy statue. "Perhaps we would be advised to consult neighbors, who may help in solving the mystery. Send servants to each palazzo, child, to inquire after our beloved flower. Surely she can be found somewhere."

"Yes, Father." Rosanna kept her head downcast, afraid to meet the old man's piercing blue eyes in case he discovered her treachery.

"Send messages to the Corellis; down the street to the Datis, and especially to the Miserotti. Think you they can help in our search, Rosanna?"

She gasped at her words, for the latter was almost a whisper, meant only for her. Warily she met his eyes, and almost imperceptibly he nodded. He knew. His knowledge was a shock, yet as she stared back at him, Rosanna realized there was no condemnation in his face. He knew only because he had been told. Then she remembered; Father Filippo was also Guido Miserotti's confessor.

"Yes, Father, perhaps they will know."

It was not till afternoon that Bianca was found. Her body, wrapped in a dark cloak, was discovered in an abandoned gondola moored at the jetty of the family warehouses. A sad, weeping procession bore the small bundle home. The emotion of the family was so moving that Rosanna managed a few genuine tears, surprised by her reaction. She even felt sorry for Uncle Ugo, who retired to his study when they reached the palazzo and locked himself in.

Later, when he emerged, he shuffled like an old man,

stooped and weary. Rosanna patted his arm in a gesture of comfort as they entered the solar where Bianca, washed and dressed in her finest gown, was laid in state on the funeral block.

To see her cousin lying in repose, almost as if she slept, was surprising to Rosanna. No one would guess she had been stabbed if they did not know, for the blood was gone; her chest covered by the stiff, pearl-embroidered brocade of her festival gown. Rosanna had not been allowed to attend the preparation of the body, all the care being performed by Bianca's old nurse, who now wept on her knees in the corner. Even Aunt Magdela had been too overcome to dress the corpse, but she had plaited her daughter's hair in an elaborate pattern, topping the mountain of braids with a simple white cap of pearls.

"She's gone, Rosanna, gone," Uncle Ugo whispered in disbelief, reverently touching the dead hands, their ivory fingers clasping a single, long-stemmed rose. "How did it happen? Who would want to do such a thing to my little girl?"

His tear-choked voice made Rosanna uneasy. Though she remembered the many reasons she had to hate him, in his loss he was bewilderingly pathetic. He clasped her against him, and she staggered under the sudden weight as he leaned on her, but there was nothing but comfort expected from the embrace. Dutifully she kissed his cheek.

"Perhaps if you lie down, Uncle, you'll feel better."

"Yes, maybe I will." Releasing her, he walked to the door, his broad shoulders slumped, his soft shod feet dragging on the tiles. At the threshold he turned, looking at the still figure on the bier; then, shaking his head, he left the room.

In the corridor Rosanna heard him ask one of the menservants if the messenger had returned from the ducal palace. It was only then Rosanna remembered the Duke. There had been so much activity she had not given him any thought. A commotion from outside drifted to her ears, and a servant's hushed voice at the door announced the Duke's arrival.

From the shadows of the room, Rosanna watched him come up the narrow staircase, striding towards the solar, his doublet a vivid splash of color against the sombre, curtain-screened passage where servants dropped to the floor, kneeling to their ruler. She shrank into the folds of the blue velvet curtains drawn across the windows to shut out the sun, giving the room a strange, unearthly appearance as murky light filtered through the heavy draperies. It was oppressive in the afternoon heat with the windows closed, and though Bianca's corpse had little odor, the heavy oil which had been used on the body gave off its own sickly perfume.

The Duke stood in the doorway, his attendants hanging back to allow him a private viewing of the body. Betraying no emotion, he stared at Bianca's stiff, brocaded figure. At last he came inside the room, his feet heavy and muffled in their soft shoes. Duke Paolo knelt on the carpeted steps leading to the bier, his head bowed over clasped hands as he whispered a prayer. When he stood, Rosanna saw his expression was of pain. The sensual fullness of his mouth was gone, his lips drawn tight in a narrow, unyielding line while on his brow the furrows were deep, far different from what she remembered. Gently he pried the bloodless fingers open, and without hesitation laid a kiss on Bianca's cold palm before reinserting the rose between her hands. For a few moments he stared at the angelic little face, now in heavenly repose beneath the pearl cap. He touched the bright, stiff-braided golden hair and bent to kiss Bianca's icy cheek, turning abruptly on his heel, not seeing Rosanna, paying no attention to the old nurse hunched on her knees before a crucifix in the far corner of the room.

When he was gone, Rosanna experienced a growing wave of nausea, until she ran from the room, fleeing before the startled eyes of the party of mourners, heading for the small closed room at the rear of the house. There she vomited down the stone basin, tears and pain mingling in blind confusion within her body.

Presently the door opened and a man came inside, securing the fastening behind him.

"Rosanna."

At first she did not hear, so occupied was she with the heaving sickness inside her.

"Rosanna."

162

His voice was close at her elbow and she recognized the special tone, one she had last heard beneath the fog-shrouded archway beside the canal. It was Sandro Miserotti.

"What do you want?"

"What does a man usually come here for?" He laughed, drawing her from her knees. "I have bodily functions like other men."

"I didn't know," she muttered, wiping her mouth dry with the back of her hand, afraid and repelled by his closeness. "Don't let me stop you. I've already watched you kill, there's no reason why you should start respecting me now."

He caught her arm, detaining her, laughing once more at her words. "Don't forget, you were the one who brought her to us—the one who lusts after his Grace. It is not I who want the heat of his bed."

Rosanna stared at him, seeing the sneer on his mouth, wondering suddenly if he would betray her. "How many others know?"

"About you, no one."

"But Father Filippo knew."

"Did he tell you?"

"Not in so many words."

"It was the goodly priest who found *La Bianca*'s body, sweeting, need I say more?" Sandro released her arm, stepping back to survey Rosanna's appearance. "You look like a bitch from the Ponte Maggiore. His Grace seen you?"

She shook her head, self-consciously patting her straggling hair in place, affronted by his statement. "My aunt dresses me little better than one. Perhaps if I earned my way I could afford richer gowns," she snapped.

"You'd probably make a fortune at it."

"I won't stay to be insulted. Get out of my way."

"You are a prickly one. You'd better trim those claws, for Paolo won't fancy a she-cat in bed. My mother has offered to house you till the period of mourning is over. We thought it a suitable plan, that way your comings and goings will not be taken note of. Already doubts have been seeded in Paolo's mind about the fair Bianca. Sordello will deny it, but who's to defend the honor of a dead

163

woman. Come, wash your face and get the stink of vomit off your lips. Before he departs I want you to speak to him to keep your memory fresh."

"Do you seek to sell me already, with Bianca not buried?"

"It will do no harm to remind Paolo there are still desirable women alive, after all, he isn't going to mourn forever," Sandro pointed out practically, wrinkling his nose at the smell of the room. "He runs hot most of the time, this will only have a temporary effect on his virility. Come on, this place smells like a broken piss pot."

Following him, Rosanna found she was feeling much better. Now she hoped she would not encounter the Duke before she had a chance to change her clothing. Sandro knew Paolo better than she. If he thought the plan wise, it probably was.

"Where's your room?"

"Upstairs."

"Can we go a back way?"

"Yes, along the balcony," Rosanna suggested, wondering if he intended to come with her.

"All right, hurry. I don't know how much longer Paolo will stay."

Rosanna raced after his long stride, panting to keep up with him. Breathless, she arrived outside her door and he marched inside, fastening the door behind them.

"Hurry up."

"I'm not getting undressed with you here."

"I'll promise not to rape you. Go behind a screen and stop being so confounded modest. He'll be gone if we aren't careful and you'll have missed a golden opportunity," Sandro suggested in exasperation, throwing himself on Bianca's bed.

Pulling a face at him, Rosanna raced to get her blue dress—the best she had. It was almost too small for her and the skirt was immodestly short. "What about this?"

Sandro surveyed the garment as she held it in front of her. "That'll be all right. Does it show some flesh?"

"In the bodice?"

"Of course in the bodice, where did you think I meant? God, sometimes I think women are born imbeciles."

"Oh, shut up," Rosanna snapped, going behind the painted screen near the dressing table.

Twice she peered between the cracks in the panels making sure he was still on the bed. He was, and he swung Bianca's pendant around on his finger, whistling a catchy tune while he waited. When she finished dressing she washed her face and hastily brushed her hair with Bianca's gold-handled brush. At last she was ready, and Rosanna stepped from behind the screen, awaiting his approval.

Sandro swung from the bed, coming towards her and with his head to one side he studied her appearance. "Perfect," he said at last, tweaking the neckline of her gown, until she pulled away from the heat of his fingers.

"I'm only making the gown more delectable, *Santa* Rosanna," he hissed.

The Duke was in the solar, preparing to depart. Sandro thrust Rosanna forward and when the Duke turned, after a farewell glance at Bianca, hers was the first face he saw.

"Your Grace, my condolences," Rosanna murmured, hoping her voice was convincingly sad.

"Thank you. It was your loss too. You will miss her as I will." There was a heavy finality in his voice, and when he extended his hand for her to kiss, Rosanna felt no response in his fingers.

"Everyone will miss her, your Grace."

Her kiss was gentle, not intending passion, yet still he caught his breath when her lips met his hand. And Rosanna was momentarily rewarded as she saw his eyes flick away from the décolletage of her gown as he concentrated on the bone clasp in her hair.

"Bring comfort to your aunt and uncle in their sorrow," he commanded, drawing her up till she stood on a level with him. "Who would have thought last night's festive meal would end like this." With a sigh he released her hand, turning to his gentlemen. "I am ready, Viverini. Tell them for me." He turned back to her, finding her eyes on his face and he was puzzled by her expression. "Whoever did this will be punished, have no fear," he assured, then in discomfort he tore his eyes from hers, his manner abrupt.

She watched him stride down the corridor, entering the

tiled, circular entrance hall, where servants and family kneeled before his passage. At the door he drew Aunt Magdela from her knees, and with a quick gesture he lightly kissed her cheeks.

"We will hold her funeral on Monday, in the Duomo. I shall proclaim a day of mourning for the entire duchy."

Aunt Magdela muttered her thanks, dropping to her knees, her cheeks wet with fresh tears. Almost thankfully, Duke Paolo departed, striding down the steps into the sunshine, his bright clothing dazzling in the yellow light, a sharp contrast to the brooding darkness of Palazzo Sordello. He passed from sight, and the courtiers followed, each offering condolences as they left.

At last the family were alone, except for Sandro Miserotti, who waited at the door of the dining room, uncomfortable to be present at their hour of grief.

"I'm sorry your lady mother could not leave her bed. 'Twill be better for Magdela not to see the girl, too much comparison. Go with him, Rosanna, and don't forget to thank *Donna* Ippolyta for her hospitality. We shall see you for our child's funeral."

Uncle Ugo brushed her cheek with his lips, the kiss slack and passionless.

"Good-by, Uncle," she whispered and with rising spirits Rosanna went down the steps into the brilliant Sunday afternoon warmth.

Chapter Eleven

If Rosanna had expected her stay with the Miserotti family to be pleasant, she would have been disappointed. Her treatment was similar to that received from her aunt and uncle. Ippolyta Miserotti treated her little better than a servant, while her daughter, Ginevra, viewed Rosanna with disdain. The younger girl, Leonora, whom Rosanna had hoped to see again, was still at the family villa in the country.

Sandro told her his father would speak with her when he returned from Padua, where he had traveled on business. As the male head of the household, Sandro represented the family at Bianca's funeral, an ordeal which Rosanna wished she need not endure. *Donna* Ippolyta lent her a black dress for the occasion, insisting it was more suitable than the one Rosanna wore. The neckline was high and the voluminous skirts swept the ground like a mammoth train when she walked, making her feel drab and ugly, almost dead herself, in the borrowed mourning.

"Thank God Paolo won't see you in that," Sandro voiced as they left the requiem mass. He shielded her from view as the Duke passed, but not once did Paolo glance their way, keeping his eyes fixed straight ahead.

"I'm still me," Rosanna hissed in annoyance, maintaining a steady, measured pace in the procession of mourners.

"Convince me," he quipped back, shushing her quickly when she would have retorted.

Uncle Ugo motioned for Rosanna to walk with the family, and casting Sandro an angry glare, she hurried to catch them.

Everyone wept as they followed the bier where Bianca lay, dressed in her festival gown. The rose in her hands had wilted, drooping dead and forlorn against the brocade skirt. Rosanna was dry-eyed, though she kept her head down, maintaining a suitable pose of sorrow as they entered the graveyard. The sun was high and as she walked beside the body, Rosanna wrinkled her nose at the odor which wafted from the corpse—sickeningly sweet and foul.

Bianca was placed outside the family crypt where Father Filippo intoned the requiem. Duke Paolo knelt beside the body and placed a wreath of roses on top of the floral tributes from the bereaved family; then, with a brief prayer, he came towards the mourners. Rosanna quickly hid behind a large courtier in voluminous purple robes so that the Duke would not see her. It seemed as if he searched the faces in the crowd and she wondered if he looked for her, though she dare not present herself; Sandro had insisted she stay in the background. Placing his black velvet hat on his head, the Duke motioned to his attendants to follow. He strode down the flagged path which twisted between crypts and gravestones, finally reaching his horse which was tethered near the entrance to the cemetery.

Guido Miserotti returned to Lorenzo on Friday afternoon, and within minutes of his arrival, he sent for Rosanna. Finding her legs shaking with fright, she went to his study at the front of the house overlooking the busy Via San Bernardo.

"So we begin," he greeted, as she entered the room.

He was standing beside a bookcase filled with leather-bound books, his clothing dusty and travel stained. His gray beard was scraggly, drooping upon his black robes like a mangled pelt.

Rosanna curtsied politely, finding his scrutiny unnerving.

"Have you seen his Grace?"

"Only at the funeral."

"Good, we don't want him to be overexposed to your charms, do we?" Miserotti turned towards the desk and taking a gilded almond from a silver bowl, he offered the dish to her. "Take one, gold is good for the body."

"No thank you."

He shrugged and replaced the dish. Pulling a scroll of parchment from his garments he said, "Here is a denouncement of your cousin's chastity, signed by many. Indisputed testimony, of course."

"Of course."

"You need not be sarcastic, Rosanna *Bruna,* everything is being done for you. Don't forget that."

"Is it necessary to say such things? They aren't true. Bianca was such a prude, she'd never have done anything like that," Rosanna protested, finding an uncomfortable sense of shame as he defamed the morals of her dead cousin.

"She wouldn't?" Miserotti questioned, humor in his voice. "I don't think you'll convince his Grace of that. He has firsthand knowledge of her immorality. Or think you that touching interlude was a dream?"

"No," she mumbled, turning to the window to watch a cart loaded with fruits and vegetables passing over the cobbles below, its toothless driver beaming in appreciation as he noticed her face at the window.

"Very well then, we shall have no further talk of it. You'd be advised to keep your mouth closed if it can only speak such idiocy."

His anger shocked her, for suddenly Miserotti went from friend to enemy. At his sharp command she turned around, seeing him smile in his evil manner, his yellow fangs discolored by specks of half-chewed almond comfit lodged between the teeth.

"That's better. Smile, your looks are greatly improved by a smile. Remember that, it will be useful to you in the future. This document will be presented to Paolo. At the moment he is likely preparing to hunt in an effort to forget his bereavement. A rider will take this to the lake."

"He's gone?" Rosanna questioned in surprise, not aware of the Duke's departure. She had thought him still at the palace. With Paolo at his hunting lodge, how could she go to him?

"It is not necessary to inform you of the comings and goings in the city."

"But I thought . . ."

"It is I who do the thinking." Miserotti came towards her, gathering his flowing robes into a train which he carried over his arm. As he approached, the strong odor of sweat and dust came to her nostrils. An effort had been made to mask the stench with a cloying perfume which only seemed to intensify it. "Do you find me repulsive?" he asked, his mouth drawing into a leer as she backed away. "If I were so inclined I could use you for whatever purpose I wished. You are completely at my disposal, dear child, completely."

His yellowed fingers stroked the soft curve of her cheek, and Rosanna blanched at the thought of forced intimacy with this human vulture. "Don't . . . don't you ever think that about me," she warned, her voice trembling with emotion.

Miserotti saw the hate in her eyes, and he dropped his hand. "A woman is not violated by thought alone. I shall think whatsoever I please. I did not bring you to this circumstance for love, only because you are valuable to me. A slaveholder is a fool to soil his merchandise."

"I'm not your slave. There's no proof of my guilt. You've nothing with which to blackmail me."

"Don't stake your life on it, unless you are immortal."

Rosanna stared at him, finding horror and fear rising in a hot tide from her stomach. On her brow, sweat beaded fine, and her hands were clammy as she wound the skirt of her dress in a sweaty spiral.

"I will tell you what to do and you will listen, and if you value your life, you will obey."

"Yes . . . tell me what to do," she whispered, mesmerized by the flickering yellow of his eyes. They were not human; more the cunning eyes of an animal, almost as if she stood face to face with a wolf trapped in the mountains, as if, gnashing those vicious teeth, he would spring and devour her.

"Good." Miserotti nodded. And suddenly his eyes changed.

At the transformation, Rosanna breathed an audible sigh of relief, stumbling to the bench he indicated beside the window.

"In one month's time you'll be taken to the lake. By then everything will have been prepared. I'll groom you, dress you, transport you . . . after that it's up to you. And Paolo."

"You mean I have to wait an entire month?"

Miserotti shook with dry laughter at her aggrieved voice, and he came to stand before the desk, his shoulders moving in silent mirth. "Mother of God, what a hot little baggage you are. Why so impatient? We must give poor Paolo time to recover. I think a month is not unreasonable to wait for him, after all we want him like this." Miserotti thrust a long, bony finger before him, erect and graphic. "Not like this." With a smile he allowed the finger to relax and droop downwards.

She turned back to the window, finding his humor crude. Below, the farm cart had stopped and three urchins pelted the ancient driver with clods of filth from the stagnant gutters. A month of this! God, it was too much to endure in the heat of the city, in this house, with these murderers. But she had no other choice.

The third week of September, 1455, was blessed with perfect weather, it seemed impossible that autumn could be just around the corner, for this seemed an extension of perpetual summer. Rosanna sighed with happiness as she mastered the rocky trail, riding beside Miserotti on a blooded mare. The animals' black flanks gleamed silken in the sun, her head tossing proud and spirited as she smelled the enticing country air.

Unfortunately, Rosanna found Miserotti a dour traveling companion. One of the grooms had ridden beside her on the first part of the journey, flattering her with his eyes, gradually allowing her to draw him into conversation. But her chaperone had considered it improper to

171

converse with a stable hand, so the boy had been dismissed to the rear of the party. Now Miserotti himself rode at her side, his conversation infrequent; confined only to the lack of drinking water. At last he sank into brooding silence leaving Rosanna free to manufacture her own thoughts.

As they neared their destination, she became nervous about the intended meeting with Paolo. What if he had no wish to see her? She thought he loved her a little, yet he had never spoken of the emotion. He had admitted he desired her, but there was no mention of love.

The tang of lake water was apparent in the breeze, and in a few moments the castle of Lorenzo's duke became visible between the trees. Rosanna straightened in the saddle, anxious to see the famed Castel Isola.

There it was, rising from the placid lake like a castle in a legend, its brown walls mellowed, golden in spots where the surface of the rock had worn away. Turreted towers stretched high to a bank of fluffy clouds. In the background the foothills of the Alps could be seen, misty in the distance. Pausing a moment to admire the scene, Rosanna realized she was happy. It was as if this place and the ancient castle were familiar to her, as if she had journeyed here before with pleasure.

The trailing clouds suddenly blotted out the sun, plunging the lakeside into gloom. In this light the castle appeared brooding and forbidding. Its massive walls cast shadows, blackening the lake. Then the clouds whisped higher and the sun came out, transforming the picture in an instant, until all was pleasant again.

"Hurry, we don't want to stay outside all day. My throat is parched," Miserotti grumbled at her elbow, and leaning forward he whacked the flanks of her mare with his riding crop. With a startled whinny the horse darted forward, covering the rocky track in a moment, snorting and hesitant at the water's edge.

Treating him to a haughty stare, Rosanna lifted her head, holding her chin high in defiance as they waited to ford the lake.

The Duke was hunting and would not be back till late afternoon, so the opportunity was taken to acquaint her with the floor plan of the castle. Miserotti made certain to point out Paolo's bedchamber set high in a tower, affording an uninterrupted view of the lake and a breathtaking panorama of the mountains to the north.

Everywhere was strange, for she had never been inside a castle. The rooms seemed huge, their rough-hewn walls hung with mammoth tapestries. The colors of the panels were drab, nothing like the brilliant murals which were painted on the walls of the ballroom at the palace. These hangings depicted biblical stories instead of the more erotic scenes from mythology, and Rosanna dismissed them as merely a covering to hide the damp walls.

There was a sunny walled garden hidden in the heart of the castle, but Miserotti would not let her explore it, only allowing her a glimpse through the windows of the solar.

"You won't have time for gardening, wench. And please God you won't need to brew a spell to snare his Grace," Miserotti growled as she requested permission to enter the garden.

With a toss of her head Rosanna snapped: "I don't brew spells."

"Your prime interest will be in that bedchamber up there." Miserotti jerked his head toward the spiral stair, ignoring her angry correction. "Come on, I'll show you your room before he rides in."

It was a circular room in one of the smaller towers, but its unusual shape pleased her. A bed and a carved chest were the only furnishings, though blue-velvet cushions had been fitted in the window alcove, adding a wide window seat. Darting to the small window, Rosanna undid the catch, flinging the mullioned pane open. Sweet, water-cooled air flooded inside, and she nodded in approval. "I like it."

"It's yours, whether you like it or not."

Pulling a face at his retreating figure, Rosanna leaned out of the window, seeing a couple of majestic swans below. The large birds glided over the water, white feathers glittering on the green-black surface, causing ripples with the graceful movement of their bodies.

From the distant trees came the strident notes of a hunting horn, and she realized it was Duke Paolo returning from the hunt. With pounding heart she waited, rewarded by the sight of riders winding through the greenery. At last they came into the open and she searched for Paolo amongst the gentlemen. He was soberly dressed in black, his voice silent, not joining with the others in their joking and laughter. The sight of him so withdrawn made her heart ache, for she longed to comfort him, to bring a smile to his lips and make them full and passionate once more.

Her clothing had been placed in the room and Rosanna took a heliotrope gown, banded in black, from the top of the chest. Miserotti must have wanted her to wear this. Her new clothing was the only thing she had to thank her benefactor for. Hopefully tonight there would be far more to rejoice in.

When she was dressed, Rosanna waited at the window for the summons to dinner. A servant girl came for her, and when she reached the dining hall, the Duke was not there.

Miserotti was seated at the head of the table, lordly and commanding, taking precedence over the other gentlemen present. The diners eyed her with approval as she slipped into the only empty place at the far end of the massive oak table. The great hall was a monstrous room, its walls cluttered with stuffed boar's heads and deer with enormous branching antlers, their eyes glassy and false. The unwavering scrutiny of the bulbous eyes made Rosanna uncomfortable, robbing her of an appetite as she found herself picturing people's heads on the walls, instead of animals'. The castle's hunting trophies were morbidly reminiscent of the severed heads which dripped and moldered on spikes across the Ponte Maggiore, displayed to remind prisoners of the fate of the condemned as they were brought along the narrow bridge from the prison to the place of execution. It was frighteningly easy to picture her own face staring obscenely from a pike, her flesh rotting and putrid. To cross Guido Miserotti could earn her that ignoble fate, for he was all powerful. A word from him swayed the opinion of his brother, Claudio, who was the Chief Justice of Lorenzo. If she was wise, she would do exactly as he requested.

Glancing up, Rosanna found his eyes on hers, breaching

the distance between them, that same animal glint to their depth. "Are you not hungry, *donna*?" he asked.

"No, it is the journey, too tiring."

"Yes, a long journey," he agreed, his eyes smiling as he read a meaning to her words she had not intended. "Come, if the gentlemen will excuse us, I'll show you to your chamber."

The others rose politely as she swept from the room, Miserotti following close on her heels, his black gown flapping against the tops of his shoes as he walked.

It was silent in the corridor and Rosanna felt compelled to whisper: "You showed me my room this afternoon."

"So I did, my memory is lapsing," he agreed, glancing down the darkened corridor. From the hall the sound of talk and laughter was muted as the meal continued, the others safely occupied for some time yet. "I had hoped his Grace would sup with us, but they say he takes his meals alone. No matter, we shall draw his attention before the night is out."

They had stopped before the door to the solar, which at this hour was unlit. A cool breeze blew through the room, wafting from the open windows leading to the courtyard beyond.

"It's that way to the garden," he said.

" 'Tis too dark to see much. I'll wait till daylight."

"Paolo walks in the garden after he sups. He stays there till it's time for bed. Now, do you understand how attractive a garden can be at dusk?" Turning her round, Miserotti examined her appearance, nodding his approval. "Smile at him, comfort him, arouse him." As she did not move, he pushed her gently. "Why are you waiting? Go to him. He's alone."

Twilight was heavy with the scent of musk, and night-blooming jasmine mingled exotically with the roses. In the distant trees, birds called, their shrill voices clear in the stillness as they winged homeward. Beyond the castle, the lake was placid—black shadowed near the bank, murky against the tall rushes. A fish broke the mirror calm, sending ripples in a widening circle and it leaped again by the willows. Far down the mountain the orange rim of the sinking sun was barely visible, soon to be extinguished by the green plain of Lorenzo.

Rosanna walked softly over the lawn, smelling the freshness of dew on the grass beneath her feet, her trailing skirts wet about her ankles. Long before she reached him, she saw the Duke. Paolo was leaning on the parapet, staring moodily at the lake, his back turned upon the precise, regimented beauty of his landscaped garden. To see him thus made her heart swell with pain. He was so alone, so sad in the enormity of the summer twilight.

For a moment she hesitated. "Go to him," Miserotti had said. But what if Paolo turned from her, then everything would have been for nought.

"Your Grace." Her voice was soft, almost a whisper. And he did not hear. Rosanna touched his black doublet, her fingers trembling against the velvet. "Your Grace."

He turned abruptly, startled by the voice. "You."

They looked at each other without moving. Her eyes were brilliant with tears, her emotion painful in its intensity. The Duke did not touch her, nor did he move away.

"Your Grace, I do not wish to intrude. If you will it, I shall go," Rosanna whispered after a long silence.

Gravely he looked at her, glancing away to the water where the last glimmer of sunlight melted in blackness. "Stay," he said simply, his voice thick and unnatural.

Then she moved, taking the short steps toward him as if he were a mile distant. It was Rosanna who put out her arms, who took his golden head against her breast for comfort. And he did not draw away. After a moment his arms went around her and pulled her close, the throb of his body music in her veins. Tears spilled down her cheeks and he kissed away the crystal rivers, holding her as if he would never let her go.

"Let me love you, Paolo," she whispered against his mouth, shuddering in the ecstasy of his embrace. "Oh, Paolo, I love you."

"Yes . . . I know," he said, searching her face, giving in to the torment of his body. It had been too long and his strength was gone. He no longer had any will against her.

"You will never need another," she promised, touching his face, his crisp waving hair.

"I know that too." Her mouth was hot, its fragrance unbearable. It was dark now, the garden plunged into

176

shadow; they were alone and, Mother of God, he needed her. "Here, in the garden?" he whispered.

"If that is your wish."

"Is it yours?" he asked, puzzled by her answer.

"You are my wish. Come, there's a grotto with night-blooming jasmine. It will be like Paradise," Rosanna whispered, shuddering as he caressed her hair.

"I love you, I swear it," he vowed in a burst of passion. "Can you be happy with me?"

"To know you love me is all I need to be happy."

Paolo kissed her again, feeling suddenly light and free. She was a goddess among women, her desire primitive and earthy, she was everything he had ever wanted. And he did love her. Now he knew it was true. He led her by the hand along the scented walkway, through the blue marble archway of the grotto, to the gates of Paradise.

It was morning when Rosanna awoke and for a moment of drowsiness she thought she was in Bianca's bed-chamber. Then, with a wave of shock, she realized she was at Castel Isola. The walls hung with tapestry were unfamiliar. With pleasure she recalled coming here last night in the black, midnight darkness, her body warmly glowing with Paolo's love. He had put her on the great bed and lain beside her.

Then he had told her all those wonderful things she had always wanted him to say, and he had never said—all the caresses she had longed for, and he had never given. Last night was the fulfillment of her dreams and today she would gladly have died in payment for the gift.

With a sigh she stretched beneath the covers, finding the sheets silken to her bare body.

"You wake like Venus."

Startled by the voice, she glanced towards the curtained windows to find him watching her.

"Your Grace," she cried, caught off guard.

"Your Grace," he mocked with a smile. "Am I not still Paolo this morning?"

Shyly she smiled back. Yes, she had called him Paolo last night and many other things beside. "If it is your wish that I call you so, your Grace."

"It is my wish, and also the other names you have for

me. I love them all, *angela mia*," he whispered, sitting beside her, his eyes soft with love. "I've never known a woman like you before." He reached for her hair, stroking the loosened braid, half spilled on the pillow. "Unbind it for me."

Rosanna sat against the mountain of down, reaching to her hair. The covers fell away and she did not pull them up, rejoicing in the adoration of his eyes, unashamed of her naked breasts.

Paolo watched her, his heart racing frantically beneath the black velvet of his bed robe. She was like some magnificent pagan deity of love, her full breasts, white against the unbound shimmer of her raven hair. And he took her hair, spreading it like a cloak about her shoulders.

"I would like a portrait of you thus—my Venus of the morning," Paolo whispered ardently. "Would you allow me to have you painted like this?"

Rosanna blinked, surprised by his request. "If you would like it."

"I'd love it. I'll speak to Ricasoli this very week. I will be jealous that he see you unclothed, but he finds the body of a boy more comely than that of a woman. Thanks be to God."

Paolo stooped to kiss her and Rosanna stroked his hair, caressing the back of his neck beneath the collar of his robe. A knock on the door, and she scrambled for the sheets as Paolo turned from her to the intruder.

A servant brought food. Crossing to the windows he drew the curtains to admit golden sunlight. All the while the man's eyes were discreetly downcast and not once did he look at the woman in the bed.

Paolo laughed at her modesty, bringing the tray to the bedside. "I shall feed you, my goddess."

With the suggestion he dipped bread in the wine in her cup, pressing it to her mouth. Laughing, she allowed him the game, in turn soaking bread for him. And he kissed her fingers as she touched his lips. There was sliced venison, but neither of them was hungry and the wine-soaked bread sufficed.

Rosanna had shaken back her cloak of hair and lay watching him, a smile on her lips. With a swift movement he drew aside the bedcovers, seeing her stretch indolently before his appraising gaze. "Will you stay with me always, Rosanna?" he asked softly, enchanted by the beauty of her limbs.

"Forever."

As he stood smiling down at her, she moved from the bed to the red-patterned carpet, kneeling before him, obedient at his feet. "I am your slave, master," she said.

Her dark eyes shone with laughter and he touched the smoothness of her hair, stroking her cool brow, his fingers tracing the prominence of her nose. Rosanna moved forward on her knees until she was close to him and she wrapped her arms about his waist, hugging him with all her strength.

"It is I who am the slave," Paolo whispered.

Tomorrow they would return to Lorenzo, a prospect which made her sad. Even the bleak, fortressed castle had grown familiar and dear, hiding within its tall stone walls the unexpected beauty of the garden, with sun-kissed benches and climbing roses. It was in the garden she had known Paolo best. There he had revealed the man behind the royal Duke as they talked and laughed, lying peacefully on the grass, his head in her lap. Rosanna had stroked his face, gazing at his pale eyes, watching her always so gravely and with such love. And she remembered the way his fingers stole into hers as they watched the sunset. A man and a woman, very much in love. . . .

"The sun's sinking, shall we return?"

Paolo's words interrupted her thoughts, and Rosanna smiled at him, as he trailed his hand in the shallow water at the edge of the lake.

"Must we, so soon? Everywhere's quiet, even the birds don't sing tonight. I'd like to make this hour last forever." She sighed, slithering over the grass to sit beside him and she plucked an arrow-slim reed from the water.

"We'll ride early tomorrow. I want to show you my palace. Everything I own will be for you, *angela*. What will you think to ride beside me through the streets?"

"I hope you'll be proud to have me there."

"Of course I will. There will be more than one spiteful tongue when you are seen, for the word will spread through the court like wildfire. Perhaps you'll set a new

179

fashion, *carissima,* with your lovely black hair," Paolo suggested, touching her thick braided locks, woven through with gold strips. "The blondes will be put to shame."

"Do you think so?" she asked with surprise, remembering how Bianca told her the court ladies had dyed their hair gold to ape Flora Dati.

"I'll always remember the first night here with you," he whispered softly, taking her hand.

"So will I, though I'd dreamed of it so often."

"Rosanna how did you know there was a grotto? You've never been here before," he asked after a moment, a frown creasing his brow.

"Perhaps I dreamed it. I just knew it was there."

He touched her face, his fingers softly caressing and his blood surged in a weakening flood. The twilight shadows had lengthened until the grass was black, the tall, encircling trees, sombre guardians around the lake.

"Lago di Paradiso," he murmured hoarsely, taking her against him, "The name is true, is it not, now we have found each other?"

She smiled her agreement nestling into the warmth of his neck, the scent of him always new and arousing.

"Will you let me make love to you here in the grass?" he asked, his voice hoarse with emotion. "Shall we lie beneath the moon like the gypsy people, and smell the scent of things growing in the night?"

"It will be our last time."

"No," he contradicted. "I will ride the miles to Lago di Paradiso if only to couple with you in the grass, my goddess, and smell the dew in your hair."

With a joyous smile, Rosanna pulled his face to her own, passionately kissing him, his laughter a love song against her ear, the lapping water in the background its accompaniment.

The moon was high, tossing fitfully against scudding clouds, when Rosanna regained consciousness to find Paolo beside her, watching her sleep, his face soft in the moonlight.

"Why did you not wake me?"

"Can't I have the pleasure of seeing you sleep with such satisfaction."

He helped her rise and they walked over the crunching shingle of the lakeshore to the moored boat, their shapes casting elongated dark splashes upon the water.

Lifting her into the boat, Paolo climbed aboard, and untying the vessel, he pushed them from shore. In a few minutes they were at the opposite bank, where he leaped ashore, pulling in the boat and helping her to the stone-paved jetty.

Then, like a man and a maid, they walked hand in hand to the small gate set in the garden wall, leaving the lake behind in the silver night.

Chapter Twelve

The royal party rode through the hilly countryside to
Lorenzo, harnesses jingling, the horses' hooves loud on
the rocky road. In an azure sky the sun shone bright,
shimmering over the sparkling pinnacles of the distant
city. Rosanna knew mounting excitement as they neared
the clustering buildings, nestled safely within the rose-
pink city walls. In a few minutes it would be known she
was the Duke's mistress, for he rode openly at her side.

A month ago the populace had wept with him for his
loss, watching as he rode sadly towards his mountain retreat; now he returned, a smile about his mouth, infectious excitement in his every move. He wanted Rosanna
to be loved by his subjects, he wanted them to adore her
as he did, rejoicing in the happiness she had given him.
Instead of sombre mourning Duke Paolo wore burgundy
velvet and white satin, his cloak blowing in the wind as he
quickened his horse's pace. A black velvet cap with burgundy plumes sat jauntily on his dark gold hair, the
feathers tossing with the movement of his body.

She watched him, loving him more for knowing at last
he was hers—his heart as well as his body. Adjusting the
sea-green skirts of her riding habit, Rosanna urged her

mare forward, overtaking him at the head of the procession. With a shout, he spurred after her, and they rode neck and neck to the gates of Lorenzo.

For Rosanna the progress through the city was a triumphant one. People lined the streets, pausing in their tasks to cheer the Duke, waving kerchiefs and caps as the royal procession moved towards the palace. The horses jostled and capered in the pressing throng and Paolo reached out to grasp her hand, reassuring her of their safety.

Down the Via San Lorenzo they passed, turning into the Piazza Neri, then two abreast through a narrow cobbled passage to the Via San Bernardo. Rosanna glanced towards the silent Palazzo Sordello, wondering if her aunt watched from behind the shuttered windows to see her triumphant return to Lorenzo. They passed the Dati home and Rosanna stared boldly at the half-hidden figure in the window, peering behind the curtains, the brilliance of yellow hair suddenly visible in the sun. And she smiled as she glimpsed Flora Dati's pale, tear-stained face before the curtains were hurriedly closed. Rosanna turned back to the crowds, smiling, acknowledging their cheers, joining Paolo's laughter as he brought his horse alongside hers until their knees touched as they crossed the narrow Ponte San Lorenzo, the wide canal beneath them shining silver in the sun.

The rider wound up the hill towards the ducal palace, coming finally into the piazza San Lorenzo, where Rosanna stared in wonder at the enormous royal palace. Now she had every right to enter those marble archways because Duke Paolo brought her here. At last she was envied. She had seen it in women's faces as they rode together through the streets. No longer was she the black outcast which Bianca had made her, but a woman in her own right.

The next hours were a whirl of happiness as she moved through the marble corridors of the palace as Paolo showed her his home. She gasped over the beauty of the rooms which were high ceilinged and immense, making her feel tiny by comparison. At last he led her to his own suite where she admired the magnificent furnishings lavishly adorned with gold tassels. His bed was gilded, the brocade draperies heavy with gold embroidery, far richer than the appointments of Castel Isola. The walls were covered with venetian glass, the rich furnishings multiplied a dozen times by the long mirrors which added depth and breadth to an already palatial room.

"How will you enjoy sleeping in that bed?" he whispered, taking her hand. "See the mirrors, we shall be completely surrounded by other lovers."

"I don't know if I'll like that."

"We can draw the curtains." He laughed, squeezing her hand in comfort. "My father had the mirrors put there so that he could watch himself making love to his mistress, but I had draperies installed, for I found it not to my taste, though sometimes I shall insist upon viewing you twenty times over, to be driven insane by your beauty."

Paolo pulled a golden-tasseled cord and red velvet curtains moved smoothly in place to hide the mirrors around the bed. Now Rosanna could understand why the royal family needed such an immense fortune to live, for it must take what her uncle made in a year to pay for the furnishing in this suite alone.

"Will I stay here with you?"

"At first, but I'll have the adjoining suite decorated to your taste, if you would like."

She said she would, and though Rosanna wondered who had occupied the rooms before her, she did not ask. Paolo was not the kind of man to be reproached about the past, or even questioned about it; so wisely she tried not to think about what happened before she knew him.

Rosanna stretched on the great bed, sinking into the vastness of the feather mattress. The bed dipped with his weight as he lay beside her, and they stared at the painted dome in the ceiling where cherubs brought a beauteous, naked Venus golden apples and bouquets of flowers.

"I'll shower you with jewels and gowns, never again will you have to bargain your body for a furred bed robe, Rosanna Sordello," he vowed softly, taking her in his arms. And she shuddered at the heat of his kiss.

The next day, while Paolo held a council meeting, Rosanna was summoned to the Duchess Maria's apartments. When the servant departed, leaving them alone, Paolo's mother scrutinized her without extending any overture of friendship, not even raising her from the floor. The Duchess stood before the kneeling girl, and Rosanna concentrated on the black jeweled slippers on her tiny feet, small and dainty as a girl's.

"So you're the new one. I must say, I don't admire his choice. Maybe Paolo is tired of our aesthetic ideal of beauty. Perhaps he wants some gypsy heat."

Though wanting to deny the fact she was a gypsy, Rosanna kept her mouth closed, shivering at the eerie sound of the Duchess's mirthless laughter.

"All right, get up."

Thankfully Rosanna creaked to her feet, her legs chilled by the cold tiles. The Duchess indicated a chair while she went to the window seat where she watched the slow moving crafts on the canal.

"You're probably wondering why I sent for you."

Perched on the edge of her chair, Rosanna nodded.

"What's the matter? Lost your tongue?"

"No, your Grace."

"I always send for Paolo's new women, I like to assess my competition. Why do you want him?"

Unnerved by the Duchess's direct questioning, Rosanna hesitated, then taking a deep breath, she spoke the truth: "I love him."

"That's a novel answer." The Duchess came to stand beside her, turning her face toward the light. Her black eyes were hard and cold, piercing like a dagger. "By God, I didn't know how novel it was. You mean it!" she exclaimed with surprise. "Your eyes are brimming with stars."

The Duchess took a pink sugar comfit from a plate beside the bed and nibbled the delicacy while she stared at Rosanna, who grew increasingly uncomfortable beneath her scrutiny.

"What other reason?"

"No other."

Raising her eyebrows, Duchess Maria tossed the confection to a beribboned lapdog, who emerged from beneath the bed. "There's no wonder he chose you. I don't think he's ever possessed a woman who hadn't some scheme for power behind her kiss. Oh, they said they

185

loved him, men are such fools, but I knew better. At least we're well rid of the Dati strumpet. Thank God her first two bastards were girls. There are rumors the boy has two men vying for the honor of fathering him—Paolo, and the Dati's chapel master."

Rosanna shifted uncomfortably in her chair, wishing the Duchess would release her from the audience. The copper-colored lapdog sniffed at her shoes, then drew back a few paces and barked, a shrill, discordant din.

"Quiet!" At the Dutchess's voice, the dog slunk to her hiding place in disgrace. "Why does Netta bark at you? Is it true what they say, are you a sorceress?"

There was a noticeable change in the Duchess's face, and her voice turned angrily demanding.

"I don't know why the dog barked, your Grace. It is not true. I'm not a witch, nor was my mother. Miserotti is the one who spreads the false rumors."

"Miserotti, and a dozen more. You're ill-fitted for this game, wench. To love my son is not protection enough at court. There are enemies waiting for us all, watching for an opportunity to knife us in the back. The only way to survive is to be one step ahead of the schemers, to stab first, and ask questions later."

Duchess Maria went to an elaborate, gold-inlaid bell pull, slipping her fingers through the filigree like a monstrous ring. "Paolo is fickle. Only if you can provide him with a new emotion, can you keep him. Your body alone won't do it."

Then a maidservant appeared at the door and Rosanna was dismissed.

It was many months before she managed to forget his mother's ominous warning. But the wonderful, exciting life at court subdued her fears—that and the reassurance of Paolo's love.

In the autumn he commissioned several portraits from the court painter, Ricasoli, the first to be of her reclining naked on a bed, his *Venus of the Morning*.

Though she had expected to dislike him, Rosanna found the artist a handsome, engaging young man who spoke intelligently about many things. She began looking forward to the portrait sittings with pleasure. At first it was difficult to overcome the discomfort of his presence while she was undressed, but when he referred to her body it was quite impersonal, as if she had been a statue instead of a woman. This professional attitude soon dispelled her embarrassment, until she too thought of her form in that manner. When she admired the blossoming painting, the woman on the canvas seemed wholly detached from herself.

When the portrait was finished, Paolo ordered it to be hung in his bedchamber, so captivated was he by Ricasoli's perfect representation of her form. The second portrait was to be of her fully clothed for public display in the reception rooms of the palace, but this was for his private collection. He was too possessive to want others viewing her nakedness.

During spring, a row of flowering trees were planted beneath Rosanna's window, so that she might enjoy their frilly pink blossoms. When the trees reached maturity she would be able to look into a sea of flowers.

Her apartments were finished the same week. The redecoration had taken longer than expected, but she had not minded the wait because her days were filled with happiness. Ignorance of the power of her enemies allowed her a brief fool's bliss.

Rosanna clapped her hands in delight as she saw the newly decorated rooms. The bedroom was especially pleasing to her, for it was exactly the way she had pictured it. The bed curtains were midnight blue velvet edged in gold and the underside of the canopy was studded with gold stars. When she lay on her back and looked up, it was like the midsummer sky winking with bright clusters of stars. She had kept it secret from Paolo. Tonight she would surprise him with it.

They supped in private in his rooms, then afterwards she drew him to the door.

"Is tonight the night?" he questioned in surprise. "You mean I can actually enter the hallowed walls of *Donna* Rosanna's bedchamber. What have I done to deserve such an honor?"

With a playful blow to his chest, Rosanna laughed at him, eagerly pulling his hand, leading him through his dressing room to her own. He looked about the scented room, remarking on the exquisite pink brocade of the walls.

"No, Paolo, this isn't my surprise. Come, close your eyes and I'll lead you to it," she invited. He laughed at her, protesting her dramatics, but nevertheless he obeyed, and stumbling over the carpets, he went where she led.

When at last she allowed him to open his eyes he held her close, thanking her for the memories of happiness the star-sprinkled canopy evoked.

"Tonight is a night for surprises. I have one for you."

With a mysterious smile, Paolo withdrew a thin rolled parchment from his robes, and going to the light, he spread the paper on her bedcover. It was a sketch for a coat of arms—a simple gold star on an azure background.

" 'Tis to remind us always of our summer love," he revealed, when she asked the significance of the heraldic arms. "The insignia is officially filed; the coat of arms is yours."

Overcome with joyous tears, Rosanna slipped into his arms, nearly swooning with the sweetness of his touch.

Her idyllic life came to an abrupt halt one hot August evening when Miserotti came uninvited to her apartments. Yesterday Paolo had been summoned back to the city on urgent business. It was with reluctance they left Castel Isola, Paolo deeply concerned over her welfare on the journey, for Rosanna was four months gone with child. The discovery of her pregnancy brought with it a soft glow, and from the first she knew the child would be a son.

The oppressive heat and the stench of the city nauseated her. Rosanna sent her supper back to the kitchens, unable to face the platter of baked capon floating in a purple sauce seasoned with Corsican wine. She went to the balcony in hope of finding a breeze, but the air was still, the tree leaves barely quivering in the twilight haze.

Her maid announced Miserotti's presence, and though Rosanna did not want to see him, she was afraid to refuse.

Sitting straight and stiff, Rosanna watched Miserotti in

anger as he related his business, listening to his silken voice. She wanted to strike him, but she dare not.

At last she said: "You deceived me. You promised his wife would be Giulietta Savarese, a girl child, and now . . . now you bring that full-blown Cione bitch as candidate."

Her final words were a minor explosion and Miserotti smiled, his evil, cunning leer. "Temper ill becomes you," he chastised, helping himself to wine. "You have what I promised—Paolo. What more do you want?"

"But you said the Savarese child," she cried, her voice cracking with suppressed anger.

"It was unfortunate the child was taken ill. I have no power over fate."

Rosanna glared at him, her heart thumping uncomfortably beneath the silk bodice of her gown. "And if I say no?"

"You cannot, 'tis already done. This past week, with Angelo of Luciano as proxy for his Grace."

Shuddering at the revelation, Rosanna was silent. Miserotti knew she was powerless to stop the marriage and once again he rejoiced at her fluttering, hopeless resistance in his trap.

"Come now, do you not satisfy him? Do you fear he will fall in love with his wife?" Miserotti asked, watching her over the crystal edge of his goblet.

"I am a fool to send a full-grown woman to his bed."

"I wouldn't say that. The Cione girl is rich and probably fertile, but I wouldn't think she's any rival. Perchance she's cold as the waters of the lake. Paolo will not tarry long in her bed. Is he already losing interest?"

"He loves me," she spat, glaring at Miserotti. "I carry his son."

"Or daughter."

"It will be a son."

"As you will, *Donna* Rosanna, as you will." Bowing, Miserotti took his leave, his black cloak fluttering like a gaunt bird of prey as he walked into the corridor.

Her anger gave way to misery and Rosanna laid her head in her hands on the table. Everything was going wrong. She had been a fool to become involved with Miserotti, though at the time she seemed quite powerless to resist. She had Paolo as he promised, but what if he enjoyed this woman? What if he tired of her now she was pregnant?

"Do you weep?"

It was his voice, and she raised her tear-stained face to meet his eyes, concerned and tender. Rosanna's smile was weak and Paolo cradled her head against the soft velvet of his doublet.

"*Cara,* please, tell me what is wrong. Am I neglecting you?"

"No. It is the babe. They say a woman is emotional at this time," she whispered, blinking away her grief.

"How is my son?" Paolo asked with a smile, slipping his hand to the hardness of her abdomen. As if it recognized the touch, the child within her womb leaped and kicked. In awe, Paolo stared at her, moving his hand again, feeling the movement of their child beneath his fingers.

"Rosanna," he breathed, "Oh, Rosanna." Tenderly he took her in his arms and she clung fiercely against him, kissing his face.

"We must not hurt the babe," he warned breathlessly, feeling his body respond to her kiss.

"He will not be hurt," she promised, smiling up at his handsome face. "Come, love me, Paolo . . . tonight I need you very much.

Chapter Thirteen

On the day the prospective bride arrived in Lorenzo, Rosanna stayed in her rooms, the hours crawling by, until it seemed as if the day would never end. She supped alone, and after the meal Paolo came to her chambers, the arrangements for Teresa Cione's accommodations complete. She was to spend the next day in meditation in the convent of Our Lady to prepare herself for the religious ceremony of her marriage.

Seeing Rosanna's pallor, he suggested they walk beside the canal in the evening breeze. The hour was enjoyable, but Rosanna found she soon tired, for her strength was diminished. Once she had sought strenuous exercise to release her energies, but now the miles of palace corridors were tiring enough.

They rested on a bench in the deserted courtyard and eventually Rosanna plucked up courage to speak to Paolo about his intended bride. "Is she pretty?"

"She is not ugly, but pretty . . . no."

"Her hair, what color is it?"

"Brown, I think. A light brown."

"And her eyes?"

"I don't know what color, perhaps they are brown

also," he said, with a smile. "You are the perfect example of a jealous mistress."

Rosanna flushed and turned away in an effort to hide her pain. To Paolo it was amusing to answer questions about his bride, for he saw none of her misery. To him Teresa was a duty. Men did not often love their wives, or women their husbands; marriage was to beget heirs, or riches—in Paolo's case, both.

"Will you enjoy her?"

"I don't know yet," he replied honestly, "I barely know the woman."

"But you will be husband to her."

"Of course. I do not have to love her for that."

Tears pounded in her throat, painful, bursting. With blurred eyes, Rosanna plucked lamely at the narrow grass strip beside the bench, taking green blades to shred in her fingers, deliberately avoiding his eyes.

"*Cara*, for a man that is automatic. It is lust."

"With me also?" she managed after a long time.

"No, you know it is not. With you it is paradise," Paolo whispered, seizing her hand, extracting the crumpled green-stained stalks. "With her it won't be the same at all."

"How can you tell? You said you don't even know her yet."

"I know. Before I'd ever seen her, I knew ... and so should you."

"I don't want you to go to her, but I know you must. You're right, I am jealous," she admitted as he held her close. "To think of her with you like that ..."

"Then don't think of it."

His solution was a typical male one, but far too hard to accomplish. Snuggling her face against his neck, Rosanna brushed her lips upon his flesh where his skin rose warmly tanned above the white frill of his shirt.

Paolo smiled, shivering at her caress. "Will you also make me swear not to enjoy myself?" he whispered with a grin.

"Perhaps I should, but I won't. I'm not that much of a fool. Though I'll will her to be cold to you, to spurn your passion as a dutiful wife should; then, within your heart you will always stay faithful to me."

On a brilliant Wednesday morning in September, 1456, Duke Paolo wed his bride. The populace went wild with joy over the nuptials, and church bells rang a deafening carillon to echo their enthusiasm. Flowers were trampled beneath the horses' hooves as the procession rode through the streets, and the fountains in the public squares ran wine instead of water. The deafening cheers of the crowd drifted to Rosanna's ears as she watched behind the curtains of her window as Paolo rode by in his wedding finery, his tiny bride beside him, blushing and shy in her flowing white gown. In sick anguish Rosanna was reminded of the day she had glimpsed a tearful Flora Dati at her window in the Via San Bernardo. Now it was she, while his child fluttered within her womb, insistent as a caged bird. Pray God, this was not the beginning of her defeat as it had been for the Dati woman, there were far too many envious courtiers anxious to hasten her downfall.

Rosanna stayed away from the banquet where the guests included envoys from the King of Naples and the nephew of Cosimo di Medici. Though Paolo had invited her, she could not bear to watch him with his bride.

In late afternoon, the meal was at an end, and the other festivities began, crowned at their finish by the task of putting Teresa in her groom's bed. The laughing wedding party would pass her door, and that would be one more agony to endure, though even then her pain would not be over, for her imagination could supply the conclusion to the day.

Curiosity drew her to the doorway when she heard their steps in the corridor. There was drunken laughter and many voices. Opening the door a crack, Rosanna peered through the slit unobserved. They were coming down the long gallery, filing past the door, gentlemen and ladies of the bedchamber, and for a moment she could not distinguish the new duchess amongst the company. Then she recognized the small figure in the midst of the procession. At close quarters she could see that Teresa Cione was not beautiful, but she was attractive in a quiet way, her features small and even. Falling from a white linen cap, her brown hair hung loose about her shoulders, shining like silk, reaching below her waist.

Gently Rosanna closed the door, feeling weak, until her knees buckled alarmingly. She sank upon the floor listening to their footsteps dying away. They were probably outside Paolo's bedchamber now. How would he look when he saw his new bride? Would he smile at her and clasp her hand, would he kiss that innocent child's face drawing her close against the fineness of his body? With a sob of anguish, Rosanna ground her clenched fists into her eyes in an effort to stop her tears, but they flowed nevertheless, hot and painful.

Twilight was gone when she finally dried her eyes. Darkness was solid in the room and stumbling to the windows she wrenched them open, stepping onto the balcony in the warm night air. The silver moon was rising behind the blue roof of the Duomo. Did Paolo and his bride lie close on the royal bed, did they kiss or stare at the rising moon? And when he joined in passion with his tiny bride did he give any thought to her waiting alone?

Hate seethed within her bosom until she clenched her fists, smiting the vine-covered wall without feeling pain. Teresa Cione was her enemy, for she sought to own her lover, did own him in the eyes of the church. Whatever children Paolo gave her would be the future rulers of Lorenzo, but the swelling seed within her own body would be nothing more than bastard. In a spasm of hatred Rosanna cursed the bride; whatever grew in her womb would wither, whatever son she produced for Lorenzo would be cursed from the day of his birth. Then she remembered Paolo. The son would be his also. Whoever the mother of the child, the son was still his. In a flicker of pity she relented, for his sake alone, glancing across the court to the windows of the bedchamber, wondering suddenly if Teresa knew about her. A smile of triumph curved her mouth at the thought. No, of course he would not have told her. There would be great pleasure in their first encounter, for whatever else Teresa might have of him, she alone had his love.

Duchess Teresa drummed her tiny foot impatiently on the floor, watching the clock. It was past midnight and still he had not come. This was outrageous. Only her third night of marriage and her husband was already neglecting her. Mother had told her to insist he come to her bed, for the first month at least, until she conceived. The bed looked so soft and inviting she was almost sorry she had promised to fulfill her mother's wishes. Although her husband was very handsome, it was really much nicer to sleep alone. In the daytime he was nicer than at night. If only he had stopped at a kiss, or a caress, she would have even enjoyed him at night. But it was that other upon which he insisted, she did not enjoy, when he touched her body in unseemly places. It was true women paid for Eve's sin by bearing children. They began to pay at conception. To think there were strange creatures who enjoyed such experiences, and with other men beside their husbands. To endure a husband was punishment enough, but to take lovers was insanity.

Teresa thrust the thoughts from her mind staring at the bright moonlight filtering through the gold damask curtains at her windows. Perhaps Paolo ... there, for the first time she had thought of him by name. With a smile of pleasure, she lay back on the bed. She was becoming used to him already. For days she had thought of him only as his Grace, even after they were married, but now that he was just Paolo, somehow he seemed nicer. Maybe he played cards with his gentlemen, for sometimes Father gambled till the early hours. If she went to him he might allow her to watch. He would probably sit her on his lap and kiss her like Father did, then pop sweetmeats into her mouth. Yes, she would go to find him.

Pulling on her crimson bed robe, Teresa opened the door, walking into the deserted corridor outside. She was not sure which was Paolo's chamber. Yesterday, when she had been walking along the palace corridors to acquaint herself with her new home, she had noticed him go through a door across the court. She would try that room.

Filled with a spirit of adventure, Teresa walked along the moonlit passages, working her way around the courtyard past dozens of closed doors until she found the right one. It was quiet inside, but light shone in a narrow banner beneath the closed door, so someone was awake. She would smile and curtsy to him, begging his leave to watch. He was really a nice husband, far nicer than some other girls' husbands. He had always been kind to her, and when he kissed her softly, her heart fluttered. After all he really couldn't help being a man. . . .

She pushed gently on the door, it was unlatched and swung quietly on oiled hinges. At first she could see no one, then she was aware of a movement from the window and saw Paolo standing there, his golden doublet bright. She was about to speak to him, when she realized there was someone else in the room.

Teresa gasped as she saw a woman move toward him, a strange woman with high cheekbones and masses of black hair hanging down her back, but strangest of all she was naked to the waist. Paolo slipped his arms about her, his hands sliding over her flesh.

Crying out in indignation, Teresa stepped forward. The occupants of the room stared at her in surprise, recognizing her anger and dismay. Her voice seemed to be frozen in her throat as she met her husband's eyes. Wantonly the woman smiled at him and without haste she removed his hands, placing them on her waist. Teresa found her tongue, her words punctuated by sobs of distress.

"Paolo . . . why . . . who . . . who is she?"

"I think you have lost your way, Teresa. Have you forgotten, your bedchamber is on the far side of the court?" he snapped, not bothering to cover the woman's nakedness. "When I want to speak to you, I will send for you. It is late. Go to bed."

"Paolo . . . I waited for you . . . I . . ."

"My time is my own, *donna,* and what I do with it is none of your affair. Now, will you go to your chamber, or shall I take you there?"

The woman disentangled herself from his embrace, and taking a cloak from a chest beneath the window, drew it about herself. A smile was on her face, lifting her eyes into a curious slant above her high cheekbones. Her mouth was full and with the red tip of her tongue she slowly wet her lips.

"Your Grace," she said, dropping a curtsy.

Affronted by her audacity Teresa backed towards the door, not knowing what to say, for the situation was a shocking surprise. There had been no word breathed to her about a mistress, though she had wondered, for it was not unusual for a man to keep several. Yet here in the palace, within sight of her own bedchamber. How could Paolo flaunt the creature before her?

"Come, I will return you to your room."

Grasping her arm, Paolo marched her from the bedchamber, propelling her rapidly along the corridor. Without a word he wrenched open the door, thrusting her inside.

"Good night, Teresa. I'll see you in the morning, then we shall discuss your rights . . . and mine."

He stalked away, his eyes hard, returning to that room across the court. With a cry of distress, Teresa fell upon the bed, burying her head upon the gold-covered pillows with the embroidered lion of Lorenzo crushed beneath her face.

When she first woke, Teresa wondered if everything had been a bad dream, but as she grew wider awake, she knew it was not. Rage possessed her, tears coming to her eyes as she recalled her terrible humiliation. What a fool she had been. How they must have laughed about her behind her back—Paolo and that woman.

A sharp knock sounded on the door and her serving woman entered bearing a tray of fresh rolls and wine.

"I don't want anything. Take it back," she mumbled, turning her blotchy face away, not wanting Anna to see her swollen eyes and know she had been weeping.

"You must eat something, your Grace."

"No, I couldn't."

"Are you not well?"

"Very well, thank you."

"Then what is it?"

"Who is she?"

"She, your Grace?"

"Stop it, you know who I mean. All of you have known all the time and no one told me. You let me find out by myself . . . and . . . I . . . almost liked him too."

Anna took the sobbing girl against her breast, comforting her mistress with soothing, clucking sounds. "There, there, don't cry. No one told you because it's not important. We weren't trying to deceive you. A man has vices a woman wouldn't understand, but it's nothing to fret over. There, you'll spoil your pretty eyes."

"Who is she?"

"She calls herself Rosanna Sordello."

"Is she Sordello's daughter, the merchant?"

"No, I don't think so, his sister's child I heard."

"Oh, Anna, I saw her .. them . . . together."

"Mother of God, together? In bed?"

"No," Teresa wailed as fresh tears spilled from her reddened eyes, "but they might as well have been."

"You can leave."

A man's voice rang out from the open doorway, startling the women, who stared round-eyed at the Duke.

"Yes, at once, your Grace." Anna curtsied, and casting a pitying glance at her tearful mistress, she scurried from the room.

Paolo closed the door and walked to the bed. Teresa looked at him, noticing how stern he appeared in his black doublet, his face set in anger.

"Good morning . . . Husband," she tendered, hastily thrusting back her dishevelled locks, attempting a smile.

"Good morning. Aren't you going to eat your breakfast?"

"No . . . I . . ."

"Eat it."

Paolo thrust the tray into her hands and strode to the window. With a crash, he drew back the heavy curtains, then flung open a window, glancing up at the cloudy sky.

"Is it going to rain?" Teresa asked, attempting to be cheerful.

"I don't know and I'm totally unconcerned with the weather," he snapped, returning to her side. "Teresa."

"Yes." The way he said her name sent a chill of fear creeping along her spine, for he made it such a harsh, angry word.

"About last night."

She looked away, not meeting his eyes, staring at the broken roll on her plate and she crumbled the bread as he spoke.

"I am entitled to my privacy. When I made you my wife I did not relinquish my right to life. What I do beyond your bedchamber is no concern of yours, do you understand?"

Miserable, she nodded, her eyes filling with tears.

"In future, you will never enter a room within my private suite unless you have my express permission. These are your apartments. They are, I believe, quite spacious and well appointed. I shall come to you when I desire, and I shall send for you when I wish to speak to you. Is that clear?"

Again she nodded, crystal drops sliding down her nose, trickling salty upon her mouth.

"You are never again to humiliate me in the presence of another."

"Humiliate you," Teresa burst, finding her voice at last. "You! What about me? I was humiliated beyond endurance, to see you with that . . that ... woman. Handling her while I watched."

"Had you been in your chamber where you belonged, your modesty would not have been affronted. I make no apologies to you, and if you are wise, you will demand none."

"I don't want apologies. I want her to leave."

"She was here before you."

"But I am the duchess," Teresa shrieked, flinging the tray from her bed to crash on the tiles in a puddle of spilled wine and broken glass.

"In the name of God, control yourself," Paolo cried, kicking aside the debris. "Do you want the servants to know what a spoiled child you are?"

"Is that worse than them knowing about her?"

He stood straddle-legged beside her bed, his arms folded across the heavy chain around his neck, obscuring the flash of jewels, and he stared down at her. "No one but you has objected to her presence," he said evenly, his brows knitted in a frown. "I love Rosanna Sordello, and I do not want her to leave. Must I remind you, Madam, you are Duchess only because I married you. I am the Duke. It is I who rule Lorenzo, not you. There are no orders to be issued by the Duchess Teresa. Is that clear?"

"Yes."

"I will keep a mistress without asking your permission. I kept one before your arrival, and see no reason to change because of it. And if you are interested, Madam, the lady carries my child." Paolo smiled at her gasp of dismay, and he stooped to take her hand, dutifully kissing her limp fingers. "Good morning, Teresa. I will tell the servants to send you another breakfast."

Chapter Fourteen

Snow lay thinly frosted over the rooftops, clinging white and fluffy to tree branches stretched bare toward the gray sky. Pink-faceted marble showed in patches, glittering damply in the struggling sunlight as the clouds parted for a few minutes, then closed, lowering with threatening cold blasts of wind.

Across the roofs of buildings at the far end of the square, the blue domes of San Lorenzo peered uncertainly from their white cover, and the great bell clanged solemnly, calling the faithful to mass. Slowly they emerged from their palazzos, reluctantly forsaking their roaring hearths—fat, red-nosed burgers in rich, fur-lined robes, urged through the snow by pious wives who clutched leather-bound prayer books in mittened hands. Children ran over the piazza snowballing each other, laughing as they gathered ammunition from the steps of the cathedral, or from the pedestal of the mounted statue of the first Duke Lorenzo who stared solemnly down at them from his war charger, huge icicles hanging from his hooked metal nose.

Rosanna sighed with pleasure as she watched the color-ful scene, and she huddled deeper inside her fur robes, pulling the soft ermine snug about her ears. Her body was swollen and it was difficult to wrap herself comfortably in the cloak. The child in her womb lurched, its foot kicking vigorously against her hip. Soon her time would come; February by her own reckoning, and she would bear a son.

The guards moved to attention on the palace steps and Rosanna saw the Duchess Teresa going to mass. Her heart missed an uneasy beat as she realized Paolo walked beside his wife, solicitously taking her arm lest she slip on the icy steps. He strode jauntily over the snow-covered piazza, a fixed smile on his face beneath his black fur hat, and though Rosanna leaned far down from her balcony viewpoint, he did not look at her window. With narrowed eyes she studied Teresa critically, finding her body much thicker beneath her purple-furred robe. It was over two months since the duchess's miscarriage. Paolo had not visited his wife since except for social visits. Could it be that tonight they would try again for an heir to the throne? Was that why he accompanied her on foot through the January snow: a humble pilgrimage to pray for her fecundity? With a twisted smile, Rosanna leaned heavily against the wall, finding her heart thumping uncomfortably as if it would leap from her breast.

Sickness, compounded by jealousy, overcame her as she pictured her lover lying beside his duchess in the gold and white bed in her lavish apartments. She told herself Teresa found no pleasure in her husband's body, only fulfilling her duty as a Christian wife by submitting to his lovemaking.

Her reason told her this, but behind it was the nagging doubt that Teresa would enjoy him, or worse still that he would enjoy Teresa. Paolo was a passionate man. Would he be content to remain celibate throughout her confinement, when she lay helplessly abed to await the impending birth? To think of him with another made her faint with jealousy. Betta Peruzzi had openly flirted with him at the Christmas ball, had he visited Luca's pretty daughter in secret when he accepted their supper invitation last week? Or perhaps Flora Dati had secured an audience with him. He had known many women, some of them still at court waiting for his eye to wander, watching for her own decline in favor, gloating cruelly over every night he stayed away from her bedchamber.

With an anguished sob, Rosanna buried her face in her hands and rushed inside to the warmth of her apartments. Her sobs were deep and relieving, until she felt drained and at last she slept to dream of the summer she went to his room at Villa Sordello, reliving that night in the firelit bedchamber while the storm raged unchecked outside.

Paolo came to her room after mass. Finding her asleep, he stooped to kiss her cheek, surprised to taste dried tears salty upon her skin. He sat beside her studying the mound of their child in the bedcovers, overwhelmed by emotion for her. One of the servants must have whispered why he attended mass with Teresa this morning, and what had been the public prayer they repeated, voicing the intention of the solemn mass. Tonight, God willing, he would beget an heir. Poor Rosanna. It was for that she wept. He would have done anything to spare her pain, but to deny Lorenzo an heir was one concession he could not make.

Drowsily, Rosanna opened her eyes, feeling his hand on her cheek. With a gasp of surprise, she grasped his fingers, kissing his hand, her eyes sparkling with happiness. "How long have you been there?"

"Ten minutes or so," he replied, stooping to kiss her, surprised when she clung to him so desperately, emotion making her lips tremble and her dark eyes fill with tears.

"Oh, God, Paolo, I've needed you with me," she whispered, her voice choked with sobs as she stroked his hair. "Please stay and share a meal with me."

He knew he should decline, for he had promised the afternoon to Teresa; then, at three, he had a council meeting. But she was so lovely, so pathetic in her need. "Yes, I'll stay, *cara,* for a little while," he assured.

Rosanna rang for her women and ordered the meal, her face lit with pleasure. Her movements were lighthearted, almost giving lie to her advanced pregnancy. She carried the child high and in the cunningly fashioned gowns she had designed for herself, her condition was almost concealed. Paolo watched her, glad that she did not mention the mass, or ask him any questions about Teresa.

With Rosanna he was at ease, relaxed in the glowing warmth of her room.

The meal was brought and a servant mended the fire till it blazed roaringly up the black chimney. This afternoon Paolo found himself falling in love with her all over again, delighting in her welcome.

The grayness of the sky was coldly forbidding and beyond the window the wind howled, buffeting the glass. And presently he noticed it was snowing. They watched the winter storm, with its swirling flakes burying Lorenzo in a shroud of icy white, which danced madly in the wind.

"Did you watch me leave this morning?" he asked unable to contain the question any longer.

"I was looking at the snow, thinking how pretty everything looked . . . yes, I saw you." She said no more and he was glad, gratitude voiced by the renewed pressure of his hand on her arm as he took her gently against him, as always the child forcing them apart. Paolo held her shoulders and smiled down at the thrusting mound of blue which parted their bodies.

"Already my son comes between us to deny his father the pleasure of his will."

She smiled at his whispered words, trembling at the happiness of her thoughts. "Am I still desirable then?"

"Yes," he laughed lightly, kissing her forehead. "Because I love you, and for you my love is always mingled with desire."

From the piazza the clock struck another hour resounding solemnly through the falling snow and he glanced reluctantly towards the door. He should have left an hour ago, yet he still did not want to go. In his mistress's chambers he was a whole man again, master of his destiny, instead of a puppet manipulated by treacherous courtiers, or deceived by ill advice from his greedy city council. With Rosanna Sordello he was a man. She allowed him the dignity of his station in public, but alone he was forever her lover.

"Can you not stay a little longer, Paolo?" she whispered, seeing his eye on the door at the clock's chime, tears coming once more to her eyes at the thought of his departure.

"Another half hour, no more, *cara*. There are duties

to which I must attend, and pleasant though this is, my council waits."

He lay beside her on the green damask coverlet, absently stroking her hair while he talked about plans for a new addition to the palace. Ricasoli was to paint the ceiling with scenes from the life of the first Duke of Lorenzo who had founded the city.

She watched him, suddenly wishing she was not pregnant, that he would make love to her. His kisses would be aflame with passion instead of turning guarded when his intensity overcame his wisdom. "I wish it was still summer," she whispered. "Do you remember how we rode to Castel Isola? How we loved beneath the stars?"

Paolo did not answer, but his breathing quickened at the memory. After a long silence he said: "Yes, I remember."

"It has been such a long time, Paolo . . ."

His eyes were grave in the firelight and she caught his hands to her face, lavishing kisses on his slender fingers that used to fire her body with passionate madness at their caressing. Presently she slept, and he slipped away, arriving at his council chamber two hours late, much to the annoyance of his councilors who had paced the chilly vestibule awaiting his arrival.

And later that night, when he completed his duty to Lorenzo in the bedroom of his wife, the coupling was no more than an obligation to his people.

February was unusually cold. The populace of Lorenzo huddled inside their homes crouched over the meager heat of the fireside, finding their palatial marble rooms as cold as a tomb in the severe winter weather.

Aunt Magdela surprised Rosanna by sending Cia to assist at her lying-in. Cia told her the Sordello finances had declined after heavy losses from a storm at sea, and a recent fire in the warehouses. She had not been issued a new gown all year, and her impending betrothal had been cancelled for want of a dowry which Ugo Sordello decided he could ill afford at the moment. Rosanna assured Cia if she wanted to marry, she would ask Duke Paolo to take her into their household and he would provide her dowry. But Cia tearfully declined the offer. In anger, Matteo had joined a pirate crew and she had not seen him for four months.

Pain was a stabbing, thrusting reality as Rosanna threshed beneath the bedcovers to escape her tormentor. Another burning thrust, and she bit her lips to keep back her cries.

"Don't stop the screams, 'twill make your labor easier," the blousy midwife suggested, with a gaping, toothless grin.

Afraid to release her slim grasp on control, Rosanna ignored the well-meant advice. Now, for a moment, the pain was eased, and she breathed a sigh of relief, relaxing her stomach muscles in blissful contentment. From beyond the window, sleet showered in the howling wind, crashing the shutters like pebbles against the wood.

Another pain rocked her hips, and this time her screams tore loose, while old Ghita nodded approval, sponging her sweating brow with a damp cloth.

"How much longer?" Rosanna managed through clenched jaws, her teeth gritted to endure the pain.

The midwife shrugged. "Who knows. An hour, a day." She thrust a burly arm under the covers to make the examination, jabbing carelessly inside Rosanna's soft body till she winced with pain. Ghita's face broke into a second toothless beam. "You're lucky. Not long now."

Rosanna braced herself trying to remember to push down with the contractions as Ghita had explained, but usually she forgot. The child within her did not and she could feel the forceful, downward thrust of its body. She was bleeding for wetness ran upon her thighs, as Paolo's child struggled to be born.

Ghita offered a sip of wine, but Rosanna refused the drink. The midwife sponged her brow, stroking back her bedraggled black hair with rough hands. "Poor little girl, a man doesn't seem so fine now, does he," Ghita crooned as she sponged, talking to herself. "All of you cry out like the devil himself was tormenting you, 'tis the payment for sin. The fineness of a summer night is fast forgot in the labor bed. But a man, that's a different side of the coin. He's probably astride another little fool, while you sweat and cry."

Rosanna told her to be quiet, not wanting to be tormented by the old woman's rambling, but Ghita was deaf to her words. Through the blinding torment of pain the midwife's face swam in waves of red and her voice echoed, sermonizing and mocking in one, while Rosanna lay helpless.

"Duke Paolo's a fine man. Make no mistake, there's many can attest to his virility. I delivered his lady mother of both her sons," she added, splashing cold water in a shocking douse on Rosanna's face, laughing when she gasped. "Tell me, was he worth this? Was lusting after the man flesh of him payment enough for this?"

Hands to her ears, Rosanna tried to drown out the old crone's words. Calling for another servant, she listened to her own voice as Ghita's cackle rose above her feeble cries, to drown them completely in a gale of laughter which joined with the wind outside. Still screaming, Rosanna was suddenly freed from pain, until she walked on the mountain with her pet goat. The wind was cool and the air clear. Below was Lorenzo with its pink marble palace, and she was singing a child's simple song . . .

"*Donna* Rosanna, can you hear me?"

Blinking, she opened her eyes, to find Cia leaning over her, gently sponging her brow. She was cold, for the bedcovers had been stripped back and roped sheets were tied to the bedposts.

"Here, pull on these. When you feel the pain, pull hard."

With the next contraction Rosanna did as she was told, finding the strength of the cloth gave her some relief.

"Oh, the *bambino,* I can see his little head, golden curls like his father's. Push harder, *Donna* Rosanna . . ."

With a final bursting, slipping thrust, the burden was expelled and Rosanna sank back, weak with exhaustion. Cia and another servant took the baby, who squalled like an angered cat, wrapping it in a blanket before they turned back to the new mother.

Rosanna watched them with blurring vision as if they attended another. The afterbirth was lifted up and she heard it plop in a bowl. It was red and bloody like a slaughtered animal and she turned away, burying her face in the soaking pillow. The cord was tied and cut, the baby cleansed. Cia was leaning above her brushing back her hair, offering weak broth, while the other girl pulled the blood-soaked draw sheets from under her weary body.

It seemed as if she had slept for hours when they brought the baby, cleansed and swathed in a soft white blanket. The bundle was tiny, warmly fragile as they placed it in the crook of her arm. "What is it?"

"A son, of course. A fine, healthy, manchild, the picture of his Grace," Cia informed proudly, tucking the infant safely against the warmth of his mother's body.

There was a commotion at the door—a man's voice, loud above the protests of the women. Then Paolo strode in the room, coming to her side where he knelt beside the bed, his face tender.

With a sigh of accomplishment, Rosanna opened the blanket and showed him his son. "A boy," she said.

"Yes, they told me."

"He is like you."

"No, he only looks like a baby, red and angry."

"Isn't he lovely?"

"Adorable," Paolo whispered, taking her hand, and with a smile of pleasure he touched the soft face of his tiny son. "What shall we call him?"

"I don't know. I could never decide."

Paolo motioned for the women to take the child. Sitting on the edge of the bed, he gently slipped his arm about her shoulders. With a worried frown he observed the pallor of her cheeks, her eyes huge dark pools in her pinched face. The labor had been long and hard, a hell of pain for her, and for him hours of worry because they would not let him near the lying-in chamber.

"Thank you, *angela,* for giving me a son," he whispered, bending to kiss her brow. "Was it terrible? If only I could have taken your pain. I wanted it to be quick for you, but it wasn't; then, when I heard you cry out, I was sorry for what I'd made you endure."

"Don't be sorry. I felt no blame towards you," Rosanna assured.

"*Cara.*" He kissed her mouth, tasting blood where she had bitten the flesh, and Paolo found tears in his eyes. How she had suffered. How very much she loved him. At last he whispered: "I'll leave so that you can rest. Tomorrow we will discuss his name. Get well, dear heart, so we can ride to Castel Isola in the spring."

Rosanna watched him leave then she turned her head into the fresh pillow and slept the sleep of exhaustion.

During the night Rosanna dreamed of her mother. It was as if she entered the bedchamber and sat beside the bed, her hand cold and thin, but when she spoke, her mother's voice was warm with love. She spoke of the child and when she stooped over the bed to kiss her, she told her to call the boy Niccolo. "It was your father's name," she said.

When Rosanna awoke to pale winter sunshine, Cia was bringing a bowl of steaming broth and a loaf of fresh bread. Finding she was ravenously hungry, Rosanna devoured the loaf, sopping up the broth while Cia beamed at her as if she was an obedient child.

"There, now your strength will come back. Do you want to see his Grace? He's been pacing the corridor this past hour. We showed him his lusty son, but he insists on seeing you."

Rosanna nodded her assent, making Cia brush her hair and bring a fresh nightgown before he was admitted.

Paolo came to the bed, his stride eager and quick. "How well you look."

"Good morning, your Grace," she whispered, with her old smile, and he squeezed her hand, coming to sit beside her. Cia politely withdrew, leaving them alone. Paolo drew Rosanna in his arms, settling comfortably upon the mound of covers.

"Did you see your son?"

"Yes, screaming loudly. He has an enormous set of lungs." Paolo laughed. "They'll bring him to you when I leave, if you wish, but you must not tire yourself with the babe. The women can tend him till you are stronger. I've arranged for a wet nurse to be brought to your apartments."

"Am I not to nurse him myself?"

"That's your decision. You must do nothing to injure your health," he insisted gravely, smoothing her hair. This morning it had regained some of its luster, not harsh and dense as it had been last night.

"I won't tire myself. I want him to be entirely our son."

"Very well, but she will stay, just in case."

Rosanna smiled at his stubborn words, caressing the bronzed skin of his hand, then suddenly she remembered her dream. "Paolo, did you select a name yet?"

"No, we were going to discuss it this morning. Don't you remember?"

"I thought perhaps you had your own preference."

"No . . . what is it to be?" He grinned, looking down at her smiling face. "I know you well enough to understand by that question you've already selected it."

"Niccolo, but we'll call him Nicci."

"Niccolo," he repeated, accustoming himself to the sound. "Yes, I like it. I had an uncle Niccolo who was killed in the war, that's why my cousin is king of Luciano. Niccolo will do handsomely. Is that all, no other names?"

"Does he need others?" Rosanna asked in surprise.

"I have five myself. Paolo Andrea Federico Mari di Lorenzo. It's impressive, is it not?"

"Yes, but so formal for a baby. I think Nicci will be enough."

He stooped to kiss the tip of her nose. "So do I. Nicci it shall be."

Chapter Fifteen

Paolo chased Rosanna over the courtyard, his laughter ringing out, carefree as a boy. With a shout of triumph he caught his quarry, imprisoning her hands above her head.

Teresa simmered with anger when she saw them, but she was unable to turn away, drawn by a morbid fascination to watch them together. When she first heard the woman's voice outside, she should have known who it was. Paolo frolicked with her like a stableboy, completely forgetting his dignity. In curiosity Teresa watched them in the shadows, staring into each others faces. Paolo released her hands and the forward hussy stroked his hair, slipping her hand inside the unfastened neck of his doublet, down under his shirt. And Paoli, who should have been ashamed of himself, drew her tight against him, pressing her body back against the pillar. The Sordello wench smiled, almost melting against him as their body contours mingled in fluid embrace. Why, it was as if she liked it, not only his kisses, but the feel of him against her too. It was disgusting.

"Good morning, your Grace."

Teresa gasped in surprise at the voice, turning to see Miserotti standing in the shadows. With a frigid smile, she acknowledged his presence. And when she turned back to the couple in the courtyard she found they were gone.

"If you are looking for your husband, *Donna* Teresa, I believe he's in his chambers."

"No, he's probably in hers."

"His, hers, they are the same. She shares them both with him."

Attempting to smile, Teresa faced him, clasping her trembling hands together in the folds of her yellow gown. "Why are you telling me this? I'm already aware of the disgraceful situation that exists in the palace."

"A man will take his pleasure, your Grace."

She did not reply, finding her lip tremble and, absurdly, tears filled her eyes.

"It is even suggested, if this child you carry does not live, he will have her son legitimized."

"Never," Teresa cried, finding her voice. "She can have all of him but that. The right to bear the heir to the throne is mine."

"Of course, *donna*. But his Grace is blind to advice from his council. Already the boy is in his will: my spiritual son, Niccolo . . . I fear he is under the spell of witchcraft. They say Rosanna Sordello is a witch. It's common knowledge her mother was one. Some say in the mountains she kept a goat. We know the devil often assumes that shape. You have a formidable enemy, *Donna* Teresa. There are those amongst us who would see the enemy vanquished. I believe it shall be, don't you?"

"I hate her."

"Then do not endure the humiliation of her presence. You are the duchess, when your husband is away next week, you can command at will. Good day, your Grace."

"Be careful, you'll step on Beppo," Teresa snapped, pushing her away as the tiny dog yapped beneath her feet.

"Forgive me, your Grace. I didn't see the dog," Rosanna apologized, dropping a curtsy, lowering her face to hide the flush of distress the other woman's sharp words caused. In the background the other ladies tittered at her reproof, glad she was once again in disfavor.

Teresa stared at the bent, dark head. Not even decently covered, she thought with a scowl, flaunting that black hair with only a gold band and ribbons in it. Her husband probably liked it that way. With a tightening of her small mouth, Teresa pictured Paolo sinking his hands into the hair, stroking it, the way he had tried to do with hers on their wedding night. That was for wantons, and wanton was exactly what this baggage was. "Get up," she snapped impatiently. "I want my embroidery brought to me."

"Yes, your Grace." Ignoring the other women's stares, Rosanna went to the velvet-covered stool beside the Duchess' chair, where she picked up the colorful embroidery in its wooden frame. The dog ran beneath her feet and trying to avoid the yapping animal, Rosanna caught a box of silks with her elbow, spilling them in gaudy disarray on the marble tiles.

Teresa screamed at her in shrill anger and Rosanna dropped the embroidery hoop. "Clumsy imbecile."

"I'm sorry, your Grace, I'll pick them up."

"Isn't it enough that I'm humiliated at every turn. Must I be waited on by my husband's whore?" Teresa demanded, her round face flushed, her mouth quivering in anger.

Rosanna straightened, up, placing the silks on the Duchess's lap, her own face colored at the insult. "I did not intend to cause your Grace any inconvenience," she said shortly, her face tight.

"To look at you causes me inconvenience," Teresa hissed, her eyes narrowed, and she snatched the embroidery from Rosanna's hand.

"Then I shall withdraw from your presence."

"Do that. You may withdraw completely from the city of Lorenzo. Only then shall I be satisfied."

A gasp went round the room and the other women waited, their eyes round and expectant, wondering what would happen next.

Rosanna drew herself up straight and tall before her seated mistress. "Very well, your Grace, the city tires me in summertime. I shall go to Castel Isola."

The others gasped again, and Teresa caught her breath in anger, but Rosanna did not give her time to speak.

"When you want your husband, Madam, you may look for him there. He has already done his husbandly duty by

213

you. Your belly is swollen, and now you bore him; so he will follow me, because even when I carried his son, *Donna* Teresa, I never bored him. Nicci may be a love child, but he is stronger than any you will give him." With this she turned, stalking haughtily from the room.

Teresa collapsed in her chair, gasping with shock at the angry speech. Her ladies clustered around her solicitously fanning her and bringing smelling salts.

Rosanna marched through the silent corridors of the palace, tears of angry humiliation stinging her cheeks. She gave no thought to the unpleasant consequence of her impassioned words; though true, it was not usually voiced so bluntly. Reaching the door of her apartment she ran inside, giving vent to her emotion in a hysterical fit of sobbing. She would leave Lorenzo and never again would she bear the insults of that woman.

Early next morning her entourage left the palace, carrying chests of clothing and boxes of household equipment. Baby Nicci rode in a litter with his nurse, while Rosanna was mounted on the magnificent chestnut mare Paolo had given her on his son's birth. She would not have hidden inside a litter for any reason. She would ride where she could be seen, proud and defiant. Hoping the duchess watched from her window, Rosanna glanced up as she passed, but could see nothing beyond the golden curtains.

This morning she was not quite as confident as she had been yesterday. She would have to wait at least another week for Paolo's return. And she hoped his anger would be directed only at his wife for ordering her banishment. Sometimes an uneasy thought entered her mind, though she forced it out. What if Paolo did not come after her? What if he was shocked by her tactless display of anger before the ladies of the bedchamber? She was sure her exact words would be related.

The party turned out of the piazza, moving downhill, the horses slow with their burden on the steep, cobbled streets. Townsfolk stared at her in curiosity, knowing who she was. Perhaps they wondered why she was abroad without male escort, but thankfully they did not yet know what had happened inside the ducal palace. They would hear soon enough.

Nicci cried shrilly from inside the litter and Caterina sang a lullaby to silence him. After a few minutes the wails subsided and Rosanna smiled to herself as she pictured Paolo's son sleeping, his little fist doubled into his eyes, already the image of his royal father. Her fears were unfounded after all. The Duke would follow her, if only to see his son. But the realization was a bleak one, for she did not wish to be merely the mother of his child—she must be his sweetheart too.

Outside the city walls her spirits lifted, for the June morning was beautiful. The sky was blue, and a cool breeze swept from the mountains, fanning their faces to assuage the heat of the sun. Along the hedgerows flowers bloomed, wild roses twined about the bushes, and the orchards hung heavy with ripening fruit. Upon the hillsides beyond the city, vines terraced the earth with green leaves, bearing heavy this year with the promise of a season of exceptional wine.

As the horses began the slow climb, winding into the foothills of the mountains, Rosanna reined in, looking behind her to the city. A pang of sadness stabbed deep in her breast at the sight of the buildings sparkling in the sun, the traffic on the canals black dots against the ribbons of water.

The foliage gave way to boulders, scattered gray amongst the chestnut and spreading oaks. As the path wound higher, tall fir and spruce blocked the horizon, and amongst the towering evergreens wild animals hid, startled by the horses. The scrambling of the shodden hooves on loose rocks sent showers plummeting from the trail, tinkling and thudding amongst the scrub. The litter creaked and swayed, waking the baby from his slumber, but his coos were of pleasure at the new surroundings, instead of anger at the disturbance.

Rosanna drew a cloak about her, finding the breeze uncomfortably chill at the mountain crest. Below, she saw the gleaming water of Lago di Paradiso, dark firs rimming the edge with black shadows, green again in the flitting rays of the sun. Birds called plaintively from the sandy lakeshore, while high above the mountain peak, a falcon circled, to drop a moment later, straight as an arrow to its prey. The smell of the water tainted the breeze and the sound of tiny waves lapping against the bank brought back a host of memories, at once painful and sweet.

The castle lay in shadow as banks of cloud passed over the burning disk of the sun, grim in stone splendor, a silent sentinel like a fortress of old. Its conical turrets, dark against the clouds, looking as they had done when a lady waved her kerchief to welcome home her feudal lord from battle. Castel Isola was no longer a fortified garrison. With a sudden chill of foreboding, Rosanna fancied she heard the loud clang of metal upon metal, the jingling trappings of many horses, and the shrill cries of the dying. She blinked, staring up at the castle. Now the sun had come from behind the clouds, washing its stone walls with light and her apprehension melted.

She was often given to fancies lately, perhaps it was because her emotions were finely drawn and strained beneath the watchful, envious eye of Paolo's wife. Here at the castle everything would return to normal. Absently she fingered the metal amulet she wore on her arm, thinking suddenly about her mother. Always in these mountains she was reminded of her mother, as if her ghostly presence hovered close in the swirling mist, or in the shrill cry of an eagle.

At the keep the party was met with hastily concealed surprise. Water level was going down at this time of year and the horses were able to ford the lake at its lowest point, crossing the shallow water to the gate of the castle itself. With ceremony she was ushered to her chambers, which were always kept in readiness for the duke's visit. No one questioned her arrival, naturally assuming their royal master was to follow within a few days. And Rosanna hoped their assumption would prove correct.

It had been over three weeks since her arrival and still Paolo had not come. Rosanna paced the sun-washed garden in nervous contemplation, wondering if he had been delayed in Venice, or whether he was happily ensconced in Palazzo Lorenzo with his pregnant wife. Surely he would make the journey to see her, or at least send a messenger, yet the summer days passed and there was no word. The fragrant pink roses had lost their scent. Even the magic of the grotto, where they had made love on a summer night long ago, was stripped of its allure. Now the blue marble archways seemed cold, and instead of inviting her to enter, the dark shadowed stillness was a stifling trap from which she fled.

Nicci had been fretful today. Instead of bringing him to play on the grass, she left him with Caterina who rocked and soothed him with cheerful peasant calm, cajoling a smile from the chubby features when his mother could not.

Rosanna lay on the grass, her pink and silver gown dappled by a shifting pattern of leaves from the tall, spreading oak growing within the garden walls. Her eyes were tight closed. At first she did not see the shadow which fell across her, not opening her eyes, but when she did, she found Paolo there. He looked down at her, his expression almost of displeasure, his eyes withdrawn. And her heart missed a beat, stifling in panic at his set face.

"Your Grace," she murmured, rising. Only to drop a deep curtsy while she stared fixedly at his feet, dusty from travel.

Paolo outstretched his hand, helping her rise, and they faced each other without speaking. There was only a short distance between them, yet neither bridged the gap. He out of anger; she out of fear.

The awesome silence was broken by a baby's gurgling, gleeful laugh. Caterina stood on the lawn, holding out Nicci to see his father. For a moment, Rosanna thought Paolo would ignore the greeting of his son, for he did not move. Then his face broke into a strained smile as he turned, beckoning to the nurse to bring the child.

"Niccolo, what a giant," he voiced with surprise as the baby grasped his fingers with a gurgle of delight. "You have borne me a lusty son, Madam."

They were the first words he had spoken since his arrival, and Rosanna found tears pricking her eyes as she answered. Her smile was brave, hopefully concealing her unease.

"He grows lustier every day, your Grace. He is the image of his father . . . and I love him the more for it."

Paolo glanced at her face, seeing the silver tracing of tears on her cheeks which she could no longer contain.

He handed the child back to his nurse, instructing the woman to leave them.

Bleakly Rosanna watched Caterina trailing over the lawn to disappear inside the building, leaving them alone. Never before had she been afraid with him, but she was today, more so than the first time she had gone to him at her uncle's house.

He strode to the wall, leaning out to survey the magnificent view of the surrounding country. She edged toward him, hesitant, wondering if he was angry.

"You should not have said what you did."

His words were a shock, for he did not turn to face her, and Rosanna stopped, tears pounding miserably in a choking lump in her throat.

"You should not have caused a scene, or the ensuing scandal."

"Are you angry with me?" she whispered, fighting for the words through trembling lips.

"I was," he began, picking at a trailing vine which grew in profusion along the stone wall, "but I am over it."

"I'm sorry to have caused you anger."

"But not for what you said?"

"No, not for one word of it."

He looked at her defiant, tear-stained face, at the quivering lips, still soft and red. Even in sorrow she was lovely, and now he had seen her his anger was totally gone, dissipated beneath the magnetic attraction she held for him. Teresa was a shrewish prude; she berated him with tearful scenes, screamed unladylike epithets about the only woman he really wanted, and her body was cold
. . .

"Come," he said softly, holding out his hand, the rings on his fingers winking in the light. "I have wanted you these weeks past, and anger makes a poor bedfellow.

His smile dawned soft, lighting his eyes, turning them limped. Grasping his fingers, she almost fell into his arms, sobs bursting forth, until she leaned against his strength for support. Paolo caressed her hair, resting his head against hers, breathing the longed for scent of her woman's body against him. Her tears wet the fine velvet doublet, ordered new in Venice, but he did not care.

Again she was in his arms, Teresa was miles away in the fetid heat of midsummer, sour and bitter in her apartments with the heavy curtains drawn against the sun's rays, while here in the clean mountain air was all he wanted, his castle, his son, and most important, his woman.

"*Cara,* I'm sorry you were hurt," he whispered, remorseful at her pain. "Your words were more indiscreet than malicious, I knew that. My mistake was in placing you in such a position.

She nodded, sniffling, afraid to raise her reddened eyes lest he find her ugly. When he tried to lift her face, she turned away. "I'm too ugly, Paolo, don't look at me. First let me . . ."

"No, to me you are never ugly. The only ugliness is the cause of your tears." Gently he brushed away her tears with his embroidered kerchief. "Smile for me, then I'll know we are both forgiven."

Obeying with difficulty, Rosanna looked up at his face, love washing through her in a pounding flood. He had come for her at last, just the way she had said he would, and she trembled with happiness.

"You were so long. I was afraid you wouldn't come."

He smiled at her whispered admission, brushing loose strands of hair from her brow where they had escaped the pink and silver circlet. "Foolishly I tried not to, an effort to appease the wagging tongues, but it was hopeless. I followed as you knew I would . . . perhaps you are a witch as my council warns."

With a smile she received his confession, not revealing her ows doubts in the matter, and she nestled against the bright crimson doublet, sighing with pleasure at the strength of his arm around her waist.

"It's summer again and I remember how well you like twilight beside the lake," he whispered, drawing her tight. " 'Twas those thoughts which drove me to this journey, until I rode like one possessed, anger warring with desire. Say I am forgiven as I forgive you, *angela mia.*"

The whisper of his words made her heart race and she twined her arms about his neck. "How long it will seem

219

till sundown," she murmured against his cheek where the prickle of golden beard began, sharp against her skin.

In late October Duchess Teresa was delivered of a still-born son, and many tongues blamed the evil eye of the Black Witch for his death.

Chapter Sixteen

Paolo crumpled the document viciously in his hand and with an exclamation of anger he thrust back his chair. "Who dares make this accusation? I'll have his life."

"The message was sent by an anonymous hand, your Grace," Miserotti supplied smoothly, watching the Duke's face, carefully assessing his humor. His master was whiter than the parchment he clutched, his eyes ice blue, his jaw clamped tight. With an angry toss of his head the Duke indicated he was to withdraw.

"Your servant, as always, your Grace. I shall be in the council chamber if you wish my service."

Impatiently Paolo dismissed him, angered by Miserotti's fawning demeanor. He paced the room, thumping his clenched fist in the palm of his hand. Rosanna accused of infidelity, and with her own cousin. It could not be true. Yet when she had first come to him she had not been innocent. Her uncle, she excused, perhaps her uncle and cousin as well, and God knows how many others.

At the window he stopped pacing, leaning on his arm against the diamond-leaded pane, emotion coursing in a sickness through his limbs. Could this accusation be founded? Could it be she came to him from Sordello's bed?

"No ... God, no," he groaned in jealous anguish. It was not so. And the child, perhaps Niccolo belonged to Sordello as well, his own likeness only the sharing of a common ancestry.

Burying his face against the roughness of his jewel-embroidered sleeve, Paolo tried to think, but his mind was a confusing turmoil of anger and pain. From the courtyard came the sound of laughter and he glanced at the sun-washed paving where the archways were reflected in mammoth black silhouette; from across the court she came, her black hair bound only with a ribbon and a circlet of wild flowers. Her wanton tresses, how many others had buried their passion-hot faces in her silken darkness? How many others had she enmeshed in its fluttering cloud, revealing with sensuous delight the ripeness of her breasts, taking eagerly the crushing demands of hands and mouths ...

"Your Grace."

He turned at the voice, ready to berate the intruder, finding only Livia, his wife's serving woman, trembling before his anger.

"What do you want?"

"Your lady wife seeks an audience, your Grace."

"Has she not courage enough to approach her own husband?"

"She was afraid of your Grace's anger," Livia whispered twisting her white apron in nervous fingers.

"I am tired. I have no wish to see her," he explained wearily. Turning back to the window he saw Rosanna chasing her son, laughing at his waddling antics as he stumbled and fell, scrambling up on his chubby legs, goading his pretty mother to pursue him. Bleak emotion made Paolo nauseous, and resolutely he turned his back upon the day.

"Paolo."

Teresa stood framed in the doorway, her dark purple dress heightening the sallow tint of her complexion.

"Did you not hear? I am tired."

"I heard." Resolutely she moved forward, while Livia quietly closed the door behind her, thankfully withdrawing. "I did not know I was to make an appointment to see my own husband. If you are tired, your Grace, perhaps a more temperate life would be the answer. A full night's rest works wonders for the constitution."

With narrowed eyes, Paolo surveyed her as they faced each other like adversaries. "If you were not my wife, I would have you beaten for that."

"If I were not your wife, I would deserve the punishment."

For a few minutes there was silence in the room, broken only by the gleeful laughter from below. In anger, Teresa marched to the window and slammed it closed.

"Is not the night enough? Must you ogle her by day as well?" she hissed, her face heightened by twin spots of color high on her cheekbones.

"Did you write this?"

Teresa took the parchment from him, smoothing the wrinkles. As she read the missive, a smile tugged at the corners of her mouth.

"No, I did not, but I wish I had. Can you not see what she is? Are you so blinded by her body you don't see what goes on before your eyes? She openly entertains young Sordello in her chambers, and heaven alone knows how many others. She's a slut. Whether you seed her or not does not change matters."

He struck her. It was a light blow, but stinging and well placed. With a gasp of shock, Teresa clutched her burning cheek, tears glazing her brown eyes.

"Never let me hear you say that again."

She gulped, warily eyeing his stormy countenance, fearful of the anger in his face. In silence she nursed her cheek, tears of humiliation on her face. "I came to give you news, Husband," she managed in a quaking voice.

"News of what?"

"I am with child. And there is no doubt to the paternity of this son. He is yours."

A flicker of pleasure lit Paolo's face, his lips parting in surprise. "We are blessed, thanks be to God," he said, taking her hand. "This boy will be strong. I need an heir, Teresa, Lorenzo needs an heir. He will be strong, won't he?"

"Yes, your Grace," she whispered, suddenly afraid of the glint in his eyes. "I promise."

"Good. When is the birth to be?"

"October."

"I'm well pleased, Wife. Let us hope my pleasure continues through November."

In misery, Teresa curtsied, backing towards the door, already dismissed. Her husband had gone to his oak desk where he took pen and paper, carefully lettering a sentence, before glancing up to see her there.

"You may go. Our business is concluded."

Blinded by tears, Teresa ran through the door, almost colliding with Miserotti, who viewed her unusual departure with surprise.

"What is amiss, your Grace?"

"My wife is pregnant," Paolo announced shortly, as if that in itself would suffice as the reason for her hysteria.

"Such a blessing, for you and the duchy, your Grace."

The Duke did not comment and Miserotti waited in the room, his mind quicksilver as he attempted to reconstruct what had occurred between Paolo and his wife.

"Here, see that young Sordello receives this invitation. You are to be on hand, and bring a couple of friends with you."

Miserotti bowed over the Duke's outstretched hand, accepting the sealed letter. "It will be done, your Grace."

"And have *Donna* Rosanna informed I will dine alone tonight."

In high spirits Marco rode through the silent streets, his servants following, a couple of link boys running ahead to light the way. The air was balmy for April with a languorous heat suggestive of summertime, tempered by a fresh breeze. He was wearing a new doublet of mulberry satin, slashed and puffed with saffron, and a jade green plume danced on the brim of his black hat. This invitation to dine with the Duke was unexpected. Perhaps Paolo wished to resume the former closeness of their friendship, a turn of events that could bring nothing but fortune. Some turn of fate was needed to uplift the sagging state of his finances, for the house of Sordello was sinking into a morass of debt. More often his father turned to the solace of the bottle, Magdela to the doubtful comfort of prayer. Only yesterday that scoundrel Miserotti had foreclosed a loan though he knew when the merchant ships weighed anchor there were goods aplenty to repay the mortgage.

God, if fortune did not smile upon him soon, he may well be sailing one of the ships for want of a roof over his head, though an infidel pirate ship would be far more dashing. Perhaps he would form his own cutthroat buccaneer crew and prey upon the mighty Miserotti. What joy to dangle that fawning vulture on the tip of his sword, to hear him plead for mercy.

Marco laughed aloud at his fancies, and seeing they were already in Piazza Lorenzo, he hastened his horses gait, arriving at the palazzo in a clatter of ringing hooves.

He was ushered inside a small chamber, lit dimly by a single flaring torch which threw flickering shadows on the walls. The duke was seated at the head of the table and he rose with a smile of greeting. It was too dim to distinguish much in the quiet room, but Marco had the uneasy impression they were not alone.

"Welcome, it has been many months since we have supped together, my friend."

"It is my honor, your Grace."

The polite greetings over, the men were seated and a servant brought dishes laden with food. The table was already set with goblets of wine. Hesitantly Marco sipped from his, wondering absurdly if it was poisoned, for there was a bitter taste not entirely masked by the sweetness of the grapes. The Duke inquired about the family business, sympathizing with him when he revealed the foreclosure on the business premises, and the balance of money on Villa Sordello hanging precariously in the future.

"You should take a rich wife, Marco. They are useful in times of need," the Duke suggested, refilling his goblet.

"I think perhaps I'll do that, though I've always allowed my heart to overrule my head."

"Your heart?" Paolo questioned, "I was under the impression it was another part of your anatomy."

With a burst of laughter, they resumed their meal, and a little of Marco's trepidation was removed by his royal master's humorous mood.

His eyes hooded, Paolo watched the handsome face

across the table, barely containing the questions which he wanted answered. There was a time for all things, and as yet, it was not come.

"Do you see your cousin often?" he asked suddenly, biting into a wing of baked fowl.

"Yes, only last week she invited me to visit my godson. He's a fine boy, your Grace. The very image of his father."

"You think so?"

"One would have to be blind not to see the startling resemblance he bears to your Grace. She is very proud of the child and I fear she'll spoil him outrageously."

"You are fond of Niccolo as well?"

"Yes, of course, who could resist his charm?" Marco asked with surprise, wondering what prompted this vein of conversation. Once more he was conscious of a movement behind him, but when he glanced quickly about, there was nothing except a flaring torch sputtering on the wall.

"You would like a son yourself?"

"Perhaps I have some already, only their mothers are too hesitant to reveal their identity." Marco laughed, attempting to bring the Duke to humor, but it was in vain.

"She's very lovely, your cousin, and most satisfactory to a man."

"I'm glad she pleases your Grace."

"She pleases me, for she is very skillful in the art of love, is she not?"

Marco looked at the Duke's face, catching an insistence in his voice that was disturbing. "Why, yes, I suppose she is passionate."

"But you do not know, you only suppose?"

"I . . . well, yes, I only suppose. Your Grace said she was pleasing," Marco fumbled, finding sweat trickling down his arms beneath the mulberry sleeves of his fine doublet.

"In all the time you lived under the same roof you did not taste her sweetness? Come now, we must not be reticent with each other. She was lovely even then. You did not kiss her, not once?" Paolo probed, leaning forward, his jeweled hand clenched tight about the slender stem of his goblet.

"Well ... your Grace, perhaps, once ... a kiss,"
Marco agreed, wiping his sweating palms upon the knee
of his saffron hose, somehow unable to think clearly. The
wine must have been drugged.

"Only once, Sordello, with your eye for the ladies?"

"Perhaps several times. I do not remember, your
Grace."

"Your memory serves you ill. Think, how many
times?"

"I don't know ... five, ten."

"So you were lying to me. It was far more than once,"
the Duke suggested, his voice softly calm, with an oiled
quality which sent fear prickling along Marco's spine.

"What is a kiss, your Grace? How many maids we kiss
and forget," he said, swallowing nervously, at once on his
guard.

"Kiss, and touch, and bed, Sordello?"

"Yes ... yes I suppose it is that way."

"And did you also touch your cousin in other places
besides her lips?"

Marco swallowed, attempting to remove the choking
lump from his throat, but in vain. He was being drawn
deeper into a trap, carefully and treacherously laid. Whatever his answer he was already condemned. "No," he protested weakly, "I swear."

"What if I say you are lying? What if I bring proof of
your indiscretion? What then?"

"There is no proof. No one can say aught against me."

"It has already been said," Paolo hissed, his hand
brushing his brow.

Too late Marco knew it was a signal. He was grasped
from behind, pinioned against the carved back of his
chair, his arms twisted until he gasped at the torment.

"Tell me the truth," Paolo pressed, leaning over the
table, his pale eyes hardened in anger. "You knew her,
didn't you?"

"No, no, I swear it."

"Liar."

His arms were twisted tighter and Marco cried out in
pain, sweat pouring from his brow.

"You knew her then, and you still go to her chambers."

227

"No, it's a lie. Nothing improper took place inside the palace. I swear it, by the cross, your Grace. I swear it."

With set mouth, the Duke motioned impatiently to the men in the shadows of the room. A knotted cord was brought and bound around Marco's head, its confining pressure a thundering agony in his brain.

"Now, the truth. You lie with her."

"No, I don't," Marco sobbed, and the cord was tightened a knot, breaking the skin, until the sweat on his forehead was mingled with blood.

"Liar," the Duke cried, striking him across the face with his own gauntlets. "Let me hear the truth. I will know sooner or later, you haven't the strength for it to be later. Your only hope lies in speaking now."

"All right . . . please, no more . . . I'll tell you."

Paolo motioned for them to loosen the band.

"It was only once, your Grace, I swear it."

The band was tightened at his crisp command, until Marco screamed in agony. "I beg you, have mercy . . . it was several years ago . . . the only time I ever lay with her."

The Duke's face was dark with anger, a mere blurring shadow in the room as Marco writhed in agony at his torture. The cord was slicing through his flesh, biting deeper at every move, but even in his torment he knew he must save Rosanna. Already he was condemned from his own mouth. There was no need for her to suffer also.

"It is the truth," Marco gasped. "In the forest . . . it was all my doing . . . I overpowered her."

"She did not wish it?" Paolo questioned, bending close, his breath a hot tide against the sweat-drenched face of his victim.

"I forced her . . . by the cross, by the cross . . ." Marco slumped forward, passed into oblivion at the severity of his pain.

Paolo ordered lights to be brought. The sight of Sordello's twisted, blood-covered face gave him no qualms, nor was there any guilt for his crime. Blood dripped in brilliant, coursing stripes upon the white frilled shirt, sweaty above bloodied mulberry satin.

"Take him out, I believe we have the truth," he said,

reaching for wine, and watching them drag the senseless body through the door, Paolo drained his glass.

Early the next morning after mass, Paolo climbed the narrow twisting staircase to the attic of the palace where Pandolfo Ricasoli was still at work on his formal portrait of Rosanna. The fourth he had painted of the Duke's mistress.

With a smile of pleasure, the painter greeted his master, surprised by the unexpected visit.

"You came to see what has taken so long, your Grace?" he asked, wiping his fingers on a soiled rag. "Sometimes the flow eludes me and I must leave my work, but today it has been good. I'm almost finished."

Paolo strode up to the easel, a smile of amazement on his face, this portrait was even more beautiful than the last, the brushwork more exquisite. The canvas was a masterpiece of life and color, vibrating with an earthy quality which made the painted woman come startlingly alive.

"Is it pleasing to your Grace?"

"It's magnificent. You've captured every detail, even her expression. I'm overwhelmed," Paolo praised in genuine appreciation.

"Then it is acceptable?"

"Certainly. When will you be finished? I can't wait to own the painting."

"A week perhaps," Ricasoli said, standing back to view the canvas at a distance. "Don't you think the mouth is a little full, your Grace? Perhaps a shadow, thus." He stepped forward and with deft brushstrokes reshaped the mouth.

"Yes, that is Rosanna."

"You should know better than any other."

Paolo laughed, gripping the painter by the shoulder.

"I should," he agreed, glancing through the high window at the fleecy clouds, scudding across bright blue sky. "When will your palazzo be ready for occupancy?"

"One never knows, your Grace, the workmen are unpredictable. They tell me a week, but they have promised as much this past month," Ricasoli confided, cleaning his brushes, the smell overpowering in the attic room.

Paolo watched him, his mind busy with unpleasant

thoughts, even now, at the last minute, hesitant to suggest his plan. "You will need a wife to grace that fine palazzo. Have you given any thought to the matter?" he asked at last.

"A wife? No, your Grace, I had not."

The painter methodically wiped spilled vermillion paint from his palette, concealing a smile at his master's question. To say he had not thought about a wife was a mild interpretation.

"Then at least a mistress?"

"No, not even a mistress. Painting is my mistress."

"Admirable, but a cold bedfellow," Paolo suggested with a trace of humor. "Ricasoli, you have been happy here with us, haven't you?"

"Oh, yes, your Grace. I could not ask for more."

"Then your loyalty is unquestionably with Lorenzo?"

"Unquestionably."

"Good, because I have a favor to ask of you."

"Anything your Grace requests, you have only to ask," Ricasoli ventured, a smile on his fair face. His hands were dirty and he cleaned them while he waited.

"I want you to marry. I'll provide you with a lovely gracious hostess for your palazzo. There will be money enough for both of you, you can be assured, and she will not interfere in your work."

Blinking in surprise, Ricasoli nodded affably. "Whatever your Grace wishes. I have so objections if I am allowed to conduct affairs in my own way."

"Yes, you shall be master of your home."

"I will continue to paint here as well as my studio?"

"This is not banishment." Paolo laughed, ruffling the other man's long, curly hair. "My God, I'm only asking you to wed."

"There will be no sons, that part of the agreement must be stipulated," Ricasoli ventured hesitantly, turning to his work, critically eyeing the unfinished canvas.

"She will understand; the marriage is in name only. I will see to that."

"Very well, your Grace, whenever you wish to arrange it . . . I think a shadow here on the cheek, don't you?"

Paolo glanced casually towards the painting, his mind elsewhere. "Ricasoli, you will make arrangements to sign a betrothal contract this afternoon. The wedding is to be in the Duomo next month."

Nodding, Ricasoli turned the easel toward the window, touching the wet oils with his forefinger, blending a lighter tint into her raven locks. "This afternoon I will be busy until three."

"At half past the hour, in my chambers."

"Might I ask who the lady is, your Grace?"

Paolo smiled, a chill expression and he stared silently at the portrait, loathe to speak the name. "Rosanna Sordello," he said.

Paolo knew he must act while he still simmered with anger, for if he delayed, her distress would move him to relent. To marry Rosanna to another would stop the dangerous slander which was being spread abroad. He was gone too often from Lorenzo to protect her as she should be protected and there was his son to think about.

With an eager exclamation, Rosanna ran to him at the door, taking his hands in her own. Paolo kissed her cheek, but she knew from the touch of his mouth, there were other thoughts on his mind.

"How wonderful to see you. I thought you'd be busy this morning and here you are after all."

"I did not come to make love."

His words cut icily through her pleasure, until her hand trembled in his. "What did you come for?"

"There are reports that you entertain men in your apartments," he began, pulling his hand from hers.

"It's a lie. You know I'm faithful."

"I hope you are faithful."

"Paolo ... oh, Paolo." In tears she sank on the bed, wounded by his lack of trust. "How could you?"

He watched her, his heart softening. They were accusations he should not have made, but in his anger he had given little thought to her distress. "What of Sordello?"

"Marco? He is my cousin," she protested, finding her heart lurch in dismay as she wondered what Paolo knew of the past.

"Many women lie with their cousins. That is no protection."

"I do not. He comes to visit me ... and the child.

231

Paolo, I've never looked at another with lust since we've been together."

Her cries were anguished and he fought the urge to take her in his arms. "Under duress Sordello confessed to his relationship with you."

The blow met her unprepared, and Rosanna gasped at the revelation, her heart leaden in her chest. "Then he lies."

"Does a man in fear of his life, lie?"

"If he says he sleeps with me, he does."

Silent, Paolo turned away, his back towards her. Rosanna watched him stride the patterned length of the carpet and back. Until at last he said: "But he did once."

Desperately searching for the right words she wondered how much he actually knew. With a sob, she nodded her head.

"I know he forced you. I understand," he said at last.

With joy she leaped from the bed to his arms, which closed about her in forgiveness. Whatever Marco had said, he had not condemned her.

Paolo kissed her mouth, drying her tears with his kerchief. "These rumors must be stopped," he whispered at last. "I cannot have you accused of infidelity, so to stop the tongues I have made arrangements for you to wed."

At first his statement did not register, then realization crept in, gripping her with fear. "Marry," she whispered, praying she had misunderstood.

"Yes, that way no one will dare accuse you. Your husband and his family will be your protectors."

"I won't."

The pressure of his arms decreased, until Paolo pulled from her, stepping back. His face was set and Rosanna knew she had angered him. "Will, Madam. I command it."

"No."

"You shall do as you are told. You have no choice."

"Oh, don't make me do it, Paolo, please." She fell pleading at his feet, but in vain; he remained adamant in his decision.

"When you are used to the idea, 'twill not seem as bad," he consoled stiffly, finding her sorrow painful to witness. With a swift gesture he brought her to her feet. "The man is Ricasoli."

"The painter?"

"Yes. He will not treat you unkindly. And your bed will be your own. He has no concern about the frequency of my visits, for painting is his only interest in life."

Her mouth opened, and she swallowed several times, attempting to speak, but her throat seemed swollen with grief. "And Duke Bernardo?" she managed at last.

"He is Ricasoli's problem, not mine, or yours."

"I'll ask you once more, dearest, don't make me do this."

"And once more I will deny the request. This afternoon you will sign the betrothal papers in my apartment. The wedding is next month. Think you that is enough time?"

"Yes," she whispered, fighting tears, wishing he would leave so she could give vent to the emotion which swelled to bursting in her throat.

"I wish you had been more understanding."

Rosanna gaped at him waiting at the door, his hand on the golden knob, every inch the Duke of Lorenzo. She could not know what prompted this visit, what lies had been spread about her, for her enemies were many, surpassing each other in treachery.

"Me, understanding! You accuse me of infidelity; then, when I am barely recovered from that barb, you wound me with another. A forced marriage, of convenience to be sure, but to whose convenience? It is not to mine."

"Your convenience is of no matter. The duchy is ruled to my convenience only. The audience will be at half-past three. Do not be late." With a curt nod, he left, shutting the door behind him and she sank to her knees, grief welling to a noisy fit of tears.

Rosanna appeared promptly at half-past three in the duke's chambers. Ricasoli was already there, his flowing hair strongly perfumed. At her entrance he turned with a smile, his curls shining auburn in the sunlight.

"*Donna* Rosanna," he began with a smile, but the stony expression on her face quenched his good humor. And she declined to take his hand.

"Is this your idea?" she demanded, her voice husky from hours of weeping.

"No, it is entirely his Grace's plan. I am merely a loyal subject, Madam, who obeys his master's wishes."

Rosanna stared at him, wondering if the agreement was as distasteful to him as it was to her. "Don't you care? We're not negotiating a purchase of painting supplies. This is a marriage contract," she snapped, seeing a smile come to his pale hazel eyes, tawny as an animal's.

"I understand the solemnity of the agreement, *donna,*" he assured, adjusting the slipping neckline of his black velvet gown. While he talked, he fingered the red embroidery on his shirt, lovingly stroking the silken flowers with long, bony fingers. "My royal master commands; I obey. You would do well to follow the same path. His Grace does not like to be crossed."

"Thank you for your warning, but I'm qualified to know his Grace. I realize you are better acquainted with Duke Bernardo."

"Need you mention that?" he asked, a flush on his cheeks. "If you'll not allude to my relationships, I'll overlook the fact you are the royal concubine. Or in gutter terms, a whore."

Anger flashed a banner across her face as she leaped to her feet. "If we speak in gutter terms, Ricasoli, there's an apt one for your perversion. I know it well."

Their exchange was interrupted by the entrance of the duke's clerk with pen and paper, accompanied by his assistant. The clerk smiled benignly, advancing age sparing him from the exchange through deafness. But the assistant snickered.

"What a beautiful partnership," the old man mused, seeing the two handsome young people. "Ah! to be young again."

Defiantly Rosanna seized the proffered pen, signing her name with a flourish, watching while the signature was sanded. Now it was Ricasoli's turn. He signed without hesitation.

"Is that all?"

"Yes, *Donna* Rosanna. Only the church ceremony is needed to solemnize the event," the assistant informed with a leer, eyeing her full bodice, until she turned haughtily from his gaze.

"Good afternoon, Husband," she said sarcastically, extending her hand.

Ricasoli took her fingers in his, brushing her hand with his lips. "Good afternoon." Drawn to her full height, burning with anger, Rosanna left the room, the three men staring after her.

Chapter Seventeen

Rosanna waited as the weeks passed. Paolo must have gone to Castel Isola by now, for it was late July. He had intended to spend a month with his cousin in Luciano, then journey to Lago di Paradiso. Not once during that time had he written to her, or had she word from the palace, though she had not expected to be contacted by Teresa. The Duchess was in her sixth month, and looking like a pregnant sow, Cia had gleefully reported.

The city was stifling, the summer days scorching under a merciless, brazen sun, the nights still and oppressive. Many of the courtiers had long since departed for their summer homes, but Pandolpho saw no need for one. He did not seem to notice the heat as he divided his life between his studio at the top of the palazzo, and his attic at the palace. Rumors reached her of Duke Bernardo's frequent demands, so that Pandolfo journeyed many nights at the summons of his royal master, who had stayed by his sister-in-law's side during her time of need.

At last Rosanna was mistress of her own palazzo, with many beautiful gowns and a baby son to play with, yet she was unhappy. The vital ingredient she needed was missing—Paolo. That he did not at least write to her was wounding, giving rise to the frightening question in her mind: Had he tired of her? She knew it was whispered abroad, for she had heard it in the palace before her marriage. Rumor said she was indiscreet with her cousin and was to be wedded to Ricasoli as a punishment. Perhaps Paolo had not intended this marriage as a punishment, but it had proved to be one. And poor Marco banished. Cia had told her his mind was unhinged by a secret incident which took place within the duke's chambers, though she did not know what happened.

Nicci was the only brightness in her life. The heat had made him fretful. Poor little darling, his skin was blotchy, his curly head forever wet with sweat. The only surprise from her marriage was Pandolfo's gentle handling of the child, for he loved her son with genuine affection which was equally returned by the little boy.

August passed with its sultry days, the unrelieved heat fading into September. Soon the leaves would flutter from the tall chestnut in the courtyard. The wind would sweep icily from the mountains across the plains of Lorenzo, bringing the dying season to a close. And still he did not come. Rosanna had grown thinner with the months of vigil, her cheeks hollowed, her eyes dark shadowed, large in her pale face. Surely he would come soon, if only to be with his wife, who next month would be confined to her chamber for the lying-in.

September brought some respite from the heat and Rosanna managed to sleep at night, though her eyes were often red rimmed from weeping. Cia had gossiped, well meaning, but nevertheless her heart was stricken at the news that Paolo entertained Betta Peruzzi at a banquet in the castle. Was that why he had not contacted her. Perhaps the Peruzzi wench could fulfill all his needs. In the evenings she watched the sky from her balcony, wondering if Paolo looked at the moon and stars. And with a stab of pain she wondered if he delighted in Betta Peruzzi by the moonlit lake. Did he make love to her the way they had done? "Like gypsies beneath the moon," he had always laughed.

Tonight the moon was full and she stared at it, feeling the flood of power she had known of old. At first it was surprising, then she remembered her mother's amulet

237

which she had placed on her arm this evening. For months it had lain neglected in her drawer. When she saw it today she thought perhaps the charm of the amulet would bring back her lover. The engravings on the metal were strange signs of a forgotten belief, old and pitted through the years, its symbolism lost in antiquity. Slowly she touched the amulet, feeling the sacred signs, whispering the chant her mother had taught her. And she was suddenly at peace.

When Cia woke her the next morning she gave her a note delivered by a courier moments before. Rosanna eagerly tore it open, for the seal bore Paolo's insignia—he would dine at their palazzo tomorrow night. A party of eight.

The dining table was set with care, light from the sconces reflecting patterns on the gleaming silver. Bowls of gold and white flowers graced the oak table, pure and startling against the burgundy cloth. Pandolfo had selected the table settings when they moved to the palazzo, but tonight was the first opportunity there had been to display them. He supervised tonight's arrangements with his artist's eye for beauty.

Standing back with clasped hands she surveyed the arrangements, allowing Pandolfo to place single blossoms carelessly at the base of the silver bowls as if they had fallen a moment before.

"Thank you, everything is beautiful. Even the progress in the kitchen is smooth. I could never have arranged everything myself," she complimented with a smile of happiness.

"I'm glad to be of value." Coming to stand behind her he placed his hand on her shoulder—one of the infrequent moments of physical contact between them. "You see, I have some uses, after all."

Before she could reply, Cia burst inside the room, her dark face flushed with excitement. "His Grace is here."

Self-consciously Rosanna patted her hair and smoothed her dress. She had chosen a pink brocade gown, remembering Paolo liked her in pink. The skirt was stiffly embroidered with pearls in an intricate design of musk roses, the hem trimmed by a narrow band of sable. A simple plaited hairdressing, adorned by a circlet of pearls, completed her costume. She prominently displayed Paolo's bracelet on her arm, but her mother's amulet was discreetly hidden beneath. In deference to her choice of color, Pandolfo wore brown velvet with an embroidered cream shirt, though he had first elected to wear crimson. And she was grateful for his thoughtful gesture.

Together, husband and wife greeted their honored guests. The cool September night was dark, the sky sprinkled with stars, and against this backdrop Rosanna saw Paolo. He wore moss green velvet with spangled sleeves, his coat and hose shimmering cloth of silver. Flustered, she dropped a curtsy, sinking gracefully to the blue mosaic floor with a billow of pink skirts, her head bowed low, her eyes fixed on the spangled green velvet of his shoes. Paolo raised her head, his touch light against her face.

"Welcome, your Grace, we are honored."

"The pleasure is mine," he replied, raising her up before him, his fingers lingering a moment against her hair.

And Rosanna smiled. The waiting was over, everything was going to be all right, after all.

"We are honored to have you as our first guest, your Grace," Pandolfo joined, extending his hand. He would have gone down on his knee but Paolo kept his hand tight, keeping him on his feet.

"After weeks of traveling and the displeasure of ungracious hosts, I'm delighted to be in your palazzo, Ricasoli. After we've dined you must show me the entire house. I insist on it."

Behind him a man cleared his throat and Paolo stepped aside to reveal his brother, Bernardo. With surprise, which was not of pleasure, Rosanna met Duke Bernardo's eyes, finding intense dislike for herself reflected in their watery depths.

"Welcome, your Grace," Pandolfo greeted. "We are doubly honored. We did not expect to be so blessed."

Gruffly, Bernardo spoke to him, staring haughtily at Rosanna as she repeated her husband's polite words, and he came inside the hallway, glancing about with appreciation at the rich furnishings. He was dressed in half purple, half white brocade embroidered in pearls, green flowered hose on his thin legs.

"Bernardo insisted on accompanying me. I suspect Teresa feels I'm in need of a chaperone," Paolo informed with a grin.

The other guests came inside—three ladies and gentlemen of the court, splendid and gaudy as peacocks. After watching her husband for a few minutes. Rosanna understood why Pandolfo was popular with ladies and gentlemen alike, for his wit was never biting or sarcastic. Each compliment seemed genuinely meant.

At dinner Rosanna sat across the table from Paolo, finding it difficult to eat beneath his gaze. Even attempting to make conversation was a strain on her emotions. Thankfully the company was witty and well primed with wine before their arrival, so her few sallies were greeted by joyous laughter. More wine was brought, and though the other guests drank copiously, Paolo's consumption was sparing. Lively talk buzzed back and forth amid hiccups and laughter, which, as the night progressed, marked the growing insobriety of the others. Above the rim of his glass Paolo watched her, and he smiled, his lips moving softly in speech. She was not certain of his words and he repeated the phrase until she read the only word which was important: Where?

Pandolfo had risen unsteadily to his feet, preparing to conduct the Duke on a tour of the palazzo.

"Husband, do not forget to show his Grace my chambers, the view of the city is beautiful from there," she suggested quickly, and from Paolo's grin, she knew he understood.

When the hour for the company's departure arrived, Paolo was insisting upon seeing the work which Pandolfo had painted during the summer heat, saying it must be a masterpiece to keep a man chained to the city in August. At his suggestion, Bernardo left without him, scowling in displeasure, admonishing him not to stay late because of the danger of the streets. Paolo assured him his bodyguard would afford ample protection from the terrors of the night. Bernardo left reluctantly, his hand lingering in Pandolfo's, the questions in his eyes going unanswered as he was bid a hearty good-night.

Rosanna found her legs shaking as the door closed leaving the three of them alone in the emptiness of the vast domed entrance hall. Their footsteps echoed as Pandolfo led the way to his studio talking rapturously about the colors he had used in his latest painting—a new technique of blending he had perfected himself which gave vivid, likelike tints.

Paolo smiled at her, helping her on the stairs, his hand warm in hers. When they paused on the balcony to view the sleeping city, she drew away, unable to control the quaver in her voice at the unspoken message in his touch.

"I do not think I'll journey up the stairs, Pandolfo, I'm very tired. Will you forgive me, your Grace, if I leave you? My room is on this floor."

"You are forgiven, *Madonna*. I remember your apartments from your husband's interesting tour, a very lovely view."

Curtsying to him, she walked towards her door, feeling his eyes on her back. She wanted to run and she fought the urge with all her strength. At last she heard them move away as she went inside her bedchamber, and she knew Paolo had waited to be certain of her room.

It was silent as the grave, her heartbeat a thudding tattoo within her breast. Beyond the open windows the branches of the chestnuts stirred, brushing against the balcony, black shadows moving over the sparkling stone. The moon had risen, and Rosanna nervously touched the amulet to reassure herself this was not a dream. The breeze was cool on the balcony, bringing the scent of flowers to remind her of the grotto at Castel Isola. The blue marble archway was cold to the touch; the dark shadowed interior was sweet scented with jasmine. And when the wind blew from the mountains the bell above the door rang a musical chime.

A step within the room. The rustle of cloth of silver as he strode across the floor. Then the longed for agony of his hands, gentle at first, caressing, coupled with his lips on the back of her neck.

"The summer has been an eternity without you."

"Oh, Paolo." She clung against him, the spangles on his sleeves cutting through her dress.

"I've wanted you so much . . . God, how much."

241

"But you did not write."

"I know. If I'd written I could not have kept my distance. Forgive me. We make vows in anger which are purgatory to endure when the heat is gone." Absurdly his hands shook as he touched her face. "I will love you like never before," he vowed.

Birds heralded the dawn, waking Rosanna from sleep. With pleasure she found Paolo had not gone, as she thought he would. A sound came from the hallway and glancing up, she saw they had not even closed the door last night. Tiptoeing to the door she looked down the passage to see Pandolfo's flowing robe disappear round the bend in the stairs. He was up at dawn as usual, anxious to catch the clear light for his painting. Never before had he worked with such zeal, but his devotion to art would serve her well. Now he would not know if the Duke left last night, or this morning.

When she returned to the bed Paolo was still asleep. Pale yellow shafts of sunlight, messengers of the new day, stole over the bedcovers, burnishing the glittering disarray of his fine clothing clung carelessly at the foot of the bed. His arms were bare, thrown free of the restricting sheets. She brushed his shoulder with her lips and he stirred in his sleep.

Paolo woke, knowing instantly why he felt the urgent pounding of his blood.

"I thought you should be awake, your Grace, it is a long past dawn," she reminded, her breath tantalizing on his flesh. "What of your council? There must be tasks waiting on such a beautiful September day."

"There is only one," he whispered gruffly, his fingers tangling in the blackness of her hair, "that cannot wait."

The joyous pealing of a multitude of bells shattered the golden calm of the misty October morning. Rosanna woke, drowsy at first, not realizing the message the church bells told, but fully awake, she knew; the Duchess Teresa had been delivered of a son. And burying her face in the pillow, she wept.

At noon Pandolfo brought her a tray of food which he arranged himself, feeling sorrow for her plight. He knew she had wept most of the morning, for he heard the muffled sounds through her closed door, coming several times to speak to her; then, thinking better of the idea, he had gone away again.

Sniffing, Rosanna brushed her hair from her eyes, accepting the plate of white fish in a silver sauce, with slices of orange floating on top. The food was good, but she had no appetite and Pandolfo finished the meal himself.

"Have you news from the palace?" she asked at last, staring through the window without seeing the clear blue sky.

"The Duchess was delivered of a healthy boy. They are both well," he replied, seeing pain in her face. "I'm sorry, Rosanna. I don't know what to say to comfort you. There's nothing . . ."

"I'll rally, 'tis only a temporary ailment," she assured, taking the hand he extended, noticing his fingers were permanently stained with color. The gesture was comforting.

"Shall I stay with you? I've an appointment at one, but it isn't important. I could bring Nicci and we could entertain you," Pandolfo suggested eagerly, his face lit with hope.

Rosanna was surprised by his offer, but when she would have declined, he appeared so disappointed she agreed to his suggestion. Pandolfo was far younger than she at heart, though his years numbered more. It was a fact she had not known until today. He was like a child eager to please his mother.

Soon she was laughing as Pandolfo crawled on his hands and knees, baby Nicci on his back, playing horses. At twenty months the little boy adored him, shrieking with delight at the game. The hours passed and Rosanna knew the birth of Teresa's son did not really matter, for she had already borne a son to the Duke of Lorenzo. Teresa could never produce a boy as lovely as Nicci.

Nurse came to put him to bed, scolding the adults for keeping him up till four and making him too excited to sleep. With the child gone the room seemed unnaturally quiet and Rosanna hummed a song to brighten her spirits, while Pandolfo brought his lute. He played a beautiful, haunting melody which he had composed himself, totally

243

forgetting the angry man who waited impatiently for him at the ducal palace.

Duke Bernardo watched the painted barges moving slowly down the canal to disappear round the bend, obscured from view by the vast hulk of the Duomo. Three hours late! In the past Pandolfo was never late, coming eagerly to his summons. That was before he married her. Was their marriage really in name only, as Pandolfo swore? God knows, Paolo lusted after her hotly enough, could Pandolfo too be infatuated with the woman? There was another time years ago, when the painter was newly come to court, that he had suspected him of infidelity. The girl was a baker's daughter, fleshy and disgusting. He had caught them embracing one afternoon when Pandolfo had used her as a model, at least that was the pretext. He had been sickened at the thought of what else had occurred in the secluded attic studio. Of course, it had been simple to dispose of the hussy. What a revolting sight she was afterwards, bleeding and whimpering, as grossly fleshed as a slaughtered cow.

In anger, Bernardo rose from the window seat. It was unthinkable Pandolfo could defile himself by lying with a woman. They were foul receptacles of lust, smelling like the animals in the marketplace. Furthermore, women were evil; they took a man's identity, emasculating him, then they laughed at the foolish simpleton he had become. Women used their foul bodies to manipulate men who were insane enough to lust after them—even his own brother. If he was ruler of Lorenzo, women would be barred from the court. It would be an exclusive company of intelligent, beautiful young men. Women would be used only to bear children. Between men, lovemaking was pure, it was not defiled by the obscenity of the rotting interior of a woman's body . . .

"Your Grace."

Bernardo glanced to the door where a pageboy kneeled, tasseled cap in hand. "Is he here?"

"No, your Grace . . ."

"What? It's past four!" Bernardo cried in anger, hardly able to believe the painter's audacity. To keep him waiting more than three hours, how dare he?

"A note, your Grace," the page proffered, warily eyeing his master's blazing face.

"From Ricasoli?"

"Yes, your Grace."

Bernardo snatched the paper with impatience, ripping it open, his hand shaking in his haste. The words stunned him, making his heart pound a deafening tattoo against his chest. "Not coming," he muttered, almost to himself, reading and rereading the beautiful script. "I regret I am unable to keep our appointment this afternoon. A matter of importance concerning my wife." God, his wife! To call that woman his wife, to write it in a note! "Where is he?" he demanded in anger and the page backed away.

"At his palazzo. A messenger brought the note, your Grace."

"Then I will see what matter of importance keeps him so engrossed he fails to keep appointments," Bernardo cried as he stormed from the room.

At the entrance to Ricasoli's home he brushed the stuttering manservant aside, marching with grim determination through the corridors, the old man shuffling after him. Bernardo knew which was her suite for he had seen her at the window holding the child. More than likely that was where Pandolfo could be found, betraying their love with that royal strumpet.

Bernardo stopped in the doorway. They were sitting on the floor like lovers, she singing, he playing a beribboned instrument in accompaniment.

"This song was written for you, dear wife," Pandolfo was saying, his eyes limpid and worshiping, until Bernardo reeled in the doorway speechless with shock and anguish. "I wrote it to show my love for you."

"No."

At the bellow of rage the couple gasped in surprise to find Duke Bernardo at the door, his face a purple mask of hate.

The late spring breeze was warm, but it struck chill through the wet bodice of Teresa's dress, and she turned from the window. Below the grand procession of servants disappeared inside the archways of the Duke's rooms and it was silent in the courtyard. Her little son was gone.

They did not even allow her to hold him more than a few minutes at a time lest she infect him with an illness. To hold Cristofano, to kiss his cherubic face, was like heaven, and her eyes misted with tears to feel the warmth of his hand around her finger. But they took him from her, the Duchess Maria scolding his nurse for even bringing him to her. She hated Paolo's mother more than his mistress. At least the Sordello wench claimed to love him.

Teresa lay across the damask bedcovers, feeling the oozing of milk from her breasts. Holding her baby had started the flow. Why didn't they do something for her? Why didn't they send herbs to dry her milk, or tell her what to do to ease the pain? If she could have nursed Cristofano as nature intended, she knew the pressure would be eased, but he was provided with a wet nurse from the royal household. A preposterous idea, and most unladylike! her mother-in-law had exploded at her suggestion that perhaps she could suckle her own infant.

Clenching her fists against the pain, Teresa threshed on the bed, tears on her cheeks. She wanted her mother. She wanted to go home. She hated Lorenzo and its Duke. All any of them cared for was the heir she had borne. Wincing in pain, she rolled on her back deciding to force out the milk herself, as she had done this past week, although it seemed to return as fast as she expelled it. Teresa peeled away the wet material of her bodice where it was matted to her skin and taking a goblet from the table she sobbed in self-pity while she worked. There was a knock on the door and she put down the goblet, reaching for her bed robe which she tied about her waist before opening the door. Rosello, the duke's new page, stood on the threshold, his face pinched and sombre.

"Your Grace, I have a message."

"Thank you. Come inside while I read it," she suggested, ushering him to a padded bench beside the window.

The note was from her husband demanding her presence at the reception tonight. It was impossible. She could not go in her present condition. Each hour would be misery in the crowded ballroom beneath the slanting black eyes of his mistress who would gloat over her discomfort.

"Tell your master I must decline," she commanded.

With a frightened start, Rosello stared at her, his velvet brown eyes tearful. "Decline, your Grace?" he questioned.

"That is what I said."

"He will have me beaten if I displease him."

"Beaten?"

"Yes, your Grace. Already today, and it was not my fault. Andrea was to blame," the boy sobbed, his mouth trembling, the pain in his heart spilling forth to the sympathetic, motherly girl before him.

"You poor boy. Oh, how could Paolo do such a thing," Teresa cried in pity at the boy's grief. "Do you bleed?"

"Not now, your Grace." He sniffled, resting his head against her outstretched arm, taking comfort from her kindness.

Absently Teresa stroked his dark hair, her own sorrow combining with his, for he was a kindred soul persecuted by the house of Lorenzo. To beat a child: the crime was unforgiveable. "Does his Grace often beat you, Rosello?"

"Only if we displease him. This is my second beating. He doesn't do it himself, your Grace. There's a master who carries out our punishments."

"Whether he does it himself or not, he is still guilty."

Rosello yielded to her mothering, relaxing against the warmth of her body, his sobs lessening and he dabbed his eyes with his sleeve. With a smile, Teresa brought out her own kerchief, gently wiping his smooth face. He was much older than her own son, nevertheless he needed her ministration. Cristofano was swamped with attendants, but Rosello was alone.

"Thank you, your Grace," he managed, "you are very kind."

Teresa felt pleasure at the touch of him, at the rounded, pliable flesh of his face under her fingers. And with a surge of affection, she drew Rosello against her breast where, unresisting, he laid his head while she smoothed back his hair.

"You must never be afraid of my husband again. I'll speak to him about your case," she promised, and he nodded assent. The movement opened her bed robe and with dismay, Teresa realized she held Rosello's smooth face against the fullness of her breast. His eyes were closed and he did not notice. She stared at him, seeing the

247

long, dark-fringed lashes, wet with tears. He was a motherless boy, alone and frightened, while she was a childless mother. "Rosello," she whispered huskily, crushing his face against her, "Rosello."

The boy opened his eyes, attempting to draw away, but she held him firm.

"It's all right, you need not go."

"But, your Grace, I ..." he stammered, closing his eyes at the sight.

Gently she turned his mouth towards her and his lips opened. At last Rosello drew from her, his face flushed, tears of shame spilling down his face.

"You must not be ashamed. You are my child now. You will be my son," she whispered, stroking his face. "Don't be ashamed, Rosello. I love you, you know that, don't you?"

He looked at her, his tears stopped, the first stirring of adolescent desire burning in his veins. "Oh, yes, *Donna* Teresa, and I love you too," he whispered.

That night Teresa went to the reception with Rosello in attendance, and her husband was pleased to see her take a lively interest in the boy's welfare. Young Rosello needed a woman's mothering.

Chapter Eighteen

The year which followed was marked by disaster. The armies of Lorenzo sustained heavy losses as they fought to protect the sister state of Luciano from invaders. Angelo, King of Luciano, demanded more and more assistance, until Paolo was hard pressed to satisfy his cousin's needs. The Government stock fund hovered on the brink of disaster, and unknown to the citizens, the privy council borrowed considerable amounts from the dowry fund to buy armaments rendering the stocks worthless.

Summer began with an outbreak of plague which grew and festered in the hovels of the Ponte Maggiore district, sending widespread fingers of death into the fashionable palazzos on the Via San Bernardo. Rich merchants and nobles alike fled the teeming city for the sanctuary of their summer villas, until Lorenzo became a city of ghosts, populated by armies of rats who came from the canals to scavenge in broad daylight.

By September the plague was abated and the upper classes returned. Rosanna had spent the summer at Castel Isola, Paolo at her side, a fact which greatly angered King Angelo who thought his cousin should provide a ready sword to defend Luciano instead of hunting at his mountain retreat.

When they rode through the gates the city was deserted. There were no cheering throngs lining the streets, for the fear of plague still lingered. Pandolfo had accompanied the royal party to Lago di Paradiso, working during the summer on a portrait of the Duke. Now he was eager to finish a dozen other paintings he had left in his studio.

When they neared the Ponte Veneto an appalling sight met their eyes. The painter's magnificent palazzo gaped smoke blackened. A mysterious fire had ravaged the richly appointed mansion leaving no trace of his unfinished masterpieces, and what furnishings were not burned had been carried away by looters.

Paolo began an immediate investigation, but he was aware that the effort was merely a gesture, for whatever evidence there had been was long since destroyed. Rosanna was deeply shocked by the fire, for she read far more behind it than Pandolfo, recognizing it for what it was—an attempt to destroy them. Though he offered his sincere regret, she was convinced Bernardo knew more than he told of the calamity.

She reoccupied her apartments at the palace while Pandolfo began his work afresh in the attic studio there. Her gowns and jewels were destroyed, even Nicci's toys which had not been taken to the castle were gone. Fortunately their traveling baggage had been ample, a fact which kept them from being totally dependent on Paolo.

The latest reports of the financial state of the duchy were shadowed with gloom and Paolo wondered if the revenue deficit was entirely due to war losses, or more the result of too many greedy hands in the coffers. Merchants pleaded lossed from plague deaths, looting and piracy, until the greatly diminished taxes caused alarm amongst the administrators of the city finances. And an emergency council meeting was called.

Clear morning light flooded the council chamber, sending dust particles dancing in the shafts which glanced across the massive table. Paolo sat brooding, his head in his hands, watching the rapid movement of a brilliant plumaged bird in its gilt cage. Lorenzo was squeezed between the powers of Milan on the west, Venice on the east; insignificant though they may be, power-hungry neighbors coveted the duchy. Like his cousin Angelo who maintained a like position, these wolves at bay made for many sleepless nights.

"Your Grace."

Miserotti stood at his elbow.

"I'm ready."

With long faces the councilors filed into the room, shuffling and rustling papers as they settled each in his place. Christ, what gloom, they were enough to sour even this fine Steptember morning. "Gentlemen."

"Your Grace." The murmur was dutiful, if not enthusiastic. And Paolo found his unease mounting as Miserotti stood to address the council.

"Your Grace, fellow council members, the situation facing the city of Lorenzo is grave. Our vessels have been preyed upon by pirate ships. There is no one in this room who has not suffered great losses. Our armies have been defeated at Santa Christina, where the King of Luciano barely escaped with his life. We have many debts, and the tax coffers are almost empty. Therefore, your Garce, it is our recommendation that many new, and far higher taxes be levied to supplement the losses."

"Never," Paolo cried. "I won't tyranize my people. We will cut expenses."

"What cuts can we make? The army has not yet been paid. We must purchase horses and new equipment to replace that lost at Santa Christina. Have you forgotten, your Grace, since the Pact of Lodi several years past, our enemies are too powerful. With the alliance of Florence and Milan to our left hand, Venice and Naples to our right, 'tis like a vise which closes about us, ready to crush out our breath. We must purchase horses and new equipment to replace that lost at Santa Cristina and perchance find a condotta for some worthy mercenary. And then there is the addition to the palace."

"I'll curtail the work. It is not of a pressing nature."

Inclining his head slightly, Miserotti managed a smile, though it was a humorless expression. "Your Grace, we do not wish to place a burden upon you. It is for the

251

council to decide such mundane matters. We do not want to place curbs on your . . ."

"You shall not control me, Miserotti. I rule alone," Paolo snapped, his face dark with anger. "Give me the figures. This afternoon you will have my suggestions." Paolo strode from the chamber, the portfolio in his hand, snatched abruptly from Miserotti's grasp.

"His Grace is overwrought."

" 'Tis the lack of sleep these nights."

A trickle of laughter sounded at the sally, but soon died.

"We will have the new taxes and retain our own immunity, Gentlemen, I assure you."

Rosanna answered the tap on her door, thinking that perhaps it was Paolo, but instead, Miserotti stood outside.

"May I speak with you, *Donna* Rosanna, it is of the utmost importance."

With reluctance she admitted him, wondering what pressing business brought him so early in the morning. He refused wine, but insisted she take refreshment.

"I trust you are in good health, *donna?*"

"Yes, thank you."

"And his Grace?"

"He was never better."

"Let us pray the situation does not change."

"What do you mean?" Rosanna was at once alert, sensing the warning in the words as Miserotti turned from the window, his sallow face twisted in a smile.

"His Grace is stubborn. There are suggestions of his council he does not wish to follow. I feel in order to maintain his present enjoyable health, he should change his mind. As I remember, you can be most persuasive."

"You want me to persuade him to accept the council's plans?"

"Exactly."

"And if I refuse?"

"You won't refuse. We have a bargain, remember?"

"No, we no longer have a bargain, Miserotti."

"I would advise you to be careful, you have many enemies."

"I am tired of the audience, good day." She opened the

door and Miserotti stared at her, white hot with anger.

"You will regret this hour. I promise you that."

Rosanna found waves of unease coming at intervals during the day as she worried about Paolo's safety and her own. There was no crime Miserotti could implicate her in; even Bianca's death was a healed wound in Paolo's heart. Twice she had yielded to Miserotti's threats, influencing Paolo in his favor, but no more. It was comforting to be free of his blackmail. Last year she had helped Miserotti secure control of the dowry bank by placing a substitute lottery box before Paolo, helping him secure vast holdings in the government stock fund by a similar ruse. These favors had brought him great wealth, until now he controlled half the money in Lorenzo—a state which pleased him, for Miserotti admired a man who kept his wits in ready cash. That was still not enough. Today she realized he would never stop, for there would ever be a prize glinting in the future.

"There she is. Burn the black witch!"

Rosanna shrank from the angry mob, threading her way hurriedly between the buildings. Her horse stumbled on the cobbles and her heart missed a beat as she feared being unseated; to ride through the crowd was frightening enough, to travel on foot would be suicide.

With heaving chest she plunged to safety into the sun-washed piazza before the palace. The epithets they had shouted echoed in her ears, loathesome and frightening. Now she knew Miserotti's revenge. He had stirred hatred for her amongst the populace using the recent calamities in the city to maximum advantage. She already stood accused of casting her evil eye on Paolo's son and causing an ailment which left him with a permanent limp, and now of bringing the plague of summer and the army's defeat. Treacherous words were spoken against her as many believed she held Paolo's affections through witchcraft. It was the amulet, they whispered behind closed doors, the amulet had the power to sway his Grace, for she was never without it. Rosanna knew Paolo was under pressure from his council to put her from him, for he was wearier these days and new worry lines etched themselves firmly on his brow.

It seemed as if circumstance was an ever tightening web to ensnare her. Now she feared the assassin's knife at every turn, the poisoner's venom in every meal. If only she could turn the years backward to that blissful beginning when everything held such hope and promise. Now there seemed to be nothing but defeat.

Entering the palace, Rosanna lifted her skirts and ran as fast as she could to her rooms. Threats sought her out even here, for impaled on the door by a gleaming dagger was a parchment, fluttering in the breeze from the windows.

With trembling hands she pulled the dagger from her door, extracting a blood-scrawled note. She darted inside her chamber, slamming the door and for the first time since she had left this room today, she felt safe, though her knees were shaking and her palms sticky with sweat.

Smoothing the crumpled parchment with damp fingers, she read the ominous threat. A single word: Death. Who had placed the dagger there? Was it Miserotti, or a member of her own household? Perhaps the fire had been set to remove her from the safety of her home, bringing her to the vast, winding corridors of the ducal palace. Here it was easy for assassins to hide in the darkened alcoves by the windows, or slip noiselessly behind the flowing draperies, waiting with unsheathed dagger for an unsuspecting victim.

God, she must think. What to do now. How to preserve the safety of her own person and that of her son. As usual her enemies were faceless, but she could attach a dozen names to them. It could even be a misguided saviour of Lorenzo who, with fanatical zeal, believed the lies spread about her and thought the misfortunes of the city would end with her death.

There must be an answer. Inside the palace her only ally lay in Paolo's love, for he would do anything for her. Unfortunately Paolo did not realize how many sought her downfall, for he trusted his courtiers, not always seeing through the treachery of the ministers who surrounded him. Duchess Maria had been right, he was a strong man, but no match for the combined slyness of the council; it

254

was she who suspected, who questioned and tortured to obtain the truth. Paolo's revenge was taken too often through anger and passion, while his mother's was with a woman's calculation, unemotional and twice as deadly.

That summer day four years ago when she had nervously attended his mother's audience in the high-vaulted chamber overlooking the canal had been useful after all. She was wrong, she had two allies in the palace: Paolo, and his mother. Dawning relief made Rosanna smile. She would reveal her fears to Duchess Maria. Between them even Miserotti could not triumph.

It was hot and stifling in the Duchess's apartments with the curtains drawn to shut out the sun. The gloomy rooms had the odor of sickness prevailing above the sweet smell of roses from a silver urn beside the Duchess's bed. Tiptoeing over thick carpets in the oppressive gloom, Rosanna could not help comparing today's visit to that other when she had been girlishly naive and so very much in love.

With a gasp of surprise Rosanna saw Paolo's mother. It was the first time for several months and she was shocked to see her sunken face, her dark eyes blazing unnaturally bright against her sallow skin. Flesh hung loose on her jaw, sagging over the sharp bone structure, falling in jaundiced folds to the soiled neck of her gown. The old woman lying helplessly on the bed was a stranger.

"I wondered when you'd come to me."

Rosanna knelt, extending her hand, which the sick woman grasped with bony fingers. Her grip was still strong, and Rosanna was surprised by the life still present in her wasted body.

"I trust you are feeling stronger after your illness, your Grace," Rosanna murmured politely. The other woman smiled grimly, but did not reply. Those coal hot eyes regarded her face intently, probing as if the strife of recent months was visible in her expression.

"You're older. Are you wiser too?"

"Yes, Madam, much wiser."

"Life takes its toll. We always pay for what we get, however sweet the taking, payment is often given in pain. We haven't been friends, Rosanna, but I think we've always understood each other. Now perhaps you can see I was right, for the stars in your eyes are extinguished. Does my son not still love you?"

"He loves me, your Grace, but his love is not enough to protect me from my enemies."

Duchess Maria studied the crumpled bed linen beneath her clawlike hand, smoothing the furrows, shaping the material to form valleys and hillocks. "I told you there were enemies waiting to devour those who climb. They lurk in the shadows watchful as jackals, ready to pounce on the wounded straggler from the chase. Are you going to let them take what you have built, by fear alone?"

"No." Rosanna paused, watching the ever moving fingers on the sheets. "That's why I came to you."

"What help can a sick woman give?"

"If any can be given, your Grace, you will know."

A smile lit the Duchess Maria's features, lifting the pale, bluish flesh of her narrow lips, and she nodded, pleased with her answer. "Aye, I've not made enemies in vain. I've learned their vulnerability in return. Is the Dati woman still trying to ignite the dead sparks of a forgotten love affair? Or is it Paolo's simpering little wife?"

"It could be either, or Miserotti, even your own son."

"Bernardo? Yes, I'd forgotten the treachery of a scorned lover, even more vile when the partners are men. Does Bernardo blame you, as well as Paolo, for taking Ricasoli from him?"

"Yes, though I don't know to what extent his hate would go."

"Bernardo's my son through and through, unfortunately he inherited none of his father's charm, Paolo has it all. In Bernardo there is only hate. Has he threatened you?"

"I found this on my door." Rosanna brought the note from the bodice of her gown and gave it to Duchess Maria.

"In blood . . . 'tis more likely the work of the Miserotti. They are born assassins."

"Miserotti threatened me several weeks ago," Rosanna supplied, sure the Duchess was right. "He has invited a company for dinner at his palazzo on Friday. I won't go. He'll probably try to poison me . . ."

"No, poison is not Miserotti's way. I know that, but Paolo doesn't."

"What do you mean?" Rosanna whispered, bending close to catch the other's whispered words.

"Are you familiar with herbs?"

"Yes."

"I'll give you a recipe to use." The duchess struggled to sit against her pillows and she pointed to a fine inlaid chest beside the window. "In the top drawer is what you need. There's a false bottom, it's under that."

Crossing to the oriental chest Rosanna opened the topmost drawer, one of twenty all inlaid with mother-of-pearl flowers. There was a spicy odor exuding from the chest, yet tinged at the same time with a strange bitterness which marred the aroma. Beneath a loose bundle of papers she found the secret compartment. Inside were several packets of herbs and she brought them to the bed. With a smile the duchess lovingly caressed the packets, studying them at length before she finally selected two. With a nod she directed Rosanna to return the others to their hiding place.

"Take this mixture and grind it fine as dust."

Rosanna accepted the first packet which was marked with a sign in black ink. "Is it poison?" she asked.

"A mild one. At the dinner table you are to sprinkle this one in Paolo's wine."

"Paolo!" Rosanna echoed in alarm. "Poison?"

"Don't be distressed," the duchess said, taking her arm, fingering the soft flesh with her own dry, clawlike fingers. "I love him too, in my fashion. No harm will come to him. The company will think the wine was poisoned by Miserotti's hand, an assumption you will encourage."

"But what of Paolo? Will he recover?"

"At first his sleep will be like death, his pulse and heartbeat weak. Have him brought to the palace where you will nurse him back to health. We'll let him sleep for several days, just long enough for the citizens to rise in outrage against Miserotti. Then you will mix this other potion to restore our duke to health. Miraculously he will be cured, and we will destroy Miserotti and raise you up in the eyes of the populace at the same time. Don't tarry past the third day, for the effects will wear off by themselves and your plot may be discovered."

Rosanna stared at the packets in her hand, contemplating the deed. Exhausted, the duchess lay back on the pillows, her heavy lids sunk as if in sleep over the intensity of her dark eyes. Her breath was rasping, quick and shallow. "Go now," she whispered hoarsely, "I'm very tired. Come to me when it is done. We'll find other ways . . . for . . . other enemies."

She lapsed into sleep and with pounding heart, Rosanna thrust the herbs inside her bodice. As she walked to the door, the stiff paper chafed her flesh, but the discomfort was almost pleasure, for with each movement came the reminder of her plan. The Black Witch would triumph after all.

Rosanna spent the next two days sequestered within the safety of her chambers, seeing only Cia, and Nicci's nurse. On Friday morning Paolo sent a basket of fruit with his condolences, hoping her indisposition would be cured in time for the Miserotti banquet. With a guilty smile, she replied to his note. An unfamiliar pageboy was the message bearer and she asked his name.

"Rosello, *Donna* Rosanna."

With a laugh she sent him on his way, remarking on the likeness between their names. And smiling, Rosello assured her the note would be delivered to his Grace without delay. Unknown to Rosanna he made two stops on the journey to the royal apartments, first to the council chamber where Miserotti waited, then to the apartments of Duke Bernardo.

Friday night threatened to be stormy and Rosanna listened to the distant rumble of thunder as she waited for the hour of departure. With trembling hands she patted the fur-trimmed edge of her sleeve, where, concealed in the folds of orange silk, was the poison draught. Twice she had put the packet of herbs back in her drawer, and twice she had taken them out. The fear within her heart was not of discovery but of giving a lethal does by accident and killing the man she loved. Duchess Maria had assured her of the safety of this potion, still her own fear made her hesitate. What if it was a trick, a counterplot of which she was unaware? Perhaps Bernardo wished to seize the throne, ruling in Paolo's stead. How ironical it would be if her beloved were to die by her own hand.

"Are you ready, *Donna* Rosanna?" Cia asked, sensing her distress. "Is anything wrong?"

"It is the storm. They say it affects one's well being," Rosanna calmly explained, taking the brown cloak Cia handed to her. If it rained on the journey and soaked the packet, her plot would be useless, so she must protect her gown from the elements. Checking once more to assure herself the poison was in place within the wide hanging sleeve of her gown, Rosanna wrapped her cloak tight, following Cia into the corridor.

She had worn this dress because of its sleeves, as they afforded the best concealment for the poison. It was not one of Paolo's favorite gowns, he always said orange made her look like a gypsy, but she hoped he would not insist she change it. The gown had been a peace offering from her uncle on Nicci's third birthday. The dress was exceptionally fine silk, figured with boughs of fruit and leaping gazelles, and around the hem was a thick band of sable. The underskirt was paler orange, shot with silver, and a narrow circlet of silver was stitched to the neckline.

The gondolas were lit by garish flashes of lightning, which struck their gilded appointments with fiery blaze. Wind rippled the waters of the canal, and the attendants voiced their concern over the prudence of the journey. The crafts bobbed in the water, creaking as they strained against their moorings with the rising ebb, banging against each other on the swell of the water.

Paolo saw her arrive, coming at once to her side. He wore black velvet over sad tawny, a plumed bonnet on his head. Two link boys followed him, and in the glare from their torches, he saw the pallor of her face.

"What is it, dear heart, are you still unwell?" he asked, taking her hand, his face grown serious in concern.

Now was the hour to begin, to speak the prologue of her play. "No, I'm recovered, it's only something I feel within, a forerunner of doom. Think you it wise to journey on such a foul night?"

"Oh, *cara*, you're a typical woman," he laughed, hugging her close. "What harm will a little rain do us? We'll be safe inside Miserotti's palazzo long before the weather breaks. We do not put out to sea, 'tis only a short distance along the canal. Come, I shall protect you."

Rosanna smiled, finding her eyes misted with tears at the warmth of his arm drawn close about her waist. He thought to shield her from all danger with the mere strength of his love.

"Then I am safe, for there are no stronger arms in the world."

With a soft smile, he gazed upon her, taking pleasure in her words. "Come," he said, taking her to the red-canopied royal gondola, its white and gold standard flapping like a sail in the rising wind.

Willing hands assisted her descent to the rocking boat, yet she stumbled against Paolo who brought her up with a laugh, steadying her on the swaying deck. When he was occupied with the boatman, she made sure the potion was still inside her sleeve.

They sat together in the small cabin beneath a gilded velvet canopy, the strong wind moving the hanging gold fringe before her face. The silken cushions were soft beneath her, yet Rosanna could not relax, holding her body tense as she waited for the deed to be done.

"I am angry with you," Paolo said after a few minutes of their journey. "You are wearing that dress and you know I don't like it."

"Oh, Paolo, when I wore it last we were very happy. Do you remember, at the banquet . . and later when we walked beneath the moon?"

He nodded, his mouth curving at the recollection.

"Besides, I wanted to compliment your choice of color. See, Sweetheart, how well it suits the sad tawny of your doublet."

"You win, *donna,* as always. Since I've known you, I never seem to win an argument. How is that?"

"Because you are the perfect gentleman and always let me win," she replied. When he would have drawn her in his embrace, she reminded, "Later. What would the guests think if I arrived with my hair tangled and my gown a mass of wrinkles. What whispers there would be, your Grace."

He laughed and stretched against the cushions. "You have just won another."

Rosanna smiled with satisfaction, looking across the canal where lights from the palazzos along the bank splashed wavering yellow puddles on the water. From somewhere music drifted, and a boy's voice, pure as an angel's, sang the words of a love song. Blowing suddenly between the buildings the wind howled like a lost spirit, sending a chill along her spine. And with it her moment of pleasure was destroyed. In that instant she had almost forgotten the deed that lay ahead.

The gondolas headed for the bank, and through the dark she saw the welcoming light of flaring torches from Miserotti's huge palazzo. A few moments more and she could distinguish his tall figure waiting on the bank. The huge doors behind him were flung open, yellow light streaming in a banner over the shallow steps, bathing him in its glow.

"Welcome, your Grace, I am honored. My household has never been so blessed," Miserotti greeted, hurrying to the edge of the jetty while the Duke disembarked, turning to assist his lady. "And *Donna* Rosanna. Ah, what beauty!"

With a forced smile, Rosanna accepted his hand, maintaining her pose as he swept her fingers to his mouth in polite greeting. Act One had begun.

The banquet table was loaded with delicacies. Huge mounds of exotic fruits spilled their colorful bounty from golden bowls, grapes trailing purple and green on the damask cloth. Platters of roast spiced meat nudged tureens of steaming sauce, their aromas blending in an irresistible savory smell that set the gentlemen eager to begin their meal.

Miserotti's pages wore new livery, black and gold with striped hose; the family's coat of arms, a gold bar over drawn swords, glittering from their paltocks in the bright torchlight. They moved amongst the guests, ushering each to his place.

Paolo was seated at the center of the table which was set on a carpeted dais, and breaking the rules of propriety, Rosanna was placed on his left. Miserotti on his right. The seating arrangements were fortunate, for now it was only a matter of opportunity for her to scatter the potion in his wine.

A band of minstrels entered the dining hall, followed by tumblers and jugglers. The company watched the entertainers while they ate their meal, applauding as each performance came to an end. Next a lithe dancing girl, accompanied by two maidens playing decorated tambourines, came floating into the room. The dancer was a Nubian slave, her dark skin visible through the white filmy draperies of her costume. The gentlemen clapped in appreciation as she began her dance, weaving and twisting, her body sinuous within the fluttering gauze. She leaped and twisted, clapping her hands in rhythm to her steps. As the tempo increased, the dance took on a more erotic aspect. She writhed sensuously before the table, bent far backwards, her hips undulating as if they were moving independently of her body.

The guests were quiet, intently watching the stirring dance. Rosanna glanced at the gentlemen seated close by, finding them mesmerized by the glistening black body, blood rising in their veins at the girl's arousing invitation. Beside her Sandro Miserotti ran his tongue over parched lips, his hands clenched on the stem of his goblet. Paolo too was spellbound by the dancer, his half full wine glass forgotten beside his plate.

Keeping a wary eye on the other guests, Rosanna reached for a bunch of grapes, the opened sachet of herbs concealed in her hand. On the pretext of saving her dangling sleeve from Paolo's drink, she caught at the fabric with the other hand spilling the contents into the dark wine in his glass.

The dancing girl threw herself limply at their feet, exhausted by her performance. Thunderous applause greeted her finale, interspersed with men's shouts for an encore, but she shook her head and skipped away. Rosanna glanced in the wine cup to see if the herbs were still visible, finding all but the merest speck dissolved in the liquid.

"Boy, fill my glass. Such a performance makes a man thirsty," Paolo demanded of a page who had come to stand behind his chair. Obediently the youth filled his glass to the brim.

With pounding heart Rosanna watched him sip the wine, wondering how long before it took effect. Paolo smiled at her, and taking a couple of purple grapes he popped them in her mouth.

"There now, sweeting, I hadn't forgotten you," he assured, taking another sip of wine. "Miserotti thinks to incapacitate me before his guests, bringing such stimulating entertainment. What say you we invite the black wench to the palace to dance?"

"Only at three in the morning, when you are thoroughly sated."

He roared in amusement at her saucy retort, his laughter taken up by the others who heard. "God, woman, am I to have no enjoyment?"

"But of course, your Grace, you won't be sleeping from midnight to three."

Again he laughed, sipping more of the wine. Now the cup was half empty. She watched with apprehension, praying the potion was as harmless as she had been told. On impulse, Rosanna took his hand, bringing it to her lips where she planted a kiss against his palm. "I love you," she vowed, her voice shaking with emotion as he questioned her action, his eyes puzzled.

"Think you I wish to exchange the black creature for you?"

"No, I only wanted to remind you of my affection."

"I've only to look in your eyes to know," he whispered, stroking her hair a moment where it peeped through the elaborate silver hairdressing. His attention was taken then by Miserotti who leaned close to speak to him.

For the next few minutes Rosanna watched Paolo closely, wary for signs of illness. Several times she brushed his hand across his brow, finding sweat trickling down his face. Then suddenly he clutched his head as the room began to sway, the lights and colors running together.

"What is it?" Rosanna cried.

"I don't know ... everything's strange. God, *cara* ... I'm poisoned."

Rosanna shrieked as he slumped against her, crying in genuine terror as Paolo lost consciousness. Amid the exclamations and commotion of the other guests she could hear Miserotti commanding his servants to carry the Duke

263

from the dining hall. He tried to calm the guests with assurances of their sovereign's safety. Too much wine ... too close an atmosphere, anything but poison.

The Duke was carried to the nearest bedchamber, his servants, who had been summoned in haste, ministering to him. His doublet was unfastened to allow him to breathe, and cold cloths were brought to revive him. Miserotti sent a rider post haste through the storm to fetch Franchi, the royal physician. Kneeling beside his bed, Rosanna wept, giving vent to her mixed emotions of the past hours, to fear and worry, guilt and love. She clung to his hand, still and cool in her own. His pulse was weak and in panic she thought it stilled, frantically she sought the throb under the frill of his shirt cuff finding it barely noticeable beneath her finger.

When Franchi arrived the other attendants left the room, but she pleaded to be allowed to remain. After a quick examination the bearded old man pronounced his diagnosis: Poisoning.

The word was carried like wildfire through the hallway, reaching the dining hall in a matter of moments. In alarm the gentlemen of the court came running to the sick chamber, demanding entrance. Rosanna watched grown men kneel weeping over their master, covering his hands with kisses. One by one they came to the bedside, gazing in horror at their dying ruler, and they vowed vengeance as sorrow gave way to anger. Whoever had done this foul deed would pay with his life.

Their vows struck fear within Rosanna's heart, as she wondered if now the plan would go astray. What if she had been observed administering the poison? She had been sure no one watched, so intent were they upon the dancing girl, yet she could have been mistaken. No one accused her, each offering his condolences, assisting her to a chair when she collapsed weeping at the bedside. The courtiers made arrangements for transportation to the palace. Though Miserotti pleaded with them to leave the Duke in his palazzo where he could be nursed, no one would listen.

It was then Rosanna knew the plot was working as designed, for on their faces was hate and accusation which no amount of pleading from the great Miserotti could erase. In the eyes of the courtiers their master was poisoned by a member of the Miserotti household, possibly Sandro, yet more likely Guido Miserotti himself. And in turn each man remembered when his own well being was at stake, and he had trembled before the treachery of the mighty house of Miserotti. Ironically, by his past manipulations, Guido Miserotti had sealed his own fate, though this time he was blameless. For once in his career the treachery was not his own, and he trembled at the sight of their stony countenances as Duke Paolo was carried slowly to a waiting gondola. Miserotti knew it was useless to plead with the young gallants who had loved their master, perhaps not selflessly, but well. Too many of them owed him money—for their palazzos fronting the fashionable Via San Bernardo, for their horses and their mistresses, and the very clothes on their backs. And so the commodity which he had gathered about him with greed, which he had sought with a true lust for possession, had manipulated, stolen, murdered to obtain, was his undoing.

"Come, *Donna* Rosanna, will you travel with his Grace?" Rinaldo Viverini asked, his voice husky with tears, as Rosanna followed the slow-moving procession.

It was pelting with rain, the wind swirling their sodden clothing against their limbs, yet the men did not hurry, moving with measured step, careful not to bounce the Duke. Their brilliant peacock's finery was bedraggled, dripping plumes curling limply from misshapen hats. Somehow in the black night it seemed like a horrible funeral masque. Rosanna had to force herself to remember Paolo was not actually dying, and to recall she was the one who had caused his coma.

"Yes, I want to stay beside him," she whispered, tears joining the passage of raindrops down her cheeks.

"Of course." Viverini squeezed her arm in comfort, his face grave. She was very lovely in her grief. Before he had sometimes wondered what Duke Paolo saw in the Sordello woman, but watching her this past hour, he knew. It was her unselfish love for his Grace which bound him to her for almost five years, long after he should have been bored with her body. She actually loved Duke Paolo, her grief more terrible than his own. "Come," he mumbled, assisting her down the slippery steps to the gondola.

"Please, *Don* Rinaldo, if you would allow his Grace to wait until the morrow, in this storm it . . ."

"He shall not spend another moment under your roof, Miserotti. And this night it would be well to enjoy the remaining hours, for you too may not spend many moments there yourself," Viverini threatened, his hand closed upon the jeweled hilt of his dagger, prominent in a scabbard at his waist. "The treachery of this night will be over the city long before dawn. Those men-at-arms, of whom you are so proud, may earn their pay before daybreak."

With this, Viverini leaped aboard the royal gondola, curtly ordering the gondoliers to make haste and return their duke to the safety of his palace.

In the cabin Rosanna knelt beside Paolo weeping in fear against the sad tawny velvet of his doublet.

The city of Lorenzo was plunged into premature mourning for their duke. Rosanna stayed at his side, night and day, sleeping only fitfully, instantly awake at the slightest movement from the bed. Paolo's duchess brought her little son to see his father, but the child did not understand and cried to be taken away. As she left, Teresa flashed Rosanna a spiteful glance, her face flushed with triumph.

Within twenty-four hours, the hot-headed courtiers had tried and sentenced Guido Miserotti to death. The execution was to be on Sunday, a choice which brought vigorous objections from the clergy. But their dissention was overruled.

Rosanna did not witness the spectacle, though crowds gathered before dawn at the place of execution, demonstrating their angry hate with rocks and insults. The menacing drum roll, followed by a triumphant roar from the spectators, had just ended, when Rosello, the page, appeared at her door.

After he left Rosanna opened the note he had brought from Duchess Maria. The paper bore one word: Victory.

On Monday morning Rosanna issued a message to the council in which she offered to mix a potion in an attempt to revive his Grace. Her own uncle and Alfonso Corelli came to her chambers without delay. The decision of the privy council was that she could use whatever methods she knew to revive him, be they by medication or black magic.

The two council members watched her prepare her potion, though Rosanna made the act far more mystical than was necessary, working under the assumption they already believed her to be a witch. The men backed away as she lit a flashing powder in a charcoal brazier, and without understanding the words, she chanted a rhyme her mother had taught her. Uncle Ugo shook visibly as she fixed him with her black eyes, and he blanched with fear as he remembered the many reasons she had to hate him.

The men assisted her with the Duke as she forced a cup between his lips. Some of the potion spilled on the bedsheets, but she hoped enough went down to be convincing.

For several hours they watched as he seemed to be awakening from a long sleep, until at last his eyes opened as she bent over him, and he smiled at her.

Chapter Nineteen

The grapes were large, purple swelling, a frosted bloom upon the skins. Teresa had remarked upon their perfection, but as Bernardo began to speak, gradually revealing the purpose of his visit, the sweetness in her mouth turned to gall.

"Rosello is a very handsome boy, is he not?"

She nodded, watching the monotonous rhythm of the pendulum on the clock, finding a wave of nausea creeping slowly through her stomach.

"He no longer waits on my brother, now he is my page, Teresa." Bernardo paused to select a large grape which he popped delicately in his mouth.

Teresa cleared her throat, for at first her voice seemed buried somewhere in her chest. "Is that so," she said, carefully, forcing her eyes from the balcony where Rosello could be seen exercising Beppo on a silver chain.

"Yes. I thought you might find it interesting, sister-in-law. We have a very close relationship, my pages and I. There are no secrets between us."

"I don't know what you mean," she whispered, swallowing the last vestige of grape which seemed to have turned to lead in her throat.

"I think you do," Bernardo contradicted, selecting another grape. "It seems strange a woman should still carry milk when her own babe is long ago weaned."

Blood flooded in a swift tide, turning her face crimson, and Teresa stared at him, struck dumb by the horror of his knowledge. Not once had she thought herself betrayed, so secure was she in Rosello's silence.

"Of course, secrets are safe with me. I never betray the confidences of a friend," Bernardo assured, reaching out to take her hand, but Teresa drew back.

"I want you to leave."

"No, you don't, for I've not yet told you what I came for."

"Haven't you said enough?"

"I've only just begun. Sit down. There's no need for haste." As he spoke Bernardo peeled the black-purple skin from a grape, revealing the pulpy interior which he ate slowly, revelling in her shock and embarrassment. "You should be more careful. I doubt if Paolo would be overjoyed to learn of the secret vices of his duchess."

"What is it you want?"

"How well you've become adjusted to court circles ... all right, I'll make the request brief."

Teresa watched him stand with a yawn, then he walked to the window making certain the boy was safely below in the courtyard. "You are well aware of the situation within the duchy. Paolo lavishes riches upon his mistress, nothing is denied her."

"You don't have to remind me of it."

"Ah, but I do, opening wounds afresh makes the pain grow bitter. And a bitter woman is a dangerous one. Paolo spurns you for the Sordello bitch. Since Miserotti's death she is treated like the Madonna. Because she does not trust the king of Luciano, all military aid has been withdrawn from that country. If we are not careful, there will be none left to oppose her."

"If you are suggesting I kill her, you had better go elsewhere. I have no stomach for murder," Teresa spat, her face pale as she ground her sweating palms together, staining the yellow fabric of her gown.

"To attempt to kill the Black Witch is useless; daggers meant for her are turned aside, poison is given to another, disaster is turned to glory. No, there is another far more vulnerable. Paolo."

"My husband!"

"Come, the time for hypocritical loyalty is over," Bernardo snapped, spinning from the window to face her. "You do not love him, and he does not love you. The only thing you have in common is the child. And if the Sordellos have their way you will not even share that bond. Why think you Niccolo is being groomed like a prince? Out of love? Ugo Sordello wants to see his family on the throne of Lorenzo."

"But Paolo would never . . ."

"Wouldn't he? What has happened to those who stood in her way? Did Paolo not have a hand in that?" Bernardo demanded, his fists clenched white and he pounded the surface of Teresa's clothes press. "First they disposed of her rivals, even her own cousin, *La Bianca*. And Flora Dati. What are the Datis now? Even young Sordello was banished. Then came the mighty Miserotti, think you he really intended to poison his Grace? For once in his life, Guido Miserotti was innocent. It was part of a plot which you are too dense to see."

"I don't believe it," Teresa cried in shock. "They're lies. Miserotti tried to gain power. He was too greedy."

"Aye, that's true, but he didn't poison Paolo, someone else was responsible. And before you call me liar again, Madam, I will remind you the Sordello bitch sat beside him that night. Two days before the banquet she held a secret audience with my lady mother, whom she had not visited in over a year. I do not have to tell you what is my mother's favorite weapon for dealing with dangerous enemies. Long ago Duchess Maria mastered the art of poison. There was never any intention to kill Paolo. We were all fools. We didn't see through it then, and now it's too late."

With parchment-colored cheeks, Teresa stared at him, suddenly afraid. "Are you sure?" she whispered.

"Positive."

"You mean she will kill me?"

"Who knows the next victim. Perhaps you, perhaps me . . . or more likely Cristofano."

Teresa cried out in terror at the mention of her son. "Not a little boy."

"Why not? If a little boy stands in the way, he is removed."

"But we are helpless against them."

"Not if we act at once. I have powerful friends, but we have not enough money to hire a large army. If I can get that money, Angelo of Luciano will join me in overthrowing Paolo, then we will put Cristofano on the throne."

"Kill him?"

"It's the only way."

"But he could abdicate. You do not have to kill him."

Bernardo laughed bitterly, his voice echoing in the silence. "You talk like a fool. We could never convince him to abdicate. To kill him and his followers is the only way.

Teresa buried her face in her hands, her thoughts in a turmoil. The mere suggestion of such a grave sin brought terror to her heart. To engineer the death of her own husband!

"Remember, a little boy stands in her way." Bernardo smiled as Teresa shuddered. "We need money."

"But I have little, not enough to hire an army."

"Your father's a wealthy man. Ask him for the money."

"I couldn't . . ."

"You will. There's something else, as long as my mother lives, we are never safe. What the Sordello bitch lacks in guile, my mother can supply."

"I heard she was near death."

"My mother clings to life with a perverseness which astounds us all. Her ailment would have killed a thousand other women. You haven't seen her for some time, have you?"

"I swore never to visit her again if I could help," Teresa replied, her voice tremoring with ill-concealed hate.

"It's a pity. She wishes to see the child. Tomorrow is her birthday. Visit her Teresa, and take Cristofano with you."

Teresa stared at him, seeing the smile which colored his

features, the expression containing something evil which she could not explain.

"I will send a gift to your apartments, the child can present it to her," Bernardo continued, turning to go. "A basket of fruit. My mother always liked fruit, especially apples. I'll see that there are several choice, rosy apples in the very top of the basket." His hand was on the door-handle and he turned to her unsmiling. "A word of warning, Teresa. There are certain times of year when apples are unhealthy. They are out of season, so to speak. They can be bitter, and sometimes they even kill."

Teresa stared after him, watching his blue silk robes flash a brilliant streak past her window, now down the steps from the balcony. Her heart thudded with a deafening boom as she reviewed his words. They could mean only one thing; Duchess Maria would be killed and she was to be the courier of death.

On his mother's birthday, Paolo went to her apartments in response to an urgent message revealing the danger of a plot. He twisted the large ring Rosanna had given him, examining the huge stone sparkling on his finger. It was said to grow dull and change color when close to poison. She had presented it to him last autumn after his miraculous escape from Miserotti's plot.

He knocked on the closed door of Duchess Maria's bedroom, wondering how accurate the warning of the jewel would be. If his mother's information was right, there would perhaps be an occasion to test the reaction of the gem.

A maid opened the door, sobbing with anguish when she saw him. "Your Grace ... your Grace. I can't wake Duchess Maria, come quickly, please."

With one glance, Paolo knew his mother was dead.

Rosanna's fear mounted when the news of Duchess Maria's death was made public, for she doubted the event was caused by nature, but rather seemed the design of an enemy who perhaps knew of this secret plot.

Pandolfo found her weeping, the message crumpled in her fingers, and he placed his arm about her shoulders in comfort.

They were unaware of Duke Bernardo watching the scene from the dark-curtained alcove at the end of the corridor. He clenched the hilt of his dagger in rage, seeing far more meaning in the gesture than it contained. Blood pounded in hot fury through his brain, as suddenly he knew what he would do.

Pandolfo received an anonymous note, delivered by Rosello who insisted he did not know the sender, though Pandolfo discounted his words. The message was obviously from Duke Bernardo—a request to meet him in the ballroom at ten. There had been many notes lately which he had destroyed, attempting to break the hold the Duke's brother had on him. He did not need Bernardo now, for Duke Paolo was his patron, providing well for his earthly needs, even to reconstructing his palazzo. Painting supplied his spiritual needs. His sexual needs were small, curiously satisfied by his adoration for Rosanna; who, though she never professed to love him, was grateful for his affection toward her fatherless son. No, he had no need for Duke Bernardo and the sooner he told him, the easier his conscience would be. Tonight he would keep the appointment.

At Pandolfo's urging, Rosanna decided to take Nicci to Castel Isola, for she was terrified of staying in the city, wondering if she was to be the next victim. Her husband did not know her fear, thinking only that she was sad over Duchess Maria's death.

The ballroom was deserted, and Pandolfo entered with apprehension, sensing danger. A figure beckoned from the shadows and he recognized Duke Bernardo. The Duke grasped his hand with a whispered greeting. Pandolfo opened his mouth to speak, but the words died on his lips, for the sudden burning, searing pain of steel tore through the soft flesh of his shoulder. He cried out in anguish, clutching the pounding wound as he found himself dragged to the floor, Duke Bernardo's strong hands crushing the breath from his throat. He tore himself free, using all his strength to dislodge the other's grasp and Pandolfo groveled along the floor, blood spurting from the wound in his shoulder, warm and sticky against his hand.

273

"No, Bernardo ... your Grace," he begged, trapped in the corner, his hand seeking a weapon of defense, but only the gilded figure of a cupid with drawn bow was to hand. Pandolfo grasped the statue, but his strength was diminished through pain and fear, so that the missile toppled harmlessly to the floor. "No, I beg you."

Bernardo leaned above him, bent upon revenge, his face distorted with passionate rage. "I loved you. You knew that," he whispered, white-lipped, his eyes glittering demonaically in the sputtering light of a single torch. "How could you lie with her ... a woman?"

"I swear there's nothing between us. Nothing's changed."

"But you wanted it changed, didn't you?"

"No ... no, I didn't," his whisper was choking as pain throbbed in a tide of hot anguish from his wound. "I love you still, Bernardo."

"You lying bastard."

The knife blade was poised and Pandolfo watched its purposeful, glittering descent, then he felt the searing pain in his arm as he twisted from his assailant. With an oath Bernardo fell upon the carpeted steps and they struggled beneath the life-sized mural of Orpheus' descent into the underworld. And it seemed to Pandolfo, fighting for his life, that the black-robed figure of Bernardo had stepped from the painting—a demon from Hades. Weakness overcame him, his resistance growing feebler, until Bernardo crushed him on the floor, half smothered in the long gold-trimmed curtains at the windows.

"Now I will have my revenge, my beautiful, unfaithful lover."

Fascinated with sick horror, Pandolfo lay still and watched the knife plunging, now silver, now red, and above the sound of Bernardo's cries of anger, came his own screams. Again and again the dagger plunged to its jeweled hilt in the soft flesh. Bernardo kissed his face, tasting the blood on his mouth and he wept at his loss. Working grimly, tears coursing down his gold-bearded face, Bernardo hacked away the curling brown hair, sodden and foul with blood. With his dagger he opened Pandolfo's tunic, cutting through his clothing, dividing the purple tights and laying aside the material. With a vicious movement he sliced swift and clean. At last vengeance was achieved; in death Pandolfo Ricasoli was emasculated.

Bernardo scrambled swaying to his feet. With a roar he flung the dismembered flesh toward the ducal throne. "A trophy, brother mine, something to remember your artist by. Perchance you can have it mounted and presented to the Sordello bitch. 'Twill be a novel addition to her collection." Then staggering backwards, he stared hollow-eyed at the body on the floor, still and very small against the lofty magnificence of the ballroom. Blindly he ran from the room, his blood-stained dagger clattering on the marble floor.

When Rosanna left the city early next morning she passed a cavalcade of riders traveling in the opposite direction, and though she did not know Angelo of Luciano, she recognized the fluttering standards of his household. There was something about the heavily armed soldiers which gave her a stab of fear. It was not unusual to travel with such a large company of men-at-arms and Paolo was expecting the visit, though she could not help feeling he had thought the stay was to be brief, while Angelo's dozens of supply wagons suggested something far more lengthy. Rosanna was undecided what to do. Her intuition told her to turn back, but her sense told her to continue the journey. The citizens of Lorenzo were loyal; the garrison was large and well armed, bolstered by the purchased might of Peruzzi's Condottieri.

Throughout the journey she experienced unease, barely noticing the color of wildflowers, nor hearing the birds in the tall poplars lining the road. Fate was rallying against her and she felt helpless, for her amulet was gone. When the bags were packed this morning she could not find it anywhere, though she had delayed the party almost an hour while she searched for it. And now she wondered if Rosello had anything to do with its disappearance. When she sent a note to Paolo to inform him of her journey, the page was in her room.

When the painter's mutilated body was discovered, rage directed against the murderer spread throughout the court. Ricasoli had been well liked. Paolo sent soldiers to question his brother about the crime, but they returned empty handed. Bernardo had fled the city at dawn dressed as a common laborer.

Ricasoli was buried with ceremony and Paolo declared a day of mourning, dispatching a messenger to Lago di Paradiso to inform Rosanna of the tragedy. He also issued an order exiling Bernardo from the duchy on penalty of death.

This task completed, Paolo turned to another which proved to be as unpleasant—the entertainment of his cousin. Angelo had arrived bristling with anger, indignant over what he supposed to be Paolo's treachery towards him, for his entire fleet had been seized by the notorious pirate, *El Magnifico*. Paolo assured him there were always pirates.

With flashing black eyes Angelo leaned across the table.

"So, there have always been pirates. Not like this one."

"He has been fortunate so far."

"He's not the only who's been fortunate. No ship under the flag of Lorenzo has been touched these past six months."

"That's not true. Many citizens have lost cargoes," Paolo contradicted, slicing a peach with the silver knife on his plate. He offered half the fruit to Angelo who pushed it away with a scowl.

"Citizens, cousin, but no ships under the royal flag. Am I correct?"

"Now you mention it, I suppose you are," Paolo agreed thoughtfully. He had not realized the fact before. It was true and quite surprising. "A coincidence."

"I think not. Do not those ships also fly the arms of your mistress?"

"Yes, but you're mistaken there. Ugo Sordello has lost five ships already this year."

"Granted, but Rosanna Sordello has lost none."

Paolo shrugged, pouring a glass of wine. "What in God's name are you trying to imply, Angelo?" he demanded, offering the decanter to his cousin who accepted the wine with a nod.

"Just this: the coincidence seems well arranged. My

276

ships go down like paper crafts while yours sail home triumphant from every voyage. It is strange *El Magnifico* allows them to pass unmolested."

"Are you suggesting I bribe an infidel dog to prey on your cargoes?" Paolo demanded in anger.

"Infidel? Is that what he is?"

"I assume he is."

"A name like *El Magnifico*. What Muslim would bear a name like that?"

Paolo shrugged. "Do I care what he chooses to call himself?"

"I say *El Magnifico* is no Muslim. I say he was born here in this city," Angelo thundered, half rising from his chair.

"In Lorenzo?"

"Aye, Lorenzo. And he was baptized in the Duomo, but then he was not called *El Magnifico*. His baptismal name was Marco Andrea Sordello."

Paolo exclaimed in disbelief, but Angelo was worked into such a state he did not accept what he determined to be part of his cousin's dramatics. In rising anger Paolo indignantly ordered his cousin to leave the city.

" 'Twill be my pleasure," Angelo cried. "I wish it was this very night, but my men are tired. We'll wait till tomorrow."

With a cold nod of parting, the two men left the table and Paolo walked outside on the balcony in a desperate attempt to shake off a sudden feeling of unease. He stared at the sky, wondering at the darkness of the night. It was still, the tree leaves unmoving. And he learned over the balcony, his hands clasped, the heavy mounting of the ring Rosanna had given him biting in his flesh. Tonight at Castel Isola there would be a breeze. It rose cool and fresh in the mountains, rippling the water, stirring the grass beneath the trees. She would walk there alone. How he wished he was with her instead of stifling in the city like a caged man. When he had given her the coat of arms of a single star, it was to remind her of their summer love . . .

He started, turning quickly, sensing someone behind him. The balcony was deserted. He had almost expected to see Rosanna there, the pull was so strong, yet surprisingly the emotion he felt was not passion but danger. His heart quickened its pace, his hand going to the hilt of his dagger as a dark shape detached itself from the bushes below the window. Then another and another, moving silently through the courtyard, to disappear beneath the archways across the court. A familiar voice sounded in the gloom. Bernardo!

Almost as if a picture was drawn before him in the black sky, the pieces of his betrayal slid into place, well seeded by alarming rumors he had heard this afternoon. Bernardo and Angelo had united against him, financed by the banker Cione, whose loyalty had been purchased through Teresa's jealousy. This must have been what his mother wanted to tell him before she was silenced.

Paolo moved swiftly through the open window. His bedchamber was deserted, for they did not expect to be discovered so early in the evening. How did Bernardo intend to dispose of him? Was it to be a knife like poor Ricasoli, or poison like their mother?

Taking his sword and buckling it on, Paolo picked up his breastplate. He struggled with the leather fastenings, wondering how much time he had before they were at his door. The darkness of the night should conceal the flash of metal, but to be sure, he hid his armor with a cloak. Cautiously he opened the door finding no one in the corridor. First he would alert the garrison, then Peruzzi. Between them their forces would outnumber Angelo's men-at-arms, but he had no idea of Bernardo's force, who were perhaps gathering in the city at this moment.

Paolo reached the garrison without incident, surprised to negotiate the journey in safety. Whatever signal the traitors awaited had not yet been given. He found Grassolini, the Captain of the Guard, asleep in his room. The snoring soldier was hard to waken. For a few moments he could not comprehend the full danger of the situation, then the jingling sound of many harnesses brought him wide awake. The alarm was given and frantically the soldiers struggled into their armor, trying to shake off the dull lethargy caused by sleep and too much wine.

Time moved in a distorted passage. Paolo was not certain how long it was before the first clash of steel erupted from the broad piazza before the palace. Men fought in the blackness, deafened by the din of steel, the cries of the dying mingled with the terrified screams of wounded horses until the sound of battle seemed to fill the night. In terror, citizens huddled inside their homes, barring their doors against the enemy, not comprehending that treachery had come from within.

With the advent of unseasonal heat many nobles had already departed for their villas, until the might of the great houses of Lorenzo was tragically diminished, unable to rally any manpower to defend the royal house. Only the swords of the Corellis and the Donatellos combined to give assistance.

Soon the peaceful alleyways leading to Piazza Lorenzo became repositories for wounded men, or the huddled refuge of crowds. The battle spread further afield, as far as the squalid dwellings of the Ponte Maggiore district, where brave workmen fought for their Duke, side by side with the liveried army of Aldo Donatello. Buildings were put to the torch, and the terrible carnage of battle was revealed by hot orange light, men garishly silhouetted against the searing flames, swords flashing in the glare.

Paolo was wounded in the arm, but he fought on, feeling little pain, attempting to reach his horse tethered at the canal steps. At his side, Rinaldo Viverini fell, slipping on the blood-slimed cobblestones. A dozen armed men leaped upon him silencing his anguished cries for help. Paolo fought desperately to save his courtier, but others dragged him away, fearful for the safety of their Duke, urging him to his mount while there was still time. The last he saw of Viverini was his slumped figure on the palace steps, clutching his wounded abdomen in hopeless effort to staunch the blood.

The thundering hooves were halted at the entrance to the Ponte Veneto by Donatello who screamed wildly above the din that they were betrayed. Peruzzi's *Condottieri* had changed sides in the heat of battle, greedily accepting the banker Cione's sacks of gold, for Duke Paolo had not yet paid them last month's wages.

This reversal of the tide of battle spelled defeat; but it was an inevitability Paolo could not accept. He fought doggedly, burning to find his brother and take his life. But Bernardo was gone an hour ago, riding with frenzied haste towards Castel Isola, taking a force to capture Rosanna and her son.

Seeing the gold lion of Lorenzo glinting against the starless sky, the handful of loyal retainers opened the castle doors in assumption the party of riders was Duke Paolo's household come to join his mistress. Too late they discovered their error, and the island castle fell without a struggle.

In the brightness of a perfect May morning, Paolo's defeated troops came upon the castle, peaceful in the center of the shining lake, birds calling from the trees. It seemed impossible that today there would be bloodshed to mar this tranquil scene, but at the battlements armed men took their places, grim faced with determination. And Paolo muttered a hasty prayer for both Rosanna's safety and the deliverance of his men.

"We cannot take the castle, your Grace, it's impregnable," Grassolini decided with set face, scanning the manned battlements, his hand to his eyes to shield them from the glare of the sun.

"Then we are not outnumbered?"

"No, but they have the advantage. Now if we were on the plain, perhaps it would be different."

"All we have to do is bring Bernardo outside," Paolo said, deep in thought, already wrestling with the problem.

" 'Twould be as easy to charm an eagle from his nest."

"Wait! Perhaps the eagle will come down of his own accord."

"Mother of God, your Grace ... come back," Grassolini cried as the Duke broke from the cover of armed men, riding alone to the brink of the lake.

Paolo studied the faces at the battlements, searching for his brother, but he could not see him. "Where are you, Bernardo? Do you cower in a corner at the sight of the enemy?"

His voice rang clear and precise over the water. There was no answer. It was unnaturally quiet and his horse shifted its hooves on the shingle, the sound crunching in the silence, broken a moment later by the shrill cry of a bird from the trees, echoing in the eerie stillness. Then there was a commotion at the battlements as men were thrust aside. Bernardo stood red faced and angry, his fist clenched on the parapet as he answered the challenge.

"So you've come at last," he shouted, while his followers cheered at his appearance before he silenced them with a curt gesture. "Welcome to your hunting lodge, Brother mine."

"What a surly host. Won't you come down to greet me?"

There was laughter at his statement, and Paolo smiled, the sun glinting on his breastplate, winking fire in a dazzling beam, arrow straight across the water.

"Greet you! Why should I? You make a perfect target where you are."

"But you won't kill me, Brother, not yet."

"Don't be too sure," Bernardo cried, his breath quickened in rising anger.

"Come out and fight, or must I come and take you like a wolf in its lair. Do you hide behind a woman's skirts? Think you I'll not make war on you because she is within? That is the coward's way, Bernardo; but then, you always were a coward."

Bernardo yelled in anger, his voice cracking with suppressed rage at the taunts. "You cannot take me. An entire army couldn't take the castle."

"Ah, there are weaknesses you do not know. Are you so sure I don't have men entering the secret tunnel this very moment while I engage you? And where is the source of your water supply? I know, do you?"

Bernardo was silent, not replying to the shouted words while his followers attempted to soothe his anger, desperately trying to persuade him his brother's words were a trap. But Bernardo shook them off. "I hold the upper hand," he shouted, "for I still have what you came for. Here she is."

Rosanna was thrust forward, her dark gown fluttering in the breeze, the sleeves blowing over the parapet as she leaned forward. Paolo caught his breath at the sight of her, wondering if she was unharmed. She appeared to be, but he could not be certain.

"If you've hurt her, I'll kill you," he threatened.

Bernardo threw back his head and laughed. "Your lust is your undoing after all, Paolo."

"No, it is yours, you treacherous coward. Fight me hand to hand, like a man, if you would save your honor. Or are you still a woman in man's clothing?"

A bellow of anger echoed loud from the battlements as Bernardo drew his sword, flashing it high above his head. "I'll prove to your my valor," he cried.

Paolo watched the action, a smile of triumph flickering on his face. "Very well, come out and do battle." Spurring his horse, he returned to his men who were grouped at the edge of the trees, watching.

"It's a miracle, your Grace, out here we can at least hold them," Grassolini enthused, his grizzled face a wide grin.

Paolo nodded, watching the noisy movements from the castle as he spoke. "Take a small force and come out on the bank by the jetty. Wait in the trees till I give the signal. The water is shallow there. I want you to ford the lake. I'll keep him occupied till you're safely across."

"No, your Grace, you'll need all the men you have. Duke Bernardo has a large force . . ."

"You're to skirt the castle walls," Paolo continued, without listening. "Enter by the garden gate. It's set in the wall past the jetty. I'm sure he's forgotten that entrance, so it's probably unlocked. Go in and get Rosanna and my son. I'll hold them till you return . . . but don't tarry. Now go!"

Unwilling, but obedient to his master's command Grassolini signaled a dozen men to follow him, and they moved quietly into the shelter of the trees.

Paolo rode forward once more, standing in the stirrups and with a mocking smile he shouted, "What now, Brother. I wait, but I'm still unchallenged."

Angry voices drifted from the courtyard and Paolo knew his taunt had reached its mark. Creaking, the castle doors were unfastened. Long ago the portcullis was rendered inoperable, and where once there would have been a drawbridge, the water had now to be forded on horseback. Quickly he signaled to Grassolini who moved stealthily into the water. Paolo renewed his shouting and his troops cheered, drowning the swishing sound of men and horses. In a few moments Bernardo's household standard was seen as he formed his men, preparing to lead them from the safety of Castel Isola. Paolo glanced across the water, seeing that Grassolini waited silently in the deep wedge-shaped shadow of the keep.

"Here I am, Bernardo, anxious to see you prove your valor."

With a shout of anger his brother charged from the gate, reining in his horse at the water's edge where he brandished his sword. "You have not long to wait, not long before you die."

Paolo laughed, his laughter taken up a hundred times by the men in the trees. And Bernardo flushed at the mockery. Grassolini moved along the edge of the wall, his horsemen riding in single file against the masonry, disappearing from view. Paolo stood in the stirrups, his drawn word catching the sun.

"Come then. I am ready."

Bernardo accepted the challenge leading his horse into he water where it floundered up to the saddle, bringing a bellow of laughter from his opponents.

"Are you to drown, or fight?"

In anger Bernardo withdrew, searching the lake for the ford he remembered from his childhood. He found it and riding slowly along the bar of land, he stopped midway, his men-at-arms hastily reining in behind him. "You need not die, Paolo. It is still not too late. Give yourself into my keeping and put Cristofano on the throne. Abdicate and live."

"I prefer to reign and die."

"So be it."

The stillness of the countryside was torn asunder by the terrifying din of battle, which sent the birds screeching overhead, flying in dark clouds of the sanctuary of the trees. Rosanna watched from the battlements, seeing Paolo engaged in combat, surrounded by the enemy, until, plowing through the mass of steel and men, Aldo Donatello came to his rescue, swirling his great sword high in the air, lopping off ears and raining blows about steel helmets with the flat of his blade. He reached Paolo's side and they fought together until a bloody swath was cut through the enemy ranks. Terror gripped her at Paolo's danger and Rosanna cried in anguish as he was unseated, his white stallion dropping to its knees, blood rushing a

283

torrent from its side. Now Paolo was lost in the melee, and she crouched against the battlements, her head in her hands.

"*Donna* Rosanna, pray God come quick. We haven't much time."

She looked up to find Grassolini, the Captain of the Guard, urging her towards the steps. Glancing toward her jailors, who were yelling encouragement to their comrades, she ran towards the swarthy soldier.

"The child, *donna*. The child?" he questioned urgently, as she fell against the hard steel of his breastplate.

"Nicci is gone already. Cia will hide him with her family in the mountains."

Grassolini nodded, drawing her stumbling down a twisting flight of steps, racing her over the uneven ground in the garden, where she tripped on her skirts. At last she was through the gate and standing on the shingle bank of the lake. Grasping her hand the Captain drew her to his war charger, hoisting her before him in the saddle. The small party of riders plunged into the cold water of the lake riding to the opposite bank where Rosanna was thrust into the arms of a young soldier who was charged with her safety. And they hid in the trees.

It was warm in the sun. Paolo could hear the gentle lapping of the water. Pine-scented air drifted over him until he passed into a dream state, and even the pain was not as great. Surprisingly it did not hurt as he thought it would, for the first burning thrusts of agony had long since subsided. It was peaceful on the shore. The others must be dead. How still they were. Was that stain browning in the sand his blood? And the black velvet of his doublet seemed a more intense color, but it did not look red like blood.

How often he had come here, riding with joy in his heart, knowing she would be waiting for him. Or sometimes they had ridden together, knees brushing on the narrow mountain trail. How beautiful was her smile, her mouth soft, yet demanding in passion. It was because of her he did not want to die. Lorenzo and its magnificent palace was glitteringly remote, like a castle in a legend rising from the clouds. Even his loyal subjects, who bled in the streets, were not real. How terrible to die . . .

"Paolo . . . Oh, God . . . Paolo."

She was here in his dream, her hand soft upon his brow. And he smiled. The day was hazy now, and even the warmth of the sun could not lessen the chill in his bones. Vainly he attempted to sit up, so that he might see Castel Isola once more. They had not destroyed it. Its impregnable turrets had withstood a hundred onslaughts in the past; Bernardo and his puppet force could not bring that bastion to its knees.

"Darling, can you hear me?"

Her voice! Somewhere from the past it came, warm against his ear. Fancying he smelled the scent of her hair, Paolo turned his face on the sand, but it was so dark. The sun must be setting, for he could not see the ring of pines at the edge of the forest, he could not even see the lake. At sunset the water was black velvet splashed with silver. Here they came and loved, Paolo and his Rosanna; here they conceived a son. Now he would never see Niccolo grown. Perhaps she would raise him to be noble as befitted his rank . . .

"Gently. God, don't hurt him."

Protesting, his voice sounding feeble in the gloom, Paolo made them lay him down. When he moved the pain was so agonizing he was forced to bite his lips to keep from crying out. Someone removed his severed breastplate, easing the lead weight on his chest. Who was it who tried to move him? A loyal kinsman or a compassionate enemy? But he did not want to be moved. It suited him to lie beside the water, for here he had been happiest. Wetness on his face, tears, but they were not his own. Dimly he saw a shadow. A face like a vision from heaven. She was here. She had found him in the carnage of battle. "Rosanna," he whispered, his lips barely moving.

"Yes, it's Rosanna."

"Come closer, *angela* . . . it's so dark . . . Are you still here?"

"I'll never leave you."

Her voice was throbbing, he knew, for she held his hand against her lips. She kissed his fingers, foul with the blood of slain men, and she put her cheek against his. At

285

last he could see her, the shimmer of her eyes piercing the gloom, her face bringing comfort through the icy corridor of death.

Rosanna watched him smile, brushing back the golden hair which straggled blood-soaked on his brow, already stiff and drying. His dear mouth where blood trickled over the lips she had kissed, his handclasp slackening, weak in her own. God . . . he was dying and she could not stop it. Her will was a frustrated, impotent force. Now his pale eyes were glazed, yet still he seemed to know her. Frantically she thrust her hand within his wet doublet, feeling the warmth from the blood of his wound. Still his heart beat, fluttering beneath her hand, but its rhythm was weak. The vitality of his youth was spent, strewn around him where his blood had soaked the sand. In her hand his fingers relaxed and desperately she kissed his mouth, tasting the blood, feeling still that faint reply. Then it was no more. Beneath her hand his heart was still.

"Paolo," she screamed in agony, her grief a terrible thing. Her voice was dark with pain as she lay on his chest and wept.

Grassolini turned away, his bearded face wet with tears. He did not watch her actions, he did not even hear her agony, for his own grief was too strong.

Paolo's dagger rested sheathed at his waist, deadly sharp, the royal arms of Lorenzo in its jeweled hilt. Rosanna drew the blade, its glittering point a balm to her grief. One thrust, deadly and true, then she gasped, her cry turning to a moan.

Grassolini whirled at the sound, leaping to her side. But it was too late. Rosanna lay across her lover's chest, her blood mingling with his in death.

They were laid side by side within the scented grotto, soon to mingle their own fragrance with that of jasmine in a sickly sweet pomander of death. The yawning opening of the archway was sealed with fallen rock from the garden walls, and the wind through the mountains played a funeral dirge in the black night.

In October the twelfth Duke of Lorenzo was crowned—four-year-old Cristofano limping in his coronation robes, glancing towards his mother for instruction while his Uncle Bernardo, the Duke's regent, smiled benignly on him. High in the mountains, the villagers said, the bell above the grotto pealed loud until it could be heard throughout the valleys. It was a ghostly warning from the grave, the ominous tolling from an unseen force who knew all past and future.

On warm summer nights for many years thereafter, no one dared go near Castel Isola, for they were too afraid of disturbing the ghostly lovers who strolled in the garden, laughing and kissing in the scented night. And some say they saw the Black Witch and her handsome Duke, brazenly making love on the lakeshore beneath the silver moon.